Victoria Pade is a *USA TODAY* bestselling author of numerous romance novels. She has two beautiful and talented daughters—Cori and Erin—and is a native of Colorado, where she lives and writes. A devoted chocolate lover, she's in search of the perfect chocolate-chip-cookie recipe. For information about her latest and upcoming releases, visit Victoria Pade on Facebook—she would love to hear from you.

Christy Jeffries graduated from the University of California, Irvine, with a degree in criminology and received her Juris Doctor from California Western School of Law. But drafting court documents and working in law enforcement was merely an apprenticeship for her current career in the dynamic field of mummyhood and romance writing. She lives in Southern California with her patient husband, two energetic sons and one sassy grandmother. Follow her online at christyjeffries.com

Discover more at millsandboon.co.uk

THE MAJOR GETS IT RIGHT

VICTORIA PADE

NOT THEIR FIRST RODEO

CHRISTY JEFFRIES

MILLS & BOON

First Published in Great Britain 2021
by Mills & Boon, an imprint of HarperCollins*Publishers* Ltd
1 London Bridge Street, London, SE1 9GF

www.harpercollins.co.uk

HarperCollins*Publishers*
1st Floor, Watermarque Building,
Ringsend Road, Dublin 4, Ireland

The Major Gets it Right © 2021 Victoria Pade
Not Their First Rodeo © 2021 Christy Jeffries

ISBN: 978-0-263-29981-6

0621

MIX
Paper from
responsible sources
FSC™ C007454

This book is produced from independently certified FSC™ paper to ensure responsible forest management.

For more information visit: www.harpercollins.co.uk/green

Printed and bound in Spain
by CPI, Barcelona

THE MAJOR
GETS IT RIGHT

VICTORIA PADE

CHAPTER ONE

"CLAIRY, HONEY, I'M HERE…"

"I'll be right down, Mim—I just need to put on some clothes," Clairy McKinnon answered her grandmother's announcement. Clairy was in the upstairs master bedroom of the small Victorian two-story house that was now hers.

From the time she was six until she'd left for college at eighteen, Clairy had lived in the house with her grandparents, occupying one of the other two, smaller bedrooms. When widowed eighty-year-old Mildred McKinnon decided to accept her boyfriend's invitation to move in with him, Mim—as everyone called her—had signed the house over to her sole heir just before Clairy's recent decision to return to her small hometown of Merritt, Montana.

She'd arrived from Denver late the night before—too late to disturb Mim at her new home with Harry Fergusen—so Clairy had come straight here, letting herself into the clutter of her own furniture and belongings that had arrived days ago, and the last of Mim's things yet to be moved to Dr. Harry's.

"I made some tea to ice—it's in the fridge," Clairy informed her grandmother in a voice loud enough to be heard as she pulled clothes from her unpacked suitcase on this blazingly hot June Saturday.

Mim wouldn't be staying—she'd already let Clairy know that she and Dr. Harry had to attend a wedding in Billings this afternoon. Clairy planned to use the day to finish packing her grandmother's things so they were ready for the last of the move on Sunday, then work to settle in herself with whatever time was left.

Aware that there was a limit on Mim's visit today, Clairy hurried.

Dressing purely for comfort and serviceability, she pulled on a too-big, too-many-times-washed gray sweat-shirt with the sleeves cut off into ragged edges at her el-bows, and a pair of faded black yoga pants spotted with ugly dots where bleach had splashed on them.

Ten minutes earlier she'd been in the shower, so her burnished copper-colored hair was still damp. Rather than wait for it to dry, she gave her shoulder-length hair a cursory brushing and gathered it into a very lopsided topknot, which kept the thick mass of naturally wavy hair contained and out of her face, but was hardly at-tractive. She didn't expect to see anyone except Mim today, though, so it didn't make any difference to her.

Her entire grooming took about five minutes and it was obvious she hadn't put any effort into it when she caught sight of herself in the full-length mirror on the inside of the open closet door. But she didn't care. She was more interested in seeing Mim for the first time since Clairy's father's funeral five months ago.

"When do you need to leave for Billings?" she called to her grandmother as she went down the stairs and made a sharp left, bypassing the living room to head for the kitchen at the back of the house.

"I didn't hear that…" Mim called back.

Clairy started to repeat her question, but before she went too far, she spotted the elderly woman.

Clairy had inherited her red hair from Mim, who still wore it in a chin-length bob—minus any gray, thanks to Mim's hairdresser. Never without fashionable clothes, earrings, several necklaces and at least three rings on each hand, Mim was decked out in a fancy paisley pant-suit, full makeup and more jewelry than usual.

"Oh, you're ready to go," Clairy said. She'd assumed she'd have most of the morning with her grandmother before Mim went back to the doctor's place to change and head for Billings, which was about sixty miles south of the small town. Obviously not…

"Harry dropped me off so I could see you while he went to pick up the present. He'll come back for me after," Mim explained. "Twenty minutes or so—his cousin wanted us to have lunch and then go to the wedding together, so we're leaving early."

Clairy reminded herself that even if she didn't have long with her grandmother right now, she'd see her frequently because they'd be living only two blocks apart. So she didn't complain. She just went to the kitchen and hugged Mim hello.

Mim hugged her in return and held on tight. "I'm so glad you're home!" her grandmother said warmly.

"Me, too," Clairy said with equal enthusiasm.

It was still another moment before Mim released the hug. Then she stepped back and said, "How are you doing?"

"I'm good. Glad to have that drive from Denver behind me, glad to be home, glad all my stuff got here okay ahead of me."

"But you must be sad, too, though—divorce is sad! You don't have to put on a good face for me."

To Mim, divorce was unthinkable. A tragedy. Mim had been married a month before she'd even graduated from high school, and she'd gone through thick and thin with a military husband until the day Walter McKinnon died six years ago.

"I'm not putting anything on—I *am* good," Clairy insisted. "The marriage was… Well, it just was what it was… Now that it's over, I'm moving on—I'm doing a reset." It was something she'd said to her grandmother several times since she and Jared had separated, trying to convince Mim that she wasn't a victim. Because she wasn't.

"You had to leave so much behind, all your friends…" Mim said sympathetically.

"There weren't really any left who were just *my* friends—Jared only socialized with his own clique, so over the years I saw less and less of my pre-Jared friends. And once the split happened, I was out of his circle—his friends went back to being *just* his friends."

"The snooty—"

Clairy cut off her grandmother to give her the brighter side. "Marabeth has been my best friend all along and is still my best friend—it'll be good to live near her again, to see her more than a few times a year, the way it's been since college. So who I left behind in Denver isn't a big deal," she assured Mim.

But her grandmother continued to see the situation as tragic, despite Clairy's best efforts. "Still, seven years down the drain…"

"Better than eight. Or nine. Or ten," Clairy said to put a positive spin on that, too. Although she *was* sorry it had taken her that long to realize she'd made a mistake.

The same mistake she'd been so determined not to make, just dressed up to look different.

"And now that's it? It's all over and done with?" Mim said, as if that, at least, brought her relief after a lengthy battle.

It hadn't been lengthy or a battle, but rather than try to persuade Mim that the whole thing had gone so smoothly it was as if the marriage had never happened, she simply said, "Yes, it's all over and done with."

"And that visit Jared wanted yesterday morning before you left town? What was that for?"

Oh, Mim was not going to like this answer…

"It was sort of a walk-through so he could make sure I wasn't taking anything I shouldn't be taking—his art-work, anything from his collection of watches, his wine collection, that stuff. I wasn't taking anything, anyway, so it didn't make any difference."

Mim clenched her teeth in anger. She'd already made clear how unfair it was that Clairy was leaving the marriage with only what she'd had going into it. "And the girlfriend, who I still think he had on the side before—"

"He didn't even have a minute for me, Mim. I *know* he wouldn't have cut in to the more important use of his time with a side dish."

"Then how do you explain how fast he found this one?"

"That's how he operates—about a year after we were married he told me that he doesn't like to be single be-cause his friends drive him crazy wanting to set him up. And he doesn't have time for it. So the minute I was out of the picture, I'm sure he looked for someone he could plug into the empty slot to avoid the setups and keep him free for what he *does* want to devote himself to. Unfortunately, my replacement doesn't know that yet. Any more than I did until later. I just feel kind of sorry for her."

Mim actually shivered with rage at that. "And why did he want your *replacement* to come along yesterday? You already met her."

"She's his fiancée now—"

"Oh, of course she is! Whirlwind Wedding Willy— three months to get you to the altar, and he'll probably have this one there even quicker."

Clairy didn't comment, hating that she'd let herself be swept off her feet and into the abbreviated court-ship that had had her married to Jared so soon after they'd met. She'd let romance override common sense and better judgment. It was something she would *never* do again.

"You know I stayed in the loft when we separated while he went to try out a two-floor penthouse to see if he might want to buy it… Well, he does—"

"Because he thinks he deserves even more."

Clairy ignored the snide remark and went on with what she was saying. "He wanted Tina to see the loft before he decided whether to sell it or not now that he *has* decided to upgrade."

"Why sell it? He doesn't need the money, and now— when the time comes—he'll have a place for her to live through *their* divorce the way you lived in it through yours. That snake!" Mim said angrily.

Clairy finally accepted that nothing she was doing to ease her grandmother's anger at her ex was working, so she decided to just try reasoning with the older woman.

"Please don't get upset, Mim. None of it is worth raising your blood pressure. I just want to put the whole thing behind me."

She thought Mim got the message when the elderly woman sighed elaborately. "I'm just glad you're home," she repeated at the exact moment the doorbell rang.

"Harry?" Clairy asked with a glance in the direction of the front entrance.

"It's not Harry—he's just going to honk."

"Company, then?"

"Not for me," Mim said. "Everyone knows I'm at Harry's now. Maybe it's Marabeth…"

"I don't think so… She was going to come by to help around here today. Then, just before I got in last night, she texted me that she couldn't make it and put a whole lot of giddy emojis at the end of the text—I don't know what that was about. Maybe she had a particularly good Friday night that was going to last through today…" Clairy mused.

"Then I don't know who this could be," Mim said with a shrug.

Both Clairy and Mim went to the front door. Clairy opened it, and standing just outside the screen door on the covered front porch was a military man—something easy to determine even from a cursory glance because of the camo pants tucked into combat boots, a khaki-green crewneck T-shirt and the ramrod-straight stance.

Before Clairy had gotten beyond the clothes and posture to look at the face, Mim said, "Quinn!"

Quinn Camden?

Oh, great…just my luck…

Quinn Camden had sucked up every minute her father had had from the General's first visit to Clairy after shipping her to Merritt to be raised by her grandparents. And he'd gone on sucking up every minute on every other visit from then on, trailing her father like a shadow.

Quinn Camden was the person her father had thought of as the son he'd never had. The son the General had *wished* he'd had.

Quinn Camden was the man Clairy continued to have more contempt for than anyone she knew, including her ex-husband. She held him at least partially responsible for her bad relationship with her father—more so than the long absences required by the US Marine Corps because Quinn had made himself a brick-wall barrier between her and the General in his pursuit of her father as his mentor. And nothing—not even begging him to stay away—had raised so much as a drop of compassion or consideration in him.

Tough luck.

That had been his smug reply to her plea and it still rang in her ears all these years later...

"Oh, I wish I had more time!" Mim's voice interrupted Clairy's thoughts. "I'll have to leave for a wedding any minute. But please come in! I'm so glad you could get here!"

Clairy stepped aside, unwilling to participate in the welcome.

"Clairy, it's Quinn," her grandmother said, likely realizing that the two had not seen each other since Quinn Camden left for Annapolis sixteen years ago, when Clairy was sixteen.

"Ahh," Clairy acknowledged—and not in a friendly way. She hadn't recognized him, even when she had had a glimpse of his face.

But Mim was so happy to see Quinn, and so eager to get him inside, that her grandmother didn't seem to notice that Clairy had turned to ice. And since Quinn Camden's focus was on the effusive older woman, he didn't seem to have noticed, either.

As he came into the house and Mim ushered him into the living room, Clairy remained near the front door, merely watching.

So this is you now... she thought scornfully, taking a closer look at the man he'd grown into as he and her grandmother exchanged pleasantries.

Sixteen years ago he'd been a skinny teenager with bad skin. It was no wonder she hadn't connected the man before her with that image, because as much as she didn't want to admit it, now he was a very, very long way from it.

He was at least six foot four, and the T-shirt he had on was filled out with broad shoulders, undeniably impressive muscles in a wide chest and biceps that were cut and carved.

His waist was trim, his hips were narrow, and the thighs in those camo pants looked strong enough to kick down a wall.

And when her gaze finally rose up the full length of him to take in the face she hadn't yet studied in any detail, it shook her slightly to discover that he was the best-looking man she'd ever seen in person.

In fact, he was so good-looking that she didn't know how *that* hadn't drawn her attention from the start. It was certainly a face any woman would stare at—high cheekbones, a razor-sharp, granite jaw, a straight, slightly pointed nose and an unmarred, squarish forehead. He was so supremely handsome it was difficult even for Clairy not to be awestruck.

He had dark, almost black, hair, cut short but still longer than her father's. In fact, the stubble that covered Quinn Camden's face and surrounded his solemnly sensual mouth was longer than the hair on the General's head had ever been.

As were the full eyebrows over those eyes that should have been a dead giveaway as to who he was the minute she'd opened the door—the Camden eyes that were a distinct, unique, bright cobalt blue.

They were eyes that Clairy remembered all too well looking at her as if she was an ugly bug he shouldn't have to be bothered with.

The sound of a car horn honking drew Clairy out of her scrutiny of the person she'd always considered her enemy.

"That must be Harry?" her grandmother said, making it a question she aimed at Clairy.

"It is," Clairy confirmed after a quick glance through the screen door and a wave to the former town doctor.

With that confirmation, Mim said to Quinn Camden, "I'll have to leave Clairy to tell you about the will, the library, the foundation…well, everything." Then the older woman turned back to Clairy and said, "Will you do that, honey?"

Clairy recoiled. "Me?" she blurted out in unveiled repugnance.

"Please," Mim said, making the single word more an edict than a request.

And what could Clairy say? That since she was six years old she'd wished this guy off the planet? That now, when the wound from her lack of any meaningful relationship with her father was reopened by his death, the last thing she needed was to have anything to do with the biggest cause of that poor relationship? That that was asking too much? That Mim should have an inkling of that and help her stay away from Quinn Camden, not shove him in her face?

No, she couldn't say any of that.

Instead, she said a chilly "I guess…"

At which point Mim clasped one of Quinn Camden's boulder-like biceps and said, "I'm sorry to have to run, but we'll talk soon. Mac would be so thrilled that you answered the call…"

Then the older woman rushed out of the living room, pausing only a split second to kiss Clairy's cheek. She whispered, "I know, I know, but please be good—it's what your father wanted," then went out the front door and left Clairy alone with Quinn Camden. And the full bucket of loathing that Clairy had for him.

Loathing and a sudden awareness of how she looked…

No makeup, her hair all askew, ragbag clothes.

Not the way she wanted to be seen by anyone, let alone by someone who had always had the advantage over her.

It was Quinn Camden who broke the silence then. "Clairy… I figured as much from the red hair."

Or from her grandmother calling her by name— which Clairy thought was more likely, because she didn't believe there was anything about her that would have spurred recognition in him when, all those years growing up, she'd been invisible to this guy. How unlikely was it that he had any recollection of her one way or another?

Oh, how she'd been hoping her grandmother would deal with him so she didn't have to!

But here he was, dumped in her lap…

For now, anyway.

Just do this and then Mim can deal with him from here on, she told herself.

So, reluctantly, she left the entryway to join him in the living room.

Still keeping her distance, she stayed standing and didn't invite him to sit down, either.

But just as she was about to get to the point, Quinn Camden said, "I'm sorry for your loss."

The obligatory condolences. Coming from him, it made Clairy bristle. "I imagine it's your loss, too, isn't it?" she said with an edge to her voice. "Everyone knows he thought of you as his son. And since you spent more time with him than I ever did—"

"Let's say it's a loss to us both," Quinn interjected.

She just wanted this guy out of her house!

And the only way to do that was to get on with her assignment from her grandmother.

So, not worrying if she was being rude, she said, "Mim didn't say whether or not she told you about my father's will." She didn't give him the opportunity to respond; she just launched into it. "I didn't know this, but a few years ago he bought the building that Merritt's original library was in. He bought it so that after his death it could be turned into the Robert McKinnon Military Memorial Library and Foundation. He left all of his money and tangible assets to that, and asked that I move back to Merritt to set it up, oversee the library and memorial, and run the foundation that he wants to aid veterans and their families."

She paused but, again, not long enough for Quinn to speak.

"The will also asks that with whatever time from your duties you can spare, you help with the inception of the library and memorial that will—first and foremost—honor him, his military career and legacy. His wishes were for you to make sure he's portrayed the way he would want to be portrayed. He also wanted you and your military service to be highlighted, and to have your family's service well represented, too. Once that's done, the rest of the library will be for Montana veterans past, present and future who would like to be a part of it—that will fall back into my job description because he didn't expect you to be taken away from your own service long enough to keep up with that," she explained, hearing the formality in what she'd said, the lack of warmth, the aloofness. And not caring that that was the way she'd said it.

For a moment, Quinn still didn't respond. He just stood in the center of the living room that was in transitional disarray, his arms crossed over his middle, his handsome face somber.

Then, with a note in his deep voice that made it seem as if he wasn't sure he should say it, he said, "I know. Mac told me when he bought the old library building and what he wanted done with it, what he wanted you to do, what he wanted me to do. We've talked about it since then. He gave me things of his that he wants put on display. He told me what he has stored in the attic here so I'd know to look for more of it... What to look for..."

"Of course he did," Clairy muttered dryly.

How stupid was she to have believed her father would have left his valued protégé in the dark just because she hadn't known a single thing about any of this until she'd read the will? And when would she learn?

"I'm sorry…" Quinn muttered.

"For what? That you were his pride and joy? That's what you worked for, wasn't it?"

Clairy regretted the outburst the minute she let it loose.

And she had no idea why it didn't raise the satisfied smirk from Quinn that it would have raised years ago. Or—even more—why it softened his expression instead.

"I wouldn't say I was working to be his *pride and joy*. And for your sake…for starters, it *is* one of the things I'm sorry happened," he said quietly.

Oh, sure, and she believed that as much as she believed she didn't look a mess at that moment.

Quinn Camden did seem to have mastered the art of appearing sincere, though. She'd give him that. Which she considered actually more dangerous than how he'd been as a kid, when he'd been too cocky to conceal anything. Now she had to wonder what he was covering up, because sincerity from him had to be camouflage for something.

"Anyway," she said, skipping past what she considered nothing more than a forced apology, "obviously Mim is happy that you're honoring my father's wishes, and the two of you can go on from here."

"Meaning you don't want anything to do with me."

It was a statement of fact that Clairy saw no reason to deny because it was the truth.

"I figured I'd left some bad blood with you," he said. "But maybe not how deep it goes."

She just stared at him.

"It goes pretty deep, doesn't it?" he observed.

Clairy didn't disabuse him of that notion, either.

He nodded slowly. "Okay," he said, seeming to accept the situation.

But why shouldn't he just accept it? How she felt, how his role in her father's life had affected her, didn't matter to him—and never had. Why should it have, when his goals were being accomplished? So what if it had been at her expense? So what if his tramping over her had left marks?

"For what it's worth," he continued, "I've taken stock of some things recently and… Well, the way things were with you and your dad and me, that's been one of them."

Sure it has, Clairy thought.

"And I'm genuinely *sorry*," he reiterated, emphasizing the word that had already been bandied about a lot.

As if her lack of belief in him and in anything he was saying showed on her face, he said, "You haven't done anything you regret?"

Opening the door just now to you.

But she didn't say that. She said, "You expect me to believe that you regret what you did—willfully—for *years*? When you got exactly what you wanted? Now, all of a sudden, you're *sorry*? Please," she said facetiously.

He nodded again. "I probably have that coming…"

No probably *about it…*

He took a breath, a deep enough one to expand his already expansive chest, and exhaled. Clairy had no idea what that meant. And didn't care any more than she'd cared about omitting niceties or being polite.

But after the breath he'd drawn, he left the subject of his regrets behind and said, "Have you talked to your grandmother about how this is going to work?"

Like his previous knowledge of the will and her father's wishes, that sounded as if he knew more than she did again.

"Mim knows how I feel," Clairy said simply.

"Maybe. But she told me I'd be working with you because this is all your baby. And I know that's how Mac wanted it—not that we work together, but that the whole project be done by you, the way you see fit. He was impressed by other work like this that you've done, and he wanted you to do something on par with that for him."

"There was nothing I ever did that impressed my father. He just didn't like that I didn't come home to Merritt after college to look after Mim. This was his way of trying to control that—it just happened to come at a time when I'd decided moving home was what *I* wanted. So you can stop trying to grease whatever wheels you're trying to grease," she accused.

Quinn Camden's bushy eyebrows arched somewhat helplessly. "I'm not trying to grease any wheels, and Mac really did admire the things you've done for vets and veterans' organizations."

"Sure," she said flippantly, clear disbelief in her tone.

"Anyway," he said, taking a turn at moving this along, "I think your grandmother isn't planning to be involved in this. I think she's counting on you and me working together."

"Well, she might have to stop counting on that," Clairy informed him.

He nodded once more. "I guess I'll leave that for the two of you to sort out."

"Do that," she said stubbornly, and with a certainty that she would not be dealing with him from now on.

"Just let me know," he said.

"Mim will."

Another nod from him. "Okay, then."

Clairy didn't verbally ask him to leave, but she did clear the way to the front door.

He got the hint and went to the entryway.

But with one hand on the screen door to push it open, he turned back to her and said, "Honest to God—"

Clairy cut him off with a glare and a raise of her chin that dared him to go any further.

He took one more deep breath, gave her one more nod that acknowledged his acceptance that there was nothing he could say to soften her and finally walked out.

Unfortunately, Clairy was left with the image of broad shoulders that V'd down to a truly great male derriere.

But none of that mattered to her.

Because regardless of what a spectacular specimen of male flesh he might be, she still resented the guy with every ounce of her being.

CHAPTER TWO

"WERE YOU THINKING you were feeding a whole battalion today, Pops?" Quinn asked his grandfather when Ben Camden called him, his older brother, Micah, and Tanner—one of the other triplets—to the table for Sunday brunch.

"How much you want to bet the three of you are all it'll take to clear this out?" the seventy-eight-year-old challenged.

The brothers laughed, but not one of them took the bet, despite the fact that the large dining-room table was laden with serving platters of cheesy, red-and-green-peppered scrambled eggs, pancakes, bacon, Ben's homemade sausages and biscuits beside a bowl of gravy.

"And how come we're in the dining room instead of the kitchen?" Micah asked.

"Wouldn't all fit on the kitchen table," the elderly man answered simply as they each took a seat and began to load their plates.

"I thought maybe Quinn rated better than the rest of us," Tanner joked.

"It *has* been too long since he's been home," Ben complained.

And if I'd come home five months ago instead of going to Camp Lejeune to visit Mac, Mac would probably still be alive...

The thought went through Quinn's mind, bringing with it a wave of the guilt he'd become too familiar with over the last five months. And since he didn't want to get into any of it, he decided to put some effort into a lighter topic.

"So where are the newest family members?" he asked his brothers. "You're *both* engaged? And, Tanner, you resigned your commission and you have a *kid*?"

"Micah's engaged, I'm engaged—yes, I resigned from the marines, and yes, I do have a kid," Tanner said, confirming everything at once.

But Quinn wanted more out of his diversion than that, so he said, "Micah, you finally won over Lexie Parker?"

"The love of my life," Micah said without embarrassment.

"Persistence paid off?" Quinn asked.

"It wasn't persistence. I gave her years and years and years between her being my high-school crush and us meeting up again now. Then I had to work hard to clean the slate before things turned around."

"And you, Tanner—a *Markham* after all Della put you through?"

"Della passed," Ben reminded him in a hurry, as if Quinn should be treading more lightly there.

Quinn did take it down a notch, reminding himself that part of his grandfather's brief update when he'd arrived last night had included a death even more recent than the General's.

But still, he said with disbelief, "Della never gave

up the ghost on you and didn't make it through giving birth to a baby that was *yours*?"

"That about sums it up," Tanner said.

"So now you're a *father* and somehow you ended up with the younger of the Markham sisters?"

"Yep."

"*And* you're resigning your commission with the marines?"

Tanner said another simple "Yep."

"You guys have been busy," Quinn said, marveling. "And where are the future wives? And…wow, I have a *niece*…"

"They had to go to a baby shower for somebody," Tanner said.

"For Shawna Schultz—we went to school with her." Micah provided the information that Tanner was vague about.

"Wow," Quinn repeated, genuinely flabbergasted by what he'd come home to. "A lot's happened around here all of a sudden."

"You can say that again!" Ben said, as if he was slightly flabbergasted by it all, too.

But then, despite Quinn's efforts to keep this a light family reunion, his grandfather said, "I was a little peeved when you decided to go to Jacksonville—to Camp Lejeune—on your last leave instead of coming home. But now I'm glad you did. It was like fate getting you there to see Mac before it was too late."

"Were you with him when he had the heart attack?" Tanner asked.

As reluctant to talk about the death of Mac McKinnon as Quinn was, he knew it was too big an event to avoid, even if he tried to pull off another diversion.

"I left him about midnight," he answered Tanner, sticking purely with the facts. "They thought the heart attack hit about three a.m.—so, no, I wasn't with him at the exact time. No one was, or help might have been called in."

"Hard for you to lose him," Ben said compassionately. As always, he was the heart and soul of the family. "You loved him like a father."

A father who probably wanted to disown me when I left him that night.

"Mac was good to me from the minute I showed up on his doorstep when I was eight," Quinn acknowledged, the truth in that making that final evening with his mentor and friend weigh on him all the more.

"Was he sick? Were there any signs?" Ben asked.

"He was as feisty as ever. Had his usual two Scotches to end his day…" *And then maybe I ended his life…* "If he was feeling anything coming on, he didn't say it or show it."

Instead, what the sixty-two-year-old Robert "Mac" McKinnon had shown was plenty of temper to rage back at the ultimatum Quinn had given him over the mistreatment of women marines that Quinn discovered in Mac's training orders.

"When your time comes, your time comes," Tanner said philosophically.

"Worse ways to go than a heart attack," Micah added.

Quinn didn't say anything, mentally reliving for the hundredth time that last monumental argument he'd had with the General. He felt disloyal—terribly disloyal to a man he owed everything to—for starting an argument that seemed to have caused the attack and made him responsible for Mac's death. Even though it was a decision that had to be made.

He took a slow drink of his steaming black coffee, kept his hand around the cup and put his focus there to anchor himself.

Maybe he could get this off his chest.

Maybe he could talk to Ben, to Tanner, to Micah, about what he'd found out, about the fight.

This was his *family*, after all. He knew none of them would judge him.

But it was still so ugly. It had brought up so much he was still trying to figure out about how Mac might have influenced him. He didn't want to get into it over this nice meal, though. Not when it was just good to be home and with his family.

So Quinn kept his mouth shut.

"And you couldn't get any more leave time for the funeral?" Ben asked.

Quinn yanked himself out of his reverie, answering a little belatedly. "No, I couldn't. I'd used it all for that visit, and since Mac wasn't technically a relative, I would have had to pull strings to get more—"

"If anyone would have understood not doing that, it was Mac—the marine of all marines, strictly by-the-book," Micah assured him.

"Mac didn't even make it back for his own father's funeral," Ben said to support that. "He was deployed at the time, and when he finally did show up, he took some flak for not getting here. And in true Mac fashion, he said his father was already dead when he heard, so there was nothing he could do for the old man, and his duty was not to leave his command."

"Service, duty—they always did come first with

him," Tanner said with more admiration than Ben's voice had held.

"That was what he was all about," Quinn said, agreeing with his two former-marine brothers. "Mac was a stubborn, tough-as-nails, old-school marine. I still can't believe he's gone."

"It's gotta be tough on you, losing someone as important as he was to you," Micah commiserated.

"Takes a while to sink in, a while more to grieve the loss," Ben added. "You still have to eat, though…"

Quinn dipped a biscuit in the gravy on his plate and pondered another diversion, so his family would see only grief and miss the guilt that came with it.

"So…am I understanding that you're here now because of Mac's will and that memorial-library thing he's having his daughter set up?" Ben said then.

Quinn nodded while he ate the bite of biscuit, then said, "I am. Mac wanted somewhere where everyone from Montana who served could be acknowledged. He asked that we make the first of the contributions from our family—Dad, us—to get the ball rolling. I know there's stuff of Dad's in the basement, Pops—if you'd dig that out and maybe go through it, see what you might want to give. And, Micah, Tanner, you guys can think about anything you have."

Quinn paused to let his words sink in, then continued with his answer to his grandfather's question. "When it comes to Mac and what I'm supposed to do, he wanted the recognition he earned—I've heard all his stories and all the stories *about* him, I've been in some of his units, been on some of his missions. I know what he was most proud of, so he wanted me to make sure it gets out there."

Maybe not *all* of it, though...

"He trusted me to get him seen the way he wanted to be seen," Quinn concluded gruffly, thinking that it was a job he would have had more heart—and stomach—for before his trip to MARSOC training camp in North Carolina, where marines became part of the elite Marine Raider Regiment.

"He wanted you in charge of that? Not his own daughter?" Tanner asked, as if it puzzled him, having no idea how touchy that issue really was.

"Yeah," Quinn answered brusquely.

"But it's his daughter who's going to run the thing," Micah contributed.

"Looks like it. Mac just figured getting his military accomplishments in the limelight was a better job for me," Quinn explained, suffering yet another twinge of guilt. "His daughter has worked for the military as a civilian. I'm not clear on the details, but she's done some things with counseling vets and fundraising for them and I don't know what all. But it's the kind of thing Mac also wanted done with this project, so he thought she could do him justice with everything else and do good for vets and their families, too. But he figured I had a better knowledge of him and his service."

"So, again, Mac thought you knew him better than his own daughter does?"

"I think he was probably right," Quinn acknowledged in an undertone that lacked the pride he would have felt once upon a time.

"But you would have to work with her, wouldn't you?" This from Tanner with some cynicism.

"I'm not sure," Quinn responded. "Mim said yes, Clairy said no way."

Tanner nodded. "That makes sense. She *really* didn't like you or how much you hung around with the General."

Being forced to recall that fact didn't thrill Quinn. "No, she didn't," he admitted.

"And you were *rough* on her."

Leave it to a brother to point that out.

"I was," Quinn agreed.

"So no surprise that she doesn't want to partner up with you on this now. What if you have to?" Tanner asked.

Quinn shrugged. "I'll do whatever I need to do for Mac's sake." But if it was Clairy he ended up working with, he didn't think it was going to be pleasant—not after what he'd seen from her yesterday. It was obvious she still had some hard feelings toward him. In fact, he'd guess that she hated his guts.

And looking at it with the clarity of hindsight, he couldn't really blame her.

Everything he'd done to get Mac to take him under his wing would have made Raina Camden proud. But now, between having come to recognize some of the flaws in the way his mother had raised her sons, and viewing the situation with Mac through the eyes of Clairy McKinnon, *Quinn* wasn't proud of it.

He'd wronged Mac's daughter in pursuit of Mac, belittling her not unlike the way Mac had belittled women.

"When will you know who you'll be working with?" Tanner asked.

"Well," Quinn answered hesitantly, "maybe this afternoon. Mim wants me at her house, which I guess is Clairy's house when Mim moves in with Doc Harry?"

"The whole town is talking about *that*," Ben said,

confirming what Quinn had asked. "Two old coots getting together—some are laughing behind their backs. But I think it's great. They're both lonely, they hit it off—what's age got to do with it?"

"Not a thing," Micah assured him to smooth their grandfather's unintentionally ruffled feathers.

"Anyway," Quinn went on, "Mim and Clairy will both be at the McKinnon place today. Mim wants to meet up there later and go to the old library so I can see the space that'll be devoted to Mac. But she wasn't clear about whether it would be her or her granddaughter showing me around. As of yesterday, I left it for them to sort through, so I suppose I'll find out this afternoon if I'll be in Mim's hands or Clairy's."

Quinn was a little shaken when the idea of being in Clairy's hands shot something through him that almost seemed sexual.

How the hell could that be? Cold, angry, spiteful receptions were hardly something that turned him on.

And it wasn't as if Clairy McKinnon had bowled him over with her beauty.

Okay, maybe that wasn't exactly true...

Yes, she'd been dressed in clothes not fit to wear, but they'd still given him a glimpse of long, shapely legs and hints that there might be something luscious hidden in that sloppy sweatshirt. He had replayed that image in his mind last night before he'd fallen asleep.

And, yeah, he did have to admit that she had skin like alabaster, to go with the delicate features of her face. It was obvious she hadn't had any makeup on, but he had to admit that thinking about her last night had jarred some late-to-the-party appreciation of her beauty.

Especially when he factored in those piercing wide

eyes that were bright emerald green shot through with streaks of silver.

How had he missed those years ago?

Plus, there was some allure to the elegant curve of her neck, the strength and poise in her straight shoulders, the graceful length of her slim arms coming out of those ugly, cutoff sweatshirt sleeves.

And while he hadn't been sure *what* was going on with that hair, which was the color of a shiny penny, he'd been able to tell that it was thick and wavy and lustrous.

He'd undone that messy nest in his fantasy, freeing it to fall past her shoulders, down her back...

And to top it all off, she'd also managed to smell great—a scent that was lemons and lavender and something else...

So, no, maybe at first sight he hadn't realized how beautiful she was. But hindsight had made things clear.

"Earth to Quinn... Come in..."

Oh, jeez, he'd completely zoned out thinking about Clairy McKinnon!

"Sorry," he said, his attention jolted into the moment again.

"You were trying to think of a way to avoid Clairy McKinnon because you know you're in for it if you have to deal with her," Tanner mocked.

"Yeah, kind of..." Quinn said, certainly unwilling to admit what he'd actually been thinking about her. Wished he *hadn't* been thinking what he'd actually been thinking about her. And still wondering why the hell he had been!

"What were you saying?" he asked Micah.

"I said, if you don't have to be at the McKinnons'

until later, you can follow me home and check out the brewery."

"And load up on some cases of beer so I can taste this swill you crapped out on the marines to make," he said, taking a brotherly jab.

"We can't all serve forever," Micah said, defending himself. "I gave over a decade and a half, and the plan was always that I'd eventually switch to brewing my *swill*. And how dumb are you to beg me to let you invest in it?" Micah retorted.

"That's right—I did, didn't I?" Quinn pretended not to remember that. "So I should have some cases coming as dividends—pay up," he demanded.

"I can use another case of the citrus dividends," Tanner said. "So I'll tag along."

"That's what you get for letting family help your start-up," Micah mock-grumbled. "I s'pose you all think I'm keeping you in beer from now on."

There was a "hell, yes," a "you got it" and an "I know I do" all at once.

Micah just laughed and conceded, "Yeah, yeah, yeah."

That launched them into a conversation about the brewery and how it was going, and Quinn was relieved to not be the center of this brunch any longer.

And if Clairy McKinnon and the image of her kept creeping into his head even as that conversation went on?

He was sure it was just because he was dreading seeing her again.

Not because he wanted to...

"You know how I feel about him! I can't believe you expect me to have anything to do with him!" Clairy said to her grandmother.

Mim and Harry had had such a good time in Billings the day before that they'd been too tired to drive home.

They'd finally returned to Merritt at three thirty Sunday afternoon and had needed to go home before coming to finish Mim's move.

By then Clairy had packed the remainder of her grandmother's things and brought the boxes onto the porch. But on the way over, Harry's truck had blown a tire and his spare was flat. So Mim had walked the last block while Harry called the local gas station to come to his rescue. Now, as afternoon turned into early evening, Clairy and her grandmother were sitting on the padded swing on the front porch with the boxes, waiting for the former doctor.

Which was when Mim had told Clairy that Clairy would need to work with Quinn Camden while he was in town.

"I *do* know how you feel about him," the older woman assured her. "I just wish you could put what happened when you were both growing up behind you." Under her breath and more to herself than to Clairy, Mim added, "I'm not even sure how much of the blame Quinn deserves."

Clairy didn't know what her grandmother could possibly think redeemed Quinn and she wasn't interested in exploring it.

Then Mim went on anyway. "I know you wanted and expected me to be the one to work with him on your dad's memorial, but the more I thought about that, honey, the more holes I saw in it. I'd just be going through old pictures and memorabilia. I don't have any idea what you or Quinn would see as important enough to be put on display, as things that would fit into your vision of this kind of thing. I was going to tell you that you needed to be in on the Quinn part even if I was."

Clairy started to speak but her grandmother cut her off. "Then I heard from Quinn two days ago—out of the blue. *Two days ago*, Clairy. You know how it is to get leave approved in order to travel—once he got it, I couldn't very well tell him and the marines that now just wasn't good for me, could I? But it *doesn't* work for me! Not when I'm right in the middle of the move to Harry's. We've torn up Harry's house to make room, and right now we're having to search through one box or pile after another to find anything we need—it's a horrible mess that we have to get on top of! So I just have to count on you, and that's what I told Quinn—"

"I'll go to Harry's and do what needs to be done there so you can deal with that Camden jackass," Clairy declared.

"Harry would be fit to be tied if it was you putting his underwear away or deciding where his denture cup should go to make room for my denture cup," Mim balked. "Besides, not only don't I have time for anything else right now, not only wouldn't I know what I was doing, but your father also wanted *you* to do this. The library, the memorial, the foundation—the whole thing!"

"Then it also doesn't need Quinn Camden's input."

"But Quinn's input is what your father *wanted*. He wanted it so much it was in his will so he could make *sure* Quinn had a hand in it—"

"Because he thought *Quinn* was the only one who really knew him and could do him justice," Clairy retorted.

"Oh, Clairy, honey… You know I can't argue that

your dad was the best dad to you—he was my son and I loved him, but I know that when it came to you, he just… He didn't know what to do with you, and instead it was Quinn who got what you should have gotten from him," Mim said, choosing her words carefully so as not to judge her son too harshly. "And since you've both grown up, it's been Quinn who had that military connection with your dad, so it only made sense to him to have Quinn be in on the memorial."

Clairy recognized what her grandmother was doing because Mim had begun doing it the day six-year-old, sad, lonely, dejected Clairy had been sent to her, and Mim hadn't stopped doing it since—Mim walked a line between wanting to console and soothe Clairy while excusing her son.

"Your dad didn't think you could have the same grasp of his work, his lifelong call to duty," Mim went on. "I couldn't, and I was a navy nurse! Your father knew that Quinn would understand the kind of thinking, the kind of derring-do, the kind of decisions your dad made along the way and what he did to earn his medals. He thought it took someone who'd also been in the trenches to know how to put him in the best light—"

"Then why not just hand everything over to Quinn Camden to do?" Clairy suggested.

"Because beyond that macho stuff, this is what you do. And your dad was green with jealousy over what you did with the Jenkins Foundation. You know how George Jenkins stuck in my Bobby's craw—the two of them competed like children, their rises through the ranks were neck and neck, and your dad was sure that George never would have kept pace with him without the Jenkins money and political connections."

Clairy was well versed in the contentions between the two men and had been surprised when the Jenkins Foundation had offered her a job. She'd been less surprised when her father had been aggravated by her acceptance of the offer, but it had been an opportunity she couldn't refuse.

"I think that was still your father's driving force in this," Mim said. "He didn't want his own career overshadowed in any way by George Jenkins, and he thought what you did with the Jenkins Foundation might make that happen. That was when he decided he wanted his own memorial and foundation, and he wanted to be sure that it rivaled George's. Until the Jenkins Foundation hired you, they weren't accomplishing much, but you turned it into a feather in George Jenkins's cap, and your dad wanted to make sure you did that same thing and more in his name. Quinn couldn't do what you'll do—your dad knew that."

And if someone else had been responsible for building up the Jenkins Foundation, it would have been assigned to them instead of me, Clairy thought, believing that—like with everything when it came to her father—sentiment or the fact that she was his daughter held no rank.

But she didn't say that. She merely said a flat, definitive "I'm not going to work with Quinn Camden."

Mim laughed. "That sounded so much like my Bobby that he could be sitting right here with us…"

"And you know that if he'd have felt as strongly about something as I feel about this, it would never have happened."

"You're right—it wouldn't have. But you're a more reasonable person than he was."

"Not reasonable enough to have anything to do with Quinn Camden under any circumstances, for any reason."

"Except if your grandma needs you to! And, Clairy, I need you to!" Mim insisted with enough forcefulness to override Clairy's refusal.

"Mim—"

"Honey, I just can't do it! So you have to!"

Clairy knew that tone, and she didn't have any recourse. She closed her eyes and shook her head in frustration.

But for her grandmother's sake, for the sake of her father's library and memory, as well as for the sake of the foundation she would now be able to spearhead— something she was excited to do—she supposed she would have to suffer Quinn and his presence.

The only comfort for her was in knowing that it would only be for a little while. Just like with her father, there was only a short window of time before Quinn Camden would return to duty.

"Oh, look, everybody's here at once," Mim said then.

Everybody? Who is coming besides Harry?

Clairy opened her eyes to find both Dr. Harry, in his old beat-up truck, and Quinn, in a much newer white truck, pulling up to the curb in front of the house.

"And why is that jackass here, too?" she asked dourly.

"I was getting to that. I'm sure Quinn won't have a long leave for this, so we shouldn't waste any of the time he has, and he'll need to know how much space you're allotting to your dad's memorial in order to decide what to include and what might have to be left out, won't he? So I thought that you could take Quinn over to the library, give him the tour and show him what he has to work with."

"Mim…" Clairy said between clenched teeth.

"The faster it all gets done, the faster he'll be out of your hair," her grandmother explained, as if she'd read Clairy's earlier thoughts.

The older woman got up from the porch swing and headed for the steps to enthusiastically greet the new arrivals.

As she had the day before, Clairy was in no hurry to go anywhere near her old foe, so after a wave in the general direction of the new arrivals—aimed primarily at Harry—she went to the waiting stacks of boxes.

Since her grandmother was forcing her into the position of dealing with Quinn again, it at least helped that today she'd paid more attention to her appearance, so she wasn't as self-conscious as she'd been on Saturday. Her hair and makeup were done, and she had on a pair of white clam diggers with a simple, pastel green funnel-neck T-shirt.

Feeling far more confident than she had the day before, she picked up one of the boxes and carried it off the porch, heading for Dr. Harry's truck, where Quinn was helping the older man lower the rusty tailgate, and she noted that he again had on camo pants and a T-shirt. The shadow of stubble on his irritatingly too-handsome face made him look rugged and so masculine that that masculinity was almost palpable, even in the open air.

As she neared the truck, Quinn met her and took the box before she could object, freeing the way for the elderly doctor to step between them and enfold her in a warm hug.

"Clairy! Welcome home!"

"Good to be home," she assured the doctor, whose white hair was still thick enough for a pompadour wave that added an inch to his height.

Still held in the hug, her eyes met Quinn's over the doctor's shoulder, and she was struck by their color all over again. But the moment it occurred to her, she looked elsewhere.

When Harry released her, he said, "Quinn has offered to help load me up, so why don't you and Mim just clear the way and let us work?"

"I didn't pack any of the boxes too heavy and I carried them all out here, so there's no reason I can't help," Clairy insisted, actually wishing the frail older man would sit on the sidelines.

"How about everyone sit it out and let me do it?" Quinn suggested.

"Oh, Harry will never do that," Mim said. "He thinks he's still a he-man."

Clairy saw Quinn fight a twitch of a smile at that, and she knew he was thinking the same thing she was— that there had never been a time when the diminutive doctor had been anything close to a he-man.

While Quinn, on the other hand...

Clairy stopped that thought the moment it popped into her head. Stunning blue eyes and he-man muscles didn't make him any less the Quinn Camden she despised.

"Let's get to it!" Harry said then, heading for the porch under the accompaniment of her grandmother's warning for him not to overdo it.

Having Quinn's help did make quick work of the chore—which was good, because Clairy had a very difficult time keeping her gaze off Quinn. Unfortunately, having the job done that much faster left her saying goodbye to her grandmother and the doctor, and now alone with Quinn, that much sooner.

"So those two are taking the leap to live together," he said as they watched the old truck go slowly down the street.

"They are," Clairy answered, unable to tell by his tone if he was for or against it.

"How old are they?"

"Mim turned eighty on her last birthday. Dr. Harry is seventy-eight."

"Your grandmother is a cougar?"

It was a joke. But was he making light of it, or making fun of her grandmother and the doctor?

"She's healthy and happy with Harry. They both figure that since they enjoy each other's company and they're good companions, they might as well spend whatever time they have left together."

"But they aren't getting married?"

"He asked and he'd like to—"

"But she wants to keep her options open?"

"She just doesn't see the point, so she's not doing it," Clairy said, still wondering if Quinn's questions were indications of the same disapproval her father had shown when Mim had announced to him that she was thinking about the living arrangement.

"She doesn't need marriage," Clairy went on, "but she's also not ready to be put out to pasture the way my father thought she should be. I'm proud of her for not letting her age hold her back." There was challenge in Clairy's voice, daring him to say anything against the elderly couple.

But rather than any kind of scorn surfacing, Quinn

said, "Hey, I think it's great that neither one of them is throwing in the towel just because they have some years on them. Good for Mim. And for old Doc Harry."

Okay, so in this he didn't hold the same opinion that her father had. Clairy doubted that there were too many more ways they weren't on the same track.

Then the marine faced Clairy and said, "So since Mim just took off, I'm guessing you lost the battle over working with me?"

"I certainly didn't win it," Clairy said flatly.

"I'll try to make it painless," he offered.

It was on the tip of her tongue to say *just make it fast and get out of my sight*.

But his tone was amiable and she decided that injecting too much venom into the situation was only likely to impede their progress, so she merely nodded.

And tried not to feel the hint of engaging appeal his comment had had.

"Mim said she got you over here tonight to check out the library and see what kind of space we're devoting to Mac so you'll have an idea of how much material there'll be room for," she said matter-of-factly.

"Seems like a good place to start."

"Let me close my front door and we can walk over through the town square. Or you can drive and I'll meet you, if you want to go home from there."

"I'm up for the walk."

Clairy thought she could feel his eyes on her as she returned to the house, but she couldn't be sure until she pulled the front door shut.

She hadn't been wrong, and despite being caught at it, he didn't stop watching her as she retraced her steps to the curb. But she wasn't going to let being studied like a new recruit shake her. She could take whatever scrutiny he wanted to dish out.

As they crossed the street and headed through the square, the centerpiece of it became more and more visible—the huge bronze statue of her father that had been erected two years earlier. Merritt considered it an honor to be the birthplace of a decorated national hero and had wanted that recognized.

"I heard when they put that statue up the town council discussed renaming Merritt," Quinn said as they neared it. "Two more votes and this would have become McKinnon."

"The town likes claiming him as their own," Clairy confirmed.

She expected Quinn to say it was because her father had been a great man—or something along that line—but for a moment he was strangely silent.

Into that silence, Clairy said, "How long is your leave?"

"I took ten days."

Clairy bristled internally at the idea of spending that long a time with him and let silence reign again.

Then he said, "So do I have this right—there will be a section of the old library that will be solely devoted to Mac's life and service, a second section that will be given over to other vets and a third division that will be for serving veterans?"

"And their families," Clairy added. "The memorial and the library will be on the ground floor and will also offer a small area for enlistment brochures and materials—"

"For recruitment?"

"My father mentioned it specifically in the will—he

wanted the glory of the military to inspire men to join, and information right there when he hoped it happened."

"Yeah, that sounds like him."

"The foundation offices will be on the second floor and separate from the memorial and library. That's where I'll be and so will whatever staff I can afford to help organize fundraising and meet with vets and the families of vets."

"For?"

"It will be a resource center to help or access outside help for benefits, housing, loans, education. We'll have counseling for any health or mental or grieving issues, for transitioning back into civilian life. Hopefully the fundraising will give us money to use not only to keep the doors open here, but to also eventually offer financial aid ourselves—grants, scholarships, support until benefits kick in. Whatever's needed, wherever it's needed, however it's needed."

"That's pretty ambitious," Quinn said as they climbed the steps to the gray stone two-story building Mac had purchased.

When Clairy unlocked the church-like arched double doors, Quinn caught and held the one she opened, and she went in ahead of him. He followed close behind into the dusty air of an old structure that had been idle and unoccupied for years.

"There's a cleaning crew coming in," Clairy said as she waved away some of the dust that the door had stirred up. Then, focusing on the first floor, she motioned to the few pieces of furniture that were scattered around. "I want to use the bookcases and tables that were left, so I'll need to reposition them before I can measure around them for display cases and pedestals, that sort of thing. I'm hoping to do some of that tomorrow when the cleaning crew finishes, and I'll be able to give you a more exact footage of the memorial space when I do that. But for now…"

Clairy walked around, explaining her vision of things as she went. "You might want to give some thought to how you think things should be displayed so I can accommodate it—again, cases, pedestals, maybe shadow boxes and frames if there are newspaper or magazine articles. You have more grasp on what he actually wanted used to memorialize him."

Okay, she'd managed to be less hostile as she'd talked about her pet project, but that last reminder that Quinn Camden had more insight into and knowledge of her father had hit a nerve once more and her resentment echoed in her voice.

But why—when Quinn muttered, "All to the glory of Mac…"—was there something in his voice that sounded as if a nerve had been hit in him, too?

"That was his objective, wasn't it?"

Quinn didn't answer her, and that, too, was curious when she expected him to launch into accolades about how much her father deserved glory. Instead, he merely went on. "I know *what* Mac wanted out there to represent him, not the best way to *put* it out there—display cases, pedestals… Hell, I know shadowbox*ing*. I don't have any idea what a shadow *box* is. So we really are going to have to work together…"

As much as Clairy didn't want to, she had to admit that Mim had been right—this was one of her areas of expertise and she was going to have to collaborate with Quinn in a way that not even Mim would have been able to.

"I guess so," she finally conceded with a resigned sigh of acceptance.

There was nothing left of the library tour and the dust was getting increasingly more irritating to breathe, so they went outside again.

They'd had such a late start that the sun had set by the time they left the old building, and as Clairy locked the doors, Quinn said, "I'm starving. Anything around here stay open on Sunday night these days?"

"I don't really know. Over the years, Mim has mainly come to stay with me in Denver. Even being back for good now, I didn't get in until late Friday night, so it isn't as if I know anything about what's here or what goes on or when."

"What would you say to a walk down Independence to see if we can find someplace to eat? My treat."

Clairy hadn't stopped packing boxes to have lunch, so she was hungry, too. And after a long day, the idea of returning to the empty house she'd been alone in for nearly two days, and fixing something for herself to eat standing at the counter, didn't have much draw. Even if the alternative was dinner with Quinn Camden.

The best she would allow was that he was better than nothing, and she told herself it would give her the opportunity to practice tolerating him. So she shrugged without enthusiasm and said, "Okay."

Independence was Merritt's main street. It ran through the center of Merritt proper to end at the town square. But Clairy and Quinn didn't head down Independence, because when they'd crossed the rest of the square to get to it, they discovered a food truck. According to the signs posted around it, the truck had come in for the weekend, offering fish and chips.

"Smells good," Quinn said as they approached it. "Want to keep going or try this?"

Quick, easy, closer to her house than if they went the rest of the way down Independence, more informal than a restaurant...

"I'm fine with this," Clairy answered. "Nobody's using the chess tables—we can sit at one of those," she suggested with a nod to the north.

"Great."

They went to the end of a lengthy line made up of people neither of them knew, and before too long, they were sitting across from each other on the cement benches, their meals in front of them on the chess table.

As they began to eat, they talked about the growth and change in Merritt that not only brought in food trucks, but also meant that neither of them recognized anyone in the square tonight. They also appreciated the food that wasn't fancy, but that they agreed was great.

Then Quinn said, "So I don't know a lot about what you've done since I left town..."

"You didn't know anything about me when you were *in* town—except that I was in your way."

His grimace showed some remorse, but was also a concession to the fact that that was true. "I know I was a jerk to you in the old days—I told you I'm sorry for that. I wish I could make it up to you, and I'd like to find a way..."

His tone and his expression were solemn, and as if to let her know how serious he was, he laid both forearms on the table on either side of his food and looked her squarely in the eye.

"But in the meantime," he continued, "maybe we could start over? Do things differently now? We're not kids anymore, Clairy. We're connected through your dad…" He added that last part cautiously. "Would it be so bad if we got to know each other? Even a little? Maybe then I'd have a clue how to… I don't know…like I said, make up for being so lousy to you somehow."

Everything about him said that he honestly meant what he was saying, and still, Clairy's first inclination was to shoot him down, to make it clear that there wasn't anything he could do—because there wasn't.

Her father was gone, and gone with him were any thoughts, any hopes, any fantasies she'd had of somehow, somewhere down the road, reaching a point where Mac might recognize that he had a daughter, that he might even appreciate that fact, that he might acknowledge her, show her some kind of affection.

Now any chance of that was lost. Lost to all those years when Quinn *had* been close to him.

"I don't know what you're thinking, but whatever it is, I can see you getting madder and madder at me," Quinn said, injecting his voice into what was going through her head. "But, *please*, can we step onto a new path here? There are things I know now that I didn't know before. Things that make me even sorrier for the way I treated you. Things that are making me take a look at myself in a pretty harsh light… But there's no question that you are where I first went off track and I really—*really*—want to do anything I can to set that right."

That was a surprise. Mr. Tough Luck was questioning something? Doubting himself somehow?

And what *things* did he know now that he hadn't known before? What things had made him sorry and caused him to see himself in a harsh light? Were they the same things that had caused that remark about the memorial being to the glory of Mac?

Quinn certainly had her curious, if not any more likely to forgive him.

"What *things* do you know now?" she asked.

He shook his head, and his expression was so troubled, it increased her curiosity even more. "I can't talk about it yet…wheels are in motion…but…" He shook his head again. "But when it comes to you…could you just give me a little bit of a break here?"

There was such distress and uncertainty in his tone, in his furrowed brow, that it gave Clairy pause. He'd always been so obnoxiously sure of himself, of what he wanted, of how to get it. This was not the Quinn Camden she'd ever seen before. The Quinn Camden she knew. And while before she'd thought that he'd merely mastered the art of *appearing* sincere, this time she thought he actually was.

"Is it something to do with my father?" she asked.

"Just…can we please have a fresh start between the two of us?" was his only response, stubbornly sidestepping her question. "Just you and me? Can you put hating my guts on hold a little? Let me sort out what I need to sort out, and while I do, maybe if we get to know each other, try with each other, things will be better…"

More *things*…

But Clairy had to admit that he'd intrigued her. And because of that—and in the interest of learning the secret that was niggling at him—if she had to let him feel as if he was getting to know her, if she had to put some small effort into getting to know more about him, she couldn't see any harm in it. It would all be superficial, and if it netted her some satisfaction to her curiosity, it might be worth it.

"Okay," she agreed.

Quinn seemed to relax enough to go on eating, and after a few minutes of silence, he returned to what he'd been saying before. "So college—did you stay here and commute to Northbridge for that? Or did you go somewhere else?"

"I went to the University of Colorado."

"For a degree in what?"

"Social work. I stayed there for my master's, with a special interest in military social work and counseling."

"You wanted to do something with the military but as a civilian?"

"You know my father hit the ceiling the few times I ever even mentioned joining the military—that cured me of that notion. So, yes, as a civilian. At first I was thinking more about doing something for the *families* of people in the military," she qualified. "And when I looked into different areas of social work and read that an understanding of the culture of the military was a big plus in that branch—"

"You knew you were tailor-made," he said, finishing for her.

"I definitely had experience," she said. "When I graduated, I did counseling on a military base for nearly a year."

"With just families or with vets?"

"Both. But I got more of an understanding of what good I could do with vets, so when I had the chance, I went from that to being embedded with a unit at Camp Lejeune in North Carolina."

"Embedded," he parroted, as if he had his own

meaning for the word and didn't know how it applied to her work. "That means you did what?"

"I was civilian personnel doing nonmedical counseling *only* with vets there—quick fixes mainly to help build skills, keep marines who hit a relatively minor glitch functioning in the job rather than needing extended psych leave or medical discharge or retirement."

He nodded, but Clairy could tell he'd never hit one of those glitches, and she had the sense that he hadn't even been aware the service was available.

"How did you get from that to the Jenkins Foundation?" he asked.

"I...had occasion to meet General Jenkins's wife at Camp Lejeune—"

"Ahh..." Quinn mused. "The youngest Jenkins son was there. Scuttlebutt had it that he wasn't thrilled to be a marine like Dad and had a lot of issues. Were you in on that?"

Confidentiality didn't allow Clairy to speak about that, so she said only, "I just met Mrs. Jenkins there. The Jenkins Foundation wasn't really a go-to then and she was trying to get word out that help was available through them. After getting to know her, the foundation offered me the position as their liaison with military and nonmilitary agencies—"

"Did who you are have anything to do with the offer? Because Mac thought they recruited you—and you took the job—just to get his goat."

"I know. He saw it as me turning traitor, for some reason." And his anger had led to one of the rare times she'd heard from him. "But it didn't have anything to do with him. It came out of Mrs. Jenkins liking me." And appreciating the help she'd given to her son.

"Did you do counseling for the foundation or just the liaison thing?"

"They were so poorly funded at the start that I wore a lot of hats—the same way I will now to get this started. I did counseling *and* the liaison thing, fundraising, everything and anything they needed. Olivia Jenkins and I worked side by side."

"That's where you learned about shadow boxes?"

"Eventually. When General Jenkins retired, his wife wanted to retire with him, and she made me head of the foundation in her place. That's also when General Jenkins wanted *his* library established. That's where I learned everything you'd ever want to know about shadow boxes."

Quinn laughed—it was a deep laugh that made some kind of strange ripple go through her, as if she liked that he'd appreciated her joke.

She didn't have time to analyze it before he said, "I think that counts as a meteoric rise through the ranks."

"And did my father think that was just to *get his goat*, too—me not only working for his nemesis, but also doing well with them?"

"What he didn't like was anything or anyone that did well *for* General Jenkins. And you did a lot of that. Before you went to work for them, word around was just that it was some vanity project to occupy Mrs. Jenkins. Then it started to gain some ground, which was apparently due to whatever you were doing, and there were kudos for the foundation and for General Jenkins as a result. And when that got topped off by the Jenkins Library? That put Mac over the top and it *did* get his goat, whether that was anyone's intention or not," Quinn said.

"It wasn't mine and I don't think it was anyone else's, either. Mrs. Jenkins genuinely wanted the foundation to do good work—she just didn't really know what she was doing. And she and I hit it off—the whole thing was *in spite* of who I was related to, not *because* of it." At least, that was what Clairy had believed and hoped was the case.

"Good work speaks for itself," Quinn said, as if he didn't doubt it or that she *had* done good work.

And she realized that somehow—along with liking that he'd gotten her humor—she also liked that acknowledgment.

But that didn't mean that she liked *him*. Or talking to him. It didn't mean that she was *enjoying* this—as if it was dinner with some sizzlingly hot guy who had accomplishments of his own, but who was interested in her and what she'd done in the past, who seemed impressed by it, respectful of it. What she was finding pleasure in was letting this guy who had always dismissed her know that she was no slouch.

Although she was also aware of the fact that his interest was unwavering and that it made his blue eyes seem even more blue when they were so intent on her.

They'd been talking for long enough to have finished eating, for the square to have nearly cleared out and for the food truck to have closed down. All without Clairy having been aware of anything but Quinn.

But now that she'd noticed, she began to gather the remnants of her meal to signal putting an end to the evening.

For a moment, Quinn just kept looking at her, a quizzical expression on his ruggedly handsome face.

Clairy didn't want to read too much into it, but she

had the sense that his eyes *were* opening to her as more than the mere obstacle she'd been in his quest to know her father.

Not that it mattered.

Then he cleaned up after himself, too, and once they'd deposited their trash in the nearest receptacle, they headed back in the direction they'd come.

As they passed by the old library, Clairy was searching for something to say to fill the silence that had fallen between them once more. "If you'd have driven around ahead of me, you'd be at your truck now."

"I'd have still made sure you got home," he said in a way that she would also have liked had this been a date.

He nodded toward the library and said, "Tomorrow when the cleaning crew finishes, do you have help moving those old tables and bookshelves in there?"

She didn't. "The floor is smooth and flat. I think I can slide them."

"The tables, maybe. But those bookshelves? They look pretty heavy. Can I come and help?"

With that abundance of muscle power she'd seen at work earlier loading Harry's truck?

That seemed like an offer too good to refuse.

Plus, she reasoned that the quicker that work got done, the quicker they would have a better picture of the space allotment for the memorial, and the quicker he could spend the rest of his time here with his family instead of with her.

"You *would* go away with the measurements you'll need," she said to make it seem as if it was to his advantage, too.

"So just give me a time."

"Cleaning will take most of the day. I wasn't planning to go in until three thirty or four, when they're done."

In other words, into the evening, much like tonight.

"That's fine. I don't have any pressing engagements," he joked.

And for some reason, that particular turn of phrase made her wonder about his personal status—if he might be involved with someone, if he might be engaged...

Which brought to light for her that she really didn't know much about him.

Not that that mattered, either, she told herself sternly.

Furniture moving—that's what you're talking about, she reminded herself.

"Okay, then, if you're willing, I won't turn down help," she agreed in a businesslike voice. "I'll text you when I know the cleaning is close to ending, and—"

"I'll meet you at your house, and we can walk over again," he said, as if he might have liked or enjoyed doing that tonight.

They'd reached his truck, which was parked in front of her house. Clairy stopped so he didn't go any farther with her.

"Okay, up to you," she said, agreeing to the walk, too, as if she didn't have any preference at all.

Again, in an effort to keep him from going all the way to her door, she said, "Good night," and headed up the walkway to her porch.

As she did, she was thinking about the hours that had just gone by, and she realized that if she *had* to be honest, her time with him tonight had been surprisingly not awful.

And that she didn't really mind that they wouldn't just be meeting at the library tomorrow.

That she didn't really mind that they'd have another walk together.

CHAPTER THREE

"ENGAGED? WOW... CONGRATULATIONS!" Clairy said to her childhood friend Marabeth Hawn.

Marabeth had made a second offer to help Clairy unpack on Monday, and when Clairy opened the front door late that morning, Marabeth had given Clairy a spontaneous hug and, rather than saying hello, said, "We're engaged!"

Now that Marabeth was in the house with the door closed behind them, flaxen-haired, freckled, girl-next-door-pretty Marabeth added, "That's why I flaked out on helping you unpack on Saturday—Brad proposed Friday night and we wanted to go to Billings to tell our parents. They're all so excited!"

"Well, sure," Clairy said, trying to hide her own lack of wholehearted enthusiasm for the joining of her best friend and Brad Nelan.

"Remember that you said you'd be my maid of honor," Marabeth said. "Or is it *matron* of honor once you've been married, even if you're divorced?"

"I like maid of honor—I'm not sure my marriage counted for much of anything, so it doesn't get to make me a *matron*," Clairy said with some humor. "And, yes,

I remember that I said I'd be your maid of honor, even if it was when we were twelve."

She stopped herself short of saying she just hoped Marabeth was making the right choice in husbands.

Clairy and Marabeth had been best friends since preschool, and that hadn't changed even when—after two years of college together in Colorado—Marabeth had decided college wasn't for her and gone home to run her parents' Laundromat so they could move to Billings.

Even though they hadn't lived in the same city since they were both twenty, they were still closer than a lot of sisters.

Having decided she could use Marabeth's help moving into the master bedroom, Clairy led the way upstairs. Once she'd explained how she wanted the closet organized, the two began to transfer clothes from wardrobe boxes into the walk-in.

"Have you set a date?" Clairy asked, still attempting to conceal her doubts.

"As soon as we can," Marabeth answered. "We're going to get a list of earliest-available dates for the church, reception venues, the catering, all that stuff. I'm so glad you're here now so we won't have to work around when you could get away from Denver as one of those earliest-available dates. And you can help me do everything!"

Clairy bypassed the wardrobe box full of floor-length formal designer dresses she would likely never wear again, thinking that she would just leave the gowns hanging in the box and put the box in the basement. Then she opened a second cardboard wardrobe with her work clothes in it.

As she handed her friend an armload of those, she said, "Helping with everything is the maid of honor's job."

She'd intended to sound enthusiastic, but it hadn't quite made it and had alerted Marabeth. "We've been dating over a year, Clairy. Every time I see you being leery of me being with Brad, I tell you the same thing—he's not the way he was when we were kids."

When they were kids, Brad Nelan had been Quinn Camden's best friend. Brad had been with Quinn—and Quinn's brother Tanner—when Clairy had begged Quinn to stay away from her father. After Quinn's refusal, when he'd mocked, "Tough luck," Brad had joined Quinn in sneering at her, and together the two of them had ridiculed her mercilessly, humiliating her in a cafeteria full of kids. It had added to her resentment and anger at Quinn and strongly colored her opinion of Brad, too.

Even though Clairy didn't say anything to her friend's chastisement and only raised her eyebrows innocently, Marabeth went on, "I know that Brad was just as awful as Quinn Camden was when we were in school. I didn't like either one of them any more than you did. They were both full of themselves. But Brad grew out of it. You'll see when you get to know him again."

More of that getting-to-know-someone stuff.

"I know you," Clairy countered, "and you're still the same person you always were. You know me, and I am, aren't I?"

"Yes, but that doesn't mean that people *can't* be different when they grow up."

Recalling something else about that confrontation

years ago, when Marabeth had been with Clairy for moral support, Clairy said, "They weren't very nice to you, either, when you told them to stop being so mean to me."

"I know—Brad called me a little bitch. We've talked about that. I guess when he did that, Tanner got on him for going too far—"

Unlike the derisive Brad, Tanner—one of Quinn's triplet brothers—had stayed silent through Quinn's response to her entreaty.

"Brad said he knew he'd gone too far," Marabeth defended her fiancé. "He apologized. He said his mouth got away from him, and if he had it to do again, he wouldn't have ever called me that. And you know we've had a few big fights—yours is the shoulder I cry on—and he doesn't fight like that anymore. He's a grown man who knows how to control his temper and his mouth. He's kinder. He's sensitive. I'm telling you, he's not that kid anymore."

For her friend's sake, Clairy hoped that was true and merely nodded.

"Go ahead, reserve judgment. You'll see," Marabeth insisted, her connection to Clairy giving her insight into Clairy's thoughts even with Clairy's attempts to conceal them.

When they were finished with the clothes that needed to be hung, they opened the boxes with shoes in them and went to work on the closet floor.

"I saw Quinn when I went in to check on the Laundromat before I came over," Marabeth said. "He was outside of the bakery with his older brother, Micah. I told you Micah and Lexie Parker both moved back to town, that he's opened a brewery and she's taking over the bakery."

"You did," Clairy confirmed.

"Anyway… Quinn… Whew! Life has been good to him in the looks department!" Marabeth said, marveling. "I'm not sure I would have known who he was if he'd been alone. No receding hairline, and what a body that guy came into!"

If there was one thing Clairy didn't need, it was to have Quinn's looks brought to mind. Regardless of how hard she'd tried since setting eyes on him on Saturday, she just couldn't shake the ever-present mental image of him.

As if Quinn's looks weren't getting to her, Clairy said, "You can't judge a book by its cover."

"Maybe you can't judge it, but you can sure enjoy the picture before you start turning the pages," Marabeth muttered.

"I think I'd rather just keep remembering what's written on those pages."

"Unless it's changed—unless *he's* changed, the way Brad has," Marabeth said stubbornly.

Quinn *had* seemed slightly different last night, Clairy thought. But she knew telling her friend that would only encourage Marabeth. And Clairy really didn't believe that any genuine change had taken place in Quinn, nor would it have carried any weight with her.

He might be astonishingly hot, and he might have somehow evolved—although she wasn't sold on that possibility—but even if he'd grown up into the perfect man, the way Marabeth seemed to believe his friend had, it wouldn't change anything for Clairy.

To her, he was still the same kind of man her father

had been, the same kind of man Jared had proved to be—someone who put everything and everyone second to himself and his career. And while the military might be an admirable career—more admirable than Jared's as a wheeler-dealer real-estate mogul—for Clairy it was a reason equal to Quinn's past bad actions to keep him at arm's length.

Certain that she was not at risk of succumbing to anything about Quinn—despite the fact that for two nights already she'd fallen asleep with thoughts and visions of him in her head—she decided to at least indulge Marabeth's belief in her new fiancé.

"The only thing that matters to me is if Brad has changed, so I'm trusting that you're right about him," she told her friend.

Then she put every effort into the right arrangement of her shoes so that maybe she could think about something—*anything*—other than Quinn Camden and how he looked.

Marabeth left at three thirty, and minutes later Clairy got word that the cleaning crew at the library was finished.

She could have texted that information to Quinn and gone on to work in the library dressed as she was—old tennis shoes, yoga pants and a nondescript T-shirt, her hair in a ponytail.

But that wasn't what she did.

Instead, she decided to shower and change clothes first.

Once in the shower she also washed her hair, and afterward, while she was bent over to blow it dry—upside down, to add volume—she gave a lot of thought to what she was going to wear.

By the time her hair was dry, she'd decided that even if her next job of the day was furniture moving, she was still going to wear one of her best butt-hugging pairs of jeans and a plum-colored T-shirt with short sleeves gathered at her shoulders and a sweetheart neckline that displayed a hand-crocheted lace insert.

She argued with herself about wearing the sandals she wanted to wear, but that she knew were a bad choice as moving-furniture footwear, and instead chose something only somewhat less inappropriate—closed-in ballet flats.

Then she applied more-than-daytime-but-not-all-the-way-to-evening makeup before she went to stand in front of the full-length mirror on the closet door for a final inspection.

She wasn't happy with herself for having had Quinn on her mind again as she'd gotten ready, but she felt good in what she was wearing, in the way she looked. Confident. And she told herself again that confidence could only help when she was dealing with him.

Then she turned away from the mirror and texted him that the library was ready for them.

Quinn had not dressed up to move furniture, Clairy thought when he arrived half an hour later. She watched him park and get out of his truck.

He had on a khaki-green, short-sleeved crewneck T-shirt tucked into tan cargo pants that could barely contain his long legs and robust thighs. Again, a sexy scruff of beard shadowed his face, but still there was nothing that said he'd put thought into what he had on, and somehow that caused Clairy to feel slightly at a disadvantage.

Not wanting that to show, she adopted an all-business attitude, squared her shoulders, grabbed her notebook, pen and tape measure, and went out to meet him.

"Do you need to go inside for anything?" she asked.

"Nope. But hello," he said to her omission of a greeting.

"Hello," she echoed as she reached back into the house to close the door, hearing the irritation in her voice that he had no way of knowing was aimed at herself for having slightly overdone it to dress as if this was a casual first date.

As they crossed the street to get to the town square again, he nodded at her three-ring binder and said, "What's that for?"

"I was here about a month ago and made some rough sketches of the library's floor plan. I've been working on the layout of this, but I have a couple of different formations—I need to see what will work best for placement, for distribution of the displays, for flow."

"But Mac will still take front and center..."

Clairy wasn't sure whether that was to verify that nothing had changed from what she'd told him about the placement of the memorial last night, or if Quinn felt the need to protect her father's interests. That possibility irked her, so when she answered, the irritation in her voice this time *was* directed at Quinn. "It's his memorial and his money paying for it, isn't it?" Clairy said as they reached the library and she unlocked the front doors.

The inside was in much better shape than it had been the night before. There was no dust in the air or on any surface and the tile floor glistened. The wood and brass of the staircase and second-floor railing, as well as the wood-and-brass doors to the old elevator, had been polished. Every window sparkled, the walls had been washed, and the air carried the scent of cleaning solutions.

"This is a big difference," Quinn commented as he closed the doors behind them.

"Are you kidding? They did a fantastic job! Way more than I hired them to do."

"Like you said, folks around here think highly of your dad—I'd say they pulled out all the stops for him."

"I guess so," Clairy said more to herself than to Quinn, having a moment like many she'd had in her life when she felt at odds with the way her father was perceived and her own experience with him. And she wondered again, too, if the blame for her problems with him rested on her...for no reason she'd ever been able to completely determine.

Certain that if she said that to Quinn he would tell her she was definitely to blame, she didn't. She did what she'd done often—unless she'd been talking to Mim— and kept quiet.

One of the smallest of the abandoned tables was near the entrance. The tables and bookshelves had also been polished to a shine, and Clairy used the first one she came upon to set down what she'd brought with her.

Then she opened her binder, released three floor plans from the rings and spread them out separately. She explained to Quinn that she needed the exact measurements of the bookcases, the tables, the walls and floor space, and they went to work.

Although it might not have been quite as precise,

she could have done the measurements on her own. But when it came time to move furniture, she quickly realized that without Quinn she wouldn't have gotten anywhere.

The tables were so heavy they would have been difficult for her to even drag, but there was no way she would have been able to budge the three bookcases.

In fact, she was awed by the fact that Quinn could. But with little more than the two of them tipping them onto his back and her guiding them as he slid them across the slick floor, that was what he did. It was a Herculean task that seemed to Clairy like asking too much of one man, but he managed it anyway.

He also shocked her by how easy he was to work with—that he didn't need to be the boss, that he took her instruction. It was one thing that was *un*like her father.

To her grandparents, Mac's visits were not the arrival of an exalted military leader—they were merely having their son home. They'd frequently asked him to do things around the house that they needed help with. Clairy had never once seen her father doing those things without Mac discrediting what they wanted done, how they wanted it done and, ultimately, either doing it the way he saw fit or hiring someone he ordered around like a mule to do it his way. And always, it was whether her grandparents liked it or not.

She'd anticipated that same behavior from Quinn and had been determined to stand her ground. But it wasn't what she got from him at all, and that was a pleasant surprise.

It was eight o'clock before they finished, and not only did Clairy end up with the work done and a slew of images of Quinn's muscles and the man himself that she knew were going to linger, but she also felt guilty because of the difficulty of the work itself and obligated enough that she thought she should at least feed him.

Which she told him when she invited him to go home with her for the beef bourguignon she'd had slow-cooking since early that morning.

"After breaking your back, I probably owe you a massage, too," she said as they locked up the library.

Not until she saw the slow smile that erupted on his usually stoic face and the extra glint that came into his blue eyes did she realize that it sounded as if she was volunteering to do the massage herself.

"Oh, I didn't mean *I'd* give it… I meant I should probably pay for you to have one—given by someone else."

Her own faux pas flustered her, cost her a measure of dignity, and she waited for the old Quinn to make some kind of embarrassing comments that would make it worse.

But as they retraced their steps across the square, he just laughed a little and said, "I'm fine."

Clairy wished *she* was and used the walk to take deep breaths and gain some control before they reached her house.

He accepted the beer she offered him as she prepared the side dishes, but Quinn insisted on pitching in, unlike her father, who would have taken his beer and sat down until he was served.

It wasn't too long before her small round kitchen table and spindle-backed chairs were brought in from where the movers had left them in the living room and Clairy and Quinn were sitting down to eat.

Quinn had high praise for her burgundy stew served

with mashed potatoes, salad and French bread. That, too, was not something she'd ever heard her father do. Criticize, yes. Compliment, never.

Then Quinn said, "The place doesn't look like I remember it."

"After Grampa died, Mim made a lot of changes, upgrades. The house was originally built by my great-grandfather on Mim's side and not much had been done to it over the years, so it needed some work. Mim said while she was at it she was going to spruce it up because she was sick of living in a barracks. It was an argument she and Grampa had over and over—I guess it was his military side coming out, but he wanted everything green or brown, and he nixed anything he considered *frilly* or *flowery* or *girlie*. He and my dad ganged up on her every time she wanted to change anything, and she gave in until after Grampa passed. Then she did what she wanted—even though my father still didn't approve."

"It isn't frilly or flowery or girlie," Quinn mused as he glanced around. "Just... I don't know about that kind of thing... Brighter, I guess..."

"Since I was next in line for the house, I got to be in on her decisions, and brighter, more open, was what we both wanted. Now I don't really have to change anything—I'm just moving in. Which is nice."

"You didn't want to feel like you were living in a barracks?" he joked.

"I was never into anything military-ish."

"Is that how you rebelled?"

"Maybe," she allowed. "I know the things that my father was more interested in than me have always just not been...my favorite things."

Quinn laughed wryly before taking a slug of his beer. "Things like me," he said. "And me not being one of your favorite things is a hell of an understatement."

He still wasn't one of her favorite things, but she had to admit that she hadn't chafed too much at the time she'd spent with him lately. In fact, she might have almost verged on liking it. A little.

It was strange. And confusing. And certainly nothing he needed to know. So Clairy ate rather than respond to his remark right away.

When she did, she decided to toss the ball in his court. "If our positions were reversed, how would you have felt? What if you'd been his son, dying for his attention, and I'd come along to take it all instead, leaving you out in the cold?"

"I didn't take *all* of his attention," Quinn scoffed, as if she was exaggerating. "I mean, whenever he was in town I was here a lot, but—"

"Every waking hour."

"No," Quinn contradicted. "I was here in the mornings before you were even up, so I wasn't taking anything away from you. Zero four thirty on the dot, which is when he told me to be here for PT—"

"PT—physical training. The way marines are trained in boot camp," Clairy said to make sure he knew that while she might not have been included, she was still well aware of that time he'd spent with her father.

"You could have joined us," he said.

"I asked to. Mac said a loud, resounding *no*, that I'd get in the way. For years—until I was a teenager and finally gave up—I got out of bed every one of those mornings hoping he'd give in and let me do it, too."

That brought a deep scowl to Quinn's face. Deeper

than seemed warranted. "I didn't know you were hanging out somewhere *wanting* to be there."

"I was sitting on the top step upstairs when he came out of his room. I made him pass by me to get to you, thinking that eventually he'd give in and tell me to come, too. But it was off-limits."

"It was just a workout, a tough one, but that's all. It wasn't anything you couldn't have done..." he said, as if questioning the reasoning in her father's exclusion of her.

Clairy didn't know why the information seemed to have struck him the way it did, but she merely went on, opting to voice her grievances since she seemed to have the opportunity.

"You showed up here the first time he came to visit me—the *first* time. My mom had just died in a car accident, and the day after her funeral he packed me up and handed me over to Mim and Grampa to take home with them. For three months after that, there wasn't a phone call from him, a letter, not even a postcard—"

"He probably had a mission or something that didn't let him contact you."

"Now you sound like Mim—making excuses for him. I felt like he'd died, too," she admitted. "Then he finally came for a visit—I was already in bed for the night, and when I heard his voice, I came running out. He barely said hello to me and ordered me back to bed, said he'd see me in the morning. But in the morning—when he was still having his coffee and reading the newspaper, and I wasn't allowed to interrupt—there you were, knocking on the door, asking to see him. He barely looked out from behind his paper, but when he saw you through the screen, *standing there like a little*

recruit—that's the way I heard him describe it once—
he told Mim to let you in. And that's all it took for *you*
to have the attention I'd been waiting for. Then and
from then on," she said, her tone heating up. "He was
going to make *his* kind of marine out of you—*because
the service needed more of them and was getting less*,
according to him."

"From my side," Quinn said calmly, "I just wanted to
be in the military like my dad had been—all my brothers did. When I started to piece together that Merritt
was the civilian home to someone who I'd heard grown-
ups say was on his way to military greatness, a bulb
went off over my head—I got this idea that maybe I
could get him to take me under his wing. I'd been waiting and waiting to hear that he'd come to town, so when
my grandfather said it over breakfast that morning, I
went running out without even eating and hightailed it
to your place."

"To announce that you wanted to be a marine just
like Mac," Clairy said, derisively reiterating what Quinn
had said that morning when Mim had let him in. "You
couldn't have said anything he wanted to hear more.
And there you were," Clairy repeated, "his own little
devotee. After that, everything was a test to see if you
really were or could be like him. A challenge that was
right up his alley, that gave him something to do whenever he was in boring old Merritt to see boring old me…
While he thought you were great."

"I just did whatever he told me to do—"

"Following him around like a shadow—"

"Not if it was during the school year—then I left
here after PT and didn't come back until later," Quinn

said, sticking with his claim that he hadn't taken up *all* of her father's attention.

"That didn't free up time for me to have with him—I was in school, too! And the minute I came home, you were here."

"Okay. But I was only here until dinnertime. Then I had to go home—"

"There were plenty of nights when you went on night maneuvers or night marches or reconnaissance or night surveillance. And even when it wasn't playing war, there were also more dinners here than I can count where you went from the dining-room table to the den for him to quiz you on strategy, tell you war stories, re-enact battles with his dumb toy soldiers. Or you just sat around watching war movies with him!" she spluttered.

"None of that happened until I was a lot older, until I had my driver's license and could go out at night. For all those years before that, I had to be home to eat and then stay there. It was family time—the same as it was here."

"Ha!"

"You're claiming I *didn't* have family time?" he asked, their debate at full steam although his voice was even and only Clairy was clearly angry.

"I'm telling you that I didn't have family time even after you left and *that* was your fault, too!"

"Come on," he scoffed again. "He was your *dad*… I didn't have a dad, but I was still hanging out with my mother, with my brothers, with Big Ben. Don't tell me that isn't what you were doing over here with a father you only got to be with when he was in town. Especially when you were little, long before he was running me through night training."

Quinn hadn't had a dad? What was that about?

Clairy wondered. Of course he'd had a dad—his father had served in the military and was slated to go into the library…

But again, she saw this as her chance to give her side of things, and she wasn't going to veer from it to ask what Quinn meant.

"There was no such thing as *family time* with my father," she said instead, as if Quinn was delusional. "If he was here on leave, he ate dinner in the dining room and he talked to Mim and Grampa—not to me, because *children were to be seen and not heard*, according to him. At least, that's how it was with me—"

"Not much different with me, then—I was just supposed to take orders."

"But he talked *about* you—he bragged about you, about the super marine he was making out of you, about how proud he was to be doing that. Sometimes he told them something funny you'd done or said that delighted him—he didn't even talk *about* me."

"But you were here and I wasn't," Quinn insisted. "That should have counted for something."

"When it was still all about you? And how could I compete with the massive number of push-ups you'd done for him that day? Or the marsh you'd slogged through even after you'd slipped and were covered in mud? Or the funny question you asked him about latrines? How could he care about helping me with my spelling words when *you* had started to understand how to tell military time? When it was 'all hail young Quinn' everywhere I turned! One night I asked him to tuck me in and he said he was sure *you* didn't need tucking in, so why should I? Family time?" she repeated. "Once dinner was over he wanted to read or watch his TV, have his Scotch, and again, I was supposed to be *seen and not heard*—*that* was my family time."

"He wouldn't have known whether I needed to be tucked in or not," Quinn said, as if there was nothing else he could think to say to all that.

But it was a weak answer and he seemed to know that. He was silent for a moment, his expression showing some guilt. Then he said, "I didn't know that was how he was with you. He was your *dad*—I was jealous of that. I figured that when I wasn't around he was *being* your dad, the way I imagined a dad would be."

As if the reality was beginning to sink in, after another moment of thought, Quinn said, "But now that you say it, I do remember you trying to tag along sometimes on my days with him—training and whatever. I remember that he was a bear to you. But he was a bear to me—that was just part of it. I thought that if you wanted in, you needed to take what he dished out the way I did. Since you always went away…" He shrugged. "I figured you didn't want in, that you had other times with him."

"Other times when he wasn't turning you into his mini-marine? Other times when he wasn't devising his next test to see if you'd pass it? Other times when he wasn't busy setting up your obstacle course for the next day? He was always only here on leave—there *were* no other times!"

"Okay. Okay…" Quinn finally conceded. "You can blame me for the time I did take up. But I'm not sure there's blame for me in working so hard for him that he talked about it. And is it really my fault that he *did* talk about me when I wasn't around? My fault that he still wasn't paying attention to you?" Quinn asked in his own defense.

Clairy had that answer at the ready because it was the answer she'd clung to since early on. "Oh, believe me, my father gets plenty of blame! I never accepted Mim's excuses for him then or now, and maybe the best I could have hoped for was that he would have eventually gotten bored enough to toss me a few crumbs of attention, a little bit of acknowledgment. But instead, he had you to keep him from even the chance of that! He didn't go looking for you…and he wouldn't have. If you had stayed away from him *period*, then I might have been able to have the time with him that you took up. He might have gotten bored enough to *notice* me. And then maybe—even if it was just by default—we might have come to have a relationship! If you had stayed away from him, there wouldn't have been anything for him to talk about and plan for and compare me to! I might never have been able to be the son he hadn't had, but he might have come to know the daughter he *did* have!" she stressed. "Instead, he had *you* to *be* that son he wanted! And I was just left being incidental to the glory that was you!"

She'd really let Quinn have it. They'd both stopped eating, and now that he was leaning on his forearms clasping his beer bottle between both big hands and looking very serious, she waited. And wondered.

Was he really as sorry as he'd claimed to be last night? Or would he do some version of what he'd done in the past when she'd aired her resentment—would he use what she'd exposed against her? Would he goad her with it? Would there be some version of *tough luck*…

Quinn sat back and met her gaze squarely. "When it started I was just a kid, too, and no eight-year-old thinks they're doing something wrong to go after what they want—especially not if they were raised by Raina Camden. But later, when you asked me to stay away… You're right. I should have. You didn't hide how important it was to you, and it was pure selfishness on my part to ignore it."

He paused, arched his eyebrows at her and added, "I know I treated you rotten. Like I said, I was so jealous that you were Mac's kid, that you had him and I didn't have a dad at all… And…" He sighed with some heavy self-disgust, shook his head and seemed reluctant to go on, then admitted, "I thought you were just a girl…"

"So I was incidental. Not as important as you—you *are* cut from the same cloth as my father," she said snidely. "I was only incidental to him, too."

Quinn frowned at his beer again for a few minutes before his eyes returned to hers. "I can apologize again—and now, knowing even more, I *am* even sorrier and feeling like an even bigger horse's ass—"

"But all the apologies in the world can't change anything," Clairy said.

"Which is why we agreed to a new beginning last night… Did you decide there's too much water under the bridge for that?"

She'd had a full head of steam. But when she considered whether or not there was too much water under the bridge for them to move on from here, she realized that it actually had felt good to let off some of that steam. She'd finally had the chance to say her piece. And she'd said it.

Okay, maybe she'd said it loudly enough, stubbornly enough, angrily enough for him to think there was no going on from here, but the truth was that she felt as if letting off that steam had cleared the way to go on from here.

She took a deep breath, told herself to dial it back and said, "Honestly, it's good to be heard for once."

He nodded. "I'm learning more and more how important that is," he said quietly before his dark eyebrows arched up and he let out a breath that wasn't quite a laugh. "And I definitely heard you," he assured her. "I heard more things for me to know now that I didn't know before. So are we…okay? I mean, are we at least no *less* okay than we were before?"

"We're the same amount of okay," she decreed, unwilling to let him know that she might be slightly better than that.

Not that she'd forgiven him, but now that he was taking accountability for what he'd done, now that he'd genuinely listened to her side and recognized what his actions had cost her, it did help.

"All right, then…" Quinn said tentatively, as if he wasn't sure he could trust that things weren't worse between them. "I guess this is part of getting to know you? Of getting to know what makes up Clairy McKinnon?"

"That was my childhood," she said.

"And now we can keep going?" he asked.

"Think you can take more?"

"I don't know. You're tougher on me than your father ever was," he joked.

"You asked for it from him. You earned it from me," she said.

"I know I did," he admitted with a mirthless laugh. He stood to gather their dinner dishes as Clairy noted another thing that made Quinn unlike her father—an ability to acknowledge he'd done something wrong.

She stood, too, and joined in the table clearing. "You're the guest and this was repayment for your work at the library tonight—you don't have to do dishes," she informed him.

"It's late, and if we do it together, it'll be done quicker."

She didn't argue. Instead, while they worked side by side cleaning the kitchen, something new cropped up for her to wonder about. "So this is another way you aren't like my father—he did *not* do dishes—"

"*Another* way?"

Of course, he couldn't have known she'd been comparing him to Mac…

But after that slip of the tongue, she decided that the differences Quinn had exhibited might have earned him a tiny concession.

"My father wouldn't have let me—or anyone else— tell him what to do at the library tonight, and he would never have accepted that he might have done anything wrong like you just did. Now you're doing dishes. That was *not* something he would lift a finger to help with."

Quinn accepted that with a nod and made a second trip to the kitchen table for things Clairy was putting in the dishwasher.

"Where has your domestic training come from?" she asked, thinking that—especially with those looks—he was bound to have had a lot of women in his life. That there were likely women—or one special woman—in his life now.

"You can thank my mother for that—she had four boys, so there was no sexism in the doling out of chores."

That was an answer to what she'd asked, just not the satisfaction to what she'd gone on to ponder.

"Has anyone else benefited from that training?" she inquired somewhat hesitantly, since she had no business going down this avenue and she knew it.

"I've done dishes before, sure. And laundry and vacuuming and mopping, and I can even cook a few things," he answered, apparently oblivious to what she was looking for.

"Which you've done for girlfriends? A wife?" she persisted.

"Not a wife—I've never been married. Girlfriends, sure."

Was it the thought of those girlfriends that caused his expression to tense up and some of the glimmer to leave those stellar blue eyes, or had it been brought on by her poking around in this?

Clairy couldn't be sure. But the possibility that it was caused by her poking around still didn't stop her. "Is there someone now who you should be doing dishes with?"

"No. And there hasn't been for a while... I guess for me relationships have been—"

"Incidental?" she goaded with the earlier hot-button word, guessing that—since relationships with women after her mother had not ever seemed to be more than that for her father—that was what personal relationships had been for Quinn, too.

"*Incidental* is the dirty word for the night," Quinn muttered. "But, no, my personal life hasn't been my priority. No surprise to you, I'm sure, but I've been married to the marines."

Clairy nodded as she put the finishing touches on the kitchen and reminded herself that this wasn't a subject she cared about.

Or at least it wasn't a subject she *should* care about, and yet regardless of how much she didn't want to admit it, deep down she liked that there was currently no one special in his life.

But only, she told herself, because she wouldn't have wanted him to be successfully in a relationship just as she'd failed out of one.

With the kitchen tidy again, she pivoted from facing the sink to face Quinn.

He was leaning with his hips against the counter next to her, his arms crossed over his expansive chest in a way that accentuated those biceps she'd put to good work earlier. And done no small amount of ogling in the process.

"I can't say relationships or marriage are my area of expertise," she admitted, putting an end to the subject.

He seemed to welcome that and offered a new one. "So tomorrow…exterminators are coming in to deal with raccoons in the library's rafters?"

The cleaning crew had made the raccoon discovery today and had notified Clairy about it. She'd had to take action from there and had filled in Quinn about it as they'd moved furniture.

"Right," she confirmed. "And until that gets taken care of, we're not supposed to be there."

"That works for me. I arranged with my grandfather and brothers to gather Camden military stuff. We're doing that tomorrow. How about if, once I get it all together, I bring it over here and you can go through it, see what you want, what you don't?"

"Great!" Clairy heard the overabundance of enthusiasm in that single word. Analyzing it, she realized it stemmed from having begun to think there wouldn't be a reason for them to see each other the next day, and then learning that there was…

What are you doing, Clairy?

She put effort into toning it down as she followed Quinn's lead to her front door, where he was obviously going to wrap up the evening. More neutrally, she said, "I need to get my own unpacking and furniture arranging done, so I'll do that. You can just let me know when you have everything ready for me, and we'll set a time. I'm glad we won't completely lose a day," she added, justifying her own enthusiasm.

"It might not be until later, after dinner even. Big Ben and I will get out my dad's stuff, but neither of my brothers are sure when they'll get me theirs. They just promised it would be tomorrow."

"I'll be busy, so anytime is fine, even tomorrow night," Clairy said, actually pleased with the thought of the two of them spending a quiet summer's evening sitting together looking through some of his family history.

But only because otherwise she'd just be spending a boring night on her own, not because she *wanted* to be with him.

Right?

They'd come to a stop in the entryway and Quinn had turned to face her, one hand on the doorknob.

It was absolutely, perfectly normal and aboveboard— just any old guest leaving.

But there Clairy was, with the sense that it was the end of some kind of date.

Of all things.

As she tried to squash that idea, the quiet that came between them—the fact that Quinn didn't immediately open the door and just go, the fact that he was study-ing her as if something about her had suddenly struck him—only contributed to that feeling.

And without invitation, Clairy's gaze went to his sup-ple and oh-so-masculine lips, and she somehow became curious about what it was like to kiss him…

Oh, no, that can't be.

She drew herself up straighter, stiffer, and stopped *that* nonsense!

"So just let me know," she said abruptly, referring to their plan for him to alert her when he was ready to bring his family's military mementos to her on Tuesday.

He really was lost in some thought that seemed to be about her, because only her words yanked his eyes off his study of her face. "I will. And thanks for the fancy stew—it was one of the best things I've ever eaten."

Clairy remembered belatedly that she should be the one thanking him. "Oh, it was nothing compared to what you did at the library—I should have had a cou-ple of movers…"

"Nah, no big deal. I'm here to help," he said as he fi-nally did open the door and step onto the porch.

Clairy went out behind him, needing a hit of cooler night air suddenly—*not* because kissing was still on her mind, she insisted to herself, only because it was warm in the house.

There was no hesitation in Quinn's departure as he simply said, "G'night," and headed for his truck.

"Night," Clairy called after him, taking in a deep breath and then exhaling in a quick huff of shock at herself.

Kissing Quinn Camden? How could that possibly *ever* have crossed her mind?

Maybe it was the fumes from the cleaning solutions at the library.

Maybe they'd given her a belated buzz.

It had to be some kind of reaction to *something* other than him!

Because there was no chance it was just him, she convinced herself.

And certainly no chance that it was anything she wanted to happen…

CHAPTER FOUR

"WHAT THE HELL are you doing?" Quinn asked his reflection in the mirror over the sink in his bathroom early Tuesday evening.

He had his straight razor in hand and he was about to shave the scruff he liked to grow when he was on leave.

And why was he on the verge of shaving it?

Because for the millionth time since he'd come home from the McKinnon place last night, he'd been thinking about Clairy and about the end of the evening. And about how tempted he'd been to kiss her. About how, if tonight should end the way last night did and he *did* kiss her, it might be better to lose the scruff.

"Where's your head?" he sneered at himself.

He opened the medicine cabinet and put back his razor, taking out the trimmer he used on the scruff to keep it neat. Then he closed the cabinet door more firmly than it deserved.

He'd spent the day with his grandfather, sorting through boxes of his father's things to find anything pertaining to Reese Camden's military service and hauling them upstairs to look over. Tanner and Micah had joined them later in the afternoon with their own contributions to the McKinnon library, and they'd also dug in to their father's mementos.

When they'd left, Ben had thrown two steaks on the grill while Quinn had loaded his truck with the boxes full of final choices for the library. Then he'd texted Clairy to say he could be there around seven thirty. She'd texted back that that worked for her, too, and Quinn had gone on to eat with his grandfather.

It was after that that Quinn had come upstairs to shower. And shave.

With the towel still tied around his waist, his hair damp, he'd stepped up to the sink to shave and—thinking about other things—grabbed the razor.

"You are *not* going to kiss Clairy McKinnon," he ordered his reflection, his fiercest glare enforcing the directive that no one in any unit he'd ever commanded would have dared disobey. "Not last night, not tonight, not *ever.*"

But damn, had he been close to it last night! he thought as he turned on the trimmer and went to work with it.

He'd been close to kissing Mac's daughter...

Mac's *daughter.*

That pain-in-the-ass kid he'd always wished wasn't around. Whom he'd been jealous of. Annoyed with. And hadn't thought of beyond that.

And now he couldn't seem to *stop* thinking about her. Ever since Saturday...

Despite the fact that her hair had been wonky and she'd been dressed in clothes she couldn't possibly have thought anybody would see her in, that first glimpse of her since he'd last set eyes on her, when she was sixteen, had stayed with him. And from then on, his attraction had just escalated—in no small part because dressed in better clothes, her hair combed and wearing a little makeup made her such a knockout he couldn't keep his eyes off her when he was with her, and then he carried every detail of the way she looked home with him.

It was as if—for some reason—she'd set up residence in his head. And not just the mental image of her. There was the sound of her voice, the memory of things she said—even the hard time she gave him. Every minute they'd been together was with him continuously, regardless of how much he tried *not* to think about her. Nothing like that had ever happened to him before.

Maybe it was guilt?

That was possible, wasn't it? Especially when learning how Mac had disrespected women had left him wondering if he might have subconsciously done the same thing. He'd come to feel obliged to look back at the way he'd thought of Clairy as well as the way he'd thought of his adult relationships, the way he'd treated her. Maybe taking a closer look at her was part of that.

But that isn't all you're doing...

In fact, it wasn't even the lion's share of what he was doing.

It wasn't guilt or reevaluation of the past that had him picturing that thick, wavy red hair of hers and wondering if it would run through his fingers like silk. There was no guilt or reevaluation in fighting to keep from letting the backs of his fingers trace her cheek to find out if her skin was as soft as it looked.

It wasn't guilt or reevaluation that was going on when he lost his train of thought looking into her eyes and wondering if he'd ever seen a green so beautiful.

Or looking at those delicate lips of hers, thinking

they were ripe for kissing, and wanting to do that kissing until she begged him to stop.

He wasn't remembering that she was someone he'd treated badly. He wasn't even recalling that she was someone who had a grudge against him that she was right to have. She wasn't even Mac's daughter.

She was just a delicately stunning, feisty little spitfire who was churning up things in him at a rate no one had ever done before, with an impact no one had ever had on him...

And for no reason he could even figure out...

But she *was* Mac's daughter, he reminded himself. He didn't really know if that should make her off-limits, but it seemed as if it might. It seemed like there should be some kind of code against it.

Especially when his thoughts about her went beyond kissing. Which they tended to do as he was trying to get to sleep the last few nights...

Mac's *daughter*...

Over the years—like a father encouraging his son to find a wife—there had been any number of times when Quinn and Mac had been in a bar and Mac had jabbed him with an elbow to draw his attention to a pretty woman whom the older man thought he should chat up. There had even been a few times Mac had arranged for him to meet someone he thought Quinn might hit it off with. But never had Mac suggested Quinn take an interest in Clairy.

"Could be he didn't want you fraternizing with his daughter," Quinn told his reflection. "Could be he saw your lousy track record with women and didn't want her in line for that."

Not that Mac had ever seemed protective of Clairy.

"You probably weren't, were you?" he asked his absent mentor, his own disillusionment with Mac coming to the forefront suddenly. As did Clairy's comment last night that it had felt good to be heard...

It had taken Quinn weeks after learning Mac put women marines in jeopardy to force them out of service—or at least out of his command—to decide what to do with that information.

Mac was dead—he wasn't harassing or endangering any more women, he'd told himself. Maybe what he'd done didn't need to be known.

But then he'd also begun to analyze his own actions toward women, his relationship failures, and it was the women Mac had wronged who started to haunt him. Those women and the idea of sweeping them under the rug along with what Mac had done to them.

It had ripped him apart to realize that his loyalty to Mac, guarding Mac's reputation, couldn't be all he took into consideration. If it was, if he ignored those women and whatever damage might have been done to them and their careers, then he really wasn't any better than his mentor...

So he'd called a friend, an attorney in the Judge Advocate General's office...

His guilt over what still felt like betrayal of the man who had shaped him and his life dogged him. But since that phone call, Jill had been doing a preliminary investigation to decide how far to take what Quinn had reported. Nothing could be done to Mac posthumously—although it was Mac's reputation and the mark against him that was difficult for Quinn to feel responsible for—but one of the main things that would come out of looking into Mac's misdeeds now would be to give those women a voice. To let them be heard…

"So maybe if that happens you'll understand?" he asked the also-absent Clairy, hoping she would.

Which was something else new.

He hadn't loved the idea of telling Mac's daughter any of this, but now it ate at him to think that Clairy might turn even more against him when he did, when he had to confess that if her father's reputation was tarnished, it would be by him…

He shook his head at his reflection in the mirror. "One more reason to keep the brakes on with her," he said, thinking that it went on the list that also included his poor relationship track record and the point he'd reached since Camp Lejeune, when he'd realized he needed to reassess the way he viewed women himself and where they fit in his life, if they fit in. Or if they should be kept on a strictly R & R basis, the way his mentor had.

One thing he already knew was that, when it came to women from now on, the only ones he was going anywhere near had to be either in the military themselves—which was preferable—or be 100 percent on board with the fact that, for him, the US Marine Corps came first.

And Clairy McKinnon didn't fit either of those categories.

Add to that the fact that she was someone he'd already hurt, and he knew he shouldn't get involved with her.

"So no kissing," he reminded himself, as if saying that settled it.

Which it did—he wasn't going to kiss her.

Then, in his head, he saw her again—soft waves of red hair, alabaster skin, those green eyes.

He saw again the look that had been in those eyes at the end of last night, when all of a sudden they'd softened somehow, when a new sparkle had come into them that had been sexy as hell. When her glance had fallen to *his* mouth for a minute in what had read as a sign and had put him completely in the mood to kiss her...

"You still can't do it," he ordered his reflection.

And he wasn't going to.

So why did he reach for the beard oil that was supposed to make the stubble kissably soft?

By six o'clock Tuesday evening, Clairy had her living-room furniture arranged the way she wanted it and was ready for company.

For Quinn's company. In order for them to work tonight on his family's contributions to the library. Not for any social kind of thing.

She'd been reminding herself of that all day long. Reminding herself that seeing him was not her preference. They were working together for a short time and that was the extent of it. She couldn't explain why seeing him kept ending with the sense that they were socializing. Socializing in a way that could end with her thinking about him kissing her. As if the socializing they were doing was dating...

But that was *not* what was going on, and as she'd worked, she'd lectured herself about it.

If it hadn't been for her father's will asking that Quinn oversee the memorial and that his family contribute to the library, she and Quinn wouldn't be having anything to do with each other.

And once his part of the job was finished, Quinn would disappear into the marines the same way he had years ago. If they ever saw each other again, it would only be by accident, when he came to Merritt to visit his family.

So by no stretch of the imagination was their being together under the current conditions *dating*, and she told herself firmly that she had to stop having any illusions about that.

It was all very clear in her head when she went to the kitchen at the end of the day. But even so, as she reheated a bowl of last night's beef bourguignon to eat standing at the counter, she went over it all again to make sure there wasn't and wouldn't be any question. There was absolutely nothing going on between her and Quinn Camden in which kissing would ever occur.

Then she hurried upstairs to the shower—again, not because she was getting ready for a date, but because she'd worked on the house all day and needed one. As well as a quick shampoo.

After that, an upside-down hair drying put waves, volume and shine into her hair before she applied evening-level makeup—only thinking of lighting and not wanting to fade into the woodwork, not considering who would be looking at her, she assured herself.

Then she chose a cream-colored crocheted top that she wore over a simple tank for modesty's sake, and a pair of denim jeans hemmed with embroidery and lace that matched the crochet pattern of the top.

Altogether it wasn't quite a sitting-around-alone-do-ing-nothing outfit, but it also wasn't anything she would wear for an evening out, either. So not-date-clothes for not-a-date, but still feminine and presentable.

And it was also in keeping with her goal of never feeling as if Quinn had an advantage over her again, she decided.

Which she felt like he'd sort of had when she'd drifted into wondering what it might be like to kiss him last night. An advantage she thought she'd gone on giving him when she had continued thinking about him—and kissing him—long after he'd left and right up until she'd fallen asleep.

But not tonight! Not after also reminding herself today of every problem he'd caused between her and her father, every single thing he'd ever done to cause her to dislike him.

And between forcing herself to recall his mistreatment of her and those reminders of what was really going on, as she slipped her feet into a pair of cream-colored fancy flip-flops, she felt sure that there was no chance of him getting to her tonight.

At least, she felt sure of it until she descended the stairs and, through the open front door, caught sight of him through the screen getting out of his truck.

He had on jeans and a white polo shirt, the short sleeves stretched firmly around those biceps making them impossible to ignore.

His off-duty military wear was simply serviceable attire, but the jeans and that polo shirt? They might not be dressy, but they weren't workmanlike, either. They were clothes he'd put some thought into. The kind of thought that went into socializing…

"It doesn't matter," she muttered to herself as she watched him take boxes out of the cab of his truck. "This is still strictly business—from the beginning to the end!"

Sticking with that, she went out the screen door and said, "I can take some of that stuff in."

"Hi," he said, for the second time giving the greeting she had omitted because to her it seemed too friendly.

"Hello," she responded with a touch of aloofness to once again send a there's-nothing-personal-to-this message.

She offered no other pleasantries, and merely picked up one of the boxes he'd unloaded and set on the lawn, and returned to the house.

She did hold the screen open for him once she got there, though, reasoning that it was a simple courtesy since he'd loaded himself up with the remainder of what he'd brought and his muscled arms were full.

"You got your living room set up," he observed when he went in.

"So we could work in there, maybe spread things out on the floor to get a full picture of what's here," she said, following behind him and hating herself for checking out how his rear end looked in jeans.

And judging it much, much too good...

Quinn deposited his boxes on the oval coffee table.

"I have iced tea if you're interested," she said, having already decided not to offer beer or wine in order to keep the tone not-date-like.

"Thanks," he said, his own attitude tonight seeming a bit more formal, too.

Clairy went to the kitchen and returned with two tall glasses of tea, setting them on coasters on the oak end tables that bookended the overstuffed sofa and matched the coffee table. Then she got right to the task at hand. Standing over the boxes, she said, "Let's start with the most recent stuff."

"That would be in those two small boxes." He pointed to two boxes sitting atop a larger box. "One is from Micah, the other from Tanner—"

"And from you and your other brother?"

"For now I'm only handing over a few pictures of me and your dad—they're in this file folder."

The file folder was in a second box. He took it out and handed it to her.

Clairy opened it, finding inside three photographs and a magazine article with a fourth picture included in it.

The article was on a conflict in the Middle East and the picture was a candid shot of Quinn and her father at a desert campsite. They were studying a map on a table outside an enclave of tents, both outfitted in heavy combat gear and paying heed only to what they were so seriously discussing, seemingly oblivious to being photographed.

"You're so young," Clairy observed of Quinn in the photo.

"It was the first mission Mac recruited me for," he said, his tone ringing with reverence and the flattery he'd felt at being chosen.

Clairy set aside the article and picked up one of the photographs. It was of Mac pinning a Medal of Honor on Quinn—Mac's stony expression still somehow managed to convey the pride that Clairy had never seen from him for herself. It raised envy and resentment in her that prevented her from commenting. She merely set the picture on top of the article.

The second snapshot was of Quinn and Mac in a bar, arm wrestling, the camaraderie of their relationship, their affection for each other, clear even as they competed.

That fierce-competitor facet of her father was yet another thing he'd relished having Quinn around for, another thing she couldn't participate in, and Clairy felt a second twinge of old umbrage as she saw evidence of it again.

Once more, she said nothing as she moved on to the third photograph. It was a posed picture of her father, Quinn and his three brothers, the five of them in dress blues.

"Wow, this was something," she observed, looking at Quinn in particular in his formal uniform, doing it justice to such a degree she couldn't take her eyes off him. "I didn't know there was a time when you and your brothers were all with Mac..." She pointed to Quinn and his older brother. "You and Micah..." Micah had attended her father's funeral, so she recognized him. "But I haven't seen the other two triplets since they left Merritt the same time you did. Plus, you all resemble each other so much—which is Tanner and which is Dalton?" she asked, needing to force her gaze from where it wanted to stay on Quinn's image.

Quinn told her, then explained, "That was the White House dinner honoring Mac. I'd come into DC especially for it, but Micah, Tanner and Dalton just happened to be in Washington at the same time. When Mac heard that, he pulled strings to get them on the guest list, too. We were surprised that you and Mim weren't there, but he said it was too soon after you'd lost your grandfather."

Clairy couldn't help bristling again. "I think he just didn't want us there. Grampa had been gone six months and Mac didn't even tell us about the dinner until it was over. Mim and I were both upset by that—I've never seen her so hurt and angry. But when we complained, he told us to quit *squawking* like two hens, that if Grampa would have been alive he would have asked him, but that Mim and I would have just been out of place with military men and politicians."

"God, Clairy, I'm so, so sorry…" he said, as if he'd genuinely been struck by the information.

"Did you have something to do with him not telling us?" she said suspiciously.

"No! That was lousy of him!"

Was Quinn actually admitting that? Clairy was shocked.

"Some military women and female politicians were included, too—" he said. "Of course the honoree's mother and daughter should have been asked to a White House honor presentation before me or my brothers…" He cut himself off, as if once the words were out he'd reconsidered the wisdom in saying them. Then, seeming to search for something to vindicate Mac's actions, he said, "Is it possible that he honestly did think you and Mim were still grieving?"

"I think he just didn't want us there," Clairy repeated. "I don't know if he thought we'd embarrass him in some way, or if he was ashamed of us… I don't know," she said with an echo of anger.

"I think it was just Mac being Mac," Quinn said almost under his breath but with an edge of disgust she wouldn't have thought ever to hear from him in regards to her father.

But that didn't seem possible and she decided she had to be misinterpreting something.

Then he said, "I didn't know he hadn't even invited you. I believed what he told me…"

There was definitely disgust in Quinn's tone this time, but she couldn't tell if it was disgust for Mac or self-disgust.

Quinn started to say something but stopped himself, seemed to change course, and as if falling again into his loyalty to her father, he said, "It *was* all military and political talk…"

"Excuses, excuses, excuses," Clairy muttered, wondering how many slights and old wounds would be re-opened for her before this project was accomplished and she could move on to what she wanted to do—her own work through the foundation.

"But I'm sure my father would want all of those pictures included, so thanks," she said somewhat begrudgingly, replacing the article and pictures in the file and setting it aside.

Unable to keep some additional stiltedness out of her voice, she backtracked. "So that's all you want to contribute now?"

"Dalton and I agree that this seems like what you do when you've resigned or retired, when the last chapter has been written," he explained, as if he was glad to move on. "Micah and Tanner sent medals and ribbons they were awarded, decorations, some photographs—mainly pictures of them with buddies they want remembered—but they're both out of the service now… Well, Micah is— Tanner's paperwork is filed and he's burning off leave time, but essentially he's done, too. Dalton and I are ongoing, so it isn't time to tell those stories."

"And your brother Dalton is—obviously from the picture—a marine, too."

"He is. There *are* a couple of things he's sent to Big Ben that he said could start the ball rolling on him—they're in here, under Tanner's and Micah's things. It's a place to start on him…or maybe a placeholder for him. But other than that—"

"It isn't time to tell his story," Clairy repeated, thinking that Quinn was talking more than usual to fill the awkwardness left by the reminder of the White House dinner.

"In the Jenkins library," she went on, "there were a few families like yours—past and present service members. The present ones were just noted as currently serving in whatever branch. We left space to be filled later." And Clairy was also eager to move on, so she opened Micah's box, then Tanner's, deciding everything they'd sent could be used. She set aside those boxes with the file folder before motioning to the rest of the boxes.

"So all of this is your dad's?"

"It is," Quinn confirmed.

"Then we can do a bigger display of his things."

"Sounds good." Quinn seemed relieved to be talking about his father rather than hers, and the change in topic also helped Clairy emerge from some of her own resurrected negative feelings.

Part of what she loved about this job was learning the unique stories of each veteran and that was what came to the surface as they began to tackle the boxes of Reese Camden's memorabilia. Her first surprise with Quinn's father was that he was in the US Air Force, when she'd assumed he'd been a marine, like her father and like Quinn and his brothers.

As the evening wore on, Clairy laid out everything, and she and Quinn debated what should and shouldn't be included. Clairy had experience dealing with vets and their families who believed everything was golden and should be put on display. When it came to his father, Quinn fell into that category. Fortunately, Clairy had success finessing him through the process, pointing out why certain things only detracted from his father's greatest accomplishments, negotiating with him when he stood his ground on a few things until they'd agreed on what would be used and what wouldn't.

Then they repacked the boxes—one with the items Clairy would keep, the rest with what Quinn would take with him when he left.

Which it was clearly time for him to do once the purpose for them getting together had wrapped up.

But despite her earlier bad reaction to the White House event, despite having passed nearly three hours in each other's company, the fact that Clairy had tried to resist it, she wasn't eager to usher out Quinn.

She should have been. But she wasn't. And before she'd figured out why, she said, "One more glass of tea?"

As if you aren't doing something you know you shouldn't do just because you're sticking with tea, she silently sneered at herself.

"I think I'm good, thanks."

"Would you rather have a beer? A glass of wine… now that we're done with work?"

She wanted to kick herself.

What's wrong with you?

But she knew what was wrong with her whether she wanted to admit it or not—she didn't want to see him go yet.

"No, thanks, I really am good," he repeated.

Maybe she didn't want him to go yet because she still had more questions about his father.

"I keep wondering why, with your dad being in the air force and you and your brothers wanting to follow in his footsteps, you all went into the marines," she said.

It was a last-ditch effort, but also something she *had* been wondering about and hadn't found an opportunity to ask.

It did the trick, because Quinn sat down on the sofa—and not just a perch on the edge to give her a quick answer. He sat at one end, his right elbow on the arm, his left arm resting along the top of the couch's back and his left calf propped on top of the opposite knee, all as if the offer of more to drink was an invitation to stay.

Which, of course, it had been.

Clairy sat in the other corner of the sofa to hear his answer, feeling a ridiculous amount of gladness that he'd accepted the veiled invitation and reassuring herself that what she'd just done was purely in the interest of getting to know each other.

Why else would the entire length of the sofa be separating them?

It couldn't be more innocent...

"I know. You'd think we all—or at least one of us—would have gone into the air force, wouldn't you?" Quinn said. "But none of us were interested in flying. I don't know whether Dad dying in a plane crash factored in for my brothers, but it did for me."

There had been no indication in any of the memorabilia that Reese Camden had died in a plane crash, so this was news to Clairy. Hearing it now, she assumed it was while he was in the service, so she said,

"Was it wartime or peacetime when the plane crash happened?"

"He was a civilian when he died—he'd left the air force," Quinn said, as if he thought she knew. "He was in the air force from 1978 to 1986, but alive and well when he resigned—just after being awarded the Meritorious Service Medal that I brought you. He died two years later from a mechanical failure flying a private plane for the other branch of the Camden family—the Colorado Camdens. My great-grandfather Hector was H. J. Camden's brother."

"I knew there was some connection between your family and the Camden-Superstores Camdens. I just didn't know how."

"That's how. When my mom found out she was having triplets—with three-month-old Micah already on her hands—Dad decided he had to be around more than he could be if he stayed in the military. But he still needed a job and flying was what he wanted to do, so he became the other Camdens' private pilot. And ultimately that was how he went—at twenty-eight—flying a Camden plane," Quinn said, some sadness echoing in his voice.

"How old were you?"

"Not quite two. Micah was barely three—"

"You were two years old?" Clairy said, surprised. She recalled Quinn's comment the night before about not having a dad and her own curiosity about what he'd meant. Now that she thought more concretely about it, she realized that she didn't have an exact timetable for Quinn's family history. She'd been just a child herself and hadn't thought about the parents of other kids— she'd just assumed they had them. Including Quinn.

Trying to understand how she'd been so off base, she said, "I remember thinking that Ben was your dad until I was about eleven or twelve—I was throwing a fit about you being around so much and asked Mim why you didn't stay with your own father instead of always coming around after Mac. She told me Ben was your *grand*father, that your dad had died. But I didn't realize it had been so long before that. I took it as something that had just happened—"

"When I was thirteen or fourteen? Hardly."

"I remember trying to be a little nicer about you coming around for a while because I felt sorry for you—"

"I know that didn't last," Quinn said with a laugh.

"Well, no," she admitted somewhat contritely. "I figured you still had your grandfather around all the time, so you shouldn't be taking what little time I had with my father when he was here on leave…"

Clairy shook her head at her own cluelessness, readjusting her thinking to incorporate this new information. "I've always thought your dad was career military who died while he was in the service when you were older—definitely not when you were *two*…"

"I don't know what to tell you," Quinn said with a shrug at her misconceptions. "But you were just a kid—younger than me—and it wasn't as if you were ever at my house, or that I ever told you about my family or who was who. I can see where you could have thought Big Ben was my dad—for all intents and purposes, he was."

"So you didn't really ever even know your father," Clairy observed, putting some pieces together.

"I don't have any memory of him, no. Not even

Micah does. When Dad died, we came here from Denver to live with Big Ben—"

"I also just assumed you were born in Merritt. I guess because you were here when I got here I thought you'd always been here."

"Nope. Dalton, Tanner and I were born in Colorado. My mom lived on base there when my dad was in the air force, and Denver is where the other Camdens were, too. When he resigned and went to work as their private pilot, we stayed there, in a suburb outside of the city."

"I really had it wrong."

"I guess you did," Quinn said, as if it didn't have any relevance to him.

"So no wonder you were hungry for a father figure."

He grimaced at that. "That makes it sound like Big Ben dropped the ball somehow, and after all he did for us, all he's been to us in place of a father, he definitely didn't do that," Quinn said, clearly making sure credit was given where credit was due.

But when he went on, it was in a confidential tone. "But for me…yeah, I guess I did want more than what my grandfather was. I love Big Ben. I'm grateful to him. I'd lay down my life for him. There's no better man. But he's a quiet, gentle guy. He was the sensitive influence in our lives—"

"Your mother wasn't the sensitive influence in your life?"

Quinn laughed. "No way!" he said, as if the idea of that was laughable. He didn't expand on it, though, but went on talking about his grandfather. "Big Ben was more our philosopher, our moral compass. And it was lucky we had him, believe me. But… I don't know… Maybe I had something to prove. I wanted a tough taskmaster to show that I could meet harder challenges, to mold me into something stronger, maybe. I'm not sure what the drive was. I just know that your old man fit the bill, that when I could meet his standards, I felt like I could do anything, like nothing could beat me, and that was the way I wanted to feel."

Clairy thought there was so much more in what he was saying that it opened her eyes to a view of a scared kid who had lost his father before he'd even known him, who had grown up with a sense of vulnerability that had probably come out of that loss even if he hadn't realized it. A scared kid who had believed that if he could make himself tough enough, he could truly feel safe. Just a kid who probably also wanted to shine especially bright for that father who wasn't there.

And it broke her heart. It made her realize all the more that little-boy Quinn wasn't at fault for her father ignoring her, that the blame for letting her down rested solely on Mac.

And it gave her a flush of guilt for resenting Quinn so much, even if that resentment *had* come out of her own family issues.

It also complicated things for her when Quinn seemed less a villain and more just another child with his own needs for a parent. When she saw things through his eyes and felt compassion for him.

Especially since that compassion opened the door for other emotions to come through. Emotions that weren't all negative. That softened the way she felt about him suddenly.

Not that she had *feelings* for him.

"I didn't understand then," she said quietly. "I just thought you were...*greedy*. That you were sucking up the time my father should have been spending with me, when you had your own father—or grandfather—to spend time with." She took a turn at shrugging. "So I was a jerk to you, too."

"Well, you weren't nice to me, that's for sure," he said without any real injury in his tone, as if he was merely cashing in on whatever culpability she was owning up to.

"I'm sorry?" she said in the form of a question, because she wasn't admitting she'd done anything wrong, just that she'd misconstrued some things in her own innocence.

"Is that supposed to be an apology?" he goaded, obviously unaware of the empathy he'd generated in her.

Clairy thought that was probably for the best, because she couldn't imagine that this man, of all men, would appreciate being felt sorry for. Even if it did put him in a better light with her.

"I *was* just a kid. And you were as obnoxious and mean to me as you could possibly have been," she reminded him. "So of the two of us, I'd say you still come out as the bigger jerk."

"Man, I can't catch a break with you no matter what," he lamented.

But the tone between them was light, teasing, when she muttered, "Let's just say it might get you a little closer to a break."

"Really…" he said, as if he saw possibilities in that, his own voice laced with interest.

"Not too close," she returned, not wanting to admit to too much.

"I'll have to keep working on it," he promised in a quieter, more intimate tone.

Their gazes stayed steadily connected for a moment before Quinn broke the connection.

"I should go. It's getting late," he said, standing.

Clairy didn't argue this time. She just stood up, too, taking the box nearest to her that held items she'd rejected. "I'll help you get some of this out," she said, even though he was leaving with less than he'd carried in and didn't need the help. But she told herself the same thing she'd told herself the previous evening—that she could use the fresh air.

Quinn put the two remaining boxes on top of each other and carried them under one arm so he still had a free hand to open her front door, then the screen door, and hold it for her.

"So," she said as she stepped onto the porch with him and they headed for his truck, "have you heard yet that your old friend Brad Nelan asked my friend Marabeth Hawn to marry him?"

"Brad and I usually see each other when I'm here, but we don't keep up in between. I didn't even know he was seeing Marabeth until he and I had breakfast this morning and he told me."

"Well, we can't get into the library again tomorrow because of the raccoons—apparently, there are more of them than the cleaning crew saw and they're a wily bunch—so I thought I'd use the day to put together an engagement barbecue for tomorrow night... Did Brad tell you that?"

"He did."

"Did he invite you?"

"He did. Is that all right?"

"Sure. That's why I'm asking, because if he didn't,

I would." Not for any reason except that he was Brad Nelan's friend, Clairy told herself.

"Then it's okay if I come?" Quinn asked when they reached his truck and he set his two boxes on the passenger seat, turning to take the third box from her.

In doing that, his big hands brushed her forearms where they were wrapped around the box.

It was nothing. Brief, scant contact. And yet it sent a ripple of something charged through her, stealing her attention from his question.

And, apparently, her lack of reply caused him to think the lack of speed in answering meant she didn't want him to come, because, before she said anything, he said, "I know that's not library-memorial work. If my coming crosses a boundary—"

"No," she said too quickly. She consciously cut back on her enthusiasm, then insisted, "Of course you should come. Like I said, I was about to invite you. You're Brad's friend."

"Still..." Quinn allowed, giving her an out.

"Definitely come," she responded, clasping her arms around herself to stop the lingering sensation of that brush of his hands.

He deposited that last box in the truck and closed the door, and when he turned back to her, he was somehow standing closer than she'd anticipated.

She considered taking a step back.

But she didn't.

"Will you have a date?" he asked out of the blue.

That caused Clairy to laugh. "I don't know who I would have a date with," she said to the absurdity of the idea.

But then she sobered when it occurred to her that Quinn might be asking because he wanted to bring one.

"You can, if you want…"

Oh, there was no gusto at all in that offer.

But Quinn smiled a thoughtful smile, his eyes on hers, and said, "How about if we're each other's?"

Dates?

That seemed like a really bad idea.

And still, she replied, "Okay."

He nodded, his expression satisfied and something else as he went on looking down at her. "Good," he almost whispered, as if it was a secret.

And something about that just-between-them hushed voice caused kissing to pop into Clairy's mind for the second night in a row.

Which was silly, she told herself, because, of course, kissing wasn't going to happen.

Until Quinn leaned forward just enough to make it happen. His mouth was suddenly on hers ever so lightly, his lips parted ever so slightly, extending an invitation of his own.

That she accepted by kissing him back.

With her eyes closed, her head tilted even more and her lips parted, too. Which encouraged him to deepen the kiss, to take away all tentativeness and make it real.

His big hands came to her upper arms to hold and caress them and send stronger, more vibrant currents all through her. She didn't unclasp her arms from around her middle, using them to provide herself with a small sense that she still had some control.

His lips were smooth. His breath against her skin was warm. Even that sexy stubble was soft. And he was such a good kisser…

Good enough that she could have gone on kissing him all night long.

Which meant that even though it was a fairly lengthy kiss, it still seemed way too short when Quinn drew it to a close and straightened up.

His eyes came to hers again with what almost looked like awe in them.

He didn't apologize, as she thought he might. He didn't ask if it was all right that he'd kissed her. He just left that kiss between them, squeezed her arms once and took away his hands.

"Tomorrow night," he said then. "I'm happy to come early and help if you can use me."

An image of *using* him flashed through her mind at that offer, but Clairy dodged it in a hurry.

"It's just a barbecue. It won't be fancy," she answered, finally taking a few steps backward, onto the lawn.

"Just let me know," he said as he went around to the driver's side and got behind the wheel, turning on the engine while Clairy merely nodded in response.

All as if he hadn't just kissed her.

And as much as she played with the thought of telling him he shouldn't have, of acting incensed and outraged, of letting him know he'd better not ever do it again, she just took one more step backward and waved weakly to send him away.

Because while something inside her shouted that Quinn Camden was no one she should be canoodling with, kissing him again was all she could think about.

CHAPTER FIVE

CLAIRY WAS UP at dawn on Wednesday. It helped that many of the guests invited to the impromptu engagement party that she was throwing for Marabeth had insisted on pitching in, but still, Clairy had a jam-packed day ahead of her.

The weather couldn't have been better for an outdoor party—sunny and warm but not too hot—so there was no worry about that.

Mim's green thumb had already made the sprawling backyard a lush venue. Marabeth's aunt owned the local barbecue restaurant and was catering. Marabeth's uncle had the best cheesecake recipe in town and had volunteered to provide cheesecakes for dessert, claiming he wanted the chance to show off. Her three bridesmaids had wanted to contribute, so they were supplying drinks—alcoholic and non. One of the groomsmen was in a band and was eager to provide music. And the wife of the best man wanted to do an appetizer platter.

Clairy was doing two more of those, but they were at the bottom of a long list of things that had to be done before. She needed to shop for the ingredients for those other appetizers along with decorations, disposable plates, glasses, napkins, silverware, serving utensils and tablecloths.

She needed to be home in time to receive delivery of the tables and chairs she'd rented, as well as the flower arrangement she'd ordered to adorn the serving table, and the Congratulations On Your Engagement banner and helium-filled balloons.

She had to arrange all the tables and chairs, set everything out and decorate before the appetizers could be made. Then she would need to shower, dress and do her hair and makeup.

With all of that on her to-do list and details galore also running through her head, it seemed as if there wouldn't be any room for thoughts of Quinn.

And yet he was there between every line on her list, there between each errand she ran and there without interruption as she worked alone in the quiet of the backyard that afternoon.

He'd done the impossible—talking about what had caused him to pursue her father as his mentor had opened up a soft spot in her for the little fatherless boy he'd been.

He'd let her see that he'd craved a father's attention as much as she had. Maybe even more.

They'd both had grandfathers in their lives—hers as gruff as her father and offering not much more of a paternal relationship than the General, while Quinn had had a closer bond with his. But still, hurt by the General's rejections and disregard for her, Clairy had merely sought refuge in her bedroom to lick her wounds. Quinn, on the other hand—and even *with* comfort from his grandfather—had toughed it out with the General.

He'd taken Mac's harshest treatment in order to have contact with him, time with him.

Granted, she hadn't had that option because her father had ordered her to go away whenever she'd tried to do anything with him, or with him and Quinn. But she'd spied on enough of Quinn's training to have witnessed just how exacting it had been and wondered why he just didn't go home and never come back, why he'd kept coming back day after day, visit after visit.

In her years of counseling family members left behind by veterans they'd lost, Clairy had seen more than a fair share of kids who had longed for that lost parent and the attention they would have received from them to somehow be replaced, for that hole in their lives to be filled.

She'd seen misbehavior and acting out in a destructive way. She'd seen kids who tried too hard to please, sometimes to the point of courting danger. She'd seen kids trying to excel in order to be noticed—to their benefit when the achievements stacked up, to their emotional detriment if they failed again and again.

And not once had she pieced together that Quinn might have been one of those kids. But now she was beginning to think that he was.

Fortunately for him, he'd fallen into the group of stacking up achievements rather than failures, and for his sake, she was glad. But her heart still went out to the little fatherless boy who had felt compelled to take the worst the General had to offer.

And, yes, that had made something shift in her—it had raised compassion for him for the first time, opening up that soft spot she'd recognized last night.

But was that what had led to that kiss?

Going into the evening with him, she'd thought that she'd had control over that. She'd been sure it wouldn't even cross her mind the way it had at the end of Monday night.

Instead, rather than merely thinking about kissing, it had happened. And she definitely hadn't been thinking of him as a little fatherless boy when it had.

But what if compassion and that soft spot for him had paved the way for more?

For attraction she didn't want to admit to. Attraction she had to be careful with.

After all, what had driven him to come between her and her father—and despite the fact that she was coming to see more and more that her father bore most of the blame—didn't excuse Quinn of everything, she thought as she spread tablecloths on all the tables.

Yes, she might have discovered she could forgive the actions of the very young Quinn, but there had also been spite and meanness in the way teenage Quinn had treated her, and for that he didn't get a free pass.

In fact, she knew she should be extra cautious because how much of that mean, spiteful, arrogant, heartless teenager might have carried over into the man?

"You should have thought about that last night before you kissed him. It might have stopped you," she told herself.

But would anything have stopped her?

Something needed to, she decided, even though rather than regretting that kiss, she hadn't been able to *stop* thinking about it since it had happened. Any more than she'd been able to keep from wanting to do it again.

And she'd already been thinking about him constantly. Falling asleep every night picturing him, fantasizing about him. On top of the fact that spending hours and hours with him still didn't seem like enough.

But what if the spiteful, mean, arrogant teenager hadn't stuck with grown-up Quinn and the man he'd become was not only a feast for the eyes, but also a genuinely good guy underneath it—the way Marabeth thought Brad had turned out?

Clairy wasn't quite sure where that notion had come from as she opened folding chairs around the tables, but she knew that thinking about that possibility certainly wasn't a good way to tamp down on an attraction to Quinn! It wouldn't leave much to resist, would it?

When she really considered the likelihood of such a drastic change in him, though, she couldn't actually believe it. Not when she recalled just how badly he'd treated her.

And none of it mattered, anyway, because it wasn't as if he was a prospect for a relationship, she reasoned as she finished setting up the serving table and went for the ladder in order to string up the banner and balloons.

A relationship?

Was that what these thoughts were inching toward?

"Oh, Clairy..." she said to herself with a sigh. "You can't be entertaining the slightest idea of a relationship—not now and not with Quinn Camden."

But the very outlandishness of that possibility made it occur to her that all of these feelings could very well be a postdivorce ripple.

She'd also done marriage and divorce counseling for veterans, for the spouses of veterans. And she'd seen divorce among friends. She knew there were many things that could show up in the aftermath of a split, including a desire to fill the gap with a new person, a new romance, a new relationship.

No, she wasn't aware of feeling any of that, but that didn't necessarily mean it wasn't simmering somewhere in her subconscious.

Especially when her marriage had turned into a situation so similar to her childhood and she'd found herself overlooked and inconsequential again.

That had to be factoring in, she realized.

Here she was, coming out of a divorce from a man who had barely been aware of her for almost the entirety of their marriage, and she was now spending time with someone who was drop-dead gorgeous and was paying attention to her, putting effort into getting to know her and clearly not overlooking her.

No matter what kind of a jerk he'd once been.

All she needed to do was ride out what was nothing more than the first postdivorce phase and stop making it a big deal.

By the time the outside was ready for guests and she'd moved into the kitchen to make hors d'oeuvres, she had herself convinced that was all that was going on with her and she didn't need to worry about whatever she was feeling toward Quinn.

And not only was this merely phase one, she decided as she hollowed out cherry peppers and stuffed them with cream cheese and prosciutto, this whole thing with him had a short shelf life because—like her father—Quinn being here was only a temporary thing. A visit on leave.

After which he would return to duty, her life would go on, and that would be that.

So whether or not she'd forgiven him or found compassion for him, whether or not she had a soft spot for him, whether or not he'd evolved into the most wonderful man on earth, it didn't make any difference. It wasn't even of any consequence if she was fixating on him a little for the moment—it was probably just therapeutic.

And if she needed something to keep her grounded in reality, she reminded herself of the one thing she did know about Quinn—he was military through and through. Like her father. Which meant that he was devoted to the marines in a way he would never be as devoted to anything or anyone else.

It was what she'd suffered as a kid, what she'd blamed—as much as she'd blamed Quinn—for not having all she should have had with the General. It was what she'd experienced again in her marriage, despite the fact that Jared was a civilian. He'd been devoted to something other than her, too. And that had confirmed in spades that she didn't ever want to be in any other relationship where she was second fiddle—not to the military or anything else.

Twice was enough.

As she finished the second appetizer tray of fresh vegetables with a spicy Southwestern vegetable dip to go along with them, she felt as if what was happening when it came to Quinn was more containable and less worrisome.

So she was going to worry less about it and contain it more.

And yet still, as she checked the time and rushed upstairs to shower and get ready for the party, she couldn't stop thinking about Quinn.

She couldn't stop wanting to be with him.

And there she was, with the hope that he might kiss her again causing a flash of excitement to run through her.

"It's just phase one and it will pass," she reassured herself.

But before it did, should she or shouldn't she indulge?

Everyone seemed to have a great time at the engagement party. The food was a big hit, there were toasts and congratulation speeches galore, sing-alongs with the band and so many engagement gifts that they filled the back seat when they were all loaded into Marabeth's car.

Marabeth's aunt cleaned up all the barbecue paraphernalia she'd brought with the food. Her uncle left Clairy half a cheesecake, but otherwise took away everything else he'd provided.

Marabeth's cousin owned the rental shop where the tables and chairs had come from, and before leaving, Maxwell folded them, loaded everything into the back of his truck and took them away.

Marabeth wanted the balloons. The band packed their own gear and in the process dislodged the banner, which Marabeth also took as a memento. Ultimately, Clairy was left with a lot of full trash bags and some cleaning to do when everyone cleared out.

Everyone except Quinn.

Clairy thought that might have been as part of his suggestion the previous evening that they attend the party as each other's dates. There hadn't been much of tonight that had even given them the opportunity to speak to each other, but maybe he still felt obliged—

in his role as her date—to insist on staying to help clean up.

Nothing she said could dissuade him, so she finally gave in.

As Clairy took in the last of the food, Quinn carried all the trash bags out to the curb for Thursday's pickup.

Then he joined her in the kitchen.

But rather than addressing the dishes in the sink or what littered the kitchen table, Clairy said, "I can do the rest of this in the morning. I'm ready to take off these shoes and have my piece of cheesecake—want some?"

She was still on the fence about whether or not to indulge in any more of the things she was fantasizing about when it came to Quinn. But what she was sure of was that after an entire evening of just being two ships passing in the night, she wasn't nearly as ready to say goodbye to him as she had been to everyone else.

In fact, when she'd been offered that half a cheesecake, she'd said yes mainly as bait, with just this moment in mind.

"Sounds good—I didn't get around to dessert, either," Quinn answered, leaving her with no clue whether he wanted a few more minutes with her, too, or just the cheesecake.

But Clairy remained glad he was there as she turned off the backyard lights and went to the refrigerator.

"It's still so warm out," she said. "How about if we sit on the front porch?"

"Sure," he agreed.

Clairy cut two pieces of super-creamy cheesecake, ladled raspberry puree over the tops and added a spoonful of fresh berries and mint to them.

"Spoons or forks, and where do I find them?" Quinn inquired.

"Spoons, I think, so we don't lose any of this sauce I've been hearing about all night. And they're in that drawer next to the fridge," she instructed, taking a dessert plate in each hand as Quinn opened the drawer and retrieved utensils.

Clairy led him from the kitchen to the front of the house. While she kicked off her sandals at the foot of the stairs, Quinn opened the screen door.

"There's only the swing, but it's big enough for both of us," she said, handing him a slice of cheesecake and accepting the spoon he traded it for once they were outside.

Then Clairy went to the padded swing hanging at one end of the porch.

"Oh, that feels good," she moaned in more rapture than was called for by merely getting off her feet, making Quinn grin a slightly ribald grin as he propped one hip on the railing nearby.

"Don't you want to sit down?" she asked.

"I'm fine," he said, making her wonder if he wanted to keep some space between them.

If that was the purpose, it was slightly disheartening to her.

But there was compensation in the fact that they weren't sitting side by side: she got to look at him.

He was dressed in a pair of gray slacks tonight, with a lighter gray shirt, the long sleeves rolled up past his forearms.

She liked seeing him in civvies. He might not look quite as rugged as he did in everything else, but there was no less appeal in the more refined version. And the well-groomed scruff kept him from looking too polished.

Since she had the swing to herself, she pivoted slightly on the seat so the full view was unhampered.

Tonight she'd chosen to wear a flowered sundress with a square-cut neckline so wide it barely covered her shoulders and only allowed for a built-in bra in the tight-fitting bodice that attached to a large circle skirt.

Not only was there a considerable amount of fabric forming the circle, but the skirt also hit just above her ankles. She draped it demurely over her legs and feet when she tucked them under one hip.

Once she was settled, she discovered Quinn watching her. Until she caught him—then he averted his gaze to his plate and tasted the cheesecake.

"Woo, old Manuel has reason to brag about this," Quinn commented.

"He told me when he offered to bring dessert that his cheesecake recipe is the best in the state—maybe in the country or the whole world," Clairy explained with some humor, quoting the older man's own words.

"I think he might be right," Quinn said, going in for another spoonful as Clairy began to eat hers.

"The sauce, too," she said with a mock swoon at the sweet-tangy puree. "He said I'd be sorry if I didn't let him bring that to put over the cheesecakes and he wasn't kidding."

As they went on relishing the treat, Quinn said, "It was a nice party."

"It seemed like everyone had a pretty good time."

"Seemed that way to me, too. How 'bout you? Did you enjoy it?"

"I did," Clairy said. "Did you?"

"I liked catching up with people I haven't seen in years. Seemed like you were getting bombarded with the same couple of questions I was, though, about what you've been up to since you left Merritt—that got a little old."

"Oh, yeah!" Clairy confirmed vigorously. "Only it's common knowledge that I'm back after getting divorced, so they were coming at you in a different tone than they were coming at me. You were getting the tell-me-about-your-adventures tone, and I was getting a whole lot of poor-Clairy stuff or fishing for dirt."

"Yeah, I heard that whenever I was in earshot of you," he replied, commiserating with her.

And he'd been within earshot most of the evening because it had almost seemed as if he was trying to get to her side the whole night.

Or was she just imagining that?

Regardless, he hadn't been too successful. He'd been the person everyone wanted to talk to, and most of the time she'd seen him headed for her, someone had way-laid him.

Although thinking about that reminded Clairy of when he had made it to her side. "Thanks for those two assists with Mrs. Rayburn. She was determined to get something juicy out of me."

Elsa Rayburn was the elderly town gossip, and on the two occasions she'd been grilling Clairy, Quinn had prematurely broken off his own nearby conversations and come to her rescue.

"I was trying for that third time, but I think she sent in Mr. Rayburn to block me, because that old bugger either couldn't hear me trying to excuse myself or just ignored me and kept talking—"

"His hearing is just fine—he probably had been given orders to nab you and not let you go."

"Well, he did a good job—he literally had me cornered. I would have had to knock him down to pass him," Quinn said with a laugh. "So I was stuck listening to his army reserve stories for half an hour."

"Marabeth saved me from that third one or I might still be stuck," Clairy said, laughing, too. "Thank goodness the Rayburns wore out early and left!"

They'd both finished their dessert and Clairy motioned with her dish. "Want a second piece of cheesecake?"

"No. It's good, but rich—one is enough," Quinn said.

If only that was true of that kiss last night…

Maybe it would be if you'd just stop thinking about it! Clairy chastised herself.

Pushing off the porch railing, Quinn came to take her plate. He set both of the small dishes on a small table near the front door.

Clairy was a little afraid he was segueing to leave, but then he turned back to her. Retracing his steps, he joined her on the swing. He angled in her direction, one arm resting atop the swing's back just behind the cap sleeve that covered her left shoulder.

Glad he hadn't been gearing up to go home yet—and not unhappy to have him seem to relax more by sitting with her even though it made not thinking about kissing him again impossible—she relaxed a bit more, too.

But when she did it created a minor problem—in order to keep her hair contained and off her neck tonight, she'd twisted the thick waves into a knot in back and held it there with a chopstick-like brass comb. As she leaned back, that brass comb got lodged in the chain holding up her side of the swing.

"Uh-oh… I'm stuck…" she said, forced to pull the comb from the knot and chain at once and leaving her hair to spill.

Without anything coy in mind, when her hair came out of the knot, she shook her head to loosen the thick strands so they could fall free.

That done, for a second time she caught Quinn steadfastly watching her.

But once more, the instant she noticed it, he stopped abruptly.

"Am I wrong or are you not a hundred percent thrilled that your friend is marrying mine?" he asked without preamble.

That was not such a light topic…

Was she going to admit to the truth or not?

She hadn't decided when he added, "I thought there was a little anti-Brad under the surface when you asked if I knew they were engaged last night and told me about the party. Then tonight—don't get me wrong, you were the perfect hostess—I still thought there might be a whiff of you liking Marabeth better than Brad. Even your toast was slanted toward Marabeth, with barely a mention of him."

"Marabeth is my best friend, so I do like her better. Brad is…just the guy she's marrying," she hedged.

She'd thought her voice had been completely neutral, the same way she'd thought she'd covered up her dislike of Brad all evening. But something about what she said caused Quinn to frown and shake his head, as if he saw through her and wasn't going to let this slide.

"You still don't like him," Quinn mused. He stalled for a moment and then said, "I was recently reminded of an incident…" He was silent again, as if he was treading lightly into this subject. "That day in the cafeteria when you tried to persuade me to stay away from Mac."

So he remembered it.

Clairy had wondered.

"Is Brad on your hate list, too? For backing me up?" Quinn asked.

"My *hate list*? I don't have a hate list."

"You do—I'm at the top of it, and unless I'm mistaken…" he said, as if he was putting things together as he spoke. "Is Brad next on the list?"

Clairy rolled her eyes as if he was delusional.

But that didn't deter him, either. "You have some reason for being down on him, too—Tanner reminded me that he and Brad were there when it all went down, that I gave you a hard time and that Brad piled on."

"Your brother didn't," she said, apropos of nothing except that she'd always given Tanner Camden some amnesty for that and it seemed worth noting.

"But Brad was almost as bad as I was," Quinn said, still piecing things together.

Clairy let silence, and the stiffness of her spine, speak for her while she thought again of why she should resist any attraction she might have to Quinn—phase one of her postdivorce life or not.

"Looking back, that whole deal was pretty bad, wasn't it? And it was worse when Brad got into it. It pitted you against both of us. And you were younger and outnumbered, and it was ugly and only got uglier when Brad chimed in and we started to one-up each other on the smart-ass snarkiness."

And clearly, Quinn didn't recall it without working at it, while it was one of the worst moments of her life and something she'd never forgotten.

Clairy only answered with an arch of her eyebrows.

"So Brad is second on the hate list," Quinn concluded. "And now he's marrying your best friend, and you've moved back to town, and that means that to be in Marabeth's life again, Brad will be in yours… You aren't thrilled with that."

"I'm more worried about the kind of person who will be Marabeth's husband," Clairy said frankly.

"O-o-h…that's even worse than you just not liking him," Quinn said, as if light was dawning. "You think she's marrying someone who showed a bad side of himself to you, and you're afraid that's how he could end up treating Marabeth when she's married to him."

"I was where Marabeth is now—freshly courted, newly engaged… It's great. Everything is rosy. But I was also married for years and I know what can happen when the bloom is off the rose. If the person you marry was different before meeting you, before they were on their best behavior and putting their best foot forward for you, that's the person they become again."

"Ouch!" he said, as if she was referring to him.

And certainly he was included in what she was leery of, and on the lookout for, because she wasn't convinced that underneath his current agreeable behavior, that mean, insensitive beast wasn't just waiting to come out again.

"Does Marabeth know where you stand?" he asked then.

"She says Brad grew out of that teenage big-man stuff, that he isn't the same person."

"You don't believe it?"

"I'm skeptical," Clairy said honestly.

"I'm sorry to hear that," Quinn said, as if he'd just taken a bit of a blow himself. "That has to mean you don't have much faith that I grew out of that stuff, either."

"Are you less driven than you were? Less bound and determined to go after what you want at any cost? If there's an obstacle in your way, is there anything you won't do to trample over it?"

"Yes and no—it depends on the circumstances now. Not letting anything stand in my way still sums me up as a marine. It's what's gotten me where I am, what makes me good at what I do. But I've learned that it isn't always the way to handle things—in fact, I've just lately seen that same philosophy in someone else go really wrong and learned a whole new lesson when it comes to that."

His voice had gone quiet at the end, into that mysterious tone he'd used when he'd told her that he knew some things now that he hadn't known before.

To Clairy, it seemed as if his mind had wandered into more than answering her questions. But he didn't give her a chance to delve into it before he came back to the moment and went on. "And, yes, that's all a part of me because my mother wouldn't have it any other way. It was how my brothers and I got what we wanted—it was at the core of your father, too."

"Who just added to it in you," Clairy said fatalistically. "It didn't make him a nice guy, either. Or someone really successful at relationships—especially with women."

Quinn closed his eyes, his brows arched, and Clairy

wasn't sure what button she'd pushed, but it seemed as if she'd pushed one. He appeared to have contained it, though, when he opened his eyes again. "No argument—your dad didn't die with a lot of friends," he said morosely, as if that admission brought some kind of remorse to him personally. "And he also didn't have a woman in his life...well, except you and Mim."

"And it couldn't be said that we were very much in his life," Clairy pointed out.

But rather than go on, she returned to what he'd said tonight, and last night, too, in reference to his mother—actually, what he'd also said on Monday night, when Clairy had aired her complaints against him and he'd said that going after what he wanted the way he had was a result of being raised by Raina Camden.

"Did your mother want you to be like the General?"

"My mother didn't know much about Mac, so it wasn't that she aimed me in his direction hoping I'd end up like him—although when she found out that I was hounding him to teach me to be a marine, she was all in favor of that because anything I wouldn't let up on got her approval. My mother wanted strong sons and she had her own method of getting us there."

His mother had encouraged her son to hound an adult for his attention?

That seemed odd to Clairy. "Her own method..." she repeated, trying to understand.

"I told you my father died piloting a private plane for the other side of the Camden family—"

"The Superstore Camdens."

"And like I said, the Superstore Camdens came from H. J. Camden, my great-grandfather Hector's brother. Not only did my mother hold my father's death against the other Camdens, but she also took an old family story about the Superstores being Hector's original idea and decided that if it was Hector's idea, he should have been in line for half of what the other Camdens made with that idea."

"It seems like there could be something to that… You don't think he should have?" she asked, interpreting Quinn's tone.

He shrugged. "It's one point of view, I guess, but she was the only one of my family who ever held it. She could never get Hector—when he was alive—or Big Ben or my dad on board with it, or with going after the other Camdens for what she thought was owed us all. And because they wouldn't fight for it, to her, that made them weak. She loved them, but she thought they let themselves be doormats to the other Camdens, and it made her hell-bent on not letting her sons be like that."

"And she accomplished that how?" Clairy asked, fearing something harsh.

Quinn must have seen that, because he chuckled wryly, then said, "She didn't do anything bad—she was a good mom, but she was a strong woman and she had a game plan to make her sons strong, too."

"And the game plan?"

"She made us compete with each other over everything. With four boys, that meant some fierce competition—over who got the last biscuit when more than one of us wanted it, over who got to choose what we watched on TV, over who had to do the worst chores. Every single thing that involved more than one of us became a contest."

"How?" Clairy asked.

"She set up obstacles we had to overcome or ways

to earn what we wanted or to prove we wanted it most, and whoever came out on top won out. And if she had so much as an inkling that we'd backed down from any challenge—at home or anywhere else—we were in more trouble with her than whenever there was a report of any one of us being too aggressive."

"She wanted you to be aggressive?"

"Yep. The more aggressive, the better," Quinn confirmed. "To her, that showed strength, and strength was what she wanted to see in us."

"So if you wanted my father's attention, you'd been taught to do whatever you had to do to get it…and it was something that made your mother proud?"

"Yes and yes. But there are a couple of things I'm getting at," he said, as if he didn't want to go into any more of this at the cost of why he was laying that groundwork. "Like I told you before, as a kid, I wanted Mac to take me under his wing and I just did what I thought I was supposed to do—anything it took to get what I wanted. By the time I was a teenager…well, we've already established that that time of life, on top of living up to my mom's expectations, didn't make me a nice guy. But I *did* grow up, and now I know when to use my powers for good and when to put them on the shelf," he said, injecting some humor into a serious subject.

Then he went back to what had gotten them into this conversation. "When it comes to Brad and that day with you that put him on your hate list, he was just doing the obnoxious-teenage-boy thing and following my lead— he was jumping on my obnoxious, bad-behavior bandwagon because that's what teenage boys do to show off and prove they're tough and cool and all that teenage stuff. Sure, sometimes it sticks with some guys who never grow up, but that isn't me and it isn't Brad, so I know you don't have to worry about what kind of husband he'll make Marabeth."

That had been a long and winding road to make his point, and it had said more about Quinn than it had about Brad, so Clairy just responded, "I hope you're right."

"I know I am," Quinn added confidently. "Brad isn't just on his best behavior and putting his best foot forward. What you see of him now is what he honestly is now—grown up and a good guy. He's a veterinarian, for crying out loud—he delivers puppies and kittens."

"And you?" she challenged, reserving judgment on her friend's fiancé and hoping her fears were as unfounded as Quinn thought they were.

"I have never delivered puppies or kittens. I did deliver a human baby once—under combat fire in a small village while my unit held off insurgents, if that gets me any leniency."

"Or are you just on your best behavior and putting your best foot forward for now?"

"If I was aiming for pulling the wool over your eyes, wouldn't I be swearing to you that I never tap into that part of me that burned you when we were kids?" he reasoned. "Instead, I've been honest. I haven't lied or pretended that I *don't* ever tap into that part of me. What I'm telling you is that when it's necessary, when it's called for, I do use it, but *not* otherwise, because I did grow up."

"Meaning that you can accept that you don't always get what you want?" she said, doubt in her voice.

"Yes," he answered. "Despite what my mother taught

me, I know when *not* to trample over people to get what I want, no matter how bad I want it."

"And you can just do that—set aside what your mother *ingrained* in you? What works for you? What's gotten you what you want since you were a little kid?" Clairy said dubiously.

"H. J. Camden was an underhanded, ruthless cutthroat. There wasn't an ethical bone in his body and that's why my great-grandfather didn't want anything to do with the building of the empire that those tactics created. Am I a hard-nosed marine when I need to be? Absolutely. Has my personal life suffered from the single-mindedness I've had when it comes to my career?" His eyebrows arched again, this time with something that looked like remorse. "It has—but in the form of neglect, not because of anything like what I did to land on your hate list. But the thing is, Clairy, time has taught me that being a marine is more than I thought it was as a kid, more than using what my mother *ingrained* in me. I guess you could say that the marines took what she trained me to be, what Mac trained me to be, and added the code of values that were lacking in my teenage brain—"

"Your mother didn't give you values?"

"Sure, the basics—don't lie, cheat or steal. Big Ben was our moral compass, but when you're a kid and strength, persistence and never backing down no matter what are first and foremost to your mother and only parent... Well, as a kid I saw the other things as...fluid, I guess you could say."

"The marines taught you to back down?" she challenged.

"It was in the marines that I was taught and held to

higher standards. Where I had to learn there was more value in earning respect than in getting what I wanted. It was where I had to learn about uncompromising integrity and unselfishness. Where I had to learn that achievements needed to come with honor, that honor was everything. So, yeah, now I *can* just set aside what my mother *ingrained* in me as a kid—what I was when you knew me before—to be the man the marines made."

He inclined his head slightly as he admitted, "Sometimes it's tough. But that's usually when it's the most important…"

Clairy couldn't deny the ring of truth to what he said, or the conviction in his voice, so she decided to let up on him. It also occurred to her that—like the timing of his father's death—the way Quinn had been raised was something she hadn't known about and it explained his actions, giving her a more complete picture of what had gone into making him who he was.

He sighed then and said, "How did we go from partying to all that?"

"You started it," she accused justifiably, since he'd initiated the talk about her not liking Marabeth's fiancé.

"I did, didn't I? Let's go back… It was a nice party."

Clairy laughed and repeated her earlier answer. "It seemed like everyone had a pretty good time."

"Seemed that way to me, too." But after that, he went on in a more serious, intimate tone. "I didn't get the chance to tell you how great you look."

The compliment might have been a little late, but she was still happy to have it from him. So much so that it was impossible for her not to smile. "Thanks, but I have to be the worse for wear by now," she said.

"No, you still look great," he assured her in a way

that seemed as if he genuinely thought so, his gaze more intent on her face than it had been as they were talking. "I keep going back through my memories of you years ago. You were kind of a gawky, geeky-looking redhead then—"

With blotchy, pale skin that she was abundantly grateful to have outgrown.

But she didn't say that. Interrupting him, she said sarcastically, "Thanks so much."

"You were kind of a gawky, geeky-looking red-headed kid," he began again, "but growing up gets the credit for improving on that, too. I couldn't keep my eyes off you tonight." Then he tempered the appreciation with a crooked smile and said, "From Saturday to this, definitely an improvement."

"I wasn't expecting company Saturday. I was packing and unpacking boxes. What do *you* wear to do that?"

"Full dress blues," he lied.

Clairy laughed, then found a way to return the compliment. "It was strange to see you in civvies. But you do them justice."

So much justice...

"I feel okay in jeans, but this kind of thing is like wearing someone else's clothes. Maybe because these *are* someone else's clothes, since I borrowed them from Tanner. But still..." he said, not taking the flattery too seriously. Then he returned to talking about the party. "My only gripe with tonight was that I didn't get any time with you. I kept trying, but Mr. Rayburn wasn't the only interception—there was one after another."

So she hadn't been imagining that he'd made attempts to touch base with her all night.

"Did you need something?" she asked, playing innocent.

"To say hello, to tell you how great you looked, to just have a minute with you."

Their previous conversation had done much to quell her thoughts of kissing him last night and repeating it tonight. But hearing him say that was all it took to bring back those thoughts.

"So you didn't just stay to take out the trash and have cheesecake?"

"That should have been why. But it isn't..." he said, as if something had gotten the better of other intentions.

Between the two of them, Clairy realized that he was being more straightforward than she was and decided he might have earned some of that from her, so she said, "Whatever the reason, I'm glad you stayed."

He smiled and his oh-so-handsome face relaxed into a pleased expression. "Wow, you said that out loud."

"Did I?" Clairy said in mock surprise.

He laughed. "Maybe I just imagined it. Don't worry, I won't hold you to it," he teased.

So much for being straightforward with him. It just wasn't easy for her to admit or accept that when it came to him, things she was thinking, feeling and wanting were heading in directions she'd never thought possible.

"Isn't this strange for you, too?" she asked quietly, all joking aside. "You didn't like me any better than I liked you."

"And now things are changing," he said, moving his hand from where it was resting on the swing's back to take a strand of her hair between two fingers. "It's definitely strange," he confirmed with some confusion and awe in his tone. "But it's happening..."

Was he resolved to that? Giving in to it?

Was she?

Clairy didn't know. Or give it much more thought as he leaned in to kiss her.

She just instinctively responded to the kiss she'd been longing for, the kiss that made her feel as if the last twenty-four hours had no purpose but to get her back to that.

Just phase one, she told herself as the kiss almost instantly evolved to where they'd left off the night before—lips were parted and every moment deepened it.

Had she ever liked kissing anyone as much as she liked it with him? she wondered, astonished and swept away by how good he was at it, by just how much she did like it.

His other hand rose to the side of her face as mouths opened wider and the kiss took a detour into something even sexier, something erotic. Something that gave her goose bumps…

She placed both palms on his chest. The chest that looked so phenomenal in the tight T-shirts he usually wore, the chest that felt even better—strapping, brawny, solid.

Then his broad shoulders and his biceps came to mind, and on their own, her hands followed that same course, upward to his shoulders, down again to those biceps, where she dug her fingers in, testing the power there.

And every inch of that path made her sizzle even more inside, amping up what was already mounting between them.

Until a car drove by, reminding Clairy that they were

on her front porch, in plain view. And this had become far, far more than a kiss suitable for all audience members.

Her next thought was that maybe she should take Quinn inside to continue it.

But was she ready for the message that could send? *Yes!*

But, no, not really…

Still, she didn't want this to end. She wanted hours and hours of just kissing him until she couldn't kiss him anymore.

Except the car had pulled into the driveway of the house next door and the engine had been turned off.

Hating herself for it, she forced her hands up those glorious biceps and over his shoulders again, drawing them down to his chest, where she pushed against him just enough to let him know it was time to stop.

He got the message, because a small groan of complaint came from his throat as he put the kiss in Reverse until she lost his mouth altogether.

"I know… Neighbors," he grumbled.

Clairy eased away, and he took his hand from her face, his other hand out of her hair and added a few more inches of distance himself.

"I should probably get going, anyway," he grumbled. "It's late…"

"And we should be able to get into the library tomorrow, so I thought we should get to work going through my father's things—"

Clairy had no idea why that brought a fleeting, but very dark, frown to Quinn's face before he nodded somberly and said, "Mac told me where to look for things in your attic. We'll need to do that, and there are other things he's given me, things I cleaned out of his office and house in Jacksonville…"

"We can take it all to the library, go through it, sort it, spread it out there," Clairy said, fighting to pay any attention to that subject, when what she wanted to do was kiss Quinn again, even though her neighbor was taking his sweet time at his curbside mailbox, going through his mail there while really sneaking peeks at them.

"Okay," Quinn agreed, taking what seemed to be a steeling breath that got him to his feet.

Clairy stood, too, and walked along in her bare feet as he went to the porch steps. "Thanks for taking out all the trash," she said.

"No problem," Quinn assured her, catching sight of her still-curious neighbor.

She had the sense that Quinn was fighting the urge to kiss her again when he cast another glance in the neighbor's direction, but he didn't do it, much to Clairy's disappointment.

"Text me in the morning when you're ready for me to come over," he said, then reached a hand to her upper arm and squeezed it meaningfully.

"Good night," she whispered with as much voice as she could muster when just the feel of his big warm hand on her arm was tempting her to ignore the nosy neighbor and initiate another kiss anyway.

Or take Quinn inside after all…

But he let go of her and the option went down the porch steps with him.

"Night," he said with some of her disappointment ringing in his voice as he headed out to his truck.

Clairy stood there watching him until he was behind

the wheel. He started the engine, then gave her one last wave that she returned.

Even after his truck disappeared down the street and her neighbor finally gave up his snooping to go in, Clairy stayed there on the porch as if it prolonged her time with Quinn for just a few seconds more.

And right then, she would have given just about anything if Quinn had driven around the block and come back.

CHAPTER SIX

"IF YOU DON'T want to hold Miss Poppy here, Quinn, then I'm taking her to sit on the porch—she loves it when we go outside and rock in the rocking chair, and I'm not passing up the chance to have a minute with my great-grandbaby."

Quinn held up both hands, palms out in surrender. "Have at it, Pops. I'm liable to break something that small."

"Coward," Tanner joked.

"Not denying it," Quinn answered with a laugh. "But I don't have to be insta-dad—you do."

"Yeah, you learn fast when you have to," Tanner said as they both watched Ben leave the kitchen with the three-month-old.

Tanner and Quinn were sitting at the table having coffee at 10:00 a.m. on Thursday morning. Tanner had shown up just to visit. His fiancée, Addie Markham, was having a spa day, and he had the baby on his own.

"So you're settling in to being a civilian just like that?" Quinn asked when they were alone.

"Yeah. Hard to believe, isn't it?" Tanner answered.

"It is," Quinn confirmed emphatically. "I mean, we knew Micah always had a time limit on his service. He wasn't going to be a lifer—he was going to stay in as long as it felt right to him, then resign so he could open his brewery. But you, me and Dalton..."

Tanner shrugged. "The road just forked."

"And you took the other route," Quinn confirmed for him.

But was it as simple as Tanner made it sound? "Did you take the other route happily?" he inquired then.

"Shocks me, too," Tanner said, as if he knew what Quinn was thinking. "But, yeah, I took it happily. Willingly. Eagerly. In fact, it was all my idea. Addie is... everything. I wake up every morning and can't believe my luck. And Poppy is mine—once that sank in, it took the blink of an eye for me to know that there was no way I could pack up and leave her behind for months at a time. No way I could miss even a day with her or being around to raise her, protect her. I just knew that not only was that what I had to do from now on, it was what I *wanted* to do. So my papers are in, I'm talking to a security company under government contract about a job I can do mainly from here, and what can I say? I'm buying civvies that you can borrow when you come to town—like you did last night."

"But I just saw you in Camp Lejeune *five* months ago, after Mac's death," Quinn commented, voicing more of his astonishment over the speed with which his brother had made such a huge decision. "Five months ago you were planning to go the distance, just like me, just like Mac."

"And if you had told me I'd be where I am now, telling you what I'm telling you, I would have said you were losing it," Tanner said, unflustered by Quinn's incredulity. Then he laughed and said, "Hell, that would have been the case even *one* month ago. For me, the marines were… I don't know…a calling, I guess. I thought I'd have that calling forever, stay in forever. Then I found out about Poppy, got to know Addie, and I started to hear a different call—"

"Out of obligation to them?" Quinn asked, trying to understand.

Tanner shook his head. "I'm not with Addie out of obligation. I'm with her because I want to be." He shrugged. "Something just happened. Something I didn't think would—or could—ever happen, and I wanted her more than I wanted to go on being a marine. I didn't want us to have a life where we're only together between missions or deployments or trainings or assignments. I wanted to be with her, with Poppy, day in, day out, through the good and the bad."

"I'm just having trouble picturing you like this," Quinn confessed.

"Maybe that's because for guys like you, and Mac, the marines are even more than a calling—they're in your blood, they go bone-deep. Mac died with his boots on. I'm sure you will, too."

Mention of Mac, of Mac's death, sobered Quinn considerably. Not only did it bring up the guilt he felt over his mentor's death, but Jill, the JAG attorney, had called just before Tanner's arrival this morning to tell him the results of her preliminary investigation and that the list of women with complaints about Mac was growing.

"Mac and I did see the marines mostly in the same way…mostly…" Quinn said, more to himself than to his brother, suffering all the heaviness brought on since his final visit with the General.

"Mostly?" Tanner caught that qualification and laughed again. "Since when?"

Quinn didn't answer. Instead, he said, "Tell me truthfully what you thought of Mac."

That turned Tanner's humor into a confused frown. "You know what I thought of him—he was a great man. A great marine."

"You and Mac crossed paths a time or two... What did you see from him?" Quinn persisted.

Tanner's frown deepened. "Are you kidding with this? I saw the toughest bastard in the corps. You know Micah and Dalton and I thought you were a glutton for punishment to go after him to whip you into shape when we were kids—experiencing it for myself when the time came made me *know* you were a glutton for punishment!"

"Living up to his standards, meeting his expectations, made you better, though, right?"

"Or else," Tanner said with another laugh, this one a pained comment on what had been required to meet the General's criteria.

"And that was true of everyone he commanded? Did you ever see him be harder on one person than another?"

"I did," Tanner admitted. "I was in a training with him about three years ago and he didn't think one of my guys was up to par. Mac rode him until he was. I almost felt sorry for the guy, but Mac did make him up his game, and believe me, we were grateful for it a couple of missions down the road." Tanner narrowed his eyes at Quinn. "Why? Was Mac losing it at the end? Getting soft?"

Quinn shook his head without hesitation. "Oh, no, not Mac."

"Why the questions, then? You want to make sure he lived up to his reputation right to his last breath?"

"Saw that for myself at Camp Lejeune," Quinn answered. He paused a moment, but felt compelled to press the matter, so he asked, "You ever think he went overboard? Hear secondhand that he had?"

It took Tanner a moment before he answered that question. "I don't know…" he said. "He demanded more than anybody I've ever known. I heard plenty of complaints about him, but I can't say it was from anyone I ever wanted to have to rely on. And you know what it's like in the trenches—you don't want to be there with somebody who *couldn't* pass muster with Mac when your life depends on it."

"So no matter how rough Mac was on anybody, you would have rather had him weed them out than not? Even if he went against protocol, regulations?"

"Protocol and regulations? Wasn't Mac about as by-the-book as it was humanly possible to be?"

"What if he wasn't? What if he thought it wasn't for the greater good to be strictly by-the-book when the book got changed?"

Tanner was staring at him, frowning, obviously puzzled by what Quinn was pressing him for.

Then Tanner said, "I don't know. I'm not even sure what you're getting at. I do know that I've butted up against new regs, new protocols here and there. Not a lot, but…" He shrugged. "I've had occasions. It isn't always easy to just swallow changes."

Quinn nodded his agreement. "Yeah, I've been there, too. But…" But what? Quinn asked himself, unsure where he was going as he struggled to wade through what his last visit with his mentor had left him with.

Rather than find a way to finish this line of inquiry, he turned more philosophical and said, "You think we ever know everything there is to know about anyone?"

"Will there ever be anyone who you let know everything there is to know you?" Tanner asked without skipping a beat.

"Spoken like somebody who's seen and done some hard things himself. Things he'll never be open about," Quinn said with an entirely humorless chuckle.

"Spoken *to* somebody who's seen and done some hard things *him*self," Tanner countered.

"For the greater good," Quinn added, repeating his own earlier words.

"So will I ever want—or let—every bit of me to be known?" Tanner said. "No. And so also, no—no one will ever know everything there is to know about me."

Quinn conceded that point with arched eyebrows, then focused his eyes on his coffee mug.

"But it seems like something pretty big is weighing on you…" Tanner commented. "We can keep it just between us if you need to get it off your chest."

Quinn shook his head. "Thanks, but…not yet…" It was all going to come out, but he thought Mac's family needed to be the first to know. "I have to pack up a ton of Mac's stuff to get to Clairy today—"

Tanner laughed yet again, this time the laugh of a prodding brother as the tone between them took another switch. "And the voice gets softer when you say her name."

"Oh, yeah, right," Quinn said, spurning the suggestion of what Tanner was implying.

Tanner narrowed his eyes at Quinn. "Are you getting some comeuppance for how you treated her all those years ago? Maybe you're a little sweet on somebody who could pay you back hard?"

"Hey, you may have been bitten by some kind of fierce lovebug, but don't put that off on me," Quinn warned.

"Wouldn't think of it. I'm sure you're above that."

"Yep."

"Even with a little redheaded beauty who could give you a run for your money," Tanner said sarcastically.

"Yep," Quinn agreed again, as if that statement was so true it didn't deserve to get a rise out of him.

Their grandfather came in from the front porch then, bringing an early warning of the reason for it.

"Uh, Dad, hope you brought a diaper," Ben said to Tanner as he approached the kitchen.

"And that's my cue to get to work loading Mac's stuff," Quinn said. He stood and took his cup to the dishwasher, then hightailed it out the back door and to the shed.

His grandfather used the shed as a workroom, but when Quinn had shipped the packing boxes filled with the General's things home, Ben had stored them in one corner of the shed to await Quinn's arrival. That was where Quinn found them now.

There were more than he remembered—too many to carry to the front of the house, where his truck was parked. So he left the shed to bring his truck as far around back and close to the shed as he could get it.

Discussing the General had allowed Quinn one of the few breaks from incessantly thinking about Clairy, but just the mention of her moments before put her back in his thoughts as he moved his truck.

It wasn't Clairy alone on his mind, though. It was also the fact that beginning that afternoon they'd be going through her father's things together, revisiting the General's entire career, his history, his decisions and actions. And it was coming after Jill's call this morning.

I'm going to have to tell you. The whole damn story...

Those early weeks after Mac's death, he'd wrestled with his own guilt over their argument possibly causing it and with keeping his mouth shut to protect Mac's memory. Then he'd decided he couldn't do that for the sake of the women marines, but he still hadn't considered airing that last fight and the potential consequences of it. But now...

Now that something was going on between him and Clairy on a personal level and he was going to have to tell her about her father, tell her that he didn't know what the outcome of a formal inquiry into Mac's actions would be, now that he was going to have to confess that he and Mac had battled, it was going to come out that that battle might have been what led to her father's death.

And now that Clairy was uppermost in every thought in his head, what was that going to mean?

Are you going to start hating me all over again?

That thought was particularly hard for Quinn to have because he didn't think it would take much to cause her to start hating him again.

And while at the start of this he'd only been interested in coming to a peace accord with Clairy to get through this memorial-and-museum work with as little fuss as possible, somehow her not hating him had become important to him.

Really important.

"But today's the day…" he told himself sternly, worrying about just how important Clairy not hating him had become.

Maybe just how important Clairy had become to him…

"That's some risky business," he warned himself on the heels of that thought, which had slipped in on its own. "You know you're not ready to get involved with anyone," he reminded himself out loud, as if it might carry more weight if he heard it rather than merely thought it. "You've blown it bad with two women already—worse than bad with Laine—and you don't have any business messing around with someone else until you figure out how much of Mac's disregard for any woman's feelings you might have channeled."

But ready or not…

Quinn sighed as he slid another box into the bed of his truck.

What was churning around inside of him when it came to Clairy shouldn't be. But Tanner's crack about him being sweet on her wasn't wrong. He didn't know if he'd fooled his brother or not, but to say that he was *sweet* on Clairy was actually way too mild a description. That kiss last night had been more hot and spicy than sweet.

Jeez, what a kiss…

A kiss he shouldn't have let go as far as it had—something he was reminded of, especially when telling her about her father nagged at him.

Nagged at him and brought up the questions he'd

been chewing on for a while now about himself and where he went going forward with his own relationships. What he really wanted.

Looking at his own history with women through the same lens he was now looking at his mentor, he'd come to realize that he couldn't keep getting involved with women in the same way he had been. It had become a pattern with him. Not consciously, not intentionally—he hadn't even recognized it until he'd begun to compare himself to Mac—but a pattern of general disregard for what was important to a woman involved with him, a general disregard for their own wants and needs. A pattern of treating them as if they weren't as important as he was, as the marines were. And it had to stop.

It had to stop, he had to regroup and he had to decide how to proceed from here. He had to figure out if he should accept that serving his country in the marines was the be-all and end-all for him forever—what he'd believed since he was a child.

If it was, then from now on he had to make sure the only women he spent any time with were women who were satisfied being relegated to recreational status. Or women who could accept never being as important to him as the marines, but were still willing to have a future with him being fully aware of that…if women like that existed.

But one way or another, until he actually figured it out, he shouldn't be messing around with any woman, let alone with Clairy.

He just couldn't seem to help himself…

But you need to!

As long as he had as much weighing on him as he did, until he sorted out everything he needed to sort out about Mac, about how much his mentor might have colored his own views and actions, he needed to keep to the straight and narrow.

And that went double—triple—with Clairy.

He was just losing confidence in his ability to stick to that straight and narrow when it came to her.

"But telling her what you have to tell her now might take it out of your hands…"

"It's up to you, honey, but I think it should be known that even big important generals start out as little boys."

"You know we would have to fight him to put it in, though—he *never* would have let us do it willingly," Clairy laughingly answered her grandmother.

Clairy had put off Quinn this morning because it was the only time in Mim's busy new schedule for her to come over to go through family photos. Clairy's goal was to find out what her grandmother might want contributed to the General's memorial.

The elderly woman had made several choices that documented the early high points and transitional moments of her son's life—graduations, awards, being carried on the shoulders of teammates after football victories, becoming school president.

But on a lighter, sweeter side, she'd also come across a picture of Mac when he was four years old. In the weathered black-and-white snapshot he was wearing his father's army jacket and cap—the jacket hung to the floor, while the cap was tipped back on the small boy's head to rest on his shoulders. And her dad was giving a touching salute.

It was a cute picture, and because it represented a branch of the service, Mim thought it should be the start of the display, to show the General's early, innocent interest in the military.

Clairy liked the idea but still felt inclined to point out that her father would have considered it undignified. That was what she was doing as they walked out to Mim's car after the lunch Clairy had made for them.

"Well, now he doesn't have a say," Mim insisted. "And I'm his mother and I want one picture of him as my little boy."

"Okay," Clairy conceded. "I'll have it framed with a plaque underneath it saying it was donated by you."

"Good."

Mim opened her car door, gave Clairy a hug and said, "I better get going. Harry is waiting."

"Tell him I said hello," Clairy instructed as her grandmother started the engine and pulled away from the curb at a snail's pace.

Then she hurried back inside with barely an hour to get ready for Quinn's scheduled arrival at three.

She'd showered early and now dressed in a pair of black ankle-length slacks and a pale blue sleeveless cotton shirt with a ruffled front edge that crossed over to close with four buttons that ran from her hip to her waist to form a modest V neckline. As the time neared, she bent over, swooshing her hair to hang free so she could brush it from underneath. Then she put the long, full mass into a high ponytail with a scarf tied around it. She added soft pink lip gloss and a pair of slip-on sandals for the final touches, then went downstairs and stopped near the living room's picture window just as Quinn drove up.

He parked his big white truck where her grandmother's sedan had been, and that was all it took for Clairy to forget what she'd been about to do and stop where she was as he turned off the engine and got out.

Was her heart actually racing?

Just because of him?

Come on, Clairy, get it together!

But her heart *was* racing and it just went on racing as she watched him come up the walkway.

Gone were the slacks and shirt of the previous evening. He'd replaced them with tan cargo pants and a navy blue crewneck T-shirt with the marine emblem over his left, well-accentuated pec.

Back to rugged, Clairy thought as she watched him approach the house, wishing she could find fault with the well-groomed stubble, the artfully disarrayed hair and the more casual clothes.

But she failed miserably.

So miserably that for a split second she fantasized about skipping what they had planned today, so she could drag him inside, close the door behind him and spend the afternoon making out with him on the couch like a couple of teenagers…

Shaking off that idea, she retraced her steps to hold open the screen door for him. "Hi. Come in," she invited.

"How you doin'?" he greeted her as he entered, both of them sounding like they were barely acquainted.

"I'm ready to dig in to my father's storied career to see what we're dealing with," she answered, having needed to bolster herself a little in anticipation of wading through the evidence of all the things her father had prioritized over her.

She had no idea why that brought a frown to that

handsome face, and it wasn't explained as Quinn came in and said only, "So, to the attic?"

He definitely didn't sound eager. But it occurred to her that while she was facing the evidence of all she'd failed to compete with in her father's career, Quinn was facing reminders of things he'd shared with the General.

They were both revisiting their separate griefs, and she realized she shouldn't expect the job ahead to be lighthearted, the way going through pictures of happy family times with Mim had been.

"I brought down everything I found in the attic," Clairy informed Quinn. "But since my father gave you instructions for where to find things, you better check it out and make sure I didn't miss anything."

"Sure."

And weren't they just so down-to-business, as if barely more than twelve hours ago they hadn't been locked together at the lips.

But getting down to business was as it should be, Clairy told herself.

Even if last night had ended the way it had.

In the attic, Quinn found only one box of her father's things that Clairy had missed. As they added her boxes to those in the back of his truck, he explained that his boxes contained things Mac had given him since putting the plan for the memorial and library in the works, as well as the contents of Mac's Camp Lejeune office and private quarters.

"I guess it was lucky you were there to pack all his things when he died," Clairy commented along the way.

That produced another dark frown and no response from Quinn.

Which was essentially the tone of the day and evening as they worked. Quinn was unusually quiet, solemn and somber.

Clairy continued to attribute it to grief—something she felt more strongly herself as they went through her father's things. Underneath her resentments and longings and regrets, the General had still been her father and she'd loved him despite it all. If she hadn't, she wouldn't have cared that she hadn't seemed important to him. And as she and Quinn went through Mac's things, it was her own grief at the forefront, too.

Late in the afternoon, they were interrupted by the delivery of the display cases she'd ordered for the memorial and the sofa designated for her office on the second floor.

Clairy tried to persuade the deliverymen to bring everything to their final destinations, but they refused, leaving it all just inside the library's front entrance.

"I'll bring my dolly and we'll do that tomorrow," Quinn promised.

Clairy had wondered if today would be the end of their work together—after all, once he made the decisions about what was to be included in the memorial and how he wanted it presented, it was just up to Clairy to carry out his instructions. Hearing him promise more of his time and physical prowess went a long way in brightening her mood as they returned to the job at hand.

For dinner they ordered pizza at eight, eating as they did a tour of everything they'd spent the previous hours setting out on the large library tables.

Because her father's final wishes were for Quinn to have the last word on what would best memorialize him, Clairy took notes on Quinn's decisions on what should be displayed, where, how and in what order.

She lobbied for a few changes, and when she did, Quinn accepted her suggestions, but on the whole, the memorial was more Quinn's vision than hers. Clairy reasoned that not only was that how the General had wanted it, but Quinn had also known and understood her father, what he wanted and how he thought better than she had.

They finished about nine o'clock and it was a relief to Clairy to have made it through the emotions this dive into her father's things brought with it. She felt as if a weight had been lifted from her shoulders.

But it didn't seem as if the same could be said of Quinn. In fact, he seemed so distracted by his own thoughts that twice when Clairy asked him something she'd had to repeat herself because he didn't hear her the first time. And more than the somber expression he'd carried throughout their hours of discussing her father, he appeared to sink even further into brooding.

Even so, rather than ending the evening when they reached a stopping point with the memorial, he measured her newly arrived sofa, the opening and inside of the elevator, and said, "I think between the two of us we could get this upstairs to your office tonight."

"Today hasn't done you in?" Clairy ventured, uncertain what was going on with him, but worrying that he might just want away from memories of her father, and maybe of her, too.

"I think I can push myself," he said facetiously.

"I'm willing," she said, flinching internally at the unintentional innuendo that hovered around the edges of that comment.

But Quinn was still so mired in whatever was on his

mind that he didn't even catch it. He just went to the tufted leather sofa so they could slide it to the elevator.

When they got it there, they upended it to get it in. Then, since Clairy alone could fit in the elevator with it, she stood alongside to steady it for the ride and Quinn met her on the second floor.

They slid it to her office, where they put it against the wall she'd designated for it.

Quinn pulled off the protective plastic and sat in the center to give it a test-drive.

"That's a lot more comfortable than it looks," he proclaimed. He patted the seat. "Try it out."

Clairy did. "It isn't bad," she said, judging for herself. "I chose it because it looked stately, something for a library or den. But when you order online, you never know how it is to sit on it. It could have gone either way."

"But this is comfortable enough to sleep on if you ever get stuck here overnight."

"I can't imagine why that would happen, but it feels pretty good now—it's been a long day."

But she didn't want Quinn to take the comment as a cue to call it a night, because she wasn't ready for that. Even if he was quiet, preoccupied company. She at least wanted the chance to draw him out of his melancholy.

So before he could use her words against her, she pivoted enough for her spine to meet the couch's corner, where the sofa's back became the sofa's arm without a change in height. Facing him, she made a guess... "Today was hard for you—going through my father's things, everything being a reminder of him."

"For you, too, wasn't it?"

"Yes..." she answered, hedging. "But it was a reminder for me of where he really lived his life, what his life really was to him and how I was a distant afterthought in it, not a part of it. For you it had to be a reminder of what the two of you have always been about, what the two of you have shared since you were an eight-year-old kid, that you don't have him to share it with anymore."

Quinn turned enough to face her, too, laying his arm along the back edge of the couch, but he still didn't respond readily. And when he did, there was some hedging in his voice, too.

"Yeah, all of that… But there's more now…more even just today."

She wasn't sure exactly what that meant. "Grief?"

"Sure…"

"But something else, too?" Clairy persisted. She recalled what he'd said on Sunday night over dinner in the square after she'd given him the first tour of the library. "Is this what you said before about knowing something now that you hadn't known before?" she asked, her curiosity about that revived.

Once more he was slow to reply, and even when he did, he didn't give her a straight answer. "It's been a rough five months, Clairy. But there's some things I have to tell you."

He stalled, looked at the floor, obviously reluctant. Then he looked squarely at her and sighed. "You're not going to thank me for the information," he warned.

Clairy's concerns were mounting, but she hid them. "I don't know what could be such a big deal—my father was about the straightest arrow who ever lived. Unless he had some kind of secret life…"

"No secret life. But something he convinced himself

threatened the foundation of the United States Marine Corps—something he was willing to bend, or break, the rules over."

"Robert 'Mac' McKinnon a rule-breaker?" Clairy laughed, albeit nervously. "Come on…"

"I never knew it of him before. But when he chose to, he did it the way he did everything—in the extreme."

Stress was making Clairy impatient. "Okay. So if you're going to tell me, tell me."

Quinn closed his eyes, arched his eyebrows and took another moment to gather himself.

After a deep breath, he said, "I think you know how Mac felt about women in the military—"

"He *hated* it with a passion. He said there was nothing a man couldn't do and in the military that's how it should be. Women were just a distraction. The one time I said I wanted to join—hoping that would make him like me as well as he liked you—he blew up!"

"I remember," Quinn confirmed. "His 'no women in the military' was a pretty regular Mac rant."

"Mac rant," Clairy repeated. "That's a good name for them. He had an opinion on everything. He never thought he was wrong, no one could convince him that he was, and he liked to hammer his point home over and over again," Clairy said.

"That's what I called a Mac rant," Quinn confirmed affectionately, as if that aspect of the General's personality had amused him. His fondness for her father was still clearly in play under the surface of this.

Whatever *this* was…

Quinn sobered again. "But when push came to shove—when regulations and protocols changed, progressed—he might have bitched, but he did what we all do. He followed orders, made the changes. Mac was old-school—"

"*Old* old-school when it came to this."

"But I never knew him not to do the right thing. So when it came to women in the marines, in combat, regardless of his opinions and gripes, when that started happening, I thought he was doing what he was supposed to do."

"You *thought* he was, but he wasn't?"

"We talked about women in the marines more times than I can count. The marines are—"

"*The toughest of the tough*—I know," Clairy said, repeating what she'd heard both her father and Quinn say.

Quinn didn't comment on that; he merely went on. "We agreed that exceptions shouldn't be given for women in the marines. We agreed that they needed to meet the same standards every marine needs to meet, that if they couldn't, they shouldn't be marines. We agreed that to be in the field with women, on a mission with women, we all had to be able to rely on them the same way we rely on any other marine."

"In other words, there were parts of what my father was against that you supported."

"Parts. Where we disagreed was that women *could* meet the standards, do the job—Mac thought that women were always a weak link. But I'd seen women who were good, capable marines and I told Mac so. I said that if they proved themselves the same way men did, they had a right to do the same jobs."

Quinn got points with her for that, even if it did surprise her that he not only held that viewpoint, but had also grown into someone who could—and would—disagree with the bullheaded Mac McKinnon. "But, of course, that didn't budge my father from his opinion because nothing and no one ever did."

"No, it didn't change his mind," Quinn confirmed. "But he had me convinced that it was all just academic—that while it might be begrudging and reluctant, while he'd likely never put a woman in a crucial position himself, he was still following guidelines, protocols, laws and regulations about female personnel."

"Only he wasn't?"

Quinn didn't seem eager to admit that. And didn't at first. "The only thing my side of the argument accomplished was to make him hide what he was doing from me. Until I showed up earlier than expected at Camp Lejeune five months ago and overheard him giving orders to someone who didn't dare buck him, someone who was trying to reason with him, who was pointing out the glaring difference—the risks, and that safety measures were being removed—in what he was setting up for the two women trainees."

"He was making it *riskier* and purposely less safe for the women than the men?"

"Mac always set the bar higher for us all, which sometimes added some risk, but it was worth it—it made us better, stronger. But this was more than that. Worse... After I heard what I heard, I asked him what the hell he was doing. It was pretty clear that I wasn't supposed to have heard. He got more defensive than I'd ever seen him. He just went off—"

"It never took much to get a rise out of him," Clairy said, familiar with her father's tirades.

"He said it was bad enough to have women marines at all, but women in special ops? They especially didn't belong there and he wasn't standing for it. He admitted to me that he was going to make them fail, come hell or high water. And once he got started on his rant, he said some things that made me think this wasn't new or just about women in special ops…"

Quinn paused, clearly not relishing speaking against his mentor. Clairy had the impression that he saw this as a betrayal.

But he seemed to push himself to do it anyway, as if he was convinced he had to. "At Camp Lejeune, the orders Mac gave would have put the two women trainees in genuine jeopardy. They were strong, exemplary marines—they'd weathered everything he'd thrown at them. So he was stacking the deck against them, and that upped the odds that they might not have come out in one piece." Quinn's disbelief that the General would do something like that echoed in his voice.

Clairy understood how difficult it had to have been for him to discover that the man he'd idolized—the man he'd fashioned himself after—had flaws. But her father having flaws was not news to her, and while it wasn't easy to learn what she was learning about the General, it didn't hit her the way it did Quinn.

Still, she wanted to make sure she understood completely. "And my father knew that he was putting the women in higher danger?"

"He knew," Quinn said, as if he wished it had been otherwise. "He knew exactly what he was doing—he said it was what he had to do."

There was a note in Quinn's voice that must have been similar to the tone her father had used, because he made it sound reasonable.

Then it was Quinn's own conscience that finished what he'd been about to say. "But this was bad, Clairy…"

Another pause, another moment when Clairy thought Quinn was struggling with his loyalty to her father. She could see how torn he was between that and doing what he thought was right.

But eventually he continued. "I thought about the other things Mac had said—they made me wonder how long he'd been at this, how far he might have already gone with women assigned to him for combat. I decided I'd better do some digging, beginning with Camp Lejeune, where I made sure the specially designed training they'd been assigned was postponed. It wasn't easy to get people to talk honestly to me, because my connection to Mac made me the last person anyone wanted to squeal to—"

"That can't surprise you," Clairy said.

"I always did have his back…" Quinn responded, as if now he wasn't so sure that had been wise. "But it wasn't only that there was suspicion that I might be testing them on behalf of Mac. I talked to one former officer who had served in a unit I'd also served in under Mac, and found out that part of Tom's orders to make life harder for any woman in the unit was to also make sure I was kept completely in the dark about it—"

"So there were times when this was being done right under your nose?"

"I guess so," he admitted reluctantly. "And that made me analyze things that I'd seen myself, incidents I'd written off, justified with my own opinion that if any woman couldn't cut it, they didn't belong with us…"

There was more hesitation, more reluctance to talk. Then Quinn again seemed to force himself.

"In retrospect, I realized that I *had* seen a few things where Mac could have been purposely putting a woman in harm's way. I remembered even questioning him about his orders once or twice, but he'd said he was giving the woman the chance to prove herself to the men, to gain their respect. I remembered thinking at the time that had validity, that whenever I was assigned a woman—while I never put them in any position that could get them killed—I did use them sparingly, hold them back until I was convinced they really could cut it, so—"

"You'd bought it."

"And I shouldn't have," he said flatly. "Looking at those times through a new lens, I started to see that Mac was setting those women up to fail, hoping to show them and everyone else that they *couldn't* do it, to scare them off. I think that if they were hurt in the process, getting them sent home or transferred out of combat duty—or at least reassigned so he didn't have to deal with them—was worth it to him."

As all of this was beginning to sink in, Clairy realized that she was less stunned by her father's willingness to take some kind of action to get women out of the marines than Quinn was. In fact, she saw an added element to it that meant something else to her.

She'd had so many years of feeling as if, to her father, she mattered less than Quinn, that she was invisible, insignificant, irrelevant. So many years when she'd felt as if her father hadn't liked her, as if she'd somehow disappointed him, as if she wasn't enough, as if there was something wrong with her.

But to hear now that he'd felt this strongly even against women striving for what his entire life had been about opened her eyes to a facet of the General that she'd never considered. And that caused her to wonder if maybe her father had been so much of a sexist that he'd seen not just her, but *all* women as having less worth than men, that in his eyes *no* woman could rise to his standards or be worthy of anything but insignificant status.

And if that was true, it shed new light on her relationship with him.

Maybe it hadn't been about her…

Maybe it hadn't even been about Quinn commandeering her father's attention.

Maybe this was wholly her father's failure.

Quinn was lost in his own thoughts and didn't seem to notice that Clairy had been, too. But then he began again. "After just the quick-and-dirty look into it that I did, after what I opened my own eyes to, I had to put a stop to it," he said, his furrowed brow even more deeply troubled with that announcement. "We had one hell of a fight that night, Clairy…"

Why did that sound like a confession with a plea for understanding? For mercy, maybe?

"I told him I knew what he'd been doing, and I gave him an ultimatum—I told him he needed to step down and put in for retirement."

"But if he didn't?"

"I said that I'd formally report him."

That hung as heavily in the air as Clairy knew it had to have felt to Quinn when he'd made the threat.

"Would you have?" she asked quietly.

"Yes."

No hesitation, no wavering—only strength, determination and sorrow.

"What did he say?"

"One hell of a fight…" Quinn repeated. "We went

back and forth until after one a.m. It was as ugly as it could have been. But ultimately, he knew I meant what I said, that I'd follow through…" Quinn smiled the saddest smile Clairy had ever seen. "He said he didn't doubt it because it was what he'd made of me…"

This pause was the longest of them all, with Quinn looking past her. She had the sense that he was reliving that night, that fight.

"Then I left," he said ominously. "And when I came back at zero six hundred, I found his aide there…" Quinn looked Clairy in the eye again, as if he had to. "Mac had had the heart attack sometime between when I left and when I went back…"

Clairy stared at him as she began to absorb what he was telling her.

She'd known that Quinn was at Camp Lejeune visiting her father when he'd died. She'd known the heart attack had happened during the night, that he'd been alone at the time. She hadn't known that just shortly before that heart attack her father had had a heated confrontation and been given a career-ending ultimatum by the man he'd considered his son.

She wasn't sure what to think, what to feel.

But as that information hit her and she analyzed her own response, she discovered that it was sympathy for Quinn and what it had to mean to him that was uppermost in her mind.

"You feel like you caused the heart attack," she commented in a near whisper.

"It was a bad fight, Clairy," he reiterated. "I was making him do something he wanted *never* to do— leave the marines."

And Quinn's remorse was so huge it was almost palpable in the air.

"There was one thing you *didn't* know about him," Clairy said. "One thing that didn't make his heart attack a surprise to Mim and me because we were the only people—outside of his doctors—who knew it. He wasn't well, Quinn."

Quinn's brow furrowed even more. "What do you mean he wasn't well?"

"A year ago he came to Denver without warning. He said he hadn't been feeling well and he wanted to see a private doctor, that he was going to pay for it out of his own pocket so it was completely off the record. He said he didn't want any decline in his health known by anyone in the marines because he wasn't going to be forced into a medical discharge."

"That sounds like Mac. But he didn't even tell me?"

Clairy heard in Quinn's voice what had been in her own so many times—the shock and disbelief at learning that the General had excluded him. So she understood what had to be going through Quinn's mind. "He knew you well enough to keep what he was doing to women marines from you—he probably knew you were by-the-book enough not to let him go on working when he shouldn't have."

Quinn's only response was another raise of his eyebrows that confirmed her theory.

"Anyway," Clairy said, to get to the point, "when I took him for his appointment, the internist sent him from his office straight to the emergency room. A cardiologist there did a full workup—his heart was in bad, bad shape. The cardiologist didn't know how he was still walking around. Apparently, he'd already had a heart attack—"

"Something he'd felt? Or some kind of silent thing?"

"He knew it. It's what brought him to Denver—apparently, he'd had a physical the January before, gotten a clean bill of health. But in late May he'd been alone, had chest pain and passed out. He was still alone when he came to, he didn't feel well, but—" Clairy shrugged "—you know how he was. He wasn't going to let it keep him down. Still, he figured whatever it had been hadn't been good. That's when he decided he was only going to see a civilian doctor—"

"And went to Denver," Quinn said.

"The cardiologist called in a surgeon—they wanted to schedule him for immediate valve replacement surgery and a pacemaker. The cardiologist said Mac needed to retire, change his diet and lifestyle, that he'd need to take medications to thin his blood, and a half-dozen other drugs if he had any hope of his heart not giving out at any moment—"

"And he wouldn't do it," Quinn said, making an educated guess.

"He wouldn't even consider it," Clairy confirmed. "Mim and I both went round and round with him, and in spite of the cardiologist telling him point-blank that he was asking for a massive heart attack that could come at any time, he said he'd rather go out that way than live twenty more years not being a marine. The most he would agree to do was take the training command at Camp Lejeune rather than more active duty—"

"So *that's* why he did that! I wondered but he wouldn't give me a straight answer when I asked him."

"He was a ticking time bomb," Clairy said, finishing what she'd been about to say.

"And I threatened him with losing what he would have rather died than give up…"

Clairy had meant to decrease Quinn's feelings of guilt, not increase them. "My point is—the blame was his own, Quinn," she said more firmly, in hopes of convincing him he wasn't at fault. "The only thing that mattered to my father was to do things his own way and, in this, that meant to be a marine right to the end—"

"Which was what he was fighting for with me."

"You offered him the option of just stepping down gracefully before what he was doing was exposed—which it probably would have been, because eventually someone would have blown the whistle—and he refused. The heart doctor offered him help and he refused. Nobody could protect him from himself," Clairy concluded.

Quinn shook his head, and Clairy had the impression that nothing she said was causing him to relinquish what he clearly saw as his part in his mentor's death. "It still shouldn't have been me, of all people, who—"

Clairy decided to take a different approach. "I understand how you see this," she said. "But it had to be you who went up against him over the women he was putting in jeopardy. No one else—*no one*—carried the weight with him that you did. No one meant as much to him as you did. So no one else could have stopped him. And if you hadn't, if you had let him go on doing what he was doing even after you knew, then any injury any woman suffered at his hands *would* have been as much your fault as his."

Quinn conceded to that only with another raise of his eyebrows, which compelled Clairy to go on trying to lessen the weight he was carrying about this.

"You told me yourself when we talked about Brad, about the way you were raised, about your mother pushing you not to let anything stand in your way when you wanted something, that you've learned that even as a marine that can't always come into play. I'm thinking that when you said you just saw that same philosophy in someone else gone really wrong, you were talking about what my father was doing…"

Clairy paused for Quinn to confirm. She got only a slow nod.

"And it was the marines—my father—who taught you how to temper that, how to use your powers only for good," she said with the same attempt to lighten the conversation that he had when he'd originally used the turn of phrase.

"That's what you did," she went on. "Difficult as it was to do with one of the people most important to you. But the bottom line, Quinn, is that you were doing the right thing. My father wasn't. His health, accepting the risks that came with not treating it, was separate. And the fact that that was when his heart gave out wasn't on you—it honestly could have happened even if the two of you had just spent the best night of his life."

Quinn smiled another small, sad smile that didn't tell her whether or not she'd convinced him.

When he didn't say anything one way or another to let her know, she decided he might need to gain some more perspective on his own now that he had the full picture.

Whether or not that was true, he went on. "And there's more," he said ominously, his bushy eyebrows heading for his hairline once more. "For a while after he died, I considered keeping what I'd learned to myself to protect Mac's reputation. But the longer I sat on it…the more wrong I saw in not looking at it from the perspective of the women. I put in a call to a JAG lawyer I know and told her…"

"So ultimately you did report him," Clairy marveled.

"I'm sorry, Clairy—"

"No! It's what you should have done! I just can't believe that you—of all people—did it!"

"I wanted to protect him…to protect his memory," Quinn lamented. "But not only did the women he might have done harm to have a right to… I don't know… some kind of justice or—like you said—to be heard, but I don't know who else might have willingly gone along with Mac, who might still be doing what Mac was doing, and I just couldn't let it go without…blowing the whistle, I guess…" Though he clearly didn't like to label himself as a whistleblower.

"My friend Jill has been looking into it," Quinn continued. "I trusted that she wouldn't open a can of worms that didn't need opening if what Mac had done was on a smaller scale than it seemed to me—"

"What you were hoping was the case," Clairy guessed.

"More than you can ever know."

"But it wasn't on a small enough scale to be inconsequential."

Quinn shook his head. "Jill called me this morning. She's found enough to open an investigation by an independent committee. Not only into Mac—it looks like he had some cohorts doing this kind of thing, too, so I guess the best I can tell you is that Mac won't be the only one whose name and reputation will take a hit for this…"

"But there will be a hit," Clairy surmised.

"I'm sorry." Quinn's tone said he was sorry for so many things. "And when it comes to the memorial... I guess it's up to you to decide what you'll do with it... It could change the way he's remembered...cast a dishonorable shadow...or you could ignore it... I don't know..."

Clairy thought about what to do, thought about the man her father had been, his accomplishments, his flaws, her own complaints with him. "He was a long way from perfect," she said.

"And this could give you a platform to air that," he said with some trepidation, still in many ways following what seemed to be an instinct to be the guardian of Mac's memory. "Just please don't forget that even though Mac screwed up at the end he was still a great marine," Quinn seemed compelled to add.

Clairy thought about it all.

Clairy did keep that in mind as she considered how to handle all this new information. Did she want to air her own personal grievances with her father in public? Would that serve any purpose or make anything better?

She couldn't see how.

Instead, it seemed to cast her as a victim and she didn't want that role. She preferred to leave the way her father had treated her as a portion of her own history, something that had contributed to who she was, a lesson she'd learned in the kind of parent she *didn't* want to be, and the kind of father she wouldn't want to give her own children.

But what about the rest? Where *did* Mac's actions against women fit into the memorial to Mac?

She didn't think it could—or should—be overlooked. That didn't seem fair or just to the women marines.

After pondering it, Clairy said, "I think it will have to be noted somehow," she concluded. "I'll have to figure out how to present it—"

"Don't forget that there *are* women marines who made it in spite of Mac's best efforts, and they see that as a testament to their strength and stamina and resiliency in the face of the worst that could be dished out to them. I get that the women who suffered and failed should have a voice, but you have to give credit where credit is due to the ones who likely suffered and still succeeded."

"I'll try to relay the facts and include that. I'll give the reasoning behind what he did and point out that it's outdated thinking rightfully having a light shone on it. I can get hold of any photographs of only women marines and I can display them above the text and the outcome of the investigation," Clairy proposed. "Hopefully I'll be able to say that the good that came out of it—assuming good will come out of it—is that this kind of thing will stop?"

"I like that. It turns a negative into a positive. Even if the negative is on Mac, I don't think it undermines the good he did. It just shows that he had flaws…"

Flaws that Clairy thought Quinn was slowly coming to admit Mac had. To accept that Mac had.

"There was nothing warm or fuzzy about my father at any time, in any way. That's what made him who he was, and this will be another facet of it."

Quinn nodded. "I can live with that."

"It goes a long way that you've set the wheels into motion to stop it, though, to give a voice to the women he mistreated. Do you want to be given the credit?"

"No, leave me out of it. I'm sorry it had to be done—

this kind of thing shouldn't be going on," Quinn said quietly. "But there's no way I want credit for something that puts a smear on Mac."

Clairy understood that, understood how difficult this had to have been for him, and she thought that what Quinn had done spoke volumes about him.

Obviously he didn't see that, but he did seem relieved as he looked at her with warmth in his eyes. "Thanks for not letting this last misstep of Mac's overshadow everything else about him. It's more than he deserved from you after being the kind of father he was."

"I had you worried, though, didn't I?" she said, to give him a hard time.

But it didn't work, because his expression relaxed even more as he looked intently into her eyes. "Nah, I wasn't worried. What I'm learning every day is that there's a whole lot more to you than I ever knew or gave you credit for. And it's making me think that Mac really missed the boat by not seeing all there is to you."

Quinn didn't seem to be missing anything about her now, because he was studying her intently. And she liked that.

Maybe too much…

It had been a long afternoon and evening of work, topped off by a stressful conversation that had taken all the fight out of Clairy.

But she wasn't alone in that. Peering into Quinn's striking face, she saw that some of the marine in him had been stripped away to expose the man who had been carrying quite a burden for the last five months and needed a bit of a break himself now that he'd shared it.

And it was as if the sharing of it had brought them closer, had cultivated something new between them.

His arm was still propped on the top edge of the sofa's back. Then his hand rose up to one end of the scarf that held her hair in the high ponytail. A tug made the knot come free, and the long waves fell around her face and shoulders at the same time he moved closer to her.

"Yeah, this couch is kind of nice..." he said. "It's not a bad place to land after a rough day. To regroup..."

Were they just regrouping?

Or were they returning to what had ended the night before? Restarting it...?

Clairy wasn't opposed to restarting it. Not only had she wanted him to kiss her again since he'd stopped last night, but the previous hour's exchange had also left her craving solace, the comfort of arms around her.

His arms around her.

So much so that she wanted to encourage whatever he had in mind and brought her feet up under her hip to alter her own position and subtract another inch from the distance between them.

Answering an urge for contact, she laid her palm to the side of his oh-so-handsome face, drinking in the warmth of his skin as his blue, blue eyes delved into hers.

"Mac's daughter..." he whispered to himself.

Clairy wasn't sure whether he was marveling at that fact, reminding himself of it or warning himself to be cautious.

But whatever the meaning, it didn't stop him from drawing nearer as if something was pulling him. Pulling him into a kiss that was soft and sweet, that answered her need for comfort and seemed to have roots in that new bond between them.

But it wasn't long before comfort was found. And

then what had been cut short the previous evening began again all on its own.

First lips parted and the kiss remained soft, seeking. Until his tongue came to say hello and hers greeted it joyously.

Quinn's arm came around her to pull her the rest of the way to him while his free hand combed through her hair to clasp the back of her head. He kissed her all the more deeply, their mouths open wider as restraint dropped away.

Clairy's hand drifted from his cheek to his shoulder as that fantasy she'd had of making out with him on the couch at home that afternoon became a reality.

A heady reality that brought her other hand to his T-shirted pec. The rock-solid feel of those muscles just fed her soul and she couldn't resist exploring them. His chest. His shoulders. His broad back. His biceps…

And with each exploration, she got a little more turned on. Then a little more. Then more still, until the idea of just kissing wasn't enough.

Her head fell farther back and Quinn went with it. His impressive torso came over her enough for her to slip lower against the arm of the sofa.

Clairy uncurled her legs and stretched them over Quinn's thighs as her arms wrapped around him and her fingers gripped his back more firmly.

Kneading, almost burrowing into him, she gave him a clue to what her own body was starting to yearn for.

He didn't seem to need much of a hint, though. He let the couch's arm brace her head and trailed that hand down one shoulder to her arm, crossing from there to the outer swell of her breast, lingering as if awaiting permission.

Clairy gave it with the faintest of pivots. Quinn took the invitation without hesitation, bringing his big hand to cup her breast completely then.

He wasn't just a fantastic kisser—he had a magic touch that kindled a fire in her.

A quiet sound she'd never heard herself make sent him a message and his hand dropped from her breast to the blouse's buttons at her side.

Fastened, those buttons made the V neckline demure. But as he opened the top button, the V widened. And widened more when he undid the next two, leaving only the bottom button to keep her shirt from falling completely open.

Then that hand went to her collarbone instead of to her breast, inspiring a minor complaint to rumble from Clairy's throat as she taunted his tongue, tip to tip, with some audacity.

She felt him smile just before he retook control of that kiss and let his hand sluice downward, his fingers easing inside the cup of her bra to finally give her that unfettered embrace of his strong, adept hand on her naked breast.

He caressed, stroked, squeezed, gently tugged and pinched her flesh—her breast seemed to expand, and her nipple turned to stone in his palm.

With his mouth still in control of that kiss and her, Clairy's body slid even more down the sofa side, more fully across Quinn's lap, where she discovered that she was not the only one of them nearly going out of her mind with wanting even more.

But where? Here on her office couch? In her father's memorial-library building?

Maybe if they were longtime lovers looking for a new titillation.

But for the first time?

The thought of that put just enough of a damper on things for something else to creep into her mind—was this wise at all? Was this something she should do and let go all the way to the conclusion her body was screaming for?

Her body *was* screaming for it.

And she could feel beneath her hip that his was, too.

But this was still Quinn Camden—was she absolutely positive she should take this step with him?

Plus, she was so fresh out of her marriage, and should phase one of her postdivorce life go this far? Should she let it if she had any doubt at all?

Whether Quinn read her mind or felt some amount of withdrawal—or had the same hesitations himself—he stopped kissing her just then.

"Okay...we shouldn't be doing this..." he said, leaving Clairy still unsure what had caused him to stop.

Still, she said, "Probably not..." as the shadow of doubt grew.

It was only then that Quinn stole one last stroke of her breast and drew his hand out from under her bra, pulling the ruffled edges of her blouse back in place.

Clairy refastened the buttons as she sat up straight and edged off Quinn's lap, turning just enough to put her feet on the floor.

Quinn dropped his head onto the sofa back, closed his eyes and took a deep breath, then sighed it out. "You're getting to me, Clairy..." he said in a gravelly voice.

"Or maybe you're getting to me," she countered, making him laugh.

"God, what's happening here?" he muttered, sounding as confused as she felt.

"I don't know," Clairy confessed.

"We're supposed to hate each other."

"It'd be a lot safer," she said, thinking out loud.

"We're only together for a few days…"

"And you're one of those macho military men," she added, unable to keep the attraction she had to him out of that criticism.

"One of those macho military men who swore I was taking a hiatus to figure out what the hell I'm doing with relationships before I screw up another one…"

"It's all just complicated," Clairy said, unsure what he meant about a hiatus and figuring out what he was doing with relationships.

"Complicated…" he repeated, as if he needed that reinforced. "Complicated enough that we need to think it through," Quinn said, sounding much more rational than Clairy felt, until he added, "Don't we?"

"I think so," she said with the same combination of certainty and uncertainty.

Quinn sighed again, this time with resignation and disappointment. Then he opened his eyes, raised his head and nodded. "Okay…"

Another moment passed before he took a third deep breath, sighed once more and stood. "Let's get out of here before I can't make myself," he said, turning to offer his hand.

Clairy took it because she couldn't deny herself, even though she knew it was dangerous to make contact again and had to fight the inclination to pull him back down to her.

Then they left her office and silently descended the library's stairs.

At the front entrance, Clairy turned off the lights. But before she could open the doors, Quinn used the hand he was holding to pull her into another kiss so heated that this time what flashed through her mind was what it would be like to just go ahead and make love on the library floor.

But then he ended that kiss, too, opened one of the double doors and held it for her to go out ahead of him.

Clairy locked up after them and they returned to Quinn's truck, still saying nothing, merely letting the night air help dissipate what was still alive between them.

Quinn held the passenger door for her, too, before he got behind the wheel to drive them back to her house.

Her house, her front walkway, her porch…where she toyed with the idea of asking him in.

But she didn't have the chance before he kissed her again—as chastely as an altar boy—then told her to let him know when she wanted him to help her move the display cases the next day, and left her to let herself into her house.

Where wanting was definitely still on her mind. And what her body was still overheated with.

But it had nothing at all to do with display cases.

And everything to do with the man who seemed like the worst choice she could possibly make…

CHAPTER SEVEN

"I LOVE THAT DRESS!" Marabeth said as she and Clairy went into Marabeth's small apartment kitchen Friday evening.

"Thanks. Me, too," Clairy said of the gray-and-white windowpane dress that was tight-fitting through the bodice and flared from her waist to her knees.

"Kind of sexy, almost off-the-shoulder—you're putting me to shame in my shorts and T-shirt," her friend complained.

"Quinn and I worked all day at the library dealing with the display cases. I had to go home and shower, and I just wanted something light and airy tonight."

Feminine—that was what she'd told herself instead of labeling it as sexy.

"And with your hair down and your makeup all done… After hobnobbing with Jared and his rich friends in Denver, you may have to tone it down for plain old Merritt salmon-on-the-barbecue summer dinners."

Clairy didn't want to tell her friend that it hadn't been this dinner that had been on her mind when she'd dressed for tonight. She didn't want to tell Marabeth that—like always lately—Quinn had been what she was thinking about.

Quinn, and the way Thursday night had ended. And all the things that ending had left unfinished. And that the only thing she'd been able to think about since then was whether or not she should let those things be finished...

"At least Quinn just wore jeans and a T-shirt," Marabeth said, casting a glance across the room and out the patio door to where he and Marabeth's fiancé were standing on the small cement slab that was the apartment's patio, in front of the outdoor grill, beers in hand.

Marabeth was right—Quinn was dressed casually. But even so, the sight of him in jeans and a navy blue polo shirt still increased her already whetted appetite.

"Is this—tonight—okay?" Marabeth asked then, sounding tentative. "Having the two of you here together?"

The newly engaged couple had invited Clairy and Quinn to Marabeth's apartment for dinner.

"We wanted to thank you for the party," Marabeth went on, "and Brad wanted to have Quinn over before he leaves town again, so we thought if we could have you both at the same time..."

"It's fine, no big deal," Clairy answered her friend.

"How's it going between the two of you?" Marabeth asked. "I never saw you together at the party, but I know he was still there when I left. And tonight he drove you?"

"Seemed silly to take two cars."

"Because you're on friendlier terms...?" Marabeth queried.

"We've been working together so much we've sort of had to be."

There wasn't much to that statement, and yet it

seemed to be exactly what Marabeth wanted to hear. "I knew it!" she said victoriously. "I told Brad when we left your house Wednesday night and Quinn didn't that *something* was going on!"

"Something has been going on—we've been *working* together. And Wednesday night Quinn stayed to help finish the cleanup and take out the party trash," Clairy said.

But her friend wasn't accepting that it was as low-key as Clairy was trying to make it sound. "And then?" Marabeth urged.

Clairy knew denial wasn't going to fool her blood-hound best friend, so she gave up the ghost and just smiled.

"I knew it! I knew it! I knew it!" Marabeth's exclamation was loud enough to stop the conversation outside and draw the men's attention.

"Everything okay in there?" her fiancé asked.

"Just fine," Marabeth called back, delight in her tone and in her face. Then to Clairy, she said quietly, "How friendly has it gotten?"

"Enough for me to learn that you *might* be right that he's not the same as he was before—"

"Like Brad. I told you!" Marabeth interrupted her with more triumph.

"Plus, I've gotten to know Quinn a little better and learned a few things that explain some of what he did as a kid. And he's bent over backward apologizing."

"And now you like him!" Marabeth concluded, sounding like a teenager.

"Now I don't think I hate him anymore." That was all Clairy would concede.

Marabeth shook her head vigorously. "You dressed

up for him tonight!" she accused. "Have you already slept with him? Did the two of you come here straight from bed? Did you get all dressed up so it didn't look like that?"

"No!" Clairy scoffed before her friend could dig in any deeper.

"But you *want* to sleep with him!"

Clairy finally caved and confessed under her breath, "So bad," giving up all pretenses and making her friend laugh.

"Then why haven't you?"

"Come on, really? There are a million reasons."

"But if you want to, that's the only reason that counts."

Clairy sighed, laughed and shook her head at that oversimplification.

"I'm serious," Marabeth said. "Just do it for fun—after Jared and seven years of uninspired, scheduled sex that had to be over in time for the financial report? You've earned it!"

Clairy and Marabeth had shared every intimate detail of their lives since they were children, including that. And especially after Clairy complaining to Jared hadn't accomplished anything, and she'd grown more and more disappointed and frustrated. Which had led to venting to her friend.

"Is that really me, though?" Clairy said. "I'm barely divorced. A week ago I still counted Quinn as my sworn enemy. Plus, there's nowhere for anything between us to go, and knowing that, wouldn't it end up seeming kind of shallow and maybe even...yucky? I mean—"

"I know. We've both always needed there to be a full-blown relationship, the potential for a future, love—or at least being on the verge of love…"

They really had been discussing this subject since puberty.

"So let's look at it like that," Marabeth suggested. "Maybe things between the two of you *could* go somewhere…"

Clairy shook her head again, a slow, definitively negative shake that allowed for no possibility.

Despite that, Marabeth went on. "What if the line between love and hate *is* thin and the two of you have crossed it? What if your dad's death is destiny bringing you together? Think how great that would be! We could do this—" Marabeth glanced out the patio door again "—we could all live here in Merritt, two best friends married to two best friends. The four of us could have dinner *every* Friday night. We could raise kids together who could all end up best friends, too—or maybe they'd fall in love and get married to each other and make us all one big—"

"Oh, we've entered fantasyland!" Clairy said.

"Stranger things have happened."

"I don't think they have," Clairy said. "Even if Quinn might have changed, he hasn't changed *that* much. He's still my father's marine mirror image—a dyed-in-the-wool *forever* marine—"

"And exactly the kind of person you swore you would never get involved with when you grew up," Marabeth said, repeating what Clairy had told her numerous times.

"The kind of person I pretty much already married, which means I had to learn all over again that it's what I don't want, because if that fantasy of yours played out with Quinn, I'd either be on a military base somewhere hoping it might give me ten more minutes with him, or here alone—raising kids alone—and not even getting that ten minutes. No, thanks."

Marabeth deflated. "I know you're right." It took only a moment, though, before she brightened again. "But then I'm back to saying just have some fun now, while he *is* around."

Brad poked his head in the open patio door. "Platter—we're getting close," he announced.

Marabeth took a serving dish over to him and kissed him, then returned to the kitchen cubicle and Clairy.

Only when she was sure her fiancé was fully outside and talking to Quinn did she go on. "If you were ever going to have a one-night stand, this is the perfect setup, isn't it?" Marabeth said in a confidential tone. "The guy is sizzling hot with a body that doesn't end. You want to. You already know there's no future in anything with him, so you don't have any illusions about anything coming of it. He'll disappear any day and you may never see him again—or at least probably won't see him again for years—so you don't have to worry about being embarrassed or awkward or anything, if or when you meet up again. And it's a great way to put Jared behind you, take that first step at moving on."

"Postdivorce phase one," Clairy said with a laugh, explaining that she'd already considered most of what Marabeth was saying.

"So you're gonna do it," Marabeth said optimistically.

"I'm not sure. And I don't think he is, either."

"So seduce him," Marabeth whispered.

Clairy laughed once more, but she didn't commit to anything.

As tempting as it was to consider that one-night stand with Quinn, she still wasn't sure she should.

Or could.

Because what if she did take that leap and *didn't* come away from it as unaffected and detached as her friend thought she would?

"Am I missing something?" Quinn said on the way back to Clairy's house when Friday evening with their friends had ended. "How come Marabeth wouldn't let you *not* take that bottle of wine and kept telling you to go home and open it tonight?"

Quick lie, quick lie, come up with a quick lie, Clairy...

"She thought you and I should celebrate burying the hatchet to work together on the memorial and finishing the project."

"Ah…" he said, seeming to accept that. "So you told her you'd buried the hatchet?" he asked, sounding very interested to hear that.

"I told her that she might be right, that you—and maybe Brad, too—aren't still the creep you used to be."

Quinn laughed. "Faint praise but I'll take it and be grateful."

There was a moment's lull that Clairy hoped put to rest his curiosity about the wine Marabeth had really given her to encourage having some *fun* tonight.

Then he said, "If you think we might not still be creeps, does that mean you're feeling better about Brad?"

"I'm hoping for the best," Clairy allowed. "Marabeth is going to marry him no matter what I think, and I don't want to see any marriage fail."

"There's always that risk, though. Relationships are tough."

"Spoken from experience?" she asked.

"To be honest, relationships have been really easy for me—even the two that went on for a while. Until the end of them, anyway. But, apparently, they have been tougher than I ever realized for whoever I've been involved with."

"Let me guess—they're easy for you because you enjoy the fruits of the relationships, then go on about your business. You get deployed or leave for trainings or missions or whatever. But the women you've been involved with are left behind, left hanging, waiting, worrying, and as alone as if they weren't involved with anyone at all."

"Well, yeah. But that's all a given, being involved with anyone in the military," Quinn said. "My two bad breakups put a whole lot more blame on me than on the military, and after this last deal with Mac, it got me to thinking—"

"Were they women marines that my father tried to push out?"

"No, both the women were civilians. Rachel was a legal secretary and Laine was a paramedic. Neither of them ever even met Mac. But after having my eyes opened to the way Mac saw women—and looking at the complaints against me through that lens—I decided that maybe I'd better figure out if being involved with me has had its own special downside."

Was that why he was taking a hiatus before he screwed up another relationship, what he'd said last night?

But Merritt was a small town and it had only been a

short drive from Marabeth's apartment, so he'd piqued
Clairy's curiosity again just as he pulled his truck up
to the curb in front of her house. And there was no way
Clairy could just end the evening and leave it at that.

She held up the bottle her friend had forced on her
as they'd left and said, "So, wine…" as an invitation to
come inside and tell her more.

Quinn's only answer was a smile before he opened
his door and got out.

Clairy got out, too, and met him to walk up to the
house.

She'd meant to turn on the air-conditioning before
leaving tonight, and remembered only after unlocking
the front door, when they went into the heat and stuffi-
ness of her house.

"It's miserable in here," she complained as she turned
on the air now. "Mim and Harry brought her old patio
glider over this morning—they didn't like the look of
it with Harry's outdoor furniture. It's in the backyard
again and I left the lights from the party up, so why
don't we take the wine out there?"

"Good idea."

Clairy gave Quinn the job of uncorking the bottle as
she kicked off her sandals and got two glasses. Once
he'd poured the wine, she led the way out the rear door.

She'd used string lights with small white round
globes to add to the festivity of the party, and they still
made a nice canopy over the yard.

The cushioned, love-seat-sized glider that was
against the house was comfortable, if not contempo-
rary. The unoiled metal base squeaked when they both
sat down, and the seat unavoidably moved backward
until they were settled, facing each other.

"Okay, explain how what you found out about my father triggered something about your private life," she prompted.

"It goes without saying that Mac was the biggest influence on me—from the time I was a little kid. When I found out what he was doing to women marines, it kind of opened a curtain on what he thought of the opposite sex in general." Quinn tried his wine, seemingly buying himself a moment.

Similar to when he'd told her about her father's misdeeds Thursday night, Clairy could see again that it was difficult for him to speak ill of her father, that it was a struggle he waged with himself.

Then he said, "You came to mind, and for the first time, I actually thought about the way he'd always treated you. I don't know why—knowing Mim, knowing how he was raised, it shouldn't have been true of him—but Mac deeply *believed* that there was something that made men better, more important, more valuable all the way around, than any woman."

Clairy breathed a wry sigh at that. "I had that same thought last night when you told me what he'd been doing. It kind of helped me to think that it wasn't only me… I've always thought it was…"

"It definitely wasn't only you. But the thing is, it got me to thinking about the way I'd treated you when we were kids and about the way I might have followed Mac's lead—"

"It seemed okay to you to be a jerk to me, to shove me aside to get to my father, because I was just a *girl* and not as good as you," Clairy surmised.

Quinn flinched. "It was never a conscious thought.

It's never been a conscious thought about any woman. But your dad was—"

"Your idol, your role model, everything you wanted to be, and if that was how he saw women, maybe it rubbed off on you."

"That's what I wondered about. Beginning with you and the way I treated you when we were kids."

"It *was* what my father modeled for you from the day you showed up at our door," Clairy confirmed, looking at the situation like that herself now. "I actually remember that morning like it was yesterday. He was reading his newspaper, ignoring me. But when you got there and said you wanted to be a marine just like him, he folded it and put it down, and suddenly he was interested in what you had to say."

"Again, Clairy, I'm sorry," Quinn said contritely. "But, yeah, Mac did act like you were just…a pet or a piece of furniture—something we didn't need to take into consideration even when you were trying to get in on his training me, or when you wanted to watch his war movies with us…"

Clairy nodded, but this time instead of getting into that part of this, she was more interested in how this had translated into Quinn's view and treatment of the women in his life.

He seemed to sense that and went on. "Even though I never consciously thought I was better than or more important than any woman, I can see where Mac's influence may have colored the way I've always gone about things with women—"

"With very little regard for them?" Another guess.

"Possibly. I know personal relationships have never had priority with me—"

"Long-or short-term ones?"

"Any of them," he admitted somewhat under his breath. "Short-term were just numbers I called or texted when I felt like it. If there was no answer, I called or texted the next number on the list—"

"Oh, nice!" she chided.

"They were doing the same thing with me," he claimed.

"And the long-terms?"

"I guess I didn't recognize that things were much different with those," he acknowledged, sobering as if thinking back on the more serious relationships really was giving him pause now.

"With Rachel," he said, "it lasted about a year, and I thought we were doing okay—I was stationed in Georgia then. After dating steadily for two months, I needed to leave on assignment for a few weeks. She invited me to stay at her place when I got back, to stay with her every time I was going to be back rather than staying on base. I thought she was being…you know, practical. I'd made it clear that I'd be in and out. She seemed to accept that, and she said she wanted to keep things going even under those circumstances, to be together whenever I was in town. I figured she just figured that it was nicer to have her place to come back to than the base, that it was for convenience."

"But she saw it differently—as the two of you living together," Clairy suggested.

"She didn't say that outright in the invitation, but she did when things blew up—she said me moving in took the relationship to another level. But I hadn't seen that…" He shook his head as if he still didn't completely see it. "I guess she expected me to propose or something… Hell, I don't know exactly. I just know I thought we were on the same page, and I didn't think it was headed anywhere close to marriage. But when things exploded, she said she'd given me hints and signs and signals, that she'd said things that—if I'd given her even a second thought—I would have caught."

His sigh sounded frustrated. "The bottom line was that she wanted more, and she'd believed when I moved in that she had the right to expect it… But I was…oblivious. And it all came to a head when I found her in bed with some other guy—"

"Oh… She wasn't expecting you?"

"She knew I was coming. She just wanted to rub my nose in the fact that she had someone else. She said it was what I deserved, that it was what it took to get me to notice her, to notice what was going on with her because I took her for granted."

That did sound like Clairy's complaint with her father, but it seemed as if Quinn was finding his way with this and she thought it might be better to just let that happen on its own rather than point out the similarity.

"I thought setting me up to walk in on her in bed with somebody else was taking it too far," Quinn continued. "But thinking about it since Camp Lejeune and Mac… I don't know… Rachel was right that she wasn't uppermost in my mind at any point, that I wasn't paying enough attention to anything she said or did or signaled for it to register. I did enjoy her company, but when I didn't have it, it didn't…bother me."

"You could take her or leave her?" Clairy asked to put it in simpler terms.

He shrugged, and it seemed to have a tinge of guilt to it. "I could. And did," he confessed. "After she'd had her

say, I packed up and left without feeling anything but…
mostly confusion at how I'd missed so much. But she
was crying and throwing things—she said she wanted
to hurt me the way I'd hurt her—"

"And that just shocked you," Clairy said.

"That I'd hurt her? It did. I didn't think I was doing
anything wrong. I definitely didn't *want* to hurt her."

And it was apparent that he was genuinely perplexed
by the fact that he had.

"Then there was Laine," he went on. "So-o-o much
worse…"

Enough for him to need a drink of his wine before
going on.

"I met her right after Rachel," he began. "I was
with her until just before going to Camp Lejeune to
see Mac—*twenty months of her life…*" He seemed to
be repeating what had been said to him.

"Almost two years," Clairy observed.

"Again, I was in and out, so it didn't seem like that
and probably didn't add up to that much actual time together. But Laine hadn't seen anyone else, so—"

"Had you?"

"No. I liked her. I was fine seeing only her."

Obviously without putting much thought into it…

"Were you *fine* seeing only her just because she always answered when hers was the first number you
called when you got to town? So you didn't have to
bother with the next number on the list?"

"Don't make me out to be a dog," Quinn said de-
fensively.

Okay, maybe there had been a bit of a bite to that.
And it wasn't really fair, she decided, because since his
personal life took a back seat to his career, she had no

doubt he didn't devote enough time or energy to dating to juggle women.

But before Clairy could retract what she'd said, he went on.

"I didn't mistreat anyone…intentionally, at least. I was just… Like I said, relationships weren't my priority. But I liked Laine, and after a couple of months seeing only her and then having to be gone, if she hadn't answered when I got back, I'd have called again and again until I got her. I wouldn't have moved on to the next number."

Clairy thought he likely saw that as the highest of regard when it came to women and relationships, but she didn't say it. She could tell that he really was suffering remorse now for doing what he hadn't seen as wrong at the time he was doing it.

"So the two of you were exclusive, too. For twenty months," Clairy said to encourage him to go on.

"Without living together—I'd learned that lesson, at least. But Laine got pregnant."

That was a bombshell Clairy hadn't seen coming.

"Do you have a kid? Or is there someone out there pregnant with your baby?" she asked, in full-blown alarm.

"No! The pregnancy was an accident. She didn't even know she *was* pregnant until pain sent her to the emergency room and they told her it was… I hope I have this word right—ectopic?"

"The embryo was in her fallopian tube," Clairy said.

"She had to go into surgery right then and they had to take the whole deal—the tube and all. I was working, busy. I'd turned off my phone, left it in my desk drawer so she couldn't reach me. I didn't see her messages, her texts, until it was all over with. A friend of hers had taken her to the hospital…" he confessed ruefully.

Clairy couldn't help feeling sympathy for these two women who had gotten in over their heads with him. After all the pain her father's neglect and disregard of her had caused, she identified with them and understood what it was to be so let down by a man who was more intent on something other than them.

But she could also tell that Quinn was agonizing over what he was just realizing about himself and his actions, and she didn't want to rub salt into his wounds, so she didn't say anything at all.

He went on even without any input from her.

"Laine was through with me when I finally did get to her. She said she'd wasted twenty months of her life on me, that her chances of having kids had been reduced and all for what… She'd been hanging on, hoping it would get better—hoping *I* would get better—but that the whole mess had opened her eyes and she knew she'd never mean as much to me as the marines did, that she'd never been that important to me, that she was so *un*important to me that she hadn't even known where I was or how to reach me other than by the cell phone I'd turned off—"

"You'd hurt her, too," Clairy interrupted, but mildly and with understanding that this had caught him as unaware as had learning how the other woman felt.

"Again, not on purpose," he said. "And at the time it happened I was sorry it had all gone down the way it had, but I still wrote off most of Laine's reaction to things other than me."

Just as her father would have done.

"But now?" Clairy asked.

"Now I'm afraid I might not be much different than the worst of Mac, even though I've lived my life trying to be the best of him..."

So not only had Quinn become disillusioned by his idol, but he was also ashamed of what the negative side of that idol's influence might have created in him.

"I think just coming to all this makes you a better man than my father was," Clairy said honestly. "And maybe it'll lead to a better, more rounded life than he had. Maybe since you know now where you've failed, you won't do it again and you can actually *have* a personal life—because whether or not my father ever realized it or cared, he didn't."

"Which brings me to the rest of what I'm trying to figure out," Quinn said more to himself than to her.

"Whether or not you *want* a personal life that might interfere with being the kind of marine my father was," Clairy ventured.

Quinn's eyebrows arched. "Oh, you're too smart..." he said with a wry laugh, letting her know her guess had been correct.

And since it had, she took a leap and said, "Speaking from my father's personal life, if you have to be the marine he was, look for a woman—like my mother, like Mim—willing to accept it, excuse it. But don't bring kids into it. Like your two long-term relationships, kids can't help hoping and trying and working for more, and then being hurt when they can't get it."

"And that's pretty rotten for the kid," he said compassionately, clearly referring to her.

That compassion brought a warmth to his eyes and they held hers for long enough to cause her to think he was finished talking. That they might be moving in that other direction she still wasn't sure the night should take.

But then he seemed to pull himself out of the moment. He took a drink of his wine and returned to talking, just not about himself.

"Okay, I've told you the dark secret of my mistakes. Let me hear yours."

"Who said I have any dark secrets or mistakes?"

"You've dropped some crumbs, some teasers," he accused. "Tell me who got you to the altar and how. And why it didn't work."

She'd heard that talking about the ex was a sure-fire way to put a damper on anything involving another man.

So maybe this was a good night for it…

"His name is Jared Byers—he's a financial and real-estate whiz in Denver. We met at an event I did to raise money for the Jenkins Foundation. I married him after a whirlwind three-month courtship and it lasted for seven years."

"Hmm… I think you left out all the important parts with that version and I'm not letting you off the hook," Quinn said of her summary. "So you were married seven years. Was it the seven-year itch that wrecked it?"

"If the seven-year itch means cheating, then no, neither of us did that. If it means seven years into a marriage is when some reassessing might happen, when someone might reevaluate, might need things to change course, then yes."

"Which of you did all that?"

"Me."

Quinn smiled broadly. "Straightforward taking responsibility—I like that. Now explain."

His reaction made her inclined to be more candid, but first she set her half-empty wineglass on the small table on her side of the glider.

"Jared has it all—he came from money that he turned into much, much more money in real estate and in two private mortgage loan groups he heads, so he's rich, charming—when he wants to be—handsome—"

As she settled again to face Quinn, she thought that her ex came up short in a comparison of his looks and Quinn's. But she didn't say that. Instead, she said, "And he swept me off my feet."

"That was bad?" Quinn asked, interpreting her tone.

"It ended up making me feel kind of stupid, like I'd fallen for a con man—"

"He was a con man?" Quinn asked with the same level of alarm she'd had when she'd worried he might have a child or have left a pregnant girlfriend.

"No, he's on the up-and-up. He's just a very high-flier. He went—goes—after things full speed ahead, and while I didn't know it until much later, he'd decided it was time for a wife. I guess I fit his qualifications, so when we met I was what he went after—"

"Full speed ahead," Quinn said, echoing her words. "But you don't think he did that because he had feelings for you? You think he just did it to acquire a wife—like a piece of property?"

"Without it taking him away from work for long," she confirmed. "And *acquired* is pretty accurate. It turned out that I was more of an acquisition than anything, and once I was on his list of assets—"

"He had to have feelings for you, though," Quinn insisted.

"Do you think my father *had feelings* for me?" Clairy countered.

"You were his daughter," Quinn answered, as if there was no question.

"And my mom was his wife. But when she died I never saw him shed a single tear—"

"I don't think that was something he would have *let* you see."

"When I got upset he got mad at me—he didn't have any trouble showing *that*. He said a McKinnon didn't cry. My mom dying in a car wreck was sad, but we had to see it through."

"But looking back on it as an adult, do you honestly believe he didn't *have* any feelings, or can you see that the man Mac was wouldn't have shown them?"

"That was Mim's excuse for him. But it just seemed to me like he didn't have much in the way of feelings for anything but the marines…and you, as the son he wanted. And I'm not sure Jared has feelings for anything except *his* work. I know that's what gives him a rush that nothing else does. But until we were actually married, he made it seem as if I gave him that same kind of rush."

"I can't imagine that you didn't," Quinn said, as if he wouldn't accept anything else. "So how did he sweep you off your feet?"

"He made it seem as if he couldn't get enough of me. There were a whole lot of picnic lunches, and dinners that were all candles and starlight and private dining rooms. There were chartered planes to weekends in Paris and Rome and London and Switzerland. There were flowers and candy and gifts. He called and texted dozens of times a day to tell me how much he missed me, how all he wanted was to be with me, how he couldn't wait until he was… It was as if *I'd* swept *him* off his feet. I didn't know it at the time, but when Jared wants something, he devotes himself to getting it. He's like a heat-seeking missile—nothing is going to stop him."

"My mother would have been impressed?"

Clairy chuckled. "It sounds like she could have raised him."

"And how did you feel about him?"

"I wasn't *instantly* in love with him, but feelings did develop fairly soon. I did fall in love with him and I started to believe there might be something to all those it-happened-so-fast-and-lasted-forever love stories. So when he proposed three months after we'd met—"

"You said yes."

"I did," she said with some self-disgust. "Jared didn't want a long engagement, and with the money he could spend to get things done in a hurry—which he was willing and eager to do—we were married two weeks later."

"A small wedding or—"

"A blowout. Three hundred people—just not my father, who wouldn't come even to give me away because he was doing something more important…" But they weren't discussing her father, so Clairy let it go and went on. "It *was* a beautiful wedding. With so many of Jared's wealthy friends there that the fundraiser in me was screaming to pass the hat. It took everything I had to just sit back and be the bride," she joked wryly to lighten the tone.

"I'm almost afraid to ask what kind of honeymoon Mr. Romance took you on."

"A week living like royalty in Banff."

"Then home to Denver?"

"To Jared's penthouse."

"Then what—he just stopped with the sweeping you off your feet and went back to business?"

"Pretty much. It was kind of a shock. A big project had come up for him two days before the wedding. He'd mostly put it on hold through the honeymoon—although he did spend more time on his phone than I'd expected. He warned me that he was going to have to dive in when we got back. I just had no idea what *diving in* really meant."

"What did it mean?"

"He worked until ten or eleven at night, seven days a week. Sometimes he didn't come home at all for days and just sent his assistant for changes of clothes. I knew the over-the-top courting wouldn't go on, but I didn't think that…well, that I'd been just another acquisition and no more thought needed to be put into me from then on. That for the next seven years I'd be to Jared what I'd always been to my father—incidental. That I'd just be The Wife."

"Just *The Wife*?" Quinn queried, trolling for an explanation.

"The person who ran the home front, took care of Jared and his home and his home life the way his assistant at work took care of him and everything he needed there. I was less *his wife* and more *The Wife*—it was like a job I'd been hired to do, not a relationship. I was who showed up on his arm at any event he needed or wanted to attend—which was particularly important because I learned about six months into the marriage that that was what made him decide he should have a wife—"

"Having a built-in date for parties and dinners?"

"He was sick and tired of being The Most Eligible Bachelor—he'd actually been named that on the cover of a Denver magazine. Single women preyed on him, all his friends badgered him with setups to help him find someone, and they insisted he take time away from work to meet whoever they had in mind. There were even a few clients—important ones—who wanted him to go out with their single daughter or niece and tried to make it part of their deal. I guess that's what brought him to me—a client really pushed him to date the client's daughter and Jared begged off and lost the project to someone else."

"So he decided to get himself a token wife? It was a business decision?"

"That's what I overheard in a ladies' room when a group of wives from his inner circle didn't know I was in one of the stalls."

"Aww, Clairy…" Quinn said sympathetically. "Did you ask him if that was true? Did he at least deny it and get rid of that inner circle?"

"Neither of those things. He did insist that it was just lucky for him that I came along when I did, but it didn't help much."

"You'd married 'Mac without a uniform' and nothing changed."

Clairy shrugged her concession to the truth in that statement. "Jared wasn't as gruff as my father. He was generous—just not with his time. He was considerate enough to have his assistant keep me up-to-date on when he'd be home, when he wouldn't be, when he'd be going out of town on business, when he had social obligations I needed to put on my calendar, too. When I got dressed for those social obligations, he complimented me… The marriage was just…cut-and-dried, mechanical…"

"That had to be a *huge* letdown after the whirlwind."

"The whirlwind definitely hadn't prepared me, no."

"But you stuck around for seven years?"

"When it started to sink in that his work was the be-all and end-all to him, like my father, I guess I did what I'd done growing up—for a long time, I tried to get back Jared's attention in any way I could. When that didn't work, I thought maybe I should try playing on his field—I thought that if I was really fluent in what he did, he might talk to me about it. So I watched and read all his financial reports, all his real-estate stuff, tried getting him to tell me about his projects. But that just irritated him the same way it had when I tried to get my father to include me in your training—he saw it as something that interfered with his focus."

"Did sex play a role?"

Clairy's initial thought was that Quinn was asking about her sex *life*. Then she realized he was referring to her father rejecting her because she wasn't male.

Her own misunderstanding made her laugh. "For a minute, I thought you were asking something else…"

Quinn smiled. "You thought I was asking how things were in bed…"

"To answer the real question—yes and no. Jared wasn't sexist in terms of believing that women couldn't be more than homemakers. There were women he worked with whom he trusted, respected. But he definitely put me in one role and left me there. He even saw my job with the Jenkins Foundation more as a little hobby that could occupy me when he wasn't around. I was The Wife and he didn't want me playing any role but that."

"And you still didn't bolt when you figured that out?"

She shrugged. "The whirlwind *had* made me fall in love with him," she reminded Quinn. "So when everything I tried failed, I spent a lot of time just working at accepting that things were the way they were. Plus, I did have my job—I was free to put in a lot of extra hours and Jared *was* great for fundraising. I had the best list of the moneyed elite in the state and access to all of them. His connections also gave me inside pipelines to things for my vets that no one else had—"

"The good with the bad?"

"That was how I tried to look at it. I also told myself that after the way I grew up, I was kind of uniquely qualified for what the marriage turned out to be. Plus," she added somewhat sheepishly, "I didn't want to be the story where I was swept off my feet into an instant marriage that ended as fast as it started. And there was my father... I didn't want to look impetuous and flighty and add a divorce to the rest of what a disappointment I was to him. So I just tried to take the marriage for what it was and be content with it while I held on to the hope that it would somehow get better—"

"Like Laine," Quinn said somberly. "Only Mr. Whirlwind didn't get any better, either. So what made you reach your limit like Laine did and decide enough was enough?"

"It was last Christmas. It was the same as every Christmas had been since we were married. Nice, very formal and stuffy because Jared didn't like *homey*—that's what he called what I wanted and he said it as if I was embarrassingly out of style. As always, we had invitations to A-list parties and dinners, concerts, plays, the ballet, and Jared would fit in a few that had business connections…" She shrugged once more. "It was nice enough," she repeated. "But I was so homesick I was miserable. It all seemed superficial and empty, cold and impersonal. I wanted to be with Mim. I wanted a Merritt Christmas with the ice sculptures and the Christmas Festival. With the cookie competition and exchanges. With the caroling and the church choir. With Marabeth. With all the *hominess*. And with a husband who was actually enjoying it with me, not sitting in the seat next to me at the symphony engrossed in what he was doing on his phone." Clairy sighed. "And I realized that I also wanted kids…"

"For the first time?"

"I always saw myself with a family, and I assumed we'd get there, even though we never really talked about it—Jared's friends had kids and that seemed to be what he took his cues from for a home life. And last Christmas it just hit me hard that I wanted that next step—"

"Even with the way things were?" Quinn asked, as if he doubted the wisdom in that.

"I guess I tapped into my old habit of trying to somehow make it better. I started to picture becoming a family and that family engaging Jared. I saw us getting out of high-rise living, moving into a house, having the life I'd thought I was going to have. So on Christmas night I cornered him in the bathroom on his way to taking a shower so he didn't have anything that could take his attention away. And I told him what I wanted for the New Year."

"It didn't go over well," Quinn said.

"Jared was calm. He took it in stride. He said he

wasn't thrilled with the family idea, but if I wanted to have a baby, it was up to me."

Quinn laughed mirthlessly. "Was he planning to be the father?"

"More like the sperm donor and sponsor. He said if I *had* to do it there was a bigger penthouse he had his eye on that could probably accommodate a nursery, but that I should know he wasn't changing anything beyond that. He definitely wasn't moving outside of the city or working any differently or any less. He said I could hire a nanny, but there was no way he was doing bottle duty, diaper duty, or getting up in the middle of the night for anything. He said he wasn't pushing a stroller through a park or going to Little League games—in case I had any illusions about that. He wasn't going to play Santa or the Easter Bunny, birthday parties would be my thing, not his…" Clairy realized her tone had begun to mimic Jared's the way Quinn's had echoed his former girl-friend's, so she cut herself off.

She merely did what she'd done with Jared—she got as calm as her ex had been.

"And that was it for me," she said resolutely. "I looked at him while he dictated his terms and it oc-curred to me that somewhere along the way my feel-ings for him had fizzled. I wasn't even angry. I realized how much Jared was like my father, and that after my father, after seven years with Jared, I was done accept-ing, adapting, trying to change anything with that kind of man. I was done *being* with that kind of man—the kind of man I hadn't wanted in the first place." Clairy sighed again. "I said no to his terms, that it was over between us. The day after Christmas, he rented the big-ger penthouse to try it out and accommodate a separation. He moved there by New Year's. I filed for divorce the week after that."

"He didn't look for a middle ground to keep you? He didn't get upset?"

She shook her head. "Like my father, the only way was his way. Lawyers worked everything out—there was a prenuptial agreement because I'd come into the marriage with so much less than he had. We didn't have kids to battle over, so it was all pretty simple—"

"When was it final?"

"Not until last week—Jared apparently liked the structure of having The Wife, because by March he had someone new—"

"Did he do the whirlwind deal again?"

"No, he actually wooed that client he'd lost when he'd refused to date the client's daughter—"

"Oh, jeez, he hooked up with the daughter to get the client back?"

"And cemented that business relationship in the process—two birds with one stone. They were engaged in May and he needed the divorce to be final, or he'd still probably be too busy to sign the papers."

"What about you?"

Clairy shook her head. "I was kind of surprised that there weren't even enough feelings left to make any of it hurt. Jared had been gone so much, he'd been so distant when he *was* around, that it was hard to tell when he wasn't living there anymore. Nothing much changed except that I didn't have to cater to him."

"So it was more like putting in notice to leave a job you'd had for seven years?"

"I never looked at it like that but it sort of was," Clairy said with another laugh. "I wish I would have thought of that earlier. Maybe I wouldn't have felt so guilty for *not* being more upset. And as for The Wife Number Two, I just hope she has more idea what she's getting into than I did."

Quinn's expression became reflective. "I guess you could say that Mac was a bad influence on both of us when it comes to our personal lives."

"I guess you could," Clairy agreed.

"But now I've woken up and will be more careful, and you won't make the same mistake again," Quinn said.

"Uniform or no uniform," Clairy said firmly.

"I'm sorry that happened to you," Quinn said compassionately. He leaned forward and reached across her to put his half-full wineglass on the table with hers, and when he straightened up again, he was nearer than he'd been before.

Looking more raptly into her eyes, he added, "I think the guy did have feelings for you, though—even if he didn't show it or beg you not to end it or try to find a compromise to keep you."

"What makes you think that?"

"He may have made the decision to find himself The Wife Number Two so he could get his client back and avoid the nuisance of fix-ups again, but I don't think he would have put so much into the whirlwind with you unless there was something else there at the start…on his part."

"He might have been infatuated, I suppose." That was as far as Clairy would go, because in analyzing it, she couldn't see that there had been more than that from Jared.

"Or maybe he just loved you as much as he was

capable of loving anything outside of what he did," Quinn suggested.

"You think that's how it was with my father," Clairy returned.

"I do. Because I don't think Mac *didn't* love you. I think he just loved you as much as he could love anything or anyone other than the marines. Maybe it was the same with this guy and his work."

"Then I'd say that I need someone who can love me more than that," she said.

"I'd say you deserve that," Quinn said quietly.

And there they were, both of them at junctures in their lives that left the future up in the air. Clairy newly divorced, armed with a lesson and resolutions but no assurance what would happen from here, and Quinn undecided about where to let his own personal life go.

But to Clairy it seemed as if they'd arrived at a moment in time, a place, that felt like a haven, suspended between their pasts and the futures that hadn't yet begun. And it was as if what had been happening between them since Quinn had arrived in town was coming awake once more in his cobalt blue eyes scanning her face, peering into her eyes, his focus solely on her...

All thoughts of the past really did fade away now.

Quinn raised a palm high on the back of her head and leaned in far enough to kiss her forehead—a kiss that consoled, that said everything was going to be all right, better.

Then, just when Clairy thought he would go on to a more potent kiss, he took his hand back, sat straight and put distance between them.

In a voice that was slightly gravelly, he said, "It's dangerous for me to stay, so I should probably take off."

Take off your shirt...take off your pants...

"You're afraid of me?" Clairy challenged.

"Yep," he answered without a qualm. "Afraid of how much you make me want you. Afraid of what I might do about it."

"Because you'd rather not?"

"Oh, I'd rather," he said emphatically. "But last night—"

"Was last night and tonight is tonight..."

She hadn't thought this through. She hadn't made a decision. So why was she flirting with finishing what they'd started the previous evening? Flirting with him?

It was because she wanted him.

Still, she reminded herself that it was Quinn who had ended things—even if she might have somehow conveyed hesitation, he'd been the one to cut it short.

"*But last night* what?" she asked, repeating what he'd said before she'd interrupted him.

"Last night I was on the verge of no return and I didn't want to do anything rash. And that's still true."

"Except that now we've lived with the idea for twenty-four hours..." she pointed out in a temptress's tone she hadn't planned.

"So it wouldn't be rash?"

Everything in her was crying out for exactly that—being rash and impulsive and just giving in to what her own body was demanding of her.

But she couldn't bring herself to admit that out loud, so she answered only with a smile and a small shrug of one shoulder.

Quinn turned his head partially to the side and gave her a suspicious glance out of the corner of his eye.

"Where're we going with this, Clairy?" he asked, insisting on candor.

"Upstairs?"

"Don't make it my call because I'll say yes." Another warning. "So be sure," he commanded.

She cocked her head and studied him, considering it all before giving another flippant remark.

Marabeth had advised her to just have fun for this one night. It was an alluring idea.

But it would be with Quinn Camden. The jaw-droppingly handsome Quinn Camden, who was *that kind of man* that she was so determined to avoid. That kind of man her father had been. That kind of man Jared had been.

Tonight Quinn wasn't that kind of man, though. And he hadn't been that kind of man since he'd shown up in Merritt last weekend. Since then—and tonight—he'd been attentive, interested in her, not at all self-involved or distracted by anything. He'd been agreeable, understanding, cooperative, caring and compassionate.

And even if he went back to being the kind of man she wasn't going to get involved with again, a single night wasn't involvement. It was just phase one of her postdivorce life. Nothing serious. Just fun...

As long as she made sure that she *did* come away from it unaffected and detached...

Could she do that? she asked herself.

After her divorce, after her father's death, after all she and Quinn had just talked about tonight, she was craving something less serious as much as she was craving him. And Marabeth's idea of just doing this for fun suddenly seemed like the best advice anyone had ever given her. So she swore to herself that she would make absolutely certain not to read anything more into it than it was, and she honestly thought she *could* keep herself from getting attached.

"Upstairs," she decreed.

Quinn laughed. "That sounded like an order. I'm good at taking orders. I'm good at giving them. But I don't think that's how I want this to go…"

"How do you want it to go?"

He smiled a sexy smile and looked into her eyes again as if there was no one else on earth. Then he replaced his hand on the back of her head to hold her to a second kiss, this one an enticing meeting of their mouths—a light, lips-parted, sweetly sensual kiss that didn't say *upstairs* at all.

It said *relax and let me do the work…*

Which was a relief to Clairy on this first foray out of a lengthy relationship that had been void of any intimate inspiration and left her a bit unsure of herself.

But not unsure of what she wanted, so she parted her lips more, beckoning his tongue to come and play.

There was no tentativeness in Quinn's answer—he instigated a game of cat and mouse that Clairy eagerly joined as her hands rose to the back of his neck, up into his coarse hair, then down again to those splendidly wide shoulders.

With one hand still cradling her head, his other arm came around her to pull her in closer, and Clairy's palms glided down to lie flat against his back as their kiss deepened.

There was something about kissing him that was so natural that it was almost as if he was the only man she was ever meant to kiss and she'd finally found him.

But the minute that thought came to her, she curbed

it, telling herself it was not one-night-stand thinking and could put her in jeopardy.

Besides, that kiss was too good not to merely enjoy on its own merit. At least for a while longer.

Until it began to occur to her that she'd never seen him shirtless and that brought back her inclination to relocate.

She didn't know if he sensed that, or if he just had the same inclination, but he looked into her eyes again.

"Still sure?" he asked.

"Still sure," she said in a whispery tone she'd never heard herself use.

Then she took the initiative, and his hand, stood and pulled him to his feet to take him into the house, through the kitchen and up the stairs to her room, where she'd left her small bedside lamp on to come home to tonight.

But now, standing beside the bed, she wasn't so sure that had been the best choice—even the faint glow of the single bulb seemed too bright to her when she thought about shedding her own clothes.

So she bent over and turned off the lamp.

When she returned to looking up at Quinn, she found a knowing smile on that handsome face that she could still see fairly well in the bright glow of moonlight coming in the bedroom's windows. But he didn't say anything. He merely kissed her again, chastely, as if taking a cue from her need for the modesty of darkness.

It didn't matter, though. Even a virtuous kiss was still a kiss, and now that they actually were upstairs, in her bedroom, containing what was between them was impossible for more than a fleeting moment.

Quinn had no problem finding the zipper of her dress, lowering it slowly.

That was all the encouragement Clairy needed. She rolled up the bottom of his shirt, breaking away from the kiss long enough to take it off over his head.

She couldn't sneak the peek she wanted, but it did give her free access to his bare back. From expansive shoulders down to his narrow waist, up his sides and forward to pecs, where the discovery of his tight male nibs made her own nipples kernel even tighter in answer.

Quinn had an agenda, too. Clasping his strong hands around both of her arms, he brought her up against him before those hands burrowed inside her dress's opening to her back.

Thick, adept fingers manipulated her muscles, loosening them, ridding them of tension at the same time he aroused her and made her itch for even more.

Then those hands went up to her shoulders, snaked under the straps and coasted downward. Her dress dropped to hang on her forearms, leaving her breasts uncovered.

A brush of cooler air turned her nipples diamond-hard and Clairy let the dress fall from her wrists to the floor around her feet, leaving her only in her lace bikinis…and feeling a bit bolder.

Bold enough that when she reached out to him again it was to the waistband of his jeans.

There was a substantial greeting waiting there behind his zipper, and Quinn helped set it free even as he disposed of his shoes.

With mouths and tongues still engaged in the kiss that was purely erotic by then, Clairy felt him take something from his pocket to drop onto the nightstand before he shrugged out of everything he was wearing.

Which meant that he was there, right in front of her, in her bedroom, stark naked.

And she just had to look.

She evaded the kiss, returned to tug at his bottom lip with her teeth as a promise of more, but then went to the limit of his arms in an effort to see him.

He didn't let her. He leaned forward to recapture her lips instead, bending her far back before he eased her onto the mattress with the escort of that kiss.

She was alone on the bed with only his hands on either side of her as he continued pillaging her mouth with his for a few minutes, teasing her.

But in a short while, he ended that kiss and stood tall and glorious.

Intent on removing her bikinis, he seemed unaware of what he was presenting for her to see. But Clairy used the opportunity to finally have that glimpse of his body that she'd been after.

It was worth the wait and she devoured the sight of a man more magnificent than any clothes had done justice to—he was lean, amazingly muscled and endowed enough to take her breath away.

Once her underwear was gone, he paused to take an appreciative look at her that actually added to that endowment before he got on the bed beside her.

He was on his side and she turned to hers, too, peering into that excruciatingly handsome face of his, into those blue, blue eyes.

But what they'd begun couldn't be denied and everything was unleashed then.

Mouths collided once more as Quinn held her in one

arm while his other hand reclaimed her breasts and brought newly delicious torment.

Sometimes light and feathery, sometimes strong and firm, sometimes his whole hand pressing her flesh and then just gentle fingers tracing contours, circling her nipples, gently pinching...

Clairy nearly shuddered with excitement, thinking that it couldn't get any better. Then he replaced his hand with his mouth and taught her how wrong she'd been. So much better that her shoulders lifted off the mattress in search of even more.

She ran her own hands over every inch of him, striving to cause a similar reaction in him, but the stalwart marine was rock-solid under even her most tantalizing caress.

Until she reached low enough to encase that lengthy staff of steel and brought a quick arch of his spine that let her know she had just as much power over him as he had over her.

So much that it drove him away, searching for the protection and pausing only to use it.

Then he came back with even more intensity, more hunger—to her mouth again, to her breasts with even more raw, wicked passion, to spots she hadn't even realized were sensitive or could make her writhe.

And when she wasn't sure she could keep herself from the brink, he found a home between her thighs.

His caution returned once he was there, though, moving into her oh-so-carefully as he kissed her with a contained hunger.

She tightened herself around him and raised her hips.

It was the only signal he needed, as he began to move with divine deliberation, in and out at first, at a pace she learned and matched. Then more quickly. More quickly still, until they established a rhythm that became so organic Clairy could just let it happen and concentrate on what it was creating in her.

Every thrust, every retreat, served a purpose, increasing the pleasure, taking her further into it, and further still until she crossed into so much more. Into a burst that carried her with it, higher and higher, to a culmination that stole her breath and held her in its grip as every nerve ending glittered in the most incredible climax she'd ever had.

And as he plunged deeply into her to find his own crest, another intense wave of pleasure swept her up and held her atop yet another peak that she hadn't known she could ever reach. Only when it, too, passed did Clairy realize her fingers were digging into his back. She let up on him and wilted into the mattress again, welcoming the weight of him as his strength drained away.

For a few minutes, that was how they remained, breathing heavily, hearts pounding hard against each other.

Then Quinn took a breath that pushed his chest even more firmly to hers, sighed into her hair and rose up onto his elbows to give her a kiss that was nothing less than a profound confirmation of the connection they'd made that seemed one of more than mere bodies.

"I don't know what to say," he whispered with awe. "I didn't know it could be like that…"

He looked confused, but she understood because it had never been like that for her, either.

She could only arch her eyebrows and nod.

"Can I stay the night?" he asked.

It wasn't easy for her to rise out of her own awe, but

she worked at it, managing a bit of glibness to camouflage it. "A sleepover?"

"I wasn't thinking about letting you get much sleep."

Clairy smiled. "Okay."

He laughed. "After a breather," he added, pulsing inside of her as a teaser of what the rest of the night would bring before he slipped out of her to escape to the bathroom for a brief moment.

Then he was there again, beside her on the bed, on his back, his arm under her to scoop her into his side so closely her leg went over his massive thigh.

He grasped it and tucked it higher, more securely to him.

"You're okay, right?" he asked, his voice thick with fatigue.

"I am" was all Clairy had the energy to answer.

"And after a ten-minute snooze?"

"I'm not going anywhere," she joked, amazing herself by how much she wanted him again already.

"Thank God," he muttered as his entire body relaxed—all but his arm around her and his hand on her leg, both of them keeping her right where he wanted her.

And as Clairy also gave in to the need for rest, she was a little worried.

Because she just couldn't be sure if anything she did could keep her unaffected and detached...

CHAPTER EIGHT

A RIDGE OF STEEP, densely forested mountains formed the western border of Merritt. After a punishing workout at the gym on Saturday, Quinn hit the most rugged trail through the roughest terrain to the top of one of them for an equally punishing run.

It mimicked a day Mac had designed for him at the start of his freshman year of high school. The only difference was that when Quinn reached the flat top, he stopped. For Mac, the training exercise was only complete when Quinn made it back down again within the assigned time, without a pause to rest.

But today he did pause to look out at the view of Merritt below, scanning it until he located the general vicinity of Clairy's house.

After his night with her, the workout wasn't actually the way he would have chosen to spend Saturday. He'd wanted to spend it in bed with her.

But she'd had plans. She'd already made a date with Marabeth to go to Billings, where Marabeth would shop for a wedding dress and ask a cousin to be a bridesmaid.

So after making love for the fourth time at dawn, Quinn had reluctantly let Clairy out of his arms to get ready for her day trip and he'd gone home.

It had been his intention to go home to sleep, but when he'd plopped down on his own bed, sleep hadn't come as easily as it had in Clairy's bed, with Clairy curled up next to him.

Instead, for some reason, he'd started hearing Mac's voice in his head, taunting him and keeping him awake until he gave up trying and put himself through one of his mentor's specially designed drills.

The drill Mac had demanded of him the day after Mac had caught him showing off for Nicole Parisi, and Quinn had confessed that he liked her and was thinking about asking her to his first homecoming dance.

"You want to be a ladies' man or you want to be a marine?" Mac had shouted. "Females are a distraction—either show me you're serious or don't waste any more of my time!"

Quinn had finished that training two minutes under what Mac had allotted, and he hadn't asked Nicole Parisi to homecoming—he'd used that evening for another of the workouts Mac assigned him.

In fact, after that, whether Mac had been around to see it or not, Quinn hadn't gone to a single school dance all the way through high school. He'd cultivated a few friendships-with-benefits that had given him a way to lose his virginity and gain some experience, but that was it. He'd been determined not to be distracted, to become a marine, and to continue to prove to Mac that he was serious about it.

"But here's the thing, Mac," he said into the quiet of the deserted mountaintop, as if his mentor was there with him. "All those years ago, this workout was enough to get Nicole Parisi out of my system. Today it didn't do anything to make me stop thinking about Clairy."

Or wanting her even more than before they'd had last night together.

Or wanting to be with her in a way he'd never wanted to be with anyone.

Between the mess with Laine and then learning what Mac was doing to women marines, he'd been left questioning so many things. But today it seemed as if everything was coming to a head. With Clairy at the center of it.

"You gave her up for the marines, Mac. You even put making me a marine before her. But she was your kid, your family, and you just blew her off…"

Not that he had any room to judge when he'd done the same thing to Rachel, to Laine, Quinn told himself.

But while Rachel and Laine had given him some small look into the way his actions affected them, listening to Clairy talk about what it had been like for her with Mac as her father had really opened his eyes to how wounding Mac's behavior—and his own—had been.

"You were important to me, you know, you old hard-ass," he said affectionately. "I wanted to be just like you. I've devoted my life to it. But when it comes to the kind of life you actually had, the kind I'm headed for…"

Quinn had no idea what his mentor's relationship with Clairy's mother had been like. But since Quinn had become an adult and more of an equal to Mac, he did know what Mac's private life had involved.

Mac hadn't had *relationships* with women. He'd had women he slept with. But that was the extent of it—satisfying physical need with women who didn't want anything more than that themselves.

And if ever one of those women changed their minds,

it went one of two ways—if a woman wanted more, she never heard from Mac again. If a woman cut him off, he couldn't have cared less because he had no attachment to any one of them—he just bided his time until someone else came along.

"And after Laine, that's what I was figuring I was probably going to do, too, to keep any woman from getting in too deep with me."

But now?

Now he'd had a taste of more…

So much more, with Clairy…

What he'd found with Clairy wasn't what he'd had with Rachel or Laine or any of the other women over the years. Looking back now, he knew that they hadn't sparked in him what Clairy had.

He'd enjoyed slightly more of the female companionship than Mac ever had—dinners and dating, meeting friends or sometimes families, some small amount of cohabitating. But he'd still never invested anything of himself.

And if he went on doing that—doing even less than he'd been doing and following more of Mac's example—he was going to end up with even less than his mentor. No wife or kids. No nothing except the marines.

Certainly no Clairy.

When considering what path to take to avoid the kinds of things that had happened with Rachel and Laine, going Mac's route had seemed like it might be the best way. But thinking about it now—knowing that it meant no Clairy—was a hard pill to swallow.

"Did you have any idea how great she is?" he asked his lost mentor. "Because she *is* great. She's…everything."

That was what Tanner had said when Quinn had

been attempting to understand his brother's resignation from the marines—he had said that Addie was *everything* to him.

At the time, Clairy had inexplicably come to mind, but still Quinn hadn't been able to see his brother's point of view. Now he was beginning to.

He'd never been a big talker, and yet when he was with her, words flowed. It seemed important that he tell her whatever he was thinking, that she see what he was about, that she know him.

That had never mattered before. In fact, he'd guarded against letting anyone get to know him too well, against being too transparent. He'd always played his cards close to the vest.

And he'd actually listened to every word she'd said. Listened, paid attention, recalled, been eager to hear more.

He knew that no other woman he'd ever been with would believe *that*, but it was true.

He wanted to know what was on Clairy's mind, how she viewed things, what made her tick. He wanted to hear her stories, her opinions, her interpretation of things. He cared what she thought. He liked the back-and-forth with her. Liked that she could admit when she was wrong, but that she held her ground when she wasn't, that she didn't retreat.

And something strange happened to him when he was around her—when she came into a room, or the minute he caught sight of her, even if there were other people around, things inside him just settled, relaxed, seemed right.

When he was with her he felt somehow stronger, more capable, more complete. He found comfort in her,

he thought, as he recalled that she'd helped him deal
with the guilt he'd felt over that last fight he'd had with
Mac before the heart attack. And support, too, when
he'd confessed his decision to put a stop to what Mac
had been doing, despite the fact that it meant going
against the man he'd never felt anything but loyalty to.

"And damn if I couldn't look at that face forever..."
And run his fingers through that red hair, search those
green eyes. And smooth the backs of his fingers over
that satiny skin.

He ached for her all over again and his hands itched
just to touch her.

Everything...

His brother's sentiment echoed in his head again, and
with it came the certainty that that was what Clairy was
to him—everything...

Everything he'd never known he wanted. That he
wanted so much now he could barely stand it. So much
that something old stirred in him—the drive, the determination to have her at all cost. At any cost. The long-
ago single-mindedness that his mother had instilled
in him, that Mac had honed, not to let anything stand
in the way of having her, of making her his own, of
never—ever—letting her go...

Which meant what? he asked himself.

Offering her his military life? The kind of life she'd
grown up with?

He knew she wouldn't agree to that. And it wasn't
what he wanted to give her. It wasn't what she deserved.
Especially not from him.

Plus, it wasn't what he wanted with her, he realized
suddenly. He wanted that *more* that they'd been having
since he'd arrived in Merritt. He wanted to be an ever-

present part of her life. He wanted a *full* life with her, without the gaps that living a military life would cause for them both.

He wanted to be *everything* to her, too.

And if they had kids—which, as odd as it seemed to him, he discovered he could actually picture—he sure as hell didn't want to be to them what Mac had been to Clairy.

"The thing is, Mac," he said now, "I *do* know how great Clairy is. And I don't want to miss a minute with her. You may have loved her as much as you could love anything or anyone other than the marines, but for me it's different."

As sure of that as Quinn was in this moment, he knew what he had to do to have her.

And although it shocked him right to the core, he realized suddenly that he was willing to do it…

Well, *that* was a sight to come home to! Clairy thought as she pulled into her driveway late Saturday evening.

After a long drive from Billings and dropping off Marabeth at Brad's house, she'd been eager to get home and fall into bed to catch up on some of the lost sleep of the previous night with Quinn.

They hadn't made plans for tonight and it was after eleven, so she definitely didn't expect to see him standing on her porch when she drove up to her house. But there he was, leaning with one tight T-shirted shoulder against the post, all but his thumbs slung in his jean pockets, that sexy stubble on that too-hot-to-believe face.

One look at him wiped away her fatigue and left her thinking about falling into bed with him again, sleep be damned.

After all, he won't be here forever. Even if I spend more than a single night with him, why not enjoy this while it lasts?

Because it wouldn't last long before his leave ended. Which meant that even if sleeping with him became a multiple-night stand, she had no illusions about it being more than a temporary tryst.

I can live with that, she told herself as she began to take off Quinn's clothes in her mind.

"Fancy meeting you here," she said, flirting when she got out of the car.

He smiled the devilish smile she'd seen so much of last night and she thought that confirmed the reason he was there.

But as she approached the house, the wicked smile turned into one that was more controlled as he said, "I just came to talk."

She didn't believe it, but she pretended to. "Okay. We do that pretty well, too."

"I'm serious," he said, pushing off the post to stand straight and strong—a force to be reckoned with.

"Okay," she repeated, suspending her fantasy of undressing him, since a rerun of the previous evening didn't seem to be immediately on the horizon. She also braced herself slightly, thinking that he could have come to tell her that he *was* leaving even though his ten days weren't over yet—that was something her father had done.

"Come in," she invited, going to the front door.

By the time she'd unlocked it, he was behind her, holding the screen open.

"How was your day in Billings?" he asked as they went inside.

"Productive—Marabeth found two dresses. The bridal shop is going to hold them for her for a while so she can make up her mind. Of course, the one she really likes costs about four times as much as the other one. We looked at bridesmaids' dresses—ugh… We had a nice late dinner with her cousin, who's excited to be a bridesmaid, and then we drove home." Clairy set down her purse and they moved into the living room, where she turned on the lamp on the end table. "How was your day?"

"Tried to go home and sleep, couldn't, got up and did Mac's get-the-girl-out-of-my-system workout that's followed by a run up to Mason's Peak," he answered.

Get-the-girl-out-of-his-system workout? Am I the girl? Does he want me out of his system?

Instinctively, Clairy took refuge in the self-protective mode she'd learned as a child to help deal with her father's attitude toward her and his ever-looming departures.

She didn't ask Quinn to sit and didn't sit herself. Instead, she stood behind the easy chair at the opposite end of the room, gripping the back of it. "And now here you are to tell me you got the girl out of your system," she declared.

Quinn shook his head slowly and let out a small chuckle. "Not hardly," he muttered more to himself than to her.

"But you came to tell me something. That you're cutting your leave short?"

"Not that, either. The exact opposite—"

"That you're going to stay longer?"

"Forever—if you'll have me."

"Come on…" she cajoled, thinking that he was joking but not quite getting the joke.

"I mean it," he said, moving to the arm of the sofa nearest the easy chair she was using as a shield. He dropped onto it, his thick thighs spread, his hands clasped between them.

Seeming more relaxed than she felt, he went on. "You know your dad was my idol and five months ago I sort of watched that idol crumble. It left me with a lot to think about. A lot about the way I've thought of and treated women myself, about how they did—or didn't— fit into my life. It's been weird," he said with the air of someone who had finally worked things out for himself.

"I was starting to figure I needed to just do what Mac did," Quinn went on. "I was thinking that playing at having relationships where I had one foot out the door didn't amount to treating women any better than he had, so I should probably just skip relationships altogether, find women who wouldn't get in any deeper than I did, and give my all to the marines without any regard to anything else, the same way I basically always have. Then our paths crossed, yours and mine…"

He paused, gave her a soft smile and explained all he'd thought about during his workout, during a rest before he ran down Mason's Peak.

"The thing is, Clairy," he said once he'd told her everything that had gone through his mind, "since I was a kid, I wanted to be what your father was. But I realized that maybe that isn't true anymore. He wasn't the man I thought he was. There were some big flaws that I was blind to. But now that I've seen them…" Quinn shook his head. "Those aren't footsteps I want to follow in, and I think I'm back to looking at following in my father's, in Micah's and Tanner's—I've served, I've made my contribution, and now maybe it's time to come home…"

He paused again for just a moment before he stood and moved to the back of the easy chair, where she was, where she had to turn to face him.

Looking into her eyes, he said in a soft voice, "I've been the marine I've wanted to be. But you make me a better man, Clairy. You make me more the man I want to be now. And being with you, making a life with you, having a family with you, is the future I want. I love you."

Oh, those three little words…

Initially it stunned her to hear Quinn say them. To hear him say them with so much sincerity that they rang as deeply true. The words sent goose bumps over the surface of her skin, made her pulse race and excitement wash through her.

Until she recalled another time when those words had swept her off her feet. When Jared had said them.

And she also recalled that she'd sworn never again to let them override her common sense or her better judgment.

She closed her eyes, forced herself to be rational, reasonable and analytical, rather than emotional. And only when she thought she had a tight grip on those things did she open them again.

"*Maybe* you don't want to be like my father. You *think* you want to follow in your father's and your brothers' footsteps. *Maybe* it's time to come home," she said, reiterating his own words, mounting an argument. "*Maybe* and you *think* equals you're not sure, you have doubts."

"I had doubts as I headed up Mason's Peak. I didn't have them by the time I came down."

It was Clairy's turn to shake her head. "I don't trust that," she said flatly.

"You don't trust me?"

"You were a little bitty boy when you came here, so sure of what you wanted to be, what you wanted from my father, and that has *never* wavered—"

"Until five months ago."

"When it wavered even more toward being who my father was and only making women recreational. But before that, before you had your faith shaken, for all these years, for what amounts to nearly your entire life, you only *ever* wanted the life my father had, to be the marine my father was to his dying day."

"I admit that," Quinn acknowledged.

"And that's it? Boom! All of that, a lifetime's goal, a lifetime of work, and it's over? It's done?"

"It's changed," he insisted.

"It's taken a hit. For now. But—"

"And you think what?" he asked. "That I'm trying to suck you in like your ex did with that flashy whirlwind courtship? That I'm trying to get you to say you love me, too, that you'll marry me, have my kids, but ultimately I won't come through for you any more than that other guy did? Any more than Mac ever did? You think I'll decide to stay a marine and you'll be stuck in the same boat you grew up in and then married into, too? That you'll just be *incidental* to me?" he said, repeating her own description of what she'd been to both men.

"Yes," she said with a staunch raise of her chin and no question in her voice.

Quinn nodded calmly, patiently, not at all like her father would have in the face of being denied something he was putting himself on the line for.

Then he said, "I understand that you're afraid of a future, or having kids with someone like your ex or Mac, with someone whose career is more important to them than you are. And you're right—that has been me. But that isn't how I want the rest of my life to be. I *don't* want the rest of my life to be the way Mac lived his. Marabeth believes Brad grew up, grew out of who he was before—just give me that much and let me take it from there."

"If Marabeth is wrong—"

"She isn't. Just give me the same chance, Clairy! I know now how much I took away from you when we were kids—let me spend the rest of my life giving back to you. Giving you what you deserve, not only because you deserve it, but because I love you with my whole heart, my whole being. And I *want* you to have what you deserve. Because I love you as much as it's humanly possible to love anyone. And I want to spend the rest of my life proving it to you. I want to spend the rest of my life *with* you, by your side, with you by my side. I *don't* want to sweep you off your feet—I want both of your feet planted firmly on the ground right beside mine."

"My feet *are* firmly planted on the ground." So firmly that she couldn't help remembering the awful teenager he'd been and fearing that that might have carried over somewhere in the man, that even if it wasn't obvious now, it could still be lurking behind the scenes to reemerge, the way Jared's obsession with work had.

Her feet were planted so firmly on the ground that regardless of how sweet his words were now, she couldn't let go of the memory of how hard Quinn had worked to become what he'd wanted to be, to become the marine her father was.

So firmly that she couldn't take the step Marabeth was taking.

She shook her head a second time, stubbornly. "I won't take the risk, Quinn. I didn't really know who Jared was until after I married him. But I *do* know who you are. I know what you've put into becoming who you are. I know what you've always wanted. And it's all the more reason I can't believe you can just say *never mind* and change."

"Not even for what we've had since I got to town? Not even to have what we *could* have?"

A third, even more resolute headshake.

Quinn stared at her as if he couldn't believe what he was seeing, what he was hearing. But she resisted seeing what was just before her in that handsome face filled with raw emotion. Instead, she saw him as the image of her father, as the image Quinn had striven for. She saw the die-hard marine. She saw another man devoted to something she could ultimately never compete with.

"You can't deny how good we are together," he said, daring her.

"Or how bad it was when we were kids, or how bad it was for me with my father, or how bad it was with Jared," she countered.

"It won't be any of that from here!" he said, frustration raising his voice.

"I won't take that risk," she said so definitively there was nothing else to be said. "You should go," she urged.

"Clairy—"

"I mean it. You should go!" she said in a louder voice of her own, because as much as she believed all that had just made her decision for her, she could still feel the soft spot she had for him and she didn't know how much longer her will to resist him could last.

"Don't do this. Don't let what's nothing but water under the bridge cost us both everything we could have together."

For a moment, Quinn went on looking into her eyes as if he still couldn't grasp that she was shutting him out.

So she raised her chin even higher to confirm that she was, and said in a voice she'd intended to be forceful but that instead came out with painful determination, "Go."

Quinn did another round of headshakes. Took a deep breath and exhaled in frustration that was now tinged with what she thought was anger.

"I've always meant what I said—when I said I wanted to be a marine, I did what I had to do to be a marine. What I'm saying now is that if you'll have me, I want to be here, with you, for you. I want to be your husband, father to your kids, until we're two ancient, wrinkled white-hairs who die together in our sleep."

What she took from that was that if she wouldn't have him, he would go back to his original course, back to his career in the marines. Back to what he'd always wanted to be and seen himself as.

So it wasn't as if he was committed to ending his career.

If a different kind of life was what he genuinely wanted, wouldn't he be doing it with or without her?

One more time she shook her head in refusal, then said, "Go now."

For a long moment, he stared at her, and Clairy met those blue eyes, fighting the thought that he was giving her the opportunity to stare into them forever, to have the sight of that staggeringly handsome face with her day in and day out.

Why did you have to come to talk tonight? Why didn't you just come to take me upstairs again so we could have had at least one more night together...

"Go," she said so softly it was almost inaudible. She felt her willpower slipping and needed him to be anywhere but there when she couldn't hang on to it any longer.

She saw his jaw clench. But this time he didn't say anything. He just turned and left her safely behind her chair.

She tried not to, but couldn't help turning enough to watch those broad shoulders as he aimed for the door.

And maybe that was when her willpower snapped altogether.

Because in that instant, something happened to Clairy. Something that took her away from the part of her that saw how handsome he was, how sexy he was. Something that wasn't connected to that urge to be back in bed with him.

It was something completely different that came over her as it registered that he really was doing what she'd told him multiple times to do—he was leaving.

But it was *Quinn* who was leaving—not the little boy who'd stolen her father's attention. Not the teenager she'd hated. Not the marine fashioned after her father. Not Jared.

Quinn.

Quinn, who had absorbed the worst of her resentment toward him, repeatedly apologized and bent over backward to make it up to her rather than striking out, the way he could have. Quinn, who Mim had said wasn't altogether responsible for Clairy's lack of a relationship with her father and been right.

Quinn, who had so gently shown her more clearly who her father had been and in the process taken away the burden of thinking she'd somehow failed as a daughter.

Quinn, who had redeemed himself, worked himself out of the hole he'd been in with her—the bad blood, the obstacles, the ugly history—and made her feel things for him that she'd never felt before for anyone.

Quinn, who had done that by listening to her, by showing an interest in what she had to say. Quinn, who had been suffering his own grief, his own letdown by her father, and had still been understanding of her.

Quinn, who had just told her that he meant what he said.

That was her father through and through. The General had always said what he meant and meant what he said.

If that was true of Quinn…

Was she taking the wrong thing from what he'd just told her? Should she have taken from it that when he said he was ready not to be a marine anymore, to make a life with her, that was as true for him now as his determination to be a marine had been for him before?

He wasn't indecisive—that was the last thing that could be said about him from the time they were small children. He knew his mind. He knew what he wanted.

And tonight he'd been telling her that *she* was what he wanted.

A life with her. A family.

And she was too afraid to believe it…

He reached the front door and raised a hand to the frame of the screen door to push it open.

He was leaving and he'd be gone and this would all be over.

And she wouldn't have him.

"Wait..." she whispered.

He stopped. Hand still against the screen, he turned only his head to look at her over his shoulder.

"It's all happened so fast, faster even than with Jared," she whispered again.

"We've known each other since we were kids," Quinn reminded her.

So while what had happened between them might have had an even shorter timeline than she'd had with Jared, there weren't likely to be any surprises. If she could accept that Quinn was ready to stop being a marine and start being devoted to her alone...

"What would you do if you resign?" she asked tentatively.

"I like the idea of helping vets the way you do," he answered with no hesitation, no question, clearly having thought it through. "I was hoping I could go to work with you for Mac's foundation."

He removed his hand from the door and turned to face her again from that distance. "I also like the idea of coming home to Merritt, being with my brothers again, with Big Ben. Being here if he needs me now and as he gets older."

"When is your contract up?" Clairy asked, knowing that after so many years in the service, his commission was continued by way of contracts.

"About five weeks. But I have more accumulated leave that I could take to run it out."

So he didn't have an obligation that would take him back for months, when he might decide to stay after all.

"I just… How could being a marine be as important as it's always been to you and now just…change?" she asked.

"Looking at Mac through a clear lens started it. It went further while I was questioning myself, realizing that I had two choices—to have Mac's life or the life I can see having with you. Last night, feeling the way being with you felt—the way *I* felt—and knowing when I sorted through it all today that *that* was what I want from here on…" His eyebrows arched. "I just knew. I *love* you, Clairy," he repeated even more firmly. "*Nothing* is more important than that to me now. The thought of not having you, of ending up like your dad…as nothing *but* a marine? That's the worst punishment you could give me for the things I've done to you."

It sounded so much like the truth.

And it came down to trusting that he really did mean what he said. And that he honestly had changed.

Marabeth knew Brad when he'd been a not-so-nice teenage boy, but she wasn't letting herself be held back by who he'd been in the past. She was looking at him in the present.

Should I follow in those?

There was nothing about Quinn that had ever left a doubt that he knew what he wanted. If what he wanted had changed, why *shouldn't* she believe it? Why couldn't she trust that he did know himself, know his own mind?

"There's nothing for me to punish you for," she said. "I know now that I wouldn't have had a relationship with my father even if you'd never come around—it was something in him that made him see me as less because I wasn't male."

Quinn took a few steps back into the living room. "I wasn't nice to you when I was a smart-ass teenage boy," he reminded her, as if he needed to be sure she could move beyond that.

"No, and I hope that isn't still somewhere inside you. But I haven't seen any signs of it." In fact, she'd seen the opposite in his patience, his consideration, his calm even when she'd lashed out. "So it doesn't seem like I should punish you for that, either."

"Then don't."

"You actually do see yourself not being a marine any-more?" she asked with a glimmer of hope in her voice.

"Once a marine, always a marine. But active? No. I see myself with you," he said simply.

Oh, it wasn't easy to let go of so much that protected her from more pain...

But her guard had dropped, and once it had, she knew why it wasn't just his looks and sex appeal that had made her stop him from leaving.

She loved him.

She came out from behind the chair and met him halfway. "You're sure?"

Quinn closed the rest of the space between them to stand directly in front of her again. "Of everything."

Clairy breathed a tiny laugh. "Maybe it's strange that I doubted that," she mused.

"Or maybe I earned some of it," he conceded. "Just say we can put this fresh start back on track and take it from here."

"All the way to the altar and kids and a whole life together?"

"All the way," he confirmed unfalteringly.

"I *do* love you," she said, as if she was helpless not to.

"I'm a lovable guy," he joked, making her laugh.

"You haven't always been," she chastised playfully.

"I will be from now on, though," he vowed.

Clairy was again looking up into those eyes, that face, and this time she was brimming with what she felt for him. "I love you," she said with some awe.

"Enough to marry me? Have babies with me? Get old and cranky with me?"

"Old, maybe, but let's try to avoid cranky."

Quinn smiled that smile that only made him all the more handsome. "I'll give it my best shot," he promised as his hands cupped the sides of her face and held it for the kiss he placed softly on her lips.

The kiss that couldn't stay that way for long before all the passion of the previous night came alive again.

And as Clairy closed her eyes and indulged in it, not only could she envision a future with him, but suddenly all the pain and struggle and offenses of the past also seemed worth it if it meant she could have the man he'd become.

* * * * *

NOT THEIR FIRST RODEO

CHRISTY JEFFRIES

To my own fairy godmother, Bonnie Johnston Holbrook.
You have boundless energy and the biggest heart.
You're the glue that keeps our extended family together
and my heart smiles every time I see you. Thank you for
always showing up (and for always buying my books).
Love you to the moon and back.

CHAPTER ONE

Marcus King hated funerals.

As the sheriff of Ridgecrest County in Wyoming, he even avoided traffic details for cemetery processions, often assigning a junior deputy for the task, just so he wouldn't have to deal with the painful reminder that death could happen to anyone at any time. A fact he knew only too well, having lost his wife five years ago.

However, Marcus hadn't been able to avoid this particular memorial service, with thousands of mourners lined up outside the crowded church and millions more at home watching live on their televisions. Celebrities, national heroes and world leaders were all crammed into the too-small First Congregation of Teton Ridge, watching somberly as the president of the United States gave the eulogy for her second-in-command.

Vice President Mitchell "Roper" King had been many things to many people, but to Marcus he'd simply been Dad.

And how did one escape his own father's funeral while hundreds of news cameras were strategically placed both inside and outside the church to capture every tear, every sniffle, every flicker of emotion that crossed the faces of those who had known and loved Roper King the most?

Well, not everyone in attendance felt that way, Marcus thought as he shifted in the tight confines of his pew to angle his head toward the opposite side of the building.

"Stop squirming in your seat," his brother Duke whispered out the corner of his mouth. "You're not five anymore."

"I'm checking on my sons," Marcus replied before giving a curt nod to his twin boys sitting with their younger cousin in the pew behind them. "They've got to be bored out of their minds."

Six-year-old Jordan and Jack were hanging in there like a couple of champs, though. Sad, but hiding their restlessness way better than their old man. Probably because their aunt had promised all the kids doughnuts and brand-new iPads loaded with their favorite video games if they could keep still during the nearly one-hour service.

Marcus glanced past his sons' honey-blond heads to the packed pews behind them and caught a glimpse of the upper corner of a woman's face.

No. That couldn't be...

Surely *she* wouldn't come to the funeral, especially knowing Marcus would be there. He craned his neck to get a better look and felt his brother's elbow ram directly into the cold piece of steel secured in place below his rib cage.

Duke stifled a curse, and their mother gave them both a withering stare through her sheer black veil. When she returned her attention to the president speaking in front of the flag-draped casket, Duke muttered, "Did you seriously wear your duty holster to the service?"

"I always wear it," Marcus said, tugging on the lapels of his uncomfortable suit. "Just in case something comes up and I need to respond to a call."

"You're allowed to take the day off."

Yet Marcus never took time away from work. At least, not mentally. This was his home, his county. These people, most of them visitors, were ultimately his responsibility until they all returned to their own worlds. He glanced down at his watch. Hopefully, that would be in less than fifteen more minutes. They just needed to get through the video montage and then the procession before he could—

"Where's Tessa going?" His brother nodded to where their sister was rushing down the center aisle toward the small vestibule that led to the front doors.

"I'll go check." Marcus began to rise, but his mother, who was on his opposite side, quickly shot her arm across his midsection, just like she used to do when she'd driven him to school or baseball practice and had to slam on the brakes.

"Don't you dare stand up and cause a bigger scene." She spoke quietly, but firmly. "We have people stationed outside who can see to her."

The Secret Service agent positioned in the shadows behind the organ put his hand over the clear wire of his earpiece. Marcus had attended the pre-op briefing earlier today with several deputies from his department, as well as numerous other law-enforcement personnel from neighboring counties. Right now, he would've given anything to know what was being transmitted over the radio communications. The agent made eye contact with Marcus and gave a very discreet thumbs-up before resuming his stance.

Which meant he had to stay put and actually deal with the grief of losing his father. Instead of thinking about something simple like logistics and security perimeters, he had to think about how much he was going to miss seeing his dad's proud, but crooked smile. How he was never going to hear that rugged, but reassuring voice give him any more words of advice. Damn it. Marcus wanted to mourn in private, on his own schedule. Certainly not in front of a crowd.

The final ten minutes of the ceremony seemed to last longer than the first fifty, but finally the pallbearers, consisting of members of each branch of the armed services, carried the casket down the center aisle. His mother followed, supported by the president who'd been sitting in the front pew on the opposite side. That left Marcus to walk next to the first gentleman while mourners nodded their condolences at them as they passed each row.

If there was anything Marcus avoided more than funerals, it was politicians. Sure, the president and her husband were polite enough, and his father had made numerous friends with elected officials and cabinet members over the years. But there were plenty of people who'd traveled all the way to Roper King's small hometown in the middle of Wyoming just for the opportunity to be seen rubbing elbows with some of the most powerful leaders in the country.

Like the senior senator from the great state of Texas. And wherever Senator Cortez-Hill went, her famous husband followed, causing even more of a stir with his celebrity status as a member of the Baseball Hall of Fame.

Perfect. The only thing that would make this day even more unbearable was if they'd brought...

Oh, hell. There she was.

Violet Cortez-Hill.

Marcus's lungs seized, and his knees threatened to buckle as his eyes locked on hers. It *had* been her sitting way back here, after all. And she was even more beautiful than she'd been the last time he'd seen her—almost fourteen years ago. Her black hair was still silky straight, but slightly shorter, and framed her heart-shaped face. Her light bronze complexion still smooth and flawless, and her narrow nose still regal. But her cheekbones were sharper and more defined, and her green eyes held more wisdom and cynicism. His gaze flickered lower to her lips, which were drawn tight, as though she was holding her breath as she boldly returned his stare.

He should've listened to his instincts earlier and volunteered for traffic detail. Funerals didn't just force people to publicly confront their grief and their own invincibility. They often forced people to confront mistakes from their pasts. And now he was face-to-face with his.

Why had Violet come? Didn't she know how uncomfortable this would be for all of them?

A hand clasped his shoulder and propelled him forward.

"Keep on moving, Lover Boy," Duke grunted from behind. Marcus hadn't heard the nickname in years, and instead of sending him on a trip down memory lane, it immediately snapped him back to the present.

Putting one foot in front of the other, he squared his shoulders and followed the procession down the aisle, outside the church and into the bright January sunshine and the even brighter lights of the news cameras. He shoved his dark sunglasses on just in time, once again wishing he could be anywhere but here.

As the casket was loaded into the back of the hearse, he felt the small hands of his boys, each on one side, taking his bigger palms in theirs. Marcus couldn't afford to think about anything but taking care of his children, being the support that they needed through the devastating loss of another family member. He'd told his children that it was okay to cry, that it was okay to be sad. They'd both been so young when their mother had died, their grieving process had been somewhat delayed. As though they'd known they were missing something but didn't quite understand who or what until later. Losing their beloved grandfather, though, had the potential to stir up all sorts of feelings they'd yet to deal with about their mom's death.

Marcus's dad had once been his rock, and now more than ever he was determined to provide the same stability to his own sons.

"Where's Aunt Tessa?" Jordan whispered, concern permanently etched across the serious boy's brow. "She left real quick, and her face was all white."

"Maybe she was hungry and wanted to get something to eat," Marcus replied, doubting the excuse before he even said it.

"Well, I have to go pee, and I don't think I can hold it," Jack announced much louder. Despite being older by three minutes, Jack was the free-spirited twin. The impulsive one that counterbalanced his brother's tendency to worry about every little thing. "She better not eat all the sprinkle doughnuts before we get there."

Marcus bit back a groan, yet he couldn't help but also feel a sense of relief. His sons were actually handling the funeral crowd much better than expected. Being a single father, he'd dealt with plenty of tears and tantrums in the past and knew it came with the territory. Today, though, he'd much rather deal with doughnuts and bathroom breaks.

He squeezed their hands and said, "Let's go back inside and use the restroom. Then we'll go see if they have any more snacks left in the MACC staging tent."

In fact, it felt good to have something concrete to focus on, to have a task at hand. Plus, it didn't hurt that his sons' requests gave him the perfect excuse to get away from everyone in the crowd and check on his sister all at the same time. While he was there, he could ask his deputies stationed in the Multi-Agency Command Center temporarily set up behind the building if they needed anything from him.

Marcus chanced a glance behind him at the guests spilling onto the church steps to see if anyone was watching them, then told his kids, "Come on. Let's hop over those bushes by the sidewalk and double back to the side door. It'll be the quickest way."

It would also be the only route that guaranteed he didn't come face-to-face with the woman who'd made him stop in his tracks earlier.

The woman who used to hold his heart in the palm of her hand.

Violet Cortez-Hill knew when she'd landed at Jackson Hole Airport it would only be a matter of time before she'd see Marcus King, the man who'd once been her best friend and her first love.

Everyone probably would have understood why she couldn't find time to attend the funeral in Wyoming. But she was in between high-profile cases right now, and after fourteen years, it felt cowardly to use work as an excuse just to hide behind all those emotions that belonged in the past. And nobody had ever accused Violet of being a coward.

Besides, she'd spent so much of her adolescent summers with the older King children when their parents had forced them to attend the same political events, and she had adored their father, Roper. How could she not be here to pay her respects in person? To offer any support she could.

Yet, when her eyes had locked on Marcus's during the final procession, she'd been slammed with a million memories. It felt as though a wave had crashed into her, practically knocking her back into the hard, wooden pew.

How was it that he'd grown even more handsome over the years? That his shoulders had gotten broader and his face had gotten more chiseled? The teenager she'd once dated used to wear ripped jeans, T-shirts with goofy slogans and an old ball cap from Dorsey's Tractor Supply. Yet the man who'd stopped in the middle of the aisle to stare at her with openmouthed shock wore an expensive tailored suit and a short, neat haircut, looking nothing like the guy she used to know. Unfortunately, his nearness still caused her pulse to spike with the same level of attraction as it had all those years ago.

His brother Duke had given him a shove and Violet was left to stand there and wonder if the few seconds they'd made eye contact was really long enough for her to conclude that his reaction to seeing her had been just as intense as hers. She fought the urge to rub away the dull ache in her temples, telling herself that Marcus's response was simply due to his surprise.

The church was small and the aisle narrow, so it took ages for the rows in front of them to empty. As the rest of the mourners filed out of the church, Violet whispered to her mother, "I'm going to use the ladies' room."

"Now?" Senator Eva Cortez-Hill said through her teeth as she nodded somberly at the other politicians and A-list celebrities making their way down the aisle. "All the networks have cameras outside, and it would be a great opportunity for you to get some coverage before my next election."

"Mom, we've already been over the fact that I have no intention of running for superior court judge. Now's not the time to rehash that argument."

"You aren't hoping to run into *you know who*, are you?" After all these years, her mother still couldn't bring herself to say Marcus's name.

"Of course not, Mom. That's all in the past."

"Fine. But be outside in five minutes. Our car will be the third one behind the president's in the motorcade, and the Secret Service won't want to wait."

Violet nodded before going in the opposite direction toward the vestibule hallway that led toward the restrooms. Her family had been in the public eye for as long as she could remember, so the cameras and parades of vehicles and formal appearances were certainly nothing new. Yet, that didn't mean she relished living her life in the spotlight, even if she was good at pretending otherwise. In fact, being a public defender, representing some of the most heinous criminals in the justice system, she'd quickly learned how to mask any facial expressions that might give away how she was truly feeling inside. Every day, she sat beside strangers in orange jumpsuits accused of an array of charges and didn't hesitate to defend their right to a fair trial.

So then, why was she currently ducking into the bathroom of a small church in the middle of Wyoming? Why was she hiding out in a cramped powder room that hadn't had its floral wallpaper or framed cross-stitch decor changed out in at least four decades?

Violet braced her hands on the pink-tiled counter and stared at her reflection over the sink. "Because the last time you saw Marcus King, your world fell apart shortly after."

Her phone vibrated in her purse, and she felt a stinging pressure building behind her eyes, the telltale sign of a migraine coming on. Yanking out her phone, she saw the text from her father asking if she was okay. She fired a quick response.

I'm fine. Go on without me and I'll catch up with you guys later at the airport.

She dug around in her purse for the pills her doctor had prescribed for migraines. Even though taking them made her feel as though she were admitting defeat, she knew that it was smart to stay ahead of the pain and the accompanying nausea before it got worse. Turning on the water, she cupped her hand under the faucet and took a deep drink.

Next, she reapplied her lipstick and tried to ignore how pale her cheeks looked in the fluorescent lights and pink-hued surrounding of the ladies' room. Checking the time on her phone, she convinced herself that the motorcade was likely long gone, hopefully with Marcus in one of the first vehicles. She could slip outside and pretend nothing was amiss.

And then do what?

Ask a reporter for a ride in a news van? Call a cab? Did they have Uber in Teton Ridge? Okay, so maybe this wasn't one of her better thought-out plans. *This* was why she tried not to let her emotions get the better of her.

"C'mon," she told herself in the mirror. There were hundreds of people in attendance at the funeral. Surely someone would be heading her way. "For God's sake, what's with you? You're smart. You're resourceful. You've just been named one of the top litigators in *Lone Star Docket* magazine. Finding a ride to the airport should be the least of your problems. Get it together, damn it."

Finally the pep talk worked. She ran a hand through her dark hair and turned to the door. Straightening her spine, she left the safety of her temporary hideout with her head held high.

Only to slam into the very man she'd been trying to avoid.

Marcus's hands were firm and strong on her shoulders as he caught her, then immediately released her when his surprised face recognized hers.

"Violet." His voice was deeper than she'd remembered, and his solemn tone was definitely less playful. But at least it wasn't accusatory, which might have been how she would've sounded if he'd shown up at her father's funeral.

She drew in a deep breath, trying to ignore his citrus and leather–scented shower gel, still familiar after all these years. "Hi, Marcus. I'm deeply sorry for your loss."

A storm of emotion passed behind those blue eyes of his, as though fighting to remember why they were both here in the vestibule of the First Congregation of Teton Ridge. Her stomach roiled and twisted in a storm of its own, and she didn't know if it was a symptom from her impending migraine or a symptom of standing inches away from her ex-boyfriend.

Finally, he rubbed the back of his neck before giving her a curt nod. "Thank you."

She wanted to ask him how he was holding up, but the slight shadow of his sunken cheeks told her that he wasn't doing well. The stiff resolve in his square jaw similarly told her that he wouldn't admit it.

Clearly, neither one wanted to be the first to run away from the history between them. She could make an excuse about needing to catch her ride, but what if he followed her outside and saw that everyone had already left?

Speaking of the motorcade, why was he still here? Why hadn't he ridden in the family limos with his mother and siblings? It was on the tip of her tongue to ask him, but he crossed his arms over his chest, his defensive posture suggesting he was more than willing to stand there silently and wait her out.

He reminded her of a court bailiff or a guard at the jail who stood by stoically as she interviewed one of her clients, annoyed by the assignment and pretending not to be counting the minutes until he could be out of her presence.

The longer Marcus remained planted there staring at her, the more her pulse pounded with annoyance. Was he not even slightly curious about what had happened to her? Or at least willing to be polite and pretend he cared?

What made it worse was that Violet desperately wanted to ask him all kinds of questions about *his* life. To find out what he'd been doing since he'd vanished from her life without so much as a *see ya* fourteen years ago.

Yet she doubted he'd be forthcoming with those answers, either. Instead she said, "I saw Tessa leave the service early. I hope she's okay."

Even to her ears it sounded like she was fishing for information rather than simply trying to engage him in conversation. But the alternative would have been to either stand there silently and let the awkward tension build or to dash away as though she had something to hide.

Plus, she had always been fond of Tessa and was legitimately concerned about his sister. Marcus might not be willing to talk about himself, but he'd never been able to hide his concern for his family.

For the first time, his eyes darted away from her, and he cleared his throat. "Tessa wasn't feeling well, and a Secret Service agent took her to the command center tent to have the medics examine her."

"Oh, no. I could go check on her," Violet said, taking a step back. In fact, the migraine medicine wasn't kicking in as quickly as she'd hoped, and the nausea bubbling inside her was growing worse. Having grown up around big events like this, she knew there'd be a staging area behind the church that would be quicker to access on foot. The thought of some fresh air and an anti-nausea pill had her pivoting to leave.

"Actually." His voice was commanding and held the slightest warning. Violet paused midturn as he continued. "I'm going to be heading that way when I get done here. I'll let her know you were concerned."

The subtle, yet presumptive, instruction wasn't lost on Violet. Marcus clearly didn't want her going in the same direction as him. Or maybe he didn't want her having any contact with his family. Which was too bad because the MACC tent was usually staffed with first responders and government employees who would be more than willing to assist her in finding alternate transportation to the airport.

Her neck stiffened with irritation, and she lifted her chin. "In that case, don't let me keep you."

He rocked back on the heels of his expensive leather cowboy boots but didn't make a move to leave. "I'm waiting for someone."

Violet felt the color drain from her face. Had there been someone else in the ladies' room when she'd been in there giving herself a pep talk in the mirror? Was it his wife? She'd inadvertently heard through the political grapevine that he'd married a while ago, but she'd stopped herself from ever confirming the fact. In fact, she'd practically made it a personal mission to avoid any news about Marcus. After their breakup, she'd told herself that she had more important things to focus on and he didn't deserve the headspace. But maybe that had been a mistake. Violet wouldn't go into a courtroom without briefing the relevant facts of the case, so why had she shown up on his home turf so unprepared?

Instead of a wife coming out of the ladies' room,

though, the door to the men's restroom sprang open, and two young boys spilled out.

"Jack didn't use any soap when he washed his hands," one of the children quickly said to Marcus.

"That's cuz I finished before Jordan and didn't touch the flusher, Dad."

"Dad?" Violet heard herself squeak as her eyes darted between the identical boys and Marcus. "They're... yours?"

She tried to swallow as a sickening wave threatened to upend the contents of her stomach. She put a hand to her lower abdomen as though she could stop the building discomfort, or at least the ghost of a long-ago pain.

"Yes," Marcus said, putting an arm around each boy as all three sets of matching blue eyes blinked skeptically at her. "These are my sons. Jack and Jordan King. Boys, this is my...uh...an old friend of the family."

"They..." Her throat spasmed, and she waited a beat before trying again. "They're twins."

It was more of a statement than a question. And an accusatory one at that.

"Yes," Marcus replied slowly, one blondish-brown eyebrow lifting. "Why do you look so shocked? It runs in my family."

She felt the perspiration dotting her upper lip even as a chill raced down her spine.

Because once, *they* were going to have twins.

She almost admitted as much aloud, but she was already shoving her way back through the restroom door, barely making it into the stall before the contents of her stomach tore through her.

CHAPTER TWO

"Hey, lady? Are you okay?"

Violet was shocked to see one of the boys holding the stall door open, watching her closely after she'd finished heaving and flushed the toilet. She was even more shocked to see his twin brother and their father behind him in the cramped confines of the ladies' room.

Marcus must've known how awkward it was for him and his two young sons to have witnessed her indelicate moment, because he said, "You left the door open. Jordan was worried and wanted to come check on you."

She nodded because what else was she supposed to say? *Get out? Leave me alone?* She might've easily been able to say something like that to Marcus, but not to his young sons, who were so obviously concerned about her. Scratch that. One son was obviously worried. The other son peeking out behind his dad's hip was wide-eyed, and his lips were curled down in disgust—as though he, too, might vomit soon.

"Is it a foodborne illness?" The one who must be Jordan asked the question. There was a small crease above his freckled nose as his narrowed eyes assessed her. "Or maybe a viral gastro-testnal infection?"

Violet blinked several times at the child's attempt to use proper medical terms. "Uh, I don't think so."

She delicately stepped around him to make her way to the sink before carefully dipping her head down to rinse out her mouth and splash water on her flushed cheeks. Yet the boy followed her, his serious expression reflected at her in the mirror as she used a paper towel to dry her face.

"Do you have a fever?" he asked. "Or diarrhea?"

"Okay, Doctor Jordan, let's give Miss Cortez-Hill some space," Marcus said as he steered both of his boys toward the door, which was still wide-open. He glanced over his shoulder and told Violet, "Sorry about the intrusion. Jordan's been really into WebMD and those emergency-room documentaries on TV lately. He ran in here before I could stop him."

"Thank you for checking on me," she told the boy. Even with all the humiliation still radiating through her, something tugged at Violet's heartstrings. Of course, she would've preferred some privacy, but she wasn't immune to the concern or the curiosity of the child, who did look pretty worried. Her hand shook slightly as she unwrapped one of the pastel breath mints some nice church lady had set out in a glass bowl on the counter. By the time she reapplied her lipstick—for a second time—her fingers were barely trembling. Her hair and eye makeup were beyond repair, she thought as she gave herself one last look in the mirror, but at least her migraine was already subsiding. The sooner she got away from Marcus and Teton Ridge, the better she would feel.

Unfortunately, that wouldn't be anytime soon. The man and his sons were still there, waiting for her in the empty lobby area. She glanced out the wooden double doors leading to the steps outside and saw that many of the cars and news vans were long gone.

"You're able to walk by yourself so far." Jordan rushed to her side with his hands up, like a pint-size spotter to prevent her from falling down. "That's a good sign."

"I'd probably get dizzy and throw up, too, if I had to walk around in those kinds of shoes." Jack, the other twin, frowned skeptically at Violet's high heels. "Maybe you should just go barefoot."

Violet bit back a smile. "I appreciate everyone's concern, but I'm fine now. I promise. I just get these little headaches every once in a while, and they make my tummy unhappy."

"Those are called migraines," Jordan said with confidence. "Our teacher gets them every time we have rainy-day schedule at school and says they're caused by stress."

"Is stress like pneumonia?" Jack asked his brother. "Can we catch it if we've been in the bathroom with her?"

As his sons began a discussion on contagious diseases, Marcus dragged his hand through his short-cropped blondish-brown hair. Violet remembered he'd once worn it much longer, and it used to hold more traces of sun-bleached blond. Now, there were several stubby gray strands near his temples.

"Sorry," he said to her over the boys' heads. "You know how inquisitive kids can be."

His words were probably well-intentioned, but they pierced her heart all the same. Actually, Violet didn't know much about kids at all. She'd grown up an only child, and after everything that had happened when she and Marcus had split up, she'd shied away from interacting with young children when she could avoid it. It was just too painful. She shook her head. "Please don't apologize for them. I think it's sweet that they care so much."

Unlike their father, who hadn't bothered checking on her fourteen years ago when she'd miscarried *their* twins.

"I'd like to say that they usually don't follow strangers into the bathroom and try to diagnose them, but this is the third time. This school year."

"Oh." She blinked several times.

"We didn't follow Mr. Burnworth into the bathroom," Jordan pointed out. "He was standing behind the bakery counter, and his face and mouth were all hard and mean-looking, and I asked him if he needed a tetanus shot because he might have lockjaw."

Violet studied the boy. "You sure know a lot about this kind of stuff for only being… How old are you?"

"We're six and three-quarters," Jordan replied proudly, revealing a missing top tooth.

"That means we're almost seven," Jack explained, holding up the corresponding fingers. "We're gonna have a big birthday party at the ranch, and you can come if you're not contagious."

"That's not for two more months, though," Marcus jumped in. "I'm sure Miss Cortez-Hill will be going back to Dallas way before then."

She jerked up her chin. "How did you know I live in Dallas?"

Marcus shrugged, but not before she caught a flicker of something in his eyes. Guilt, maybe, because he quickly masked it by saying, "I figured it was a safe guess, seeing as how you were never one to stray too far from where your parents wanted you."

The pointed jab was a red herring meant to distract her from the fact that he was trying to downplay something—likely the fact that he'd just overplayed his hand. Some of the best attorneys in Texas had tried the same diversionary tactic in the courtroom with her and failed miserably. She wasn't about to let the guy who broke her heart get away with it. She crossed her arms over her chest. "Or maybe you've been keeping tabs on me, Marcus King."

His eyes rolled a bit too dramatically and she had her answer, even if he tried to deny it. "It's hard not to when our parents have always run in the same political circles. Or at least used to." Marcus glanced away a little too quickly, but not before she saw the shift of emotion pass across his face. He cleared his throat, then added, "Speaking of which, we really need to get going. We're due at the ranch for the graveside service."

"Of course. Please give your mom my condolences and tell her… Wait. The motorcade already left. Shouldn't you have been in one of the family limos?"

"Dad hates limos," Jordan said. "We hadta come in the patrol unit because Dad is always on duty. You want to ride with us?"

"Yeah," Jack added before either of the adults could respond. "You can sit in the front seat and turn on the siren if you want."

Patrol unit? Siren? Violet reassessed Marcus's dark tailored suit, his broad shoulders narrowing down to his waist and the shadow of a bulge directly above his right hip. Her ex-boyfriend was now a cop. And he was currently wearing a gun and holster at his own father's funeral. He'd always been a fun-loving yet responsible guy. But perhaps he was taking his job a little too seriously.

She was about to explain that she hadn't planned to attend the graveside service—which was supposed to only be for family and close friends—but before she could politely decline, Marcus answered on her behalf. "Boys, I'm sure Miss Cortez-Hill has other plans."

She realized this was the third time he'd referred to her as *Miss*. Either he was assuming that she couldn't possibly be married—which was a little insulting—or he knew her marital status the same way he'd known where she was living, which made her wonder what else he knew about her. Suddenly, she didn't feel like allowing him to have the upper hand anymore. Or dictating her plans.

"Actually, I'd love a ride," she told the boys. Then she looked their father directly in the eyes and said, "Thanks for the thoughtful offer."

Marcus steered his county-issued SUV through the gates of the Twin Kings Ranch, nodding at the Secret Service agents stationed at the front entrance. His family's working cattle ranch was over fifty-five thousand acres, and it took almost ten minutes to follow the main road past the house where he'd grown up, and then wind up to the private cemetery plot on a grassy bluff overlooking the Snake River.

His jaw throbbed from the way he'd kept his back molars clamped into place, nearly grinding them together as he tried to ignore the familiar scent of Violet's jasmine perfume. The same one she'd worn when they'd been eighteen. Or maybe his head was just pounding from his sons' incessant chattering the entire ride from the church.

Apparently, Violet's migraine had eased up. She was facing the back seat as much as her seat belt would allow and patiently answering the twins' rapid-fire questions about her favorite ice cream (mint chip—no surprise), her favorite superhero (Wonder Woman—again, no surprise), her dog's name (she didn't have a pet—somewhat of a surprise considering the fact that she'd always loved animals) and if she played any sports (running—very surprising since she'd always hated going for jogs with him when he'd been training for boot camp).

The one question that his children didn't ask was if Violet had any kids. Marcus should've been thankful that his normally inquisitive twins weren't bringing up such a painful subject. After all, he'd tried to put that unfortunate business behind him, even when he'd occasionally hear news about her from his parents or his sister Tessa, who'd interviewed Senator Cortez-Hill several times on her show. But when he'd introduced her to Jack and Jordan, her face had gone completely pale, as though she'd seen a ghost.

It could've been a simple case of her not feeling well, because she'd rushed into the bathroom right after. Yet there had been something else. He could sense it, lurking beneath the tension of their already-uncomfortable reunion. Marcus was suddenly dying to ask her about it. Even if it meant reliving the past.

He backed into the last turnaround spot on the dirt road leading up to the cemetery. It was unseasonably warm for mid-January in Wyoming. Most of the snow from the New Year's storm had already melted, but they'd still have to hike a few hundred yards in the uneven terrain to reach the gravesite.

"I'm sure there would've been room for more vehicles up ahead," Violet said as she tried to navigate around a mud puddle in the middle of their path, her expensive-looking high heel sinking into the damp earth.

"In case of an emergency, though, I need to be able to get my car out quickly."

She made a deliberate show of scanning the dozen or so Secret Service agents surrounding the immediate area, before jerking her chin toward several military personnel dressed in full uniform. "You think you're the only person here who can respond to an emergency situation?"

"I'm the sheriff of Ridgecrest County and responsible for the safety of all the residents and businesses. So my duty extends well beyond this ranch."

"You're also Roper King's son. I'm sure you can take a day off for your father's funeral," Violet said, right before stumbling when her heel caught on a hidden rock.

He quickly grabbed her elbow to steady her, and a current of electricity shot through his hand and up his arm. Marcus nearly released her just as quickly but thought that would suggest he couldn't handle his response to touching her. Instead, he commanded his brain to think of her the same way he'd think of old Mrs. Crenshaw, who held up traffic for at least five minutes every time she slowly crossed Stampede Boulevard, the main street running through town. "Like my son said, I'm always on duty."

She paused to stare at him, and he forgot all about traffic and little old ladies as his pulse picked up speed. To Violet's credit, she didn't pull away from him, either.

But he could tell from the rosy-bronze hue spreading along her upper chest and neck that she was equally affected by his touch. It was the same way she used to flush with heat when they were younger and he'd kiss her just above her—

"Why is your skin all reddish like that?" Jack asked Violet before Marcus's inappropriate thoughts could gain any more steam.

"It looks like a rash. Do you have any allergies?" Jordan wanted to know, and Marcus silently cursed himself for allowing his young son to spend so much time researching medical ailments.

Violet cleared her throat, but her blush only intensified. "None that I know of."

Marcus felt his mother's eyes on them and realized the minister was already speaking to the much smaller crowd who'd arrived from the church before them.

He nudged his sons forward toward the two rows of chairs. "There's a couple of empty seats behind Gan Gan. Why don't you guys go sit down? Quietly," he added. "I'll be right behind you."

Thankfully, Jack and Jordan obeyed, which only happened about 75 percent of the time. Probably because they were too overwhelmed by the sadness of all the adults around them.

The boys sat next to their young cousin and their Aunt Finn, who was great at whispering jokes and keeping the tears at bay during the most solemn of ceremonies.

Marcus didn't want this building tension between him and Violet adding to his sons' distress on an already emotional day, so he didn't immediately follow them. But that left him standing beside Violet during the most emotional and intimate part of the funeral proceedings. Not just beside her but mere inches away since his hand was still on her elbow.

He could hear her soft breathing during the gospel singer's rendition of "Amazing Grace." He could feel the rigidity in her arm during the bugler playing "Taps." He flinched with her during the twenty-one-gun salute. And somehow, he found his own hand intertwined with hers as they lowered his father's casket into the ground. Just as his throat constricted with emotion, Violet lightly squeezed her fingers around his palm, giving him a boost of strength.

Roper King's death had been quite a shock for all of them, but even more so for Marcus, who was still angry at himself for not being more aware. Even though Roper had been bigger than life and damn near invincible, he was also older and they all should've been better prepared for the inevitable. Especially coming only a few years after another loss that had been much more life-altering.

In fact, the family burial plot was the last place he should be holding hands with Violet. Shame immediately washed over him, overshadowing his grief. He quickly untangled his fingers from hers and edged away, unable to keep the gruffness from his voice when he said, "I have to go."

His footsteps were heavy and weighted with guilt when he joined his mother and siblings as they filed into a line to pay their final respects to his father—the man who had taught Marcus how to be a man, how to be a husband and, most importantly, how to be a dad.

Truckloads of flowers had been delivered to both the ranch and the church and were still being silently unloaded behind a cluster of mourners. His immediate family made their way to the cars that would take them back down the hill to the main house and the catered reception his mother had planned for only their closest relatives and friends. However, Marcus grabbed an arrangement of pale pink roses and walked over to a headstone, feeling the weight of his sadness settle deeply onto his shoulders.

Violet stood there awkwardly as the remaining mourners filed past Roper King's open grave. Once, she'd thought of the younger Kings as the siblings she'd never had, but who knew what Marcus had told them after he'd all but abandoned her all those years ago.

Not that any of them would ever be less than cordial to her if she was to approach them. But at that moment, she didn't feel right intruding on their grief just to ease the guilt of attending such an intimate service that was clearly only meant for close family and friends—neither of which she could claim. At least not anymore.

She saw Tessa King walking with a man she didn't recognize but looked to be Secret Service. A second man she *did* recognize—a young up-and-coming congressman from California—approached Marcus's sister, and Violet heard a camera shutter clicking away behind her.

Only preapproved members of the press would be allowed to be here to document the private ceremony, so Violet didn't think anything of it. Instead, she tried to focus on how she was going to get back down the hill and possibly catch a ride to the airport.

There were several men wearing cowboy hats standing around a late-model pickup with the Twin Kings

Ranch logo on the door. Roper had been loved by everyone, especially his private employees, so it would make sense for many of the ranch hands to be in attendance. Maybe she could ask one of them for a lift, because she certainly wasn't going to ask Marcus for one.

Her palm was still tingling from where his hand had clung tightly to hers during the final moments of the service. She'd seen a tear slip beneath the rim of his dark sunglasses, and despite all the heartbreak he'd once caused her, she couldn't make herself walk away from him when he'd seemed to need support most.

Not surprisingly, when everything was said and done, he'd dropped her hand and simply walked away from her. Just like he had all those years ago. Leaving her all by herself, to figure out where to go from here.

Jordan, the twin with the seemingly encyclopedic knowledge about medical conditions, approached Violet cautiously. "Are you still having your migraine? If your blood pressure feels high, you might need to sit down." The boy scrunched his nose at the folding chairs now being loaded into the back of the ranch truck. "Or I can walk you back to the car."

Actually, Violet's head had been the least of her worries this past hour. Her medication had thankfully taken effect before they'd left the church, and she didn't have to force a smile at the sweet boy who seemed to genuinely care about her health. "No, I'm all better. In fact, I was just thinking I feel so great I might walk down to the main house."

Then she could ask someone in the stables to call her a cab.

"But that's, like, fifty miles away," Jack, the other twin, said as he approached with much less caution, narrowly missing tripping over an old wooden headstone. "And our aunt says there's only *one* chocolate cake at the house without nuts. I hate nuts, so we have to get down the hill fast before all the good desserts are gone."

Most of the cars were already pulling away, and she finally noticed that it was just her and the twins left. She looked to her right and left, then asked, "Where's your dad?"

"He's over there with our mom." Jordan pointed to a spot behind her, and Violet squeezed her eyes shut, not wanting to look. Was Marcus still married? He hadn't been wearing a ring, but some men didn't wear them. Maybe their mother had ridden here in a family limo. Maybe she'd been sitting in the second row with the boys the entire time.

Violet slowly turned around, bracing herself for an awkward introduction. But instead of seeing Marcus speaking to a woman, she saw him standing under the shady branches of an old sycamore tree, placing a spray of pale pink roses in front of a white marble headstone.

Jack slipped his smaller hand in hers, and she was surprised that her fingers reflexively curled around his. "Now Grandpa is in Heaven with Mommy."

CHAPTER THREE

MARCUS WAS SERIOUSLY looking forward to grabbing a bottle of sixteen-year-old single barrel bourbon and heading straight into his own wing of the house to zone out in front of the television with the boys as they re-watched one of their favorite movies. It had been a hell of an afternoon and they all needed a comforting, yet familiar distraction. But first he needed to figure out what to do with his ex-girlfriend.

After a silent ride down the hill from the cemetery, the boys eagerly ran inside the main house to join their Uncle Duke, who'd been waiting for them on the porch. His brother must've seen them together before leaving the cemetery and known Marcus would need a few moments. Now it was just him and Violet standing in front of his SUV in the wide parking area near the steps of the kitchen porch.

"Uh…do you want to come inside?" he asked against his better judgment. After all, his mother would give him hell if she knew that Violet was here and he didn't at least extend an invite.

"I really shouldn't," she said. "In fact, I already missed my flight back to Dallas and should get to Jackson Hole soon if I'm going to try and get another connection tonight."

He nodded, equally disappointed—and oddly relieved.

"Listen," she started, then tilted her head and paused. As though she was thinking better of whatever she'd been about to say. He lowered his chin and was about to encourage her to keep going when her soft lips parted. "I'm sorry about your wife. I saw you," she explained when he blinked several times, clearly startled. "You were placing flowers on a grave, and one of the twins told me—Jack, I think. I know it's none of my business, but how did she pass away?"

"He told you?" Marcus experienced the sour taste of dread every time someone mentioned his wife. Part of the reason he hated funerals so much was because it not only reminded him of what he and his sons had lost but how everyone had treated them afterward. Marcus hated reliving all the pitying looks and tut-tuts about how tragic it was for him to be a widower so young and for the boys to be without their mother. While he wanted to appreciate their well-meaning sympathy, all it did was reinforce his own doubts about his ability to be a single father. Over the years, though, he'd found the best way of dealing with questions about Brie's death was to be as matter-of-fact about it as possible.

"She had a brain aneurysm. The twins were only eighteen months old, and yeah, it was quite a shock. One of those freak things that nobody can explain. I think that's why Jordan is so obsessed with medicine. He's naturally curious and started reading at a young age. He had all these questions about his mom and why she died, and I guess none of our explanations made sense to him. So he started looking for his own answers."

"Your sons are very caring and kind and thought... thoughtful." Her voice quivered, and she drew in a deep breath before she continued. "You're very lucky to have them."

"That's what everyone told me after Brie died." He lifted his face to the afternoon sky, the sun starting to make its way closer to the Teton mountain range. "How lucky I was to still have a piece of her."

"No, I meant you're lucky to have them, period. Even if your wife was still here, I would tell you the same thing. Your children are a blessing. You're a very fortunate man, Marcus. Not everyone will get to have that same experience, let alone twice."

His heartbeat stopped before picking up speed. "Back at the church, right before you uh...threw up... you seemed really surprised that I had twins."

She tilted her head and narrowed her eyes at him, as though the answer should have been obvious to him. "Because *we* were supposed to have twins. There were two babies when I miscarried."

Marcus's knees buckled, and his hand propped against the hood of the SUV was the only thing that kept him from going down.

"You...*miscarried*?" His voice was much louder than he'd expected, and one of the caterers carrying a stainless-steel tray from their van looked across the driveway at them.

"Of course I miscarried." Violet blinked several times, her black spiky lashes like tiny daggers to his heart. "Wait. You didn't think I...that I had an abortion?"

Marcus scrubbed a hand over his face in frustration. "I didn't know what to think because I never heard from you. All I knew was that you took the pregnancy test right before I left for boot camp, and then nothing else. At my graduation, I asked my parents if they'd heard from you, and my dad said your mom had gone out of her way to talk to him on Capitol Hill. She wanted to pass along a message that you'd made a *tough choice*—" he used his fingers for air quotes "—but were so glad you did because you were loving college life and could finally focus on your future. At first, I was so pissed, and then the betrayal set in. Not at your decision, but at the fact that you couldn't even bother to tell me yourself."

Her tone grew steely. "I *did* make a tough choice, Marcus. I *chose* to have your babies. But in the end, the decision was out of my hands. Either way, how could you think that I wouldn't have told you what happened?"

Confusion snaked through him, making everything go blurry, and he shook his head to clear his thoughts. All these years, he'd assumed Violet had changed her mind about him and the future they'd discussed. He'd believed she'd moved on with her life, and even though he'd been hurt, he hadn't judged her. They'd only been eighteen, after all. "Then why didn't I know?"

"I knew they'd taken away your phone in boot camp. It wasn't like I could call you and talk about it. The best I could do was send you a letter right after it happened."

A letter? He began pacing as he absorbed her words. He'd gotten only a few letters from his parents, but none from anyone else. Not even his friends back home.

His hands flew up in the air in frustration before

clasping on top of his head as he stretched out the tension exploding in his shoulders. "I never got it. I swear, Violet, if I had known you'd miscarried, I would've gone AWOL to be by your side."

Suddenly, his frustration turned to a sharp anger. How could she have thought so little of him? He was about to ask her exactly that when his youngest brother came slamming out of the kitchen door.

"Hey, Violet, what are you doing here?" Mitchell Junior, better known as MJ to his older siblings, was the baby of the family. "I haven't seen you since that time you and Marcus took me to the Spring Fling Festival, and you guys made me sit by myself on the Ferris wheel so you could make out."

"I don't remember that," Marcus snapped, annoyed at his little brother's interruption of their emotionally charged conversation.

"Unfortunately, I *do* remember that." Violet's frown made it look as though she was cringing. "That was pretty selfish of us. Didn't you end up puking halfway through the ride, and the operator made us hose out the car where you were sitting?"

Now, *that* part Marcus remembered. Violet had taken MJ to the bathroom to clean him up, and Marcus had been left with a traveling carny named Smoke or Blade or some other nefarious moniker who took a cigarette break as Marcus fought an old garden hose to scrub out his kid brother's mess. It was what he'd deserved for not taking better care of his younger brother.

"Where are you going?" Marcus asked his brother.

"Aunt Freckles doesn't like Mom's soy butter, so she gave me some money to go to the store and get some special brand. She said to sneak out of here before Uncle

Rider finds out where I'm going and asks me to get him a can of dip."

Uncle Rider, their dad's twin brother, was a tough-as-nails eighty-year-old cowboy struggling to follow his doctor's advice to quit chewing tobacco. Aunt Freckles, Rider's estranged wife, loved cooking for her extended family almost as much as she loved driving her former husband crazy.

It wasn't until the kid drove away that Marcus remembered the market in town had been closed today for the funeral. The only businesses that had stayed open were the gas station and the liquor store.

That should've been Marcus's first clue that things were only going to get worse from here.

Violet was still reeling from the revelation that Marcus hadn't known she'd miscarried.

She was even more upset that he'd spent all these years assuming she hadn't wanted their children. So much hurt and heartache could have been cleared up if only they'd been able to talk to each other all those years ago. She'd been about to say as much when his younger brother had come outside and interrupted their heated conversation.

Which was probably for the best. Clearly, the day of his father's funeral wasn't the best time or place to argue about the secret they'd hidden from his family or to angrily rehash all their old mistakes. She looked at her watch. Damn. She should've asked MJ for a ride into town. No way was she going to make the last flight out at this rate.

The kitchen door opened, and Jordan poked his head

outside and looked directly at Violet. "Are you getting another migraine?"

"Who has a migraine?" a woman asked. Violet would have recognized that voice anywhere.

Sherilee King.

Marcus's mom had been the quintessential politician's wife. A woman with impeccable manners and no tolerance for anyone who didn't have her family's best interest at heart. Despite her closeness with the rest of the King family all those years ago, Violet had never been able to tell if Sherilee liked her or hated her—probably a little of both—and always wondered if Marcus's mother had somehow influenced his decision to not contact Violet after the miscarriage. Obviously, she didn't have to wonder about the second part any longer. According to Marcus, it was her own mother who'd caused the damage. Still. The protective matriarch of the King family was a force to be reckoned with.

Growing up the daughter of the powerful and vocal Senator Cortez-Hill, Violet was well-accustomed to female role models with strong opinions. But Sherilee King was one of the few women who Violet considered downright intimidating. Or at least she used to feel that way when she'd been a teenager and had binge-watched all *The Godfather* movies with her father. Marcus's mom had the uncanny ability to give off a serious mafia boss–type of vibe while looking like an upscale suburban housewife. Like she could order fancy designer cupcakes for the women's-club luncheon just as easily as she could order a hit on someone for daring to wear sneakers under their gown to one of her black-tie galas.

When the older woman stepped around her grandson and out onto the porch, Violet managed a weak smile and a wave.

"Hi, Mrs. King." Violet didn't dare address her by her first name. "I'm very sorry for your loss. Mr. King was always so kind to me whenever we saw each other, and I'll always have fond memories of him."

Sherilee's face softened into a brief smile, but then her professionally styled hair stayed in place as her head moved right to left, scanning the long driveway and parking area the size of a strip mall. "Your mother isn't here, is she?"

"No, ma'am." Violet shook her head quickly, her own uncombed hair falling into her face. It was no secret that Sherilee King and Eva Cortez-Hill were friendly with each other when the media was present, but when the cameras were gone, they were like a pair of rival gang leaders waiting for the other to throw the first verbal punch. "My parents left after the church service. I was just about to call for an Uber or a cab so I could catch a later flight."

"Don't be ridiculous," Sherilee said, causing Violet to immediately feel ridiculous. The woman put an arm around her grandson, lovingly pulling the concerned boy against the side of her tailored black pencil skirt. "And don't be so formal. One of Marcus's deputies or our stable foreman can give you a ride to the airport. Unless you have your dad's private jet on standby, you might be hard-pressed to find an open seat on a commercial flight. But if you have a migraine, you should come into the house and lie down. Marcus, go get Violet a glass of wine or something stronger to take the edge off."

Jordan lifted his serious face to his grandmother's. "Actually, Gan Gan, alcohol wouldn't be very good for Miss Violet if she has a migraine."

"What about a soda?" Sherilee consulted the young child as though he was wearing a white lab coat and had an advanced medical degree. "The caffeine might help?"

"You know, my headache is long gone," Violet said before Marcus's mom and son could finish their unsolicited medical assessment. "Truly, I'm fine and don't want to impose any more than I already have—"

"Dear," Sherilee said as she put up a palm, her enormous diamond ring flashing in the afternoon sun as she interrupted, "it's been a rough day for all of us, okay? Now, Jordan here is worried about your health, and he's going to keep coming outside to check on you until he's convinced you're better. You've always been a good girl, despite having a hardheaded shark for a mother. You don't want to worry the boys needlessly, do you?"

Violet's mouth was hanging open as she tried to figure out if she'd just been praised or chastised. Likely both.

"Marcus, why are you still standing there?" Sherilee asked. "I said bring Violet inside."

"Mom, please. She's a grown woman." Marcus crossed his arms over his chest. "I'm not going to throw her over my shoulder and carry her through the door if she doesn't want to go."

"Do you see what I have to put up with, Violet dear?" Sherilee rubbed her smooth forehead, which was reputed to have been surgically enhanced by some of the top cosmetic surgeons in the world. "The older my kids get, the more rebellious they are."

That was twice Sherilee King had called her *dear*, making Violet much more tempted to accept the offer of a cold drink and maybe even the piece of chocolate cake without walnuts Jack had mentioned earlier—if any was left. Plus, drowsiness was one of the side effects from the medication she'd taken earlier and was just now starting to kick in. She could use some caffeine, come to think of it…

"You think *I'm* rebellious?" Marcus asked his mom, who flicked her wrist dismissively at him. Clearly, this was an old argument she didn't have the patience to hear again. Yet, her son was determined to continue as though he was itching for a fight with someone and anyone would do. "What about Finn and Dahlia? What about MJ? Did you know he just—"

"Stop," Violet whispered, cutting Marcus off midsentence. "If you start listing all of the transgressions your siblings ever committed, we'll be here all night. Besides, your mom's right. It's been a long day for everyone. I'll come inside for a bit and get something to eat and drink, and then I'll be on my way."

He threw his hands in the air and shrugged. "Fine. But I have every intention of finishing our earlier conversation."

An hour later, Violet had been heartily welcomed into the bosom of the King inner circle as though she hadn't been gone for fourteen years. All three of Marcus's sisters—Tessa, Dahlia and Finn—hugged Violet the moment they saw her.

His brother Duke, still wearing his Navy dress uniform, lifted her off her feet and spun her around. When he set her on her feet, he whispered, "I was waiting for Marcus to get over the shock of seeing you again before coming over and saying hi. Thanks for coming. It means a lot to have you here."

Duke was only a year younger and, as far as she knew, had been the only King who'd known about her pregnancy. It was likely he'd also assumed the worst about her just as Marcus had. So it gave her a boost of confidence to know that he was glad to see her.

Duke introduced her to his handsome and charming husband, Tom, who was a surgeon in the Navy. After Jordan's insistent prompting, Tom asked Violet a few routine questions before assuring his young nephew. "It is my professional opinion that the patient is not suffering any long-lasting effects of her earlier migraine."

"I think someone should go tell Dad," Jack said. "He keeps staring over here at Miss Violet and frowning."

Duke chuckled. "Don't worry about your dad, kiddos. He's probably just grumpy all the brownies are gone already. Why don't you go see if the caterers put out any more?"

Marcus's boys finally went off to the dessert table with their cousin Amelia, and Violet was surprised to realize she was actually way more comfortable than she'd expected to be. Surrounded once again by the family she'd loved so much, she finally began to relax. There was no way he would bring up the subject of her miscarriage or their breakup with so many witnesses.

The main house at the Twin Kings was nearly twelve thousand square feet, and there were still plenty of friends and neighbors in attendance at the reception following the funeral. She ate a little food, said hello to a few of the people she already knew and then found an unoccupied sitting area in the corner where she could escape from the curious glances and scroll through her phone as she tried to hold back several yawns. As long as Violet pretended to ignore his stormy stares from across the hotel lobby–sized living room, she was able to avoid Marcus—for the most part.

Thank God he had his back to her when he took off his suit jacket and rolled up his shirtsleeves, because it was the one time she hadn't been able to look away. His shoulders rolled back in circles as he stretched, and her palms suddenly itched to feel the tense muscles underneath and slowly massage away the day's stress.

Instead, she chugged her watered down iced tea in an effort to make her mouth less dry and her cheeks less warm. She needed to get out of here before she lost complete control.

Eventually, Violet was able to catch the attention of a Secret Service agent who was going off duty, and she snuck out of the Kings' house through the busy kitchen without so much as a goodbye.

It was better this way, she thought, as she rode in the back seat of one of the catering vans that was returning to Jackson Hole. No awkward goodbyes, no promises to keep in touch when everyone knew they wouldn't.

Plus, she wanted to talk to her mother in person and ask her if she'd really implied that Violet had had an abortion. Not that she didn't believe Marcus, but she wanted to find out why on earth her mom had done such a thing.

Oh, who was she kidding? The woman would argue that she'd been trying to protect Violet. And the truth was that her mom had been the one to physically take care of her when she'd slid into a postpartum depression afterward.

But confronting anyone would have to wait another day.

Sherilee King had been right when she'd warned that most of the commercial flights out of town were full. Even most of the hotels were packed with avid skiers who'd booked their vacations in advance, as well as guests who'd come to pay tribute to the former vice president. Violet was lucky to get a room at a nondescript chain motel and hoped she'd be able to rent a car the next day and drive to an airport in a bigger city.

Even though the medication she'd taken earlier had wiped out the worst of the headache, it had left her a little groggy, especially after the events of the day. It also helped her fall asleep the moment her head hit the pillow. When her cell phone rang early the following morning, Violet struggled to open her eyes and tapped the green button before her brain had the chance to wonder who was calling her from a Washington, DC, area code.

"Violet! You haven't left town yet, have you?"

"Mrs. King?" Violet squinted at the bedside clock that read 7:03 a.m. "What's wrong?"

"I need a criminal defense attorney."

Technically, Violet was a public defender, which meant she wasn't for hire. But if Sherilee King had the resources to track her down, then the woman already knew that fact and wasn't about to let a little thing like retainer fees or state bar requirements stop her. Violet sat up in bed and asked, "For yourself?"

"No, not for myself." The woman muttered a curse.

"For MJ. Marcus went and arrested his own brother last night. How soon can you get down to the Ridgecrest County Courthouse?"

"I know what you're trying to do, Mom, and it won't work," Marcus said as he followed his mother up the wide back-porch steps of the main house on the family's ranch later that morning. "Hiring Violet to represent MJ is *not* going to make me drop the charges."

"I'm trying to save my youngest son from being framed for a crime he didn't commit," Sherilee snapped back at him before stomping into the kitchen. "You know what would happen to a young, impressionable kid like MJ in prison."

"MJ is *not* going to prison," Marcus practically growled in frustration. "He was charged with underage drinking and resisting arrest. It's a misdemeanor."

His mom's professionally shaped eyebrows lifted. "If it's no big deal, then why are you still holding him in a jail cell?"

"I didn't say it wasn't a big deal. MJ went out drinking with Deputy Broman's eighteen-year-old daughter last night. When her dad busted them, MJ punched the man—a sworn peace officer on duty."

"So says Deputy Broman." His mother pointed a manicured finger at Marcus's chest. "You know that guy has it in for our family. How do you know he isn't making this up to make you look bad before next year's election?"

"Besides the fact that Broman has a black eye and MJ had a blood alcohol level of twice the legal limit? My deputies wear body cameras, and I saw the video footage."

"Damn it!" His mom picked up one of Aunt Freckles's famous homemade biscuits, slathered it with honey butter and then loaded it down with a couple of cold pieces of leftover bacon before shoving half of it in her mouth. So much for her claimed vegan lifestyle. Sherilee King only ate like this when she was under extreme stress. Her lipstick was still covered in crumbs when she asked, "Okay, so how about we compromise. You give MJ a warning or a ticket or something and release him to my custody?"

"As if that'll teach the kid a lesson." Marcus snorted. "Listen, Mom, I know you don't want to hear this, but MJ has been flying under the radar and getting away with stuff us older kids never would have gotten past you and Dad. Do you have any idea how blatantly biased it would be for the county sheriff to turn a blind eye to illegal behavior just because it's his kid brother doing it? If we don't make him face the music now, his next arrest could possibly be a felony. Is that what you want?"

"What I *want* is for my kids to look out for each other. To protect each other."

Marcus refused to cave. "Well, this is my way of looking out for him. Consider it an intervention."

Marcus suddenly realized that none of his adult siblings were stepping foot in the kitchen right now. What did they know that he didn't?

"And that's why I hired Violet to represent him." His mom put her hands on her hips, and he saw a quick flash of a knowing smirk, a determined glint in her eye. "Because maybe you need an intervention of your own."

A cold shiver raced down the back of Marcus's neck. "What's that supposed to mean?"

"You were in the briefing room with the Secret Service agents just a few minutes ago." His mother jerked her head toward the custom-built bunkhouse across the main road. The one that housed their father's assigned security detail whenever he'd traveled from Washington to visit the family home. "This has the potential to become a really big deal, and you can't be on duty all the time. You can't designate yourself the family protector when there is too much other stuff going on. If it wasn't tough enough dealing with your father's death and funeral, now we've got the media scandal of the year with Tessa fainting in that agent's arms yesterday. It's only a matter of time before all those reporters lined up outside the gate find out about MJ, too." Her tone softened. "Look, Marcus, I get it that you want to teach him a lesson, and I'm sure you're right. But now's really not the best time to do it."

Marcus rolled his eyes. "Then maybe MJ should have picked a more convenient time to polish off a liter of vodka before trying to make it to second base with Deputy Broman's daughter."

"Allegedly," someone said in the doorway behind Marcus. He turned to find Violet following his aunt Freckles into the kitchen, and his adrenaline spiked at the sight of his ex-girlfriend.

Her jet-black hair was in a high ponytail on top of her head, and her beautiful face didn't have a trace of makeup, causing her to appear just as young and carefree as she had been all those years ago when they'd naively thought they'd be together forever. However, her professional tone and the adversarial squaring of her shoulders reminded him that she was all grown up now and clearly ready to go to battle against him.

"Excuse me?" he asked, realizing too late that he should have kept his mouth shut.

"My client *allegedly* drank vodka with Deputy Broman's daughter. Although, he might be willing to stipulate to the circumstances surrounding the second-base allegation, since it will prove that the arresting officer had questionable motives for making the arrest in the first place."

So that's how she wanted to play this. Marcus drew in a deep breath, trying to ignore the unexpected sting of betrayal. Unfortunately, he opened his mouth once again before his emotions were completely under control. "I'm not shocked that an attorney would twist the facts to their advantage. What's shocking is that my mom got you to agree to this."

"You can call it twisting the facts." Violet lifted one shoulder in a shrug, and he noticed she was wearing the same clothes she'd had on yesterday. "I call it a fair trial, something everyone is entitled to under the United States Constitution. There's this little part in there called the Sixth Amendment, which guarantees all defendants a right to an attorney. Even when those defendants are little brothers who piss you off."

Marcus felt his nostrils flare as he expelled a frustrated breath. "I never said MJ doesn't have a right to a fair trial. Or to a lawyer. I just don't see why it has to be *you*."

"Because if *you* were arrested, Marcus, you would want the best representing you."

"The best?" Marcus knew she'd always been wickedly smart, but when had she become so presumptuous? Or so full of herself? The Violet he'd once known had been sweet and humble and slightly shy. In fact, she'd been scared to death to tell their parents after they'd sat staring at that positive pregnancy-test stick for what had seemed like days. However, now she was anything but shy—proudly facing off against him in the heart of the King domain, looking like she was ready to start her cross-examination. And apparently he'd somehow managed to land himself in her witness stand.

She gently clasped her hands in front of her, a tactic he knew was meant to seem disarming, and asked, "You mean to tell me that when you were keeping tabs on me all these years, you never came across my acquittal record at trial?"

"I wasn't keeping tabs," Marcus defended himself. He knew he'd slipped yesterday when he'd made a reference to her living in Dallas and introduced her to the boys as *Miss* Cortez-Hill. But it wasn't like he'd actively searched for information about her. "It just so happens that I follow a lot of baseball commentators online, including your dad. It's not my fault that he posts about you a lot on his social-media page."

"Oh, I heard about people doing that online-stalking thing." Aunt Freckles's eyes widened knowingly, which caused her unusually long false lashes to flicker against the brightness of her heavy green eye shadow. "They get these fake accounts so they can secretly follow people and snoop around in their business. I think the kids call it catfishing."

"I think you mean creeping." Marcus cringed as he shook his head. "But I wasn't doing that. Or catfishing, or anything else so desperate."

"No one said you were, darlin'." His aunt tutted through her bright magenta lipstick, then adjusted the cropped lime-green sweater that didn't quite meet the waistband of her jungle-print yoga pants. The woman had to be pushing eighty, yet had a tendency to dress in tight, revealing clothes that would make most eigh-teen-year-olds blush. "I was just pointing out to Violet that us single gals always have to be on the lookout for men with bad intentions."

"Oh, no, Aunt Freckles!" Violet turned to his aunt before Marcus could further defend himself or his in-tentions. "I didn't realize you were single now. I thought for sure you and Uncle Rider were going to get back together."

"Why do you care?" Marcus asked, not bothering to hide the annoyance lacing his voice. Of all the things he and Violet should be discussing, this was a topic that could wait a bit longer. "Are you a divorce attorney now, too? Maybe my family can get some sort of group rate."

"Nobody has time for your snide comments right now, Marcus." His mother reached for another biscuit and the butter knife. "Violet needs to go to her room and change so we can get to the courthouse in time for the bail hearing this afternoon. We need to make a strong defensive case right out of the gate so I can get my baby home where he belongs."

"It's more of a formality than a hearing," he cor-rected, trying to ignore the muscle ticking beside his eye. In fact, once Judge Calhoun sets the bail amount, Marcus had planned to post the bond himself. That way, MJ would be released to Marcus's custody, and then he could drive the boy home and have a heart-to-heart talk with him. "Besides, I thought you wanted to keep the arrest out of the media. Having Violet there would only draw more attention to... Wait. Did you just say she was going to *her room* to change?"

"Well, I certainly can't change here in the kitchen," Violet replied, placing her hand over the wide V of her exposed neckline. Marcus's eyes drew to the soft, tanned skin there before immediately pushing away the sudden inappropriate thought of her taking off that rumpled black dress.

"I meant a room *here*." Marcus's muscles flexed instinctively. "At *this* house?"

"You know there isn't a suitable hotel in Teton Ridge," his mother said, her slight smirk flickering again. "Naturally, Violet is going to be staying with us at the Twin Kings."

Freckles clapped her hands together before reaching for an apron. "It'll be just like old times."

"Yeah, except you're all forgetting that things didn't end so well back then." Marcus heard his mother's angry gasp, as well as a tsk from Freckles. Yet his boots echoed his own annoyance with each angry step across the polished wood floors as he stomped to the door, determined to get as far away from this potential disaster as he could. "And that was back when we were at least on the same team."

When he yanked down on the handle to make his escape, his sister, brother and uncle—who'd apparently been pressed against the other side of the door listening—tumbled into the kitchen together.

Marcus muttered a curse, then strode to his SUV without so much as a goodbye.

It looked like he and the twins would temporarily be moving into their old cabin on the ranch. Because there was no way he was staying under the same roof as his ex-girlfriend.

His life was complicated enough as it was.

CHAPTER FOUR

VIOLET SPENT THE morning filing paperwork with the Wyoming Bar Association to allow for pro hac vice status so she could temporarily practice law in the state. Since she was licensed in Texas, Roper's trust and estates attorney in Cheyenne had agreed to act as her local cocounsel, which really just meant that he was vouching for Violet while not coming to Teton Ridge himself.

Then she texted one of her coworkers who lived in the same condo complex back home, asking her to ship some of Violet's professional attire to the Twin Kings Ranch so that she wouldn't have to continue borrowing Sherilee King's couture designer suits. Although wearing Chanel to the county courthouse might not cause as much scandal as the cheetah-print sequined tube top Freckles had lovingly loaned her this morning.

In between all the busy work, Violet had also spent a significant amount of time wondering why she was even going through all this trouble when it was so clear that Marcus didn't want her there. Not that she cared what Marcus wanted. She wasn't doing this for him.

And yet, the more he opposed her presence, the more Violet was determined to stay. So what did that say about her? That she was spoiling for a fight, as well?

Maybe. Maybe, after all these years without answers, she was.

Clearly, though, she wasn't the only one with a chip on her shoulder. There was no way Marcus would've responded with such hostility if his mother had hired any other defense attorney. So then, why was he so angry that it was Violet who'd be doing their family this favor?

Probably because he was harboring some other sort of resentment toward her. The old Violet would have wanted to talk to him, to get to the root of the matter and try to resolve whatever issues were coming between them. But the new Violet had spent the last fourteen years fighting to make herself heard, and she was no longer in the mood to listen. At least not to Marcus, who'd never bothered to contact her after he got out of boot camp to hear what she had to say.

So now that she was standing behind the defense table inside one of the few courtrooms at the Ridgecrest County Courthouse, Violet was even more annoyed to see her ex-boyfriend on the opposite side of the aisle.

"Your Honor," Violet faced the older, gray-haired judge sitting on the bench, "my client is a young man with a promising future and long-standing ties to the community. In fact, he lives in the same house as the sheriff seated behind the prosecutor. Their property is currently under the protection and surveillance of several federal agents, who have been assigned to trail the defendant wherever he goes. Mitchell King Jr. is neither a flight risk nor a danger to the community at large and should be granted bail while he is pending trial."

"Miss Cortez-Hill," the judge said patiently, "the court is well aware of who the defendant is related to and where he lives. In fact, one judge already had to recuse herself from this case because she was the team mom for the defendant's Little League team ten years ago. So unless the parties are going to file a motion for a change of venue, I'm going to allow bail, as is standard for similar charges. But I'm also going to add a gag order restricting all parties from speaking about the case to the media or anyone else outside of this courtroom. I'm not going to have this esteemed institution turn into a full-blown circus just because of the defendant's famous family name. If there's nothing else pending, court is recessed for the day."

Judge Calhoun left the bench, his high-top sneakers under his robe suggesting that he was on his way to the rec center to play pickup basketball. At least, that's what she'd gathered from her earlier meeting with the prosecutor who'd purposely let it slip that he played in the same senior league with the judge and they often traveled to tournaments together.

This was a small town, and she was the outsider.

MJ, who had been allowed to change into the clean clothes his mother had brought him, sagged back into his wooden seat as he rubbed the dark shadows under his eyes. "Does this mean I get to go home?"

"Yes." Violet nodded at him and then leaned closer as she lowered her voice. "But as long as I'm your attorney, you are going to be *staying* at home and staying out of trouble. No more drinking, and no more dates with that deputy's daughter. In fact, consider yourself on quasi–house arrest."

MJ jutted his chin across the courtroom at Marcus. "Is that what big brother told you to tell me?"

"No. That's what *I'm* telling you. If I'm going to represent you and put my professional reputation on the line, then you're going to act like the model citizen that I know your father raised you to be."

At the mention of the late Roper King, his tall eighteen-year-old son slouched sheepishly in his chair. But then something sparkled behind his tired eyes. "Is it true that Marcus didn't want our mom to hire you?"

Violet could deny it, but it was important to establish honesty in an attorney–client relationship. If she wanted MJ to be honest with her, then she needed to be truthful with him. Besides, she was staying at the family ranch, and he was a smart kid. He'd figure it out for himself soon enough. "That's correct."

"Fine. I'll do whatever you say as long as it pisses him off."

"Whatever is going on between you and your brother is between the two of you." Violet stacked a file onto her notepad, making a mental note to have her friend send her briefcase, as well. "I'm not going to tell you that you need to get along. But I will strongly warn you that it is not in your best interest to purposely antagonize the man who eats lunch with the district attorney at Biscuit Betty's every Wednesday."

"You've been in town less than twenty-four hours, and you already know my schedule?" Marcus asked as he casually planted a hip on the defense table.

Refusing to let him tower over her from his perch, she stood and collected the leather tote bag she'd borrowed this morning from Tessa. But standing only brought their faces closer together. She gulped before squaring her shoulders. "I make it my business to know everything I can about my opponents."

"Really, Violet? Opponents? You make it sound like

we're enemies when, at the end of the day, we both want what's best for MJ."

Now MJ rose to his feet. The teen was taller than Marcus by a couple of inches, but the gangliness of youth was still present in his thinner frame. "What's best for me is that you stop treating me like a little kid."

"Yeah, well, this is what happens to grown-ups when they break the law, MJ." Marcus stayed comfortably seated, suggesting to his younger brother that he wasn't the least bit threatened by his height or his irritation. "They go to grown-up court and face grown-up consequences. Welcome to adulthood."

Out of the corner of her eye, Violet saw MJ's fist clenching, and she immediately put a calming hand on his tense arm. "MJ, will you please go check on your mother? Someone needs to intercept her before she tries to follow Judge Calhoun out to his car. Let me handle your brother."

Sherilee King had never met someone who didn't soon owe her a favor, and small towns like this were already ripe for issues of alleged impropriety since everyone knew everyone. The last thing she wanted was a hint of any additional scandal. If Violet was going to win a case, she was going to do so on the merits of the case and her arguments—not on any accusations that outside influences swayed the judge.

MJ gave a tense nod before going after his mother, leaving Violet alone with Marcus.

"And how exactly do you plan on *handling* me, counselor?" He crossed his arms across his chest, the bulge of his biceps pushing against the fabric of his tan county-issued shirt. Why did he have to look so damn good in his uniform?

"It's a figure of speech, Sheriff. Don't make it awkward." She slung the leather straps of her borrowed tote over her shoulder and started walking toward the exit.

She wasn't surprised to find Marcus on her heels, holding one of the narrow courtroom doors open for her, as he replied, "Then don't make this into some sort of battle where one of us has to lose."

"This battle between you and MJ was obviously brewing well before I got here." She held her breath as she squeezed past him, knowing she'd be a goner if any part of her body so much as grazed against his. "So unless you're following me to offer a sweet deal on behalf of the prosecutor, someone is going to eventually lose. I assure you that it won't be me."

"You may have one of the highest acquittal rates over in Dallas, but even the best criminal defense attorneys can't win them all." He must've seen the shock on her face when he caught up to her because he added, "You're not the only one who knows how to research your so-called opponent."

The fluttering sensation in her stomach was probably due to her missing lunch and not the way his eyes drank her in as he admitted that he'd also spent some time this morning researching her. Or at least her court record.

Luckily, the cool mountain air snapped her back to reality as she stepped outside the courthouse. "At least you can admit that we're on opposing sides. Just remember that it's your brother at the center of this fight, Marcus. Not me. When all of this is over, I'll be back in Dallas with another acquittal under my belt, and you'll still be here in Wyoming dealing with the fallout of your already strained family relationships."

Marcus made an unconvincing harrumph sound.

"Unlike some people I know, I've never been afraid of challenging my family members. Tell me, Violet, does your mother know you're staying in Teton Ridge for the foreseeable future?"

"Look, I know that my mom wasn't always welcoming to you when we were younger."

"She led me to believe you had an abortion, Violet. That's how badly she wanted to get me out of your life."

"Trust me, I have that on my list of things to discuss with her. I will do that in my own time and in my own way." She narrowed her eyes. "Is this the road you want to go down, Marcus? Because as soon as you challenge someone, they're bound to challenge you back. Then you'll have to explain why it was so easy for you to believe her and walk away."

"You think I—"

"Violet!" One of the twins yelled from the sidewalk at the bottom of the concrete stairs. It was Jack, because he shook free of Dahlia's hand and accidentally stepped on Sherilee's foot as he rushed by his grandmother to sprint up the steps. Jordan was the rule follower and stayed safely at his aunt's side, licking a vanilla ice cream cone while sending Violet a happy wave.

Jack had what looked to be melted chocolate ice cream around his mouth, and Violet tried not to wince as he hurtled into her with a tight hug. Should she hug him back? It wasn't that she was opposed to physical displays of affection or to chocolate stains. But this was a borrowed suit, and she hadn't seen a dry cleaner on Stampede Boulevard.

When Jack looked up at her, he smiled his gap-toothed grin. "I thought you left yesterday without saying goodbye to us."

At that, she did hug him back, rather awkwardly with a pat on his head. She was equally touched by his words, yet slightly confused. The poor child had been growing up without a mother, and he'd recently lost his grandfather. Of course he would have some separation-anxiety issues, although Violet would never have anticipated he'd react so strongly to a random woman he'd just met yesterday. Still, he deserved to be comforted.

"I'm so sorry, sweetie. I was in a hurry to catch my ride and shouldn't have been so thoughtless. Will you forgive me?"

"Okay," the boy said simply. "Can I sit next to you at dinner tonight?"

Violet glanced at her watch. To her surprise, it was nearly four in the afternoon.

"Here you go, Jack." Marcus pulled a clean napkin out of his back pocket and casually handed it to the boy. Clearly, he kept a supply of them on hand for this exact purpose. "I don't think we're going to have dinner at the main house tonight."

"But we always have a fancy sit-down dinner when Gan Gan is in town."

Marcus's sigh reverberated in his throat. "I know. But with Aunt Tessa and Aunt Freckles and now Miss Cortez-Hill staying there, it's kind of a lot of people."

As though hearing her grandson invoke her name, Sherilee limped up the few stairs separating them, pretending she didn't have a dusty sneaker print covering the expensive Italian leather toe of her high heel. "Don't be ridiculous, Marcus. Of course you and the boys will still be having dinner with—" she paused just long enough to give Violet a pointed look that brooked no argument "—*all of us* at the main house."

"Yes!" Jack pumped a fist in the air before yelling back to his twin. "Hey, Jordan, Violet is gonna sit by us at dinner."

At least someone was happy about it, she thought, trying not to let the excited boys see an ounce of apprehension on her face. Now she would have to endure another round of dysfunctional family dynamics with the Kings.

"You apologized to my son earlier today," Marcus said to Violet later that evening as they were having predinner cocktails in the great room of the main house. He took another drink from his bottle of craft ale, his second of the night.

Violet's hair was out of that ridiculous tight bun and hung softly down her back. She shoved a loose strand behind her ear, and despite the taste of beer still fresh on his tongue, his mouth went dry. All too swiftly, he recalled the silky feel of her hair in his hands as he... *Ahem. She's speaking, idiot.* "Of course I did. It was rude of me to leave last night without saying goodbye."

"It's weird, though. Usually he has a short attention span when it comes to new people." In fact, neither of his sons had mentioned Violet yesterday after she'd left, and Marcus had assumed they'd easily forgotten about her until his sister Dahlia had dropped them off at the courthouse after school. But saying as much would be admitting that he didn't have a good read on his own children. Because clearly, they did remember Violet, especially Jordan, who'd spent the last fifteen minutes quizzing her on the side effects of her migraine medication. Instead Marcus clarified what he meant.

"Adults normally don't go to great lengths to apologize for something kids are likely to forget anyway."

"No? Well, they should."

He'd noticed that she was somewhat stiff when Jack had hugged her earlier on the courthouse steps. Even now she looked as though she would rather be wearing anything other than the painted macaroni necklace that Jordan had made at school today. His son had ceremoniously given it to her just before joining his brother in the dining room to make sure the place cards their cousin had drawn were still in the right spots. "Do you spend much time around children?"

"I'm an only child, remember?" Violet looked away quickly, refusing to meet his eyes. "No nieces or nephews or big family gatherings like this."

"Yeah, but surely you have friends with kids?"

Her knuckles were white as she gripped the stem of her wineglass. "Um, I guess."

"You don't know if your friends have kids?" he asked playfully, trying to ease this growing tension between them. "Or you don't have friends?"

Her eyelids lowered slightly, and her lips pursed together, as though she was about to deliver a scathing remark. Warmth flooded Marcus's bloodstream, and he wished he could take a picture of her in that exact second because she was absolutely gorgeous when she was in lecture mode.

"Of course I have friends." She didn't bother to hide the annoyance in her tone. But at least she was no longer trying to ignore him. "But the ones I spend the most time with don't usually bring their children with them to work."

"You mean your coworkers?" He wasn't sure if he

wanted to antagonize her or pity her right that second. "Don't you ever hang out with people outside the job?"

"I don't do much hanging out at all, Marcus. Or is this your way of asking me about my dating life?"

"Well, I wasn't asking about it specifically, but if you want to talk about it, we can." Although, he honestly didn't want to hear about any other guys who might be after her. He was sure there were plenty.

Before she could reply, though, his sons ran into the room with Aunt Freckles on their heels.

His aunt cupped her hand around her mouth and hollered, "Dinner's ready, gang!"

"Really, Freckles?" His mother chastised her former sister-in-law. "I've seen farmers call their pigs to the slop troughs with a more civilized tone."

"If you're more comfortable with me treating you like a pig, Sherilee, I'm happy to oblige." Freckles winked a bright blue eye-shadowed lid at Finn, who hooted with laughter at their mother's sputtering.

Finn and Freckles seemed to share the same desire to shock Sherilee King whenever the chance arose. And Marcus adored his aunt and his sister for it. Sure, he loved his mother, but the King matriarch needed to come off her high horse every now and then. As long as the two women didn't team up against him, he was fine.

"Now, now, ladies." Duke took their aunt's arm and twirled her toward the dining room, leaving Finn to walk with their frowning mother. "I've been waiting nearly five years for your famous chicken-fried steak, Freckles. I'm sure the only pig at the table will be me as I load up my plate."

Marcus's brother was the consummate peacekeeper of the family. He was the perfect son who could never fail at anything. Finn was always attempting to dethrone poor Duke from his good-natured pedestal with her smart-alecky comments and constant teasing, but he usually shrugged her off like a pesky fly.

"Hurry to your chair, before Dad gets there." Jack and Jordan each took one of Violet's hands in their own and tugged her toward the dining room. "He'll put all the mashed potatoes on his plate if you don't get some before him."

Violet threw a look over her shoulder at Marcus, a smirk tugging one corner of her lip upward. "Oh, he still does that?"

It wasn't until they were all seated at the table that he was able to defend himself. "What do you mean 'he still does that'?"

Instead of speaking directly to him, though, she told his sons, "One summer when we used to be in the Junior Diplomats Club, we were at a fancy state dinner for this group of foreign dignitaries and their children. The servers brought out our plates while I was still on the dance floor. When I got back to my seat, half of my potatoes au gratin were missing. Your dad denied it was him, but he still had cheese on his fork as he tried to quickly swallow down the evidence."

"What kind of junior diplomat steals food off someone else's plate at a state dinner?" Finn tsked, pretending to be scandalized.

"I was a sophomore in high school and going through a growth spurt. Besides, as I recall, Violet was so busy dancing with the French ambassador's son and swooning with the rest of the girls over his accent that I didn't think she'd notice."

Violet gasped. "You were jealous of Jean-Henri?"

At this point, everyone at the table was watching them, and Marcus hated being the center of attention. His incredulous sniff caused his chest to jut out in defiance. "No, I wasn't jealous of that guy. He might've had all the girls convinced he was a decent dancer, but he couldn't dribble a soccer ball to save his life. The European delegates lost the final match that year, and everyone probably forgot all about him after he flew back to Paris."

"You mean Jean-Henri Laurent?" Duke refilled Violet's wineglass. "He's a professional soccer player now. His team won the international finals last spring. So you must be the only one who forgot about him, big brother."

Violet laughed at that.

Dang. Now Marcus couldn't decide if she was more beautiful when she was angry or when she was laughing. Probably when she was angry because he could still remember her laughter when they were younger. But this level of heat was a new side to her he hadn't quite grown accustomed to.

Not that he was accustomed to seeing her at all lately. Luckily, he was able to sit across the table from her and silently study her as everyone else around them talked and argued and put on quite the display of squabbling and teasing.

He forgot how overwhelming his family could be to outsiders, although Violet wasn't technically an outsider. They'd spent many of their adolescent summers together, so she certainly had no trouble interjecting into the multiple conversations going on around the noisy table.

"So how long is everyone staying in town?" Violet asked.

"Well, I was hoping to return to my ship yesterday afternoon, but the former second lady over there—" Duke used his fork to gesture toward their mother at the head of the table "—made a call to one of her buddies at the Pentagon, and now my commanding officer insisted I take another week of leave."

Tessa, whose panic attack yesterday had resulted in quite a media scandal involving the handsome and heroic Special Agent Wyatt, buttered a freshly baked roll. "I was also supposed to be back in Washington today, but our strong-willed mother insisted that I stay on the ranch and keep a low profile. Hopefully, the press finds something new to interest them soon, and I can leave in a couple of days."

"I'm not going anywhere," Finn said around a mouthful of fresh green beans. "I live on the Twin Kings, and I oversee the cattle operation. Which surprisingly lowers our mother's ability to control my life."

"How? I live on the ranch, too," Marcus pointed out. "Yet that doesn't stop Mom from her attempts to interfere in *my* job."

"I'm not interfering *or* controlling." His self-proclaimed vegan mother scraped her fork along her gravy-smeared plate with a bit too much force. "I'm simply orchestrating better options for my children."

"What about you, Aunt Freckles?" Violet smoothly shifted the subject before all the King siblings could voice their objections to their mother's careful rephrasing of history. "I heard you have a successful restaurant in Sugar Falls now. When do you have to go back to Idaho?"

"Oh, I'm here for as long as my kiddos need me," Freckles explained as she passed a second gravy boat containing the untouched vegan version to Uncle Rider. He sniffed it then grimaced before passing it off to Sherilee.

Marcus's uncle twisted an end of his bushy gray mustache and winked at his estranged wife. "And here I thought you were staying because you couldn't get enough of me and my skills in the bed—"

"Whoa, you two!" Finn interrupted. "There are young children present."

Marcus tossed his white linen napkin onto his plate in surrender. "That's probably my cue to get the boys home."

A defiant crease appeared between Jack's tired eyes. "But we want to hear more about the famous soccer player Violet got to dance with."

"He wasn't famous when Violet danced with him," Marcus said before realizing how petulant he sounded. "It was way back when we were still in high school."

"Did you and my dad go to school together?" Jordan asked Violet.

"No, I went to a boarding school near Washington, DC, and your dad went to Teton Ridge High."

"So then, how did you used to hang out all the time if you lived in different places?" Marcus could see the wheels spinning in Jordan's mind.

"We actually only saw each other once or twice a year at these boring events for children of politicians. Your dad and I were mostly pen pals."

"What's a pen pal?" Jack asked before using his sleeve to wipe the fruit punch off his upper lip.

"It's someone who lives far away, but you keep in touch by exchanging correspondence with them,"

Violet said, likely not realizing that she was speaking to a six-year-old with a limited vocabulary.

"What's *correspondence*?" Jack clearly wasn't letting up.

Jordan stage-whispered to his twin, "That means Dad slid into her DMs."

Several gasps came from the adults at the table while Finn snorted rather loudly. MJ finally looked up from his phone with a huge grin across his face. Apparently, the boys' vocabulary wasn't as limited as it should be.

Marcus jerked his head sideways at his little brother. "I'm assuming you're the one who taught my impressionable children that expression?"

MJ's grin immediately turned into a snarl. "So now you're blaming me for that, too?"

Violet sat up straighter, as though she was going to defend her client from Marcus's latest allegations. But before she could launch her opening defense, Finn made a chopping motion with her palm, like a referee trying to break up a fight.

"It was me, Marcus," Finn said with an unapologetic grin. "The boys overheard me and Freckles talking about… Well, suffice it to say that we didn't know they were listening."

"What's a dang *DM*?" Uncle Rider asked, causing another snort from Finn.

"It means *direct message*, you old coot." Freckles rolled her eyes. "When you're interested in talking to someone on social media, but you don't want everyone seeing what you write, you slide into that person's direct messages. That way you can have a private conversation."

"Well, nobody better be sliding into *your* DMs,"

Rider told Freckles, not picking up on the fact that the twins still only understood the literal definition instead of the more commonly known flirtatious implication. "You're still a married woman. Technically."

"Are *you* married, Violet?" Jordan asked.

She took a rather long gulp of her wine, and Marcus realized he was holding his own breath waiting for her to answer. Finally, she shook her head. "No, I'm not married."

"Do you have kids?" Jack asked next and Marcus's heart twisted.

"Boys, it's not polite to ask so many personal questions," he quietly cautioned his sons. Especially when Marcus already knew the painful answer.

"It's okay." Violet's half-hearted smile didn't quite reach her sad eyes. "I appreciate their curiosity. No, I do not currently have any children."

They still hadn't really talked about the babies they'd lost, and Marcus swallowed the guilt rising in his throat.

"Do you ever slide into anyone's DMs?" Jordan asked, causing Marcus to nearly choke.

"I go out on dates occasionally. But I'm usually too busy with work and don't have much time for social media."

Ah ha! It only took forty-five minutes of uncomfortable family bantering and an inquisition by a couple of six-year-olds to get the answer she'd dodged earlier.

"Dad says he's too busy to go out on dates, too," Jack replied. "He used to be married to our mom, but now he's called a widow. Like the black poisonous spider."

"Widower," Jordan corrected.

"Yeah," Jack nodded. "He's like a black widower, but

not poisonous. So that means that you can slide into his DMs again if you wanted to."

This time, Finn wasn't the only one at the table who snorted. Even diplomatic Duke didn't bother to hide his laughter. Marcus thought he was immune to being embarrassed by his family, but a flame of heat seared the skin of his neck and shot to his face.

Violet toyed with her macaroni necklace, causing the paint to smear on her fingers and her white blouse. She didn't seem to notice, though, because her eyes were too busy darting from the faces of his eager sons back to his.

Great. She was probably thinking this was some sort of setup. That he was a lonely, single father using his kids to pick up women because he couldn't get a date on his own. In fact, he'd had plenty of offers from plenty of women, but with two young sons at home, the timing just never felt right. He wanted to set the record straight; however, it had been a long day, and he was on the verge of saying something that Violet could later hold against him.

"Okay, nobody is sliding into anyone's DMs. Boys, thank your aunt Freckles for a lovely dinner. You have school tomorrow, and we still have to go over your math worksheet before bedtime."

Or before his family came up with more random comments that would make Marcus seem additionally ridiculous and pathetic. Violet already thought badly enough of him as it was.

Unfortunately, he couldn't quite subdue that unexplainable need to prove himself to her. As his sons were making their way around the table distracting his family with goodbye hugs, Marcus stopped behind Violet's chair on the way out and lowered his head until his mouth was level with her ear.

He heard her sharp intake of breath, then whispered, "Just so you know, I'm not some sorry sack who can't get a date. I'm just careful with who I bring home to meet my over-the-top family."

Her head tilted slightly, but she didn't turn to look at him. Probably a good call considering her lips weren't all that far from his as she replied somewhat breathlessly, "It's none of my business, either way."

"Well, I'm making it your business. You said you like to have all the facts, and those are the facts." He couldn't stop the suggestive tone creeping into his voice as he added a parting shot. "Use that information however you see fit, counselor."

CHAPTER FIVE

"THERE'S JUST NOT a lot of room at Gan Gan's house right now," Marcus told his sons Tuesday morning when they asked why they had to remain with him at the cabin for the whole week. In reality, even with Tessa and Aunt Freckles temporarily staying there, there was plenty of room. The truth was Marcus didn't want to keep running into Violet.

Besides, the cabin wasn't really a cabin at all. It was a house of nearly three thousand square feet in a secluded area less than a mile from the main driveway on the Twin Kings Ranch. And technically, it was their home. Marcus and Brie had built it right before their wedding, and everything inside—from the custom-designed drawer pulls on the kitchen cabinets to the floral upholstered rocker in the den—had been picked out by his wife.

Twice now, he'd been embarking on what he'd thought was a new journey with a woman he loved, eager to share his life with someone. And twice those relationships had ended in disaster. Different journeys and different disasters, obviously. Yet both times he'd had to move forward on his own, which was always easier if he didn't look back at what he'd lost.

He'd thought about redecorating a few times, to make it seem like less of a shrine to his late wife; however, he'd never gotten around to making any changes. Partly because Marcus had needed so much help with the pair of toddlers—and managing his grief—after Brie had passed away.

As a single dad, he'd become increasingly dependent on his family for backup. His sister Dahlia, who lived in town and had a five-year-old daughter, usually picked up the twins after school and brought them to his office. Uncle Rider loved entertaining the boys with riding lessons and old rodeo stories, and Finn was always happy to keep an eye on her nephews whenever Marcus had to work late.

Although, his youngest sister's inappropriate sense of humor was proving to be more of a bad influence now that the kids were repeating the outlandish things she said. And then there was Marcus's mother, who was a little *too* supportive when she was in town for occasional visits. Now that his father was gone, it was time to accept the fact that Sherilee King had returned to Wyoming full-time. She doted on her grandkids even as she drove her own children crazy with her unsolicited opinions and high-handed interference in every aspect of their lives.

"But everyone at Gan Gan's will miss us," Jack pointed out.

"I'm sure they'll get used to it." Marcus looked at the twins' pouting faces in his rearview mirror. "We have a perfectly good house that nobody is using, and you guys are getting old enough to ride your bicycles to the main house to visit whenever you feel like it."

"I don't like my plain ol' bike anymore." Jack crossed

his arms under the shoulder strap of his seat belt. "It doesn't go as fast as a 50cc-engine motocross dirt bike would."

"Motorcycles are dangerous," Jordan reminded his brother for the hundredth time.

"Only if you crash them."

"Jack, you crash everything." His twin wasn't wrong. Jack was not only impulsive, he was also the most accident-prone child in the history of Teton Ridge Elementary School. And he was still in the first grade. The school nurse had Marcus on speed dial. They'd taken so many trips to the nearby hospital for sprains, stitches and casts, the staff informally referred to the pediatric exam room as the Jack King Suite.

Sure, Jordan first took an interest in medical conditions after learning about the cause of his mother's untimely death. But then Jack's frequent visits to urgent-care offices and emergency rooms really took that fascination to a whole new level.

"Aunt Finn said she'd teach us how to drive a Polaris," Jack said, referring to the smaller all-terrain vehicles the ranch hands sometimes used for hauling supplies. "Could we get one for me and Jordan to drive to the main house? I'll wear a helmet."

"I'm not riding with you on an ATV." Jordan shook his head. "Even if Dad says yes, I won't go. Not even with a helmet."

"Fine, then." Jack stuck out his tongue at his brother before plopping his elbow on his windowsill, stubbornly cupping his chin in his hand. "I'll just take my slow, boring bike to the main house to see Violet then."

"Why do you want to visit Violet so badly?" Marcus

asked as he pulled his SUV into the drop-off line at the elementary school.

"Because she doesn't ever get to be around kids," Jack said, as though that explained everything.

Marcus reached for the stainless-steel travel mug in his center cupholder. He was going to need a lot more coffee this morning to decipher the logic of an almost-seven-year-old. "So you think you two are doing her a favor by rewarding her with your presence?"

"Gan Gan says we're a delight," Jordan replied, not picking up on the sarcasm. "And Aunt Freckles says being around us keeps her on her toes. Don't you think Violet wants to be on her toes?"

Suddenly, Marcus flashed back to a memory of the summer before his senior year in high school. He and Violet and two thousand other so-called junior global ambassadors had been invited to attend the International Summit at Sea. The event sounded prestigious but really was just a bunch of teenagers attending lectures and seminars all day on a cruise ship anchored in international waters with no cell-phone service. He and Violet had been so bored with the evening's organized activities that they'd snuck off in search of an adventure and stumbled upon the ship's beauty salon, which had been closed since there weren't any paying customers on that particular trip. There'd been a bet—for the life of him, he couldn't remember what it was—and he'd lost and had had to paint Violet's toenails for her.

Social Scene Red.

That had been the color she'd selected from the wall of nail polishes. Unfortunately, the end result looked more like Crime Scene Red after he'd made a sloppy mess with his too-big fingers and the way-too-tiny brush. But Violet had only laughed and proudly worn her flip-flops the rest of the weekend, showing off those smudged red toenails like they were works of art.

Now, all these years later, it finally occurred to Marcus that Violet hadn't been proud of his paint job. She'd been proud of winning whatever bet they'd had. Had she always been this competitive and he'd never noticed it? He was still wracking his brain for the terms of that wager when a horn blasted behind them.

All the cars in front of him had pulled forward, and the crossing guard was waving for him to follow along. Most of the time he parked and walked the boys to their classroom. But yesterday, Jordan had commented on how all the big kids got dropped off at the curb. Now Jack was begging for a motorcycle, of all things. What would they ask for tomorrow? Probably a six pack of beer. Or, in Jordan's case, a 401(k) plan.

Why did it feel like his babies were in such a hurry to grow up? And why did the realization suddenly make him feel so lonely?

Sighing, Marcus put the SUV in Park and turned to give them each an awkward half hug through the narrow opening separating the front seat from the back seat. "Good luck on your spelling tests. And eat the celery sticks I packed in your lunch."

"Did you put peanut butter and raisins on them like Aunt Freckles does?" Jack, the picky eater, asked. Thankfully, they weren't trying to grow up too fast.

"Yes," Marcus said, trying not to think of how old the raisins he'd found in the cabin's cupboard were. He really needed to go to the market instead of picking up last-minute supplies from the pantry in the main house like he'd done last night. "Don't forget. Aunt Dahlia is picking you guys up again today."

He gave the boys a final wave before driving to the county building that housed both the courthouse and the annexed sheriff's station. Deputy Broman had just returned from his overnight patrol shift, still sporting the black eye from MJ's attempts to resist arrest. The man was also still carrying a decade-old grudge from the safety academy when Marcus had beat him out as the top-scoring recruit, earning the Chief's Commendation Award at their graduation. Things hadn't improved in their professional relationship when Marcus had later won the election for county sheriff in a landslide and become Broman's boss.

Despite his deputy's attitude toward Marcus, though, the man was a dedicated cop and followed procedure by the book. He also knew how to write an ironclad arrest report that Violet, or any other attorney, would be hard-pressed to dispute in the courtroom.

"Morning, Broman," Marcus said as he used his electronic key card to open the secured back door only accessible to employees. "Uneventful shift, I hope?"

"As much as can be expected. It'll be nice when all those media vans camped outside the Twin Kings get whatever story they came for and leave." Broman had been complaining about the influx of news reporters snooping around town since before the funeral. Each time he commented on it, Marcus heard the underlying implication that it was somehow the King family's fault that the department's limited staff and even more limited budget had to be stretched thin to cover the additional patrol duties. Luckily, most of the local shops and restaurants appreciated the extra business, though. "Oh, and we got a noise complaint about Jay Grover again. Apparently he fired his fourth divorce attorney and went on another Taylor Swift binge. The neighbors are getting pretty tired of him getting drunk and blasting bad breakup songs at three in the morning. He was already passed out by the time I got there, and his Bluetooth speaker battery had died, so I left it for you guys on the day shift to handle."

"Okay. I have a few calls to make this morning, and then I'll drive over to Grover's house and have another chat with him. Speaking of lawyers, though, MJ's defense attorney is meeting the prosecutor here this afternoon to look at the body-cam footage from the night of his arrest. Can you make sure the toxicology reports are printed out before you leave?"

"No problem." Broman shifted his gear bag higher onto his shoulder as he passed through the door and inside the building. "Hey, is it true that your baby brother's lawyer is also your ex-girlfriend?"

Marcus clenched the door handle tighter before forcing his fingers to relax. It was bad enough that his law-enforcement duties were suddenly completely at odds with his brotherly duties, and that no matter what he did in this situation, someone would be pissed at him. Yet now he had the unfortunate bonus of dealing with Violet, on top of an already-precarious balancing act. All he could manage was a tense nod of acknowledgment before he retreated to his office.

The bulk of Marcus's morning was spent dealing with a sullen and hungover Jay Grover; pulling over the mayor's wife to give her another ticket for blowing through the new stop sign at Frontier Drive and Stampede Boulevard; responding to a call at Burnworth's

Bakery where Mrs. Crenshaw was refusing to leave until Mr. Burnworth, the notoriously temperamental baker, honored an expired coupon for 50 percent off a blueberry muffin; and explaining to Mr. Watterson at the Weathered W Ranch that his overweight pygmy goat (and not a rogue gang—as he had called them—of vegan teenagers) was responsible for tearing up his vegetable garden.

At one o'clock, Marcus grabbed a chicken sandwich to go at Biscuit Betty's, then buried himself in his office to finish reviewing operation reports from the prior weekend. Next, he went through his employees' time sheets and approved the overtime pay for the extra shifts they'd had to pull for all the Secret Service task-force meetings and security briefings related to the funeral. Due to Tessa's little media scandal with Agent Wyatt and all the lingering news agencies sticking around, his deputies had earned some hefty overtime checks this week.

By the time Rod D'Agostino, the front-desk volunteer, announced Violet's arrival, Marcus was already regretting his decision to hold this particular meeting at the station.

"The DA called to say he can't make it, but that other attorney is here." Rod had been a homicide detective in Chicago before retiring and moving to Teton Ridge with his wife, who wanted to get away from the big city. Unfortunately, the small-town life didn't hold much interest for an old-school cop like Rod, and Mrs. D'Agostino was so sick of listening to true-crime podcasts at home, she'd begged Marcus to let her husband volunteer at the station a few days a week.

"The junior cadets from the high-school program

are holding their monthly training in the community room," Rod reminded him. "Do you want me to put her in the interrogation room? I can come in there with you as your backup in case she gets a little slippery with all that fancy lawyer talk."

"It's called the interview room," he corrected Rod, who was clearly missing his days as a detective on the police force. "And since we aren't charging her with any crimes, it's probably safe enough for me to meet with her in my office."

"Suit yourself." Rod shrugged. "I'll be out here listening to the feds on the encrypted scanner if you need me."

As he straightened his desk, Marcus made a mental note to call the Secret Agent in charge at the ranch and advise him that Rod had figured out how to hack their frequency.

When Violet walked in, Marcus almost dropped the stack of time sheets he'd just signed. Someone must have sent her some clothes, because the outfit she had on definitely wasn't from Sherilee King's closet.

The silky-smooth fabric of the black pants hugged every curve, from the low-riding waistband all the way down to the cropped ankle length, showing off spiky five-inch heels. The matching jacket was fitted and hinted at being professional if it wasn't for the daring V-neck of the blouse under the four buttons holding the outer garment closed.

Technically, one might be able to call the articles of clothing a business suit. But the way Violet wore it gave Marcus very unbusinesslike thoughts.

"What's wrong?" Violet immediately asked. "Your

nostrils are all round and huffy, like you can't get enough air."

Marcus sniffed and shook his head. "Uh, nothing. I was just thinking that your outfit doesn't look like anything I've seen in a courtroom. At least not here in Ridgecrest County."

"Considering the fact that our judge was wearing sneakers and basketball pants under his robe at the last hearing, I'll consider myself overdressed. Besides, only one box of my clothes arrived and the dressiest material in Finn's closet is flannel. I had to borrow this shirt from your aunt Freckles."

That certainly explained the plunging V-neck. Marcus shook his head to clear it.

Violet placed her briefcase on the floor and gestured to the chair across from his desk, reminding him of his manners.

He extended his hand. "Sorry. Please have a seat."

She sat down and crossed her legs, drawing his attention to the high heels that would become highly impractical as soon as the next snow fell. Her shoes made him think of her toes, which made him think of what nail-polish color she had on underneath, and before he could stop himself he blurted out, "What was the bet that I lost?"

She lifted both eyebrows. "You're going to have to narrow that down for me. You used to lose bets to me all the time."

He frowned. "First of all, that's highly unlikely, since I rarely take bets that I might lose. Second, I'm talking about the one at that Summit at Sea cruise. Right before our senior year in high school. Remember that empty beauty salon?"

Violet's cheeks turned an adorable shade of pink, and she quickly busied herself with searching for something in her briefcase. "Are we here to talk about some old bet or about your brother's case?"

"Well, we *were* going to talk about the case. But now that it's obvious you're trying to avoid the subject, I would much rather discuss that bet."

"Fine." She finally dragged her eyes to his. "We'd snuck off from that global pyramid team-building workshop, and you were making fun of me for bringing my Shirley Temple with me."

"That's right! They closed all the bars on the ship and were only serving preapproved mocktails. I remember my roommate was the Secretary of State's son. He smuggled a bottle of tequila in his suitcase and was charging kids to spike their drinks. So did I dare you to chug it or something?"

"No. You bet me that I couldn't tie a knot into the stem of a cherry. With my tongue."

Now he felt the heat rise to his own cheeks. And other parts of his body, as well. He remembered her skillful mouth and her agile tongue oh so well, and his body was responding as if he was eighteen all over again.

As if to drive him further to distraction, she opened her soft lips ever so slightly and let out a breathy sigh. Her next words snapped him right back to the present, though.

"So am I here to talk about a past bet you lost to me, or am I here to talk about a *current* case your absent prosecutor is going to lose to me?"

Violet would've had to be blind not to see how uncomfortable Marcus was as he shifted his weight in his office chair. His eyes kept dropping to her mouth, and despite their growing animosity toward each other, the attraction was clearly still there. Her stomach did a little dance at the realization that she was having such a physical effect on the man who had let it be known to everyone at the ranch that he didn't enjoy having Violet in town.

The only time she ever used her looks or her femininity to gain the upper hand—either in her personal life or in her career, which took up most of her personal life—was when she wanted to lure some good ol' boy attorney into underestimating her. Then she could strike when they weren't paying attention and win an argument or even an entire case.

It was tempting to use the same strategy against Marcus because all his focus seemed to be on the personal history between them. He might want to secure the upper hand in some sort of imagined verbal battle between them, but that desire was distracting him from the only issue that mattered.

MJ.

She cleared her throat. "So I hear you have a body-cam video of my client that the prosecutor is planning to introduce as evidence."

"Yes." Marcus straightened his already-straight shoulders. "Along with witness testimony."

"Who is the witness?"

He rubbed the back of his neck before admitting, "Kendra Broman."

Violet frowned. "The daughter of the deputy who made the arrest?"

"She's also MJ's girlfriend."

"So you're admitting she has divided loyalties.

Why would she be willing to testify against her boy-friend?"

"She's not testifying *against* him," Marcus tried to reason. "She's only testifying to what she saw."

"Was Kendra drinking that night?" Violet asked rhetorically. She knew the answer because MJ had admitted as much to her.

Marcus straightened some already-neat papers on his desk. "I believe the arrest report implies that she was."

"Right. The arrest report that her father wrote. Interesting that there was no Breathalyzer done on her, yet there was one done on my client. So how much did Kendra drink that night? How often does she normally drink? And with whom? Has her dad ever caught her drinking before? How does her dad feel about her dating MJ? Has she ever heard her father talking about his distaste for my client or for my client's family?" Violet paused only long enough to let her rapid-fire questions sink in. "Do you see where I'm going with this, Marcus? If the prosecution puts Kendra on the witness stand, I'm going to have to ask her these questions. In public and under oath. She's barely eighteen and in love with a boy her father disapproves of. We both remember how that feels. Don't make me put Kendra through a cross-examination when the body camera can deliver the exact same evidence."

Marcus studied her, the deepened crease above his nose highlighting his serious blue eyes. "Your father disapproved of me?"

Of course that was the part of her speech he focused on. Violet rolled her eyes. "No, my dad adored you. It was my mom who had an issue with our relationship. Although, to be honest, she would've disapproved of me having *any* boyfriend that distracted me from my future prospects. She still does."

"Well, she got what she wanted in the end, didn't she?"

Violet swallowed down the sting. "You mean when I miscarried her grandchildren? Or when she had to take an emergency absence from the Senate to take care of me when I was on bed rest for two weeks afterward? She never left my side, crying whenever she thought I was asleep. I know what she said to your dad that day was unconscionable, but she was also the person who told me not to be disappointed with you, Marcus. She reminded me that you were going through a lot of stress with boot camp, dealing with the added worry that you were risking your life joining the military. I know you don't like my mother, Marcus, but even she's not that much of a monster."

He shoved a hand through his short hair. "No. God, no. I just meant that her plan for you and your life wasn't derailed too much by our relationship after all."

"Derailed?" The stinging sensation didn't go away. "That's how you want to describe what happened? I was in the hospital for three days, and the father of my children never so much as called." She held up a hand when he opened his mouth. "Yeah, I know you didn't get my letter. But learning that now doesn't lessen the pain I felt back then."

"I felt plenty of pain back then, too, Violet."

She sucked in a deep breath, but the air between them was so thick with tension, it didn't bring her any clarity. "Listen, we can't keep bringing up our past every time we see each other. We're both here to do a job. Even if we can't agree on how the other should do *their* job, we should at least agree to put on our professional pants and try to act civil. For MJ's sake."

His eyes dropped to her hips, then traveled slowly down her legs. "You call those your professional pants?"

A jolt of electricity shot through her limbs, and she immediately stood up as though she could shake away the feeling.

"What's wrong with these pants?" Following his gaze, she ran her hands along her hips to check for rips or stains. His soft groan was barely audible, making her suddenly realize his issue. "Wait. You haven't suddenly become ultramodest in your old age?"

"No. Of course not. I just meant that it was easier to think of you a certain way when you were wearing my mother's clothes."

"What a woman wears shouldn't affect how you think of her."

"I know that. And if you were any other woman, keeping my thoughts under control wouldn't be an issue. Unfortunately, I have the privilege of already knowing exactly what is under those pants. So it's a lot more difficult setting those kinds of thoughts aside when my brain and that tight fabric is so intent on reminding me."

A shiver raced through Violet at his admission, and instead of retreating and putting some distance between them, she took a step forward and placed her hands on his desk. "You think you're the only one who has to deal with thinking about what someone looks like under their clothes?"

That didn't exactly come out the way she'd intended, which made her all the more defensive.

He stood and adjusted his black leather duty belt.

"You mean my county-issued uniform I'm required to wear for my job?"

"Uniforms are supposed to fit...well...uniformly. But your biceps look like they're going to bust through the sleeves at the slightest flex. And unlike you, I don't have the luxury of already knowing what's under that poly-ester-blend fabric because you clearly weren't bench-pressing as much back when we were eighteen."

This time, his groan was louder when he stepped around his desk. Violet's brain was shooting up all the red flags it could muster, but her legs were acting of their own accord. Before she knew it, she'd met him halfway and was in his arms, her lips pressed to his.

Oh, hell. She was kissing Marcus King.

Again.

It felt so familiar and yet so new and thrilling all at the same time. They had been each other's first so many years ago, learning how to kiss with just the right amount of pressure and curiosity. Clearly, their mouths hadn't forgotten all those stolen minutes of practice and eagerly molded together as their tongues made up for lost time.

His hands spanned around her waist, and her fingers dug into his shoulders as the rest of her body melted against his. She sighed as he angled his head and deep-ened the kiss. He tasted like coffee and misspent youth, and she was at risk of drowning in that familiar pas-sion all over again.

She pulled away only slightly, needing to give her-self a second to think about what had just happened. Her heartbeat pounded in her ears as his warm breath fanned her forehead.

"God, was it always this good between us?" he asked, resting his lips against her temple.

"I think so." She shuddered, letting her palms slide down to his defined pectoral muscles. "But we were both so young back then and didn't know anything else. I remember being able to feel your heart beating in double-time against my skin, just like it is now. Except we were usually wearing a lot less clothing. And there wasn't usually this coming between us."

Tucking his chin, Marcus watched as Violet's finger traced along one of the points of the star-shaped badge on his chest. She lifted her face to his and was about to pick up where they'd left off when an announcement blared over the intercom.

"We gotta Code Twin heading your way, Sheriff."

CHAPTER SIX

MARCUS HAD ONLY seconds to jump away from Violet before his office door busted open and Jack spilled the contents of his rocket-ship backpack all over the floor. Jordan was right behind with their aunt Dahlia and little Amelia bringing up the rear.

"Oh, hi, Violet." Jack smiled before dropping to the floor to collect his scattered belongings. "I didn't know you would be here."

Violet smoothed her slightly tousled hair and blinked several times. "I, uh, didn't know I'd be staying this long."

"Why're your lips all red, Dad?" Jordan asked as his brother shoved a handful of crumpled-up papers and a half-eaten banana back into his backpack. "Do you have a fever?"

"Or did you get a frozen slushy at the Mighty Mart?" Jack, whose brain went to sugar before medical conditions, was now intently staring at him, as well. "I thought Mrs. Contreras said they were out of the cherry flavor."

"Uh, no," Marcus said before dragging the back of his hand across the lower half of his face. Judging by the absence of any lipstick left on Violet's full lips, he knew exactly why his mouth was so red. And so did his sister.

Dahlia gave a little snort before depositing a lunch box in the shape of a T. rex on the chair. "Sorry to interrupt what must be an important and, by the looks of it, very *professional* meeting. But Amelia has her ballet lesson in about five minutes, and she refuses to do her pirouettes when her cousins are there to distract her."

"I don't blame her." Marcus winked at his niece, then shot his sister a warning look. "Obnoxious family members getting all up in your business are the worst."

Steering her daughter toward the door, Dahlia paused and looked back over her shoulder. "Hey, Violet. Tessa and Finn are coming by Big Millie's for happy hour this evening if you need a girls' night out."

"Can we come?" Jordan asked his aunt.

"Then it wouldn't be a girls' night out." Dahlia wiggled her eyebrows. "Maybe your dad could take you guys to get a slushy at the Mighty Mart, instead. He looks like he could use a bit of cooling down."

When their aunt had left the office, Jack turned to Marcus. "But I wanna go with Violet to happy hour."

"Oh, I don't know if I'm going yet," Violet replied before Marcus could. "I have a lot of work to do."

"To keep Uncle MJ out of Daddy's jail?" Jordan asked.

"That's right," Violet nodded.

The back of Marcus's throat vibrated as he swallowed down a frustrated groan. "For the record, I'm trying to keep Uncle MJ out of my jail, too. And any future jails. By teaching him a lesson."

"You mean like when Coach makes us run extra laps when we mess up at soccer practice?" Jordan asked.

"Yeah, kind of like that."

"How does that teach you not to mess up?" Violet's

smooth forehead, the one he'd just pressed his own against, creased with confusion. "It seems like it would only make you tired and prone to make more mistakes."

Marcus shook his head. "But if there aren't consequences for your actions, what's to stop you from making the same mistakes over and over again?"

"How about having a patient coach or mentor or maybe even…oh, I don't know—" Violet dramatically shrugged her shoulders "—say, a big brother who *guides* you and steers you in the right direction?"

"So this is my fault?" Marcus crossed his arms across his chest and tried to ignore the way her eyes widened at his biceps. Remembering her earlier admission, he flexed his muscles slightly. "I'm supposed to be *babysitting* MJ, in addition to dealing with the rest of my family's antics? All while working sixty-plus hours a week at my job and raising my kids on my own?"

Violet's gaze snapped back to his face. Possibly at the reminder that he was a single dad. "Nobody said *babysitting*."

"Keegan's mom did," Jordan announced out of the blue. "At the bake sale, I heard her tell the other parents that you needed to hire a real babysitter so you could go out with a real woman like her."

Violet arched a brow at Marcus, and he resisted the urge to tug at his collar as he explained, "Their friend Keegan's mom has been very determined lately to get me to join this little group she formed called Single Socials. It's not really my scene, though. Just in case you thought it was."

"From what MJ tells me, you don't have much of a social scene at all." Violet smirked, and Marcus silently cursed his baby brother for opening his big mouth.

"I told Ms. Parker we didn't need a babysitter because we weren't babies," Jack said, while balancing on his knees in his father's office chair and spinning fast in circles. "But then she said that all grown-ups need to spend alone time with other grown-ups."

"You're a grown-up and a real woman," Jordan told Violet. "Maybe you should spend alone time with my dad."

After the DM-sliding conversation the other night, Marcus should've been immune to his sons' embarrassing announcements. He wasn't. And neither, apparently, was Violet. Her eyes went wide, and her mouth opened and closed several times as her face went nearly crimson. Ha. That's what she got for implying that he needed to socialize more.

"Actually, uh, your father and I, uh, have already spent plenty of alone time together for the day," she finally managed.

Marcus's mind immediately skipped back to the kiss that had been interrupted when the boys had arrived. He cleared his throat and added, "In fact, it'd probably be better if we didn't spend any alone time together at all."

Her head gave the slightest twitch, as though his words had stunned her. Hell, he'd stunned himself with the harshness of his statement. But the truth was that he couldn't trust himself around her. And if he wanted to keep her at a distance, then it was better that he maintain some sort of battle line between them.

"You're probably right." Violet's smile was polite, but her eyes held a note of calculation. "After all, I already accomplished what I came here to do."

She said goodbye to the twins and was gone for a full five minutes before Marcus realized he'd might've just been played. It was two hours later when he confirmed it.

Marcus had been so distracted by Violet's visit to his office, he'd driven the boys home without remembering to stop at the grocery store. He was standing in front of the still-empty fridge contemplating going to the bunkhouse for dinner when his cell phone rang.

"So I just had an interesting chat with defense counsel in your brother's case." Reed Nakamoto, the prosecutor who hadn't shown for the meeting earlier today, jumped right into it. "I thought you said she was your *ex*-girlfriend."

"I don't think I said either way." At least not to Reed or to anyone else. But small-town news traveled fast. "Why? What's up?"

"Well, Miss Cortez-Hill seems to think that you and she have some kind of understanding. That you're on the same page and don't want me calling Kendra Broman as a witness."

"I don't know if I'd call it the same page." Marcus swung the fridge door closed, annoyed that he didn't even have so much as an expired bottle of beer in there. "Violet made some good points about the damaging effects it could have on Kendra if she has to suffer an embarrassing cross-examination."

Reed tsked. "I told you from the get-go that there was a lot of potential for conflicts of interest in this case, Marcus. You insisted we treat your brother the same way we would treat any other defendant and not give him any special favors. So I'm going to insist that you don't do any more favors for your pretty little girlfriend without running them by me first."

"I didn't do anyone a favor, and I didn't agree to anything. She came to see the body-cam footage, a meeting that you were supposed to attend, by the way." If Reed had been there, there definitely wouldn't have been any heated looks or make-out sessions.

"Yeah, sorry about that. I ran into Judge Calhoun at Biscuit Betty's, and a group of us headed over to the rec center for a game of three on three."

So the DA shooting hoops with the judge in the case wasn't considered a conflict of interest, but the sheriff meeting with the defense attorney in a county office was? Small-town boundaries were more of a suggestion than a written rule, but the man was right. Marcus had always done things by the book, and he didn't appreciate anyone suggesting the hint of impropriety. Even if the one doing the suggesting was doing the same thing or worse.

Marcus pinched the bridge of his nose. "Anyway, Miss Cortez-Hill brought up not needing Kendra's witness testimony, and I didn't agree or disagree. That was the gist of our meeting."

Well, that wasn't exactly it. Other things had happened in that office, as well, but Reed didn't need to know all of that.

"Okay, good. Just between you and me, the defense counsel is probably right. In this instance. But we need to be careful with these big-city attorneys coming into town and sweet-talking us into deals."

"Nobody's sweet-talking me, Reed."

Marcus's fingers were gripping the cell phone so hard, it was a wonder the thing hadn't snapped in half before he could disconnect the call. Normally, he was proud of his department's three-year record for not having any complaints or lawsuits filed against them due to deputy misconduct. He wasn't about to have his ethical standards called into question because his ex-girlfriend had distracted him before going over his head to get what she wanted.

Right now, he needed a burger, he needed a beer and he needed to have a few words with Violet Cortez-Hill, Esquire.

"Come on, boys," Marcus called down the hallway, grabbing his coat. He might have to forego the beer since he didn't want to waste time changing out of his uniform. "We're gonna go to Aunt Dahlia's and crash the girls' night out party."

After leaving Marcus's office, Violet had gone straight to the tiny one-room law library in the basement of the courthouse building. The phone reception down there must've been terrible because her phone pinged to life with notifications as soon as the elevator doors opened onto the lobby floor two hours later.

The first voice mail was from her mom. She could listen to that later. She tapped on the screen to hear the second message, which had just come in fifteen minutes ago. "Hi there, Miss Cortez-Hill. It's Reed Nakamoto calling you back again. Listen, I just got off the phone with Sheriff King and, as much as I'm willing to cut young MJ a deal and avoid a trial, I just don't think I'm gonna be able to get the sheriff on board. Let's talk more tomorrow and see if we can find some common ground."

It could be that Reed was just that bad at plea deals, trying to play the good cop to Marcus's bad cop. Or it could be that Marcus was seriously being this stubborn. Probably it was a little bit of both. Either way, she wasn't in favor of any deals that didn't include the dismissal of all charges. And if she could ever get Marcus and the district attorney in the same room together, she'd tell them both exactly that.

Clenching her jaw in frustration, Violet was really in no mood to deal with her mom's message at the moment. Yet as she shoved open the heavy door leading outside to the courthouse steps, she couldn't stop the uneasy feeling that something was wrong. That there might be some sort of accident or emergency, since her mother usually only texted between their weekly calls. Sighing, she put the phone back to her ear.

"Hey, angel. It's Mom. I was just thinking that once my campaign kicks off in a couple of weeks, I'm not going to have much time off. What do you think of a girls' trip? Remember that time we took off and went to Punta Cana? Just the two of us? That was fun." It was also the first June after the miscarriage, and her mom had known that it would be a difficult time for her daughter since summers had always been a big deal for Violet and Marcus. "Anyway, look at your schedule and get back to my aide, Yvonne, with your availability. Oh, and maybe we should bring Senator Valdivia with us. She has a daughter your age and, coincidentally, has just been appointed chair of the senate judiciary committee. I told her you might be interested…"

Violet groaned, cutting off the message before the end. Her relationship with her mom was complicated, with equal parts of love and frustration. When Eva Cortez-Hill was being just a "normal mom," things were great. They could do regular mother-and-daughter things together—shopping, spa days, vacations—and they got along fine. But when her mom was being "the senator," she was nearly insufferable. The tricky part was knowing when one role was about to switch to the other so Violet could get out in time to save herself.

The old-fashioned streetlamps had just come on, and looking down Stampede Boulevard, Violet saw the vintage sign for Big Millie's Saloon in the distance. Yep, she definitely needed a cocktail after today's events. She also needed to vent to any King whose first name wasn't Marcus.

"Hi, Vi." Dahlia extended arms in welcome from behind the hundred-year-old refinished walnut bar she now owned and ran. "Let me get you a drink as a thanks for helping my baby brother out of his latest scrape with the law."

"Much to the annoyance of your *big* brother," Violet responded. "He isn't here, is he?"

"Not yet." Tessa smiled and patted the empty seat beside her.

Violet let out a deep breath as she plopped herself onto a gold leather–covered bar stool. She'd heard that the Wild West–era saloon and former brothel had been fully refurbished, but she was impressed with how Dahlia had managed to make the place seem trendy while keeping the decor true to its historic roots. "In that case, I'll take a glass of any wine you already have open."

Dahlia drew a bottle from under the bar, and Freckles breezed out of the kitchen carrying two double burgers loaded with every possible topping listed on the limited bar menu.

"Hey, Aunt Freckles," Violet said, immediately feeling more relaxed at the sight of the older woman's friendly face. "If I'd known you were here cooking, I would've left the courthouse earlier. Did Mrs. King kick you out of her kitchen?"

"No, darlin'." Freckles wore a crisp white apron over her tight zebra-print blouse and even tighter jeans. "I needed a break from Rider. That old coot has been getting a bit frisky lately. Trying to prove there's still a little gas left in his tank, if you know what I mean."

Marcus's three sisters covered their ears, despite the fact that they should've been well-accustomed to the older woman's candid comments.

"Aunt Freckles," Dahlia scolded as she lowered her cupped palms, "we can't unhear those sorts of things."

Violet hid her smile behind a large sip of wine while the King women continued to banter. Someone asked where Duke had gone, and she didn't have the heart to rat their brother out and admit that she'd seen him on her way into the building. He'd been standing outside the heavy oak front door, huddled under his puffy down jacket and quietly arguing with someone on his cell phone.

Violet's guest room at the ranch was next to Duke's, and two nights ago, she'd accidentally overheard him pleading with someone on a video call to let him be the one to tell Tom what had happened. Her interest had obviously been piqued, but then her own phone had rung with an incoming video call from her mom, and she'd spent the next ten minutes strategically holding the camera lens at an angle that wouldn't give away her location.

Not that she was keeping her presence on the Twin Kings a secret from her mother. In fact, it could be that her mom already knew something was up and that's why she'd called again today with the idea for a mother-daughter vacation. Guilt. She was still process-

ing Marcus's claim about the senator leading him to
believe Violet had had an abortion all those years ago,
and she wasn't yet sure how she wanted to confront
her mom. Until then, Violet wasn't going to mention
the name Marcus to either of her parents.

As if her thoughts had summoned the man, Marcus's
twin boys tore through the entrance of Big Millie's.

"We're here for girls' night," Jordan said by way of
greeting.

"Will you watch our jackets?" Jack flung their coats
at the empty bar stool near Violet, before both boys ran
toward the billiards table. Their father was right behind
them, still wearing his sheriff's uniform. His face was
drawn tight, his lips pressed together. He was pissed
about something and headed straight for Violet. His
sisters immediately stood up, as though they intended
to intervene.

Marcus rolled his eyes, shaking his head at their
united front. "Now you've got my sisters protecting
you?"

"I only need protection from *credible* threats." Violet
rose to her feet and stepped between Tessa and Finn.
"And you, Sheriff King, are no threat."

Agent Grayson Wyatt, who was assigned to tail
Tessa, appeared out of nowhere and asked, "Is everyone okay over here?"

Marcus gave a tense nod but didn't break eye contact with Violet. Her heart thrummed in anticipation
of whatever verbal confrontation he'd come to wage.
With so many witnesses currently surrounding them,
they could engage in a true sparring match and not get
sidetracked into another distracting make-out session.

"You know what this party needs?" Aunt Freckles

clapped her hands together so hard Violet feared one of the woman's false red fingernails would fly off. She pointed at the jukebox that was playing a fast-tempo George Strait song. "Dancing!"

Freckles, using a surprising amount of strength, shoved Tessa directly into Agent Wyatt's arms. Dahlia, the only single woman safe behind the bar, had the audacity to smile in amusement.

"Finn, you go with Agent Doherty," Freckles continued, and Violet's blood drained from her face because she knew exactly what was coming next. "And Marcus, you and Violet can talk about whatever you need to talk about on the dance floor."

Talking one-on-one with Marcus was the last thing Violet wanted to do. Standing so close to him as he whirled her around a bunch of barroom tables was even less appealing. Unfortunately, though, she was now stuck doing both.

The only alternatives would be to fake an injury, which would worry Jordan, who kept glancing in her direction. Or to refuse, which would be the same thing as admitting that Marcus had any sort of effect on her. There was no way she would give him the satisfaction.

"I thought this was supposed to be a girls' night out," she said when they were finally out of earshot.

"And I thought that you would fight fair," Marcus replied before spinning her under his arm and deftly pulling her back without missing a step. He was surprisingly more adept at leading her in a fast-paced two-step than he had been during their first waltz at her *quinceañera*.

"First of all, why does everything have to be a fight with you?" Before he could answer, she added, "And who are you to decide what's fair?"

"Okay, so maybe I phrased that wrong," Marcus admitted, his jaw tight. "But you showed up at my office looking hot as hell and maybe I'm a little pissed at myself for thinking things could be different when you kissed me like that."

When her brain finally processed what he said, he was twirling her under his arm again. She ducked her head for a second spin and *accidentally* brought her high heel down on top of his boot. He flinched but didn't stop dancing.

"I didn't kiss *you*. You kissed *me*." Violet forced a smile at Jack and Jordan, who waved to her from the billiards table where they were playing pool with a couple of off-duty Secret Service agents. "And how would one kiss make a difference between us? Did you think it would erase everything else that has happened?"

"That's another thing. We've never even talked about what exactly happened fourteen years ago. Every time it gets brought up, someone interrupts us."

"So is that why you're here?" Violet pivoted on the two count, forcing him to go backward so that she was leading. "You came tearing through those doors all hell-bent on rehashing our past? Because I really don't think *now* is the best time to have that conversation with half of your family as an audience."

"No, I came here because Reed Nakamoto thinks you sweet-talked me into not calling Kendra Broman as a witness."

"The way he tried to sweet-talk Judge Calhoun into extending the preliminary hearing during their impromptu basketball game today? I don't care how many free shots Reed purposely misses, my motion to dismiss has already been filed."

"Was that before or after you made that comment about letting my badge come between us?" Marcus asked, then quickly continued, "Because I might get easily distracted by your kisses, but at the end of the day, I still have a job to do."

"I filed it this morning, and how you do your job really isn't any of my concern. I meant the badge was *literally* coming between us, Marcus. I could feel the points of your star poking into my boob."

Maybe mentioning her breasts was the wrong thing to say right that second, because his eyes dropped to the open lines of her suit jacket where her skin was flushed, rising and falling with each angry breath expanding her rib cage.

He made a growling sound before quickly looking at something off in the distance. The song on the jukebox changed, but he continued to dance, albeit at a slower pace. She should pull away, but deep down Violet liked the power she had over him. Maybe subconsciously she *had* been trying to seduce him. She'd certainly thought of it for a split second. But he was also trying to seduce her with the way his forearm locked around her waist and skillfully held her in place against him.

"I have a serious question," Marcus said, as though their conversation up until now hadn't been all that serious. "And it's a little off topic."

Normally, she'd welcome the chance to switch the subject; however, she had a feeling this one wasn't going to be any less antagonistic. Or personal. But she wasn't about to back down now. "Go ahead."

"What do you think your mom is going to do when she finds out you're still here with me?"

"I'm not *with* you. Why would she think that?"

He rolled his eyes. "You know what I mean. The judge issued a gag order, and we've managed to keep things out of the press so far. But eventually the senator is going to find out you're here in Teton Ridge."

"Of course she's going to find out. And it won't be from the press. I'll tell her when I decide it's the right time."

"Will she make you go home to Texas?"

"Marcus, I'm a grown woman. I pay my own bills and make my own decisions. Nobody makes me do anything I don't want to do. Including my mother."

He made a scoffing sound. "I don't know why you're getting so defensive. You have no problem telling me how I should feel about *my* family. Hell, you're being paid to interfere in my relationship with my mom and my brother."

Violet shook her head. "I'm not being paid. I agreed to represent MJ pro bono."

"Oh, come on. My family has more money than they know what to do with, and public defenders are notoriously underpaid." He paused a beat, as though he'd just recalled that her family was nearly as wealthy as his. "So what's in it for you? The chance to get me back for something I never even did?"

"That's cute how you think my being here has anything to do with you," she replied. "I'm simply helping out an old family friend by using my legal expertise and doing what I was trained to do. Pissing you off in the process is just an added bonus."

"What an interesting coincidence that your job involves freeing the very same people who break the laws that my job requires me to enforce."

"Coincidence? Again, you're giving yourself too

much credit if you think my career choice had anything to do with you. Unlike you, I hadn't been creeping around on the internet trying to figure out what you did for a living."

"I wasn't creeping." Marcus's expression was so insistent, he looked like his sons when they asked for seconds of dessert. "But speaking of what you do, whatever happened to your dream of becoming a prosecutor?"

"That dream crashed around the same time my dream of becoming a mom was shot down."

"You mean when *we* lost the babies?" His quiet statement caused the righteous air to suddenly whoosh from her lungs.

She quickly recovered, though. "You say *we*, as though both of us went through such a traumatic experience together."

"Physically, no. Obviously, you had it way worse than me, and now I have to live with the fact that I wasn't there for you when you needed me most. But just because I didn't know all the circumstances at the time doesn't mean I didn't suffer a loss." Marcus's eyes seemed to glisten, and his voice grew wobbly but more passionate as he stopped dancing altogether. "Vi, I wanted our babies as much as I once wanted you."

Her knees gave out, and she might've stumbled if he hadn't been holding her so firmly against him. She'd been so hurt by the silence all these years that she'd never really considered the possibility that he would've been equally upset about losing the babies—the ones that he'd apparently wanted. All this time, Violet had assumed he'd been relieved to dodge the young-fatherhood bullet.

No wonder he'd made those earlier comments about

her relationship with her mom, considering her mother was the one who'd led him to believe the worst. Violet was pretty damn mad at the woman herself. But like she'd told Marcus earlier, she would deal with her mom in her own way. This wasn't the best time or place to be unpacking all these emotions they'd never fully processed.

Finn and Duke crashed into them as they attempted an ill-fated swing lift. When had the song changed to a fast-paced one again? And when had Duke come back inside the bar?

Violet quickly glanced around the room to see if anyone had been watching their tense exchange. Yep. Several pairs of eyes were, in fact, on them. Including Jack's and Jordan's. She cleared her throat and stepped out of his arms. "I think that should be enough dancing to satisfy Aunt Freckles. I'm going to go finish my wine."

And maybe a shot of something stronger.

For the millionth time that week, Violet silently cursed herself for not leaving Teton Ridge when she'd had a chance. She liked it better when she didn't have to think about running into Marcus King on a daily basis.

CHAPTER SEVEN

MARCUS'S PAIN-FILLED WORDS were still playing in Violet's head later that following week as she set up a temporary workstation inside the unused pool house at the Twin Kings. Not that MJ's case required that much time or effort since they were still in the pretrial stage. Normally, Violet managed several ongoing cases at once, and most of them involved much bigger charges and stakes. But since she'd taken a personal leave of absence from her job to handle MJ's case, she had to be in constant communication with the other attorneys in her office who were covering the clients on her caseload.

Tessa had claimed her father's old study for research, and Sherilee had set up some sort of public-relations headquarters in the west wing of the house. So that left the glass-enclosed pool house that wasn't in use during the winter months. The temporary office smelled faintly of chlorine and sunscreen yet had a massive custom-built river-rock fireplace taking up an entire wall. The design was intended to be used during the seasons when the weather allowed for outdoor entertaining, but it worked well for keeping the place heated now that they were well into February.

Violet moved a few pool noodles off a chaise lounge

and fired up her laptop. Of course, the first email she responded to required her to type the word *once* and she immediately lost her train of thought.

Once.

I wanted our babies as much as I once wanted you.

That's what Marcus had said to her when they'd been dancing. Clearly, he didn't want her anymore. Not that she wanted him. Obviously. But it'd be nice if they could at least get along.

She'd thought they'd turned a corner that night at Big Millie's when he'd let his guard down and opened up about losing the babies. But then the following day, she'd run into him at Burnworth's Bakery and he'd pretended he didn't even know her. In fact, several times last week she'd seen him on duty patrolling the small town of Teton Ridge, and the most he'd been able to manage was a brief nod in her direction.

It was almost as though he didn't want anyone in town seeing them being even slightly friendly toward each other.

Then, last Sunday, she'd gone out for a run on one of the many trails crisscrossing the vast ranch and saw him and the twins riding their bikes toward the main house. The boys were excited to see her and Jordan immediately wanted to know if she wanted a tour of their "brand-new" cabin.

"Well, it's not real brand-new," Jack clarified. "We used to live there before when our mom was alive, but me and Jordan don't remember that from way back when. But we have a Nintendo Switch and you can play the red controller if you want. It has motion controls and rumbles in your hands so you can feel when you go over the bumpy track."

Violet had tried not to blink too much at the casual mention of their mom in passing. "I think I may have to brush up on my video game skills before I take on the responsibility of the red controller. Maybe some other time?"

Marcus had let out the breath he'd been holding, looking visibly relieved. "Speaking of added features." He nodded at her smartphone on the elastic holder around her bicep. "How's your GPS reception on that thing? The open pastures on the west side of the ranch make it hard to get lost. But the trails on this side are way narrower and confusing for people who didn't grow up here."

"Well, maybe you'll get lucky, and I'll wind up lost," she'd retorted. He hadn't cared about her safety or her sense of direction all last week when he'd ignored her in town. Yet now he suddenly felt the need to patronize her with his knowledge of the rugged tree-lined terrain.

So now that she'd set up an office in the pool house and wasn't in town at the law library as much, she was making more of an effort to be the one who ignored him. Violet responded to several emails and had a video conference with one of her clients turned state's witness housed in protective custody at the West Tower Detention Facility. When she ran out of tasks, she returned to the main house to find out Sherilee had insisted Marcus and the twins come for a family meal that night.

The twins, as usual, had been excited to see Violet, regaling her with stories about their school day. Their father, as usual, was much harder to read. Marcus's family might be a little pushy, but nobody was forcing him to be here. She had to give him credit for at least making the attempt to keep things as normal as he could for his children.

As they took their places in the dining room, Violet watched Marcus reach across the table to help Jack pour his lemonade into one of the fancy crystal goblets Sherilee insisted everyone use. Then he silently helped Jordan spread the cold pat of butter across his crumbling biscuit. Violet wondered if he would've been as gentle and loving as a father to her twins, had they survived.

Guilt caused her chest to tighten. Of course he would have been. The man was born to be an amazing dad. It was his role as ex-boyfriend and big brother that could use a little work.

"You have any plans this weekend, MJ?" Freckles asked.

"No!" both Marcus and his mother said in unison.

MJ threw his napkin on the table. "So I'm a prisoner in my own home now?"

Sherilee returned MJ's napkin to him as if he'd accidentally misplaced it. "I thought we agreed that you'd keep a low profile and not leave the ranch until things calm down."

"You mean you and Sheriff Trust-No-One over there agreed," MJ replied, displaying his most angst-filled teenaged glare in Marcus's direction.

"I'm pretty sure your defense attorney would recommend the same thing." Great, now Marcus was drawing Violet into their petty squabble.

Violet took a sip of her ice water, wishing she hadn't declined the predinner cocktail hour, before speaking directly to MJ. "Only because I think the judge would look more favorably on you not drawing any attention to yourself by leaving the ranch. Unless, of course, you were going to a job or a college class, perhaps."

"Yeah, well, I don't have a job. And I'm not going to college," MJ announced, making his mom gasp. He looked Sherilee in the eye and added, "Ever."

"I can give you a job," Uncle Rider offered. "Plenty of stalls need mucking."

"So my only choices are house arrest and forced labor. I'd probably have it better in prison."

Violet's left eye twitched. She thought about the client she'd just spoken with via video chat. The woman had been in and out of institutions since she was twelve years old and was facing ten more years if she didn't cooperate with prosecutors to implicate her pimp as the head of a human-trafficking ring.

The young man sitting before her had no idea what a real prison smelled like, let alone felt like. MJ's pessimistic attitude—while understandable—was probably the biggest contributor to his current predicament. He was young, privileged and way too sheltered to have such a big chip on his shoulder. He was also drifting through life aimlessly with no goals and way too much free time on his hands, which only gave him more opportunity to stew.

"Peyton's mom's boyfriend was in prison," young Amelia said. "She went to visit him every month, and there was a big, mean dog that sniffed her mom to make sure she didn't sneak any keys or bad stuff into him."

"Really?" Dahlia tilted her head at her daughter. "Peyton's mom told me that her boyfriend lived in Montana."

"They have prisons in Montana," Rider said. "Got an old rodeo buddy who did a dime in the state pen back in the seventies. Said it was the worst stretch he's ever done. But he did meet his wife there. She was a guard. So I guess it worked out for him."

"Anyone else see a problem with the direction of this conversation?" Duke nodded subtly at the wide-eyed expressions on his nephews' faces. "Maybe we should change the subject to something that is a little less *Shawshank Redemption*."

"So if I can't leave," MJ said returning the topic back to himself, "can I at least have some friends over to hang out?"

"Like who?" Sherilee might've lifted a sculpted brow if her Botoxed forehead would've allowed it.

MJ shrugged. "Like Kendra?"

"No!" Marcus and Sherilee said in unison. Again.

MJ turned pleading eyes toward Violet, who seemed to be his only ally at the table. Or at least the only person legally contracted to represent him. She sighed. "I don't see a problem with Kendra visiting as long as you guys are properly chaperoned and only engaging in activities suitable for teenagers."

Finn plopped another spoonful of chicken and dumplings on her plate. "Violet, you might need to define what your expectations of a suitable activity is."

"I don't know. What do eighteen-year-olds do for fun nowadays?"

"The same thing *we* used to do when we were that age." Marcus stared expectantly at her, and Violet's face felt as though it was going to catch on fire.

Sherilee choked on her wine, while Freckles and Finn giggled like schoolgirls.

"In that case, count me out as a chaperone." Duke sat back in his chair and rubbed his flat stomach. "Mom and Dad used to make me tag along with Vi and Marcus to keep an eye on them, but I always ended up getting ditched."

"Why would they ditch you, Uncle Duke?" Jordan wanted to know. "You're the funnest one in the family, and you're real good at playing football and Uno and video games."

"Because back then, your dad and Miss Violet preferred to play a two-person game called—"

"Twister," Violet interrupted Duke just in time, which made Finn and Freckles giggle even more. Even Dahlia had to cover her mouth to keep from laughing.

Duke held up his hands innocently. "Hey, I was going to say Battleship. But that might be a better description for the game you two are *currently* playing."

Marcus narrowed his eyes at his brother but didn't dispute the fact that he and Violet were, in fact, acting like adversaries who wanted to sink each other.

"Yeah, we get it. Marcus and Violet hate each other," MJ said, causing Jordan to gasp with concern. "But can we focus on me and my situation for a second?"

"It's okay," Marcus said softly as he patted his son's shoulder. "Violet and I are old friends who just squabble sometimes. We don't really hate each other."

Jack's eyes sought Violet's across the table, and she nodded in confirmation. At least she could reassure the boys, even if she couldn't reassure herself.

MJ, though, continued, "You guys can't keep me and Kendra away from each other forever."

Rider wiped some sauce off his bushy mustache. "I think your girlfriend's dad might have something to say about that. Or did you forget that you sucker punched her old man?"

"I apologized. Besides, it's not my fault Deputy Broman hates our family. At some point, he's gonna have to get over it because I love his daughter and eventually we'll find a way to be together no matter what. We're like Romeo and Juliet."

"Did you ever actually read *Romeo and Juliet*?" Marcus asked.

"I read most of it. We had to do a book report on it my sophomore year."

Violet felt another migraine coming on and pinched the bridge of her nose. In an effort to present her client in the most favorable light in court, she'd gone through MJ's high-school transcripts and was disappointed to see so many below-average grades and comments from his teachers about how smart he was but how rarely he turned in assignments.

"Yeah, well, if you'd ever finished something you'd started, you'd know that things don't work out too well for that particular pair of star-crossed lovers." Marcus tilted back the rest of his beer and swallowed before adding, "In fact, it rarely does."

Whoa. That second dig was definitely directed at her. Forgetting her earlier reassurance to Jordan and Jack about not hating their father, Violet narrowed her eyes at Marcus. "Do we really need all your extra judgments thrown in for dramatic flair?"

"What extra judgments?"

"Oh, you know, the dig about MJ not finishing what he starts. Then the bonus commentary about young love rarely working out."

He held up his open palms. "I was merely stating the facts. Romeo and Juliet were in love, and it didn't end so well. I'm sorry if that hits a little too close to home for you, Violet."

"Well, if we're going to state *facts*, then let's talk about how Romeo totally overreacted. If he had just been patient and thought things through instead of jumping to conclusions, Juliet would've gotten up and explained everything. But your boy had to act all rash and assume the worst and turn the whole thing into a tragedy."

"How do you know Romeo wasn't also dealing with Juliet's mom planting seeds of doubt in his head?" Marcus argued. "Telling him that her daughter was better off without him?"

"If that was the case, then he should've realized her mom didn't want them to be together in the first place," Violet countered. "The seeds of doubt should never have taken root."

"All I'm saying is that it might've been nice if she'd written him a note or something letting him know what was going on."

"She *did* write a note. How was she to know that he never got it?"

"Wait. Are we still talking about Romeo and Juliet?" Rider asked. "Freckles made me watch the movie once, but I fell asleep before it got to all of that."

"Yeah, this story sounds boring," Jack said while trying to balance his spoon on his nose. "Is it time for dessert yet?"

And just like that, Freckles retreated to the kitchen to serve up the banana cream pie to the kids. Sherilee followed to make sure her sister-in-law was only using the dairy-free whipped topping instead of real cream.

Apparently, nobody else wanted to listen to Marcus and Violet rehash the story of their breakup using euphemisms from a literary classic, either. The entire King family jumped at the chance to clear out of the dining room without bothering to make a single excuse for their abrupt exits.

Violet and Marcus remained in their seats across the table from each other, the tension between them having been stretched to their limits, but now sagging. Like a deflated party balloon.

"We never used to fight like this before." Marcus finally broke the silence. "It doesn't feel right to be at odds this way. But at the same time, I can't stop myself from getting sucked into even the slightest argument. I'm really sorry, Violet. I don't know what the hell I'm doing."

"Do you remember the first time you asked me out?" she shifted forward in her seat.

He tilted his head at her before staring up at the ceiling for several seconds. Finally, he shook his head. "I remember going to the movies a handful of times, and playing mini golf, and driving to Six Flags when we tried to set Duke up with your roommate from boarding school and he came out to us before we got on the first roller coaster. Oh, and that one time you talked me into taking you to the Justin Timberlake concert and caught me singing along to all the lyrics I pretended I didn't know. But I can't think of the first time."

"That's because you never did ask me out, Marcus. It just sort of happened, like it was a given that we were together. We never really had to work at having a relationship before." She sighed. "Every time I look at you, I see the boy you used to be. I mean, in a more manly body, but it's still you. Except it's not, because you're so different now. We both are so much more cynical, for good reason, which means being around you isn't as natural as it used to be. The problem is that my brain doesn't want to accept that, so my tongue lashes out."

His chest expanded, and even from a distance she could see his pupils dilate. "Maybe your tongue needs something else to keep it occupied?"

Adrenaline spiked through Violet, causing her to briefly calculate whether it would be faster to walk around the table or to just hurdle over the draped white linen tablecloth and crystal goblets to get into his arms.

Luckily, the sudden appearance of Jack and Jordan carrying two plates of pie into the dining room saved her from doing something she'd later regret.

Having been both an eighteen-year-old virgin and now a thirty-two-year-old experienced man, Marcus had never wanted a woman more than he wanted Violet Cortez-Hill. He was no longer an impulsive youth, though, and knew full well the potential consequences of allowing history to repeat itself.

Not that Marcus wanted to go down that road again. Especially not after the unwarranted lecture he'd gotten from Reed Nakamoto about not letting Violet sweet-talk him into anything. He'd purposely stayed away from her every time he'd seen her in town, just so that nobody could say something was going on between them.

Still, it was getting awfully hard to avoid the woman when they were living on the same damn ranch. Especially when his sons loved seeing her so often and his mom kept insisting on her torturous and chaotic family dinners. Plus, deep down, he didn't really want to avoid her. He wanted to go back to how things used to be. But that would never happen until they got everything off their chests.

On his way home from work Tuesday, he was driving past the main house and saw Violet walking from the stables in the direction of the pool house. The kids had told him all about her new office space and how they'd helped her decorate with their homemade art and trail finds. Oh, and some colorful beach towels to make her feel like she was back in sunny Texas. It sounded like she was already homesick.

Violet waved, so he slowed the cruiser and asked, "Have you seen the boys? My mom picked them up from school, but she isn't answering her cell phone."

"Mrs. King said she had some sort of meeting with Special Agent in Charge Simon in the conference room attached to the agents' bunkhouse. She asked me to watch the twins for a few minutes, and they wanted me to see their new horses."

Marcus put the SUV in Park and climbed out. "So they're in the stables?"

"Well, they were. But then Uncle Rider offered to take them out on the trail. I hope you don't mind that I didn't go with them, but I didn't have any suitable shoes or riding clothes, so I decided to stay back."

He glanced at her fitted black pants and suede fashion boots with the fur trim. Nobody was going to confuse her for a cattle hand, but he'd seen people climb into the saddle wearing a lot worse. Then a memory clicked into place. One of him taking a sixteen-year-old Violet out on her first ride. Marcus had stupidly wanted to show off one of their prime stallions, a young, spirited buck who, unfortunately, attempted to mount Violet's mare. While she was riding her.

But that was so long ago. Plus, she'd gone to an elite boarding school in Virginia with a world-famous equestrian program. Surely she couldn't be…

"Wait. Are you still afraid of horses?"

"I'm not *afraid* of them," she said, then lowered her voice as a gelding in the outside corral passed by. "It's just that they don't really like me all that much."

"How can an animal not like you?"

"I don't know. Maybe they sense my nervousness."

Marcus bit back a grin. "Have you ever gotten back in the saddle again?"

"Of course. When I was in college, I decided to conquer my fear once and for all. It was spring break, and a group of us went to Cancún. The resort had horseback riding on the beach, so I figured having a change of scenery wouldn't trigger my traumatic memory of that awkward day with Fabio."

Marcus winced. "Yeah, the name of the horse should've been my first clue that he wasn't ready for a leisurely trail ride."

"If it's any consolation, I chose a small, unassuming-looking horse named Gidget the second time around and she wasn't much better." Violet must've seen the confusion on his face because she held up a hand. "No, she didn't try to mount anything. She just thought she was a surfer and kept rushing into the waves and rolling around in the sand. Again with me on her back. So suffice it to say that horses are one of the few creatures who refuse to acknowledge my commanding presence."

Marcus allowed his eyes to wander down the snug fabric encasing her long legs. Violet certainly had a commanding presence that was becoming increasingly more difficult for him *not* to acknowledge.

"You know, Fabio's still here. He's an old man now and sired so many colts, we had to finally retire him. He's over in Shady Acres." Marcus put his arm over her shoulders to steer her away from the outer corrals. "Come on. I'll take you to see him, and you'll realize that he's not so threatening anymore."

"Shady Acres?" Violet angled her head sideways as she questioned him, but she didn't pull away.

"Yeah. You know, from the TV show *Golden Girls*? Finn loves to name the horses and the different wings of the stables after her favorite sitcoms. If I remember correctly, the horse you were riding that day was also named after a character in that show. Blanche. Which explains why Fabio couldn't stay away from her."

Violet let out a full-bodied laugh, and Marcus instinctively pulled her in tighter. This. This is what it used to feel like between them. They would playfully tease and crack jokes and walk completely in step with each other. Violet fit perfectly beside him.

In fact, he was tempted to take her the long way around the stables just so they could keep walking like this. But Finn had carved wooden signs above each row of stalls, and Rider believed in putting the older horses front and center so that nobody forgot how hard they'd once worked for the ranch. So Shady Acres was the first section they came across, and Fabio was in the third stall down.

"No way," Violet said when she saw the once-palomino-colored muzzle was speckled with gray. "This can't be him. What happened to his flowing golden mane?"

"Let's just say that, nowadays, he likes his food much more than he likes the ladies. He managed to get his head stuck in one of those self-feeding hay nets. His mane was all tangled up in the netting, so we had to buzz it off. It hasn't grown back yet."

"He certainly looks way less threatening now. Don't you, boy?"

"Here." Marcus pulled an apple-flavored oat biscuit out of his inside jacket pocket. "Give him this, and he will love you forever."

Violet wrinkled her nose. "You keep horse treats in your uniform pocket?"

"I'm a sheriff in a small ranching town. Half of my job consists of interacting with citizens who are either riding livestock, herding livestock or complaining about someone else's livestock. I've got dog treats in the other pocket. Now, hold your fingers out straight like this."

Violet's palm was stiff when he handed her the biscuit, and Marcus slid his hand under hers to coax her into relaxing. A zing of awareness shot through him at the feel of her warm skin. She must've felt it, too, because she shuddered delicately. Or maybe she was afraid of Fabio's protruding teeth coming her way.

"It's okay. Just hold yourself steady." Standing behind her, Marcus put his other hand on her waist so she'd know he was right there with her to intervene in case something happened.

But as expected, Fabio took the treat, smacked his lips as he chewed, then snorted in appreciation. Violet's body relaxed against Marcus, and he let his fingers splay around the curve above her hip, his thumb grazing along the soft, stretchy fabric toward her waistband.

"That wasn't so bad." She sighed, and it took him a second to realize she was talking about the horse.

Or maybe she wasn't.

The back of her neck was resting against his shoulder, so when she tilted her face to look at him, her smiling lips were inches from his. Marcus groaned before claiming her mouth with his own.

Unlike two weeks ago in his office, though, this kiss started out tentative and slow. As if neither one wanted to be the first to lose control.

But as their tongues explored deeper, his fingers followed suit, and soon his hand was nudging under the hem of her sweater. Violet gave a breathless moan and twisted so that she could face him, which only pressed their bodies closer together.

The unmistakable whirling of an engine sounded outside, and Violet pulled away slightly. Her breath was warm, and her voice was raspy as she whispered, "Is that the helicopter?"

"Probably." He moved his lips to her cheek and pressed light kisses along her jawline. After a daring paparazzo had chartered a local sight-seeing chopper to get some long-range aerial photos of Tessa, the Secret Service agents had been doing routine air patrols around the ranch twice a day.

When his mouth dipped lower to her neck, she threw her head back and moaned. Her fingers were stroking underneath the lined collar of his jacket, holding his head in place as she gave him full access to the tender spot where her pulse was beating out a frenzied tempo. Marcus was so intent on what he was doing, he barely heard her whisper, "What if someone catches us?"

"Come on, we can go in here." Marcus had noticed that the stall across from Fabio's was empty, and he pulled her inside. He rolled the solid wood sliding door closed, but that only hid them from the chest down.

There was a pile of straw in one corner that looked clean, and he steered her in that direction. "We're going to have to hunker down if we want to stay out of sight."

Violet's laugh was low and throaty as she sank into the pile as though it was a regal throne. "This reminds me of the time our families were both staying at Camp David for that Department of Defense conference, and we snuck out of our cabins and hid in the archery shed. Except you're a much better kisser now."

"That's because I remembered to take out my retainer this time." Marcus lowered himself over her, determined to prove how much better he was at everything. She eagerly embraced him, lifting her arms around his neck and pulling him closer. Her sweater rose, and he slid both of his palms higher, caressing the silky warmth of her bare skin until his hands were just below her breasts.

They were lying side by side, facing each other, and his arousal strained against his uniform pants as she pressed herself against him. Without breaking their kiss, Violet's fingers began to work at the heavy clasp of his leather duty belt.

But before she could get it undone, they heard voices entering the stables. Violet's eyes flew open, and she put a finger to her lips, as if Marcus needed the warning to stay quiet. He was rock hard, and there was straw sticking out of Violet's hair at all angles. Anyone who saw them would know exactly what they'd been up to.

The voices—at least three of them—grew closer. Violet whispered into his ear, "Do you think you can shift your weight back the other direction? Your gun is digging into my hip."

He responded through clenched teeth. "If I shift back to where I just was, it won't be my gun pressing into you."

Squeezing her eyes shut, she reminded him of Jack when he was a toddler and thought that if he couldn't see anyone around him, then nobody could see him, either. Marcus used his elbows to lift his torso enough to roll away but then froze at the rustling sound of the straw surrounding them.

"Shhh," she said. He didn't think it would be possible to make her blush more than she already was, but then he realized the rosy color spreading up her neck wasn't from embarrassment. It was whisker burn.

The voices were now right outside their row of stalls. He recognized the annoyance in his sister Tessa's tone before realizing who she was talking to. He slowly shifted to his knees so he could see out one of the slats.

Congressman Davis Townsend, better known as Congressman Smooth to the rest of their family members. Nobody understood what Tessa saw in the up-and-coming politician, who was clearly using her to get closer to the famous King name.

From the sound of things, the congressman was upset about all the media hype surrounding Tessa and Agent Wyatt, who was now standing by quietly as Tessa rejected Townsend's not-so-romantic proposal. Suddenly, the conversation turned angry.

"Together, we could've gone further than Roper King could ever have hoped," Townsend said, and Marcus's blood rang in his ears. Nobody was going to disrespect his dead father on the very ranch that his legacy had been built upon.

Marcus started to rise, but Violet tugged on his hand.

Her whisper was hushed yet firm. "Let your sister handle this, Marcus. She's been bottling everything in lately and needs to speak her piece."

As if to prove Violet right, Tessa finally snapped. "My dad got exactly as far as he wanted, Davis. And, for the record, he hated people who needed to use someone else to get ahead."

"I was never using you. At least, not any more than you were using me."

"How did I use you?" his sister asked. She was a political analyst with a prime-time show interviewing some of the most powerful world leaders. At least she was finally acting like herself again. "I'd love to hear this."

"Tessa King had the reputation of being a cold, cutthroat bitch before I came along. I humanized you. Being in a relationship with me made you at least seem like a real woman."

Marcus was on his knees and ready to spring into action, his fists clenching at the insult to his sister. He didn't think he could stay silent much longer.

"I think you need to leave now, Congressman Townsend," Tessa said.

"But your mother invited me—"

"Miss King has politely asked you to leave," Agent Wyatt interrupted in a direct, deliberate voice. "I'll have the command center radio your pilot so you can fly out of here on your own accord."

"Or else what?" Davis's chin lifted.

Oh, hell no.

Wyatt was more than trained to handle the situation on his own, but Marcus was a law-enforcement officer as much as he was a brother. Challenging a sitting member of the House of Representatives would be a risky career move for the agent, who'd already gone above and beyond his duty keeping Tessa safe.

Plus, Marcus was not about to let some sanctimonious prick stay on his family's property a second longer. He was out of the stall before Violet could pull him back.

It took every ounce of training for Marcus to keep himself reined in as he purposefully approached the congressman. "Or else we can escort you from the premises in the back of the Ridgecrest County Sheriff's unit."

She should've stayed put, but Violet stepped to his side, risking her own reputation by backing him up. Marcus's chest swelled with pride and appreciation.

Three pairs of eyes darted back and forth between them. Instead of giving anyone the chance to question what he and Violet were doing there in the first place, Marcus continued, "Before you make your choice, it's only fair to warn you that the back seat of my squad car doesn't have tinted windows. I'm sure the press stationed outside the gates would love to get a great shot of you back there."

Townsend took a step back in retreat and flashed his ridiculous fake grin. "We're good. I was just leaving."

The congressman turned to go, and Marcus followed to make sure the man actually left the premises, not just the stables. Violet kept up with Marcus's determined strides, and right before they exited into the daylight, she slipped her palm into his, gave his hand a firm squeeze and then dropped her arm to her side before they went outside.

He wished he could've glanced in her direction to

see what she was thinking, but he had to keep his eyes trained on the back of Townsend's head.

Initially, he thought the hand squeeze was a silent promise to finish what they'd started back in the horse stall. But then, in his peripheral vision, he spotted his sons and Uncle Rider cooling down their horses in the outer corral.

More than likely, she was simply giving him the warning that they now had an audience. Playtime was over, and they were back to being adversaries.

CHAPTER EIGHT

VIOLET FINISHED HER list of exhibits for the pretrial hearing and closed her laptop before deciding to take a long run to clear her brain. She'd tried to put Marcus out of her mind for the past few days but couldn't stop thinking about how close they'd actually come to both literally and figuratively having a roll in the hay.

She especially couldn't stop thinking about how his initial response had been to protect Tessa during his sister's argument with her ex-boyfriend. Even with emotions running high, Marcus had been extremely professional in the way he'd handled the trespassing congressman, considering the fact that Violet herself had wanted to punch the jerk.

Marcus truly did have his family's best interests at heart, and it was becoming increasingly apparent that he just wanted to protect his siblings. All of them. Including MJ. Now if she could only convince him that the way he was going about looking out for his brother would surely backfire.

She passed an old tree with a faded carving in its trunk along with an arrow. *RKx2 was here.* Finn had explained to Violet that as boys, their father and Uncle Rider used to carry pocketknives and scratch their initials into trees along their favorite trails so that they would know where they'd already explored.

"*RKx2* is a lot shorter to write than spelling out *Rider King and Roper King* every time," Finn had said. "If you follow the arrows below the initials, they'll always point you toward the stables so you can't get lost. They were adults, though, when they purchased the western acres. So if you ever end up on that side of the ranch, you better have a GPS because there aren't any RKx2 markers over there."

Every time Violet went for a run, she always tried to follow the marked trees on the east side, since it gave her a better sense of direction. However, seeing the carving today gave her an unexpected sense of comfort, as well. Marcus's father had been one of the smartest and most diplomatic men she'd ever known. Sure, he was a politician and could smooth talk with the best of them. Yet, he always knew the right thing to say and exactly when to say it.

"Hey, Mr. King, if you're up there listening, maybe you could give me the right words to talk to your oldest son." She felt silly making the request aloud. Mostly because her job was to come up with convincing arguments. So she added, "Preferably at a time when he's willing to actually listen."

She was only a mile into her run when she passed the small road leading to the family cemetery and saw Marcus's patrol vehicle parked at the top. Her heart skipped several beats. She hadn't expected the opportunity to talk to the man to pop up this soon.

Violet paused, jogging in place. She shouldn't interrupt him while he was visiting his father's grave. But then again, she *had* asked Roper King himself for a sign. What should she say, though?

After arguing with herself for several minutes, she finally decided to continue her run, taking the two-mile loop path skirting a cluster of trees. She told herself that if Marcus was still there when she returned this way, then she would approach him.

Violet wasn't the fastest runner to begin with, and despite slowing her pace, his vehicle was still there when she finally made it back to the crossroad. Ugh. Even though she'd yet to come up with the right words, she was going to have to say something. Otherwise, she'd regret wasting the opportunity and then spend the rest of the day kicking herself for not having the courage.

And Violet didn't want any more regrets when it came to Marcus King.

Rolling her shoulders a few times before walking through the gated path, she expected to find him standing in front of the newest—and biggest—granite headstone in the cemetery. When she realized he was standing in front of his wife's headstone, though, Violet froze before trying to quietly backtrack her steps.

Unfortunately, Marcus had already turned his head and spotted her.

She lifted her hand in a wave before realizing that maybe that wasn't the most appropriate greeting under the circumstances. "I didn't want to interrupt you. I was just hoping to catch you..." *Not alone. Don't say alone.* "I should've waited until you were done with your visit."

"I was pretty much done." Marcus rocked back on his boot heels. "What's up?"

Violet should've brought up the subject of MJ, but instead said the first thing that popped into her head. "Tell me about her."

Judging from the surprised expression that crossed his face, he clearly hadn't been expecting her to say that. "About Brie?"

Damn it. Maybe that was out of bounds. "I mean, only if it's not weird."

"Everything has been weird since you arrived, Vi. So why would we want to go back to normal now?" Marcus let out a deep breath and shoved his hands in his pockets. "I might as well tell you all about her since she knew all about you."

Now it was her turn to be surprised. "You talked to your wife about me?"

"Yeah. I used to talk to her about everything. I mean, not initially. We'd gone to high school together but never really hung out back then. According to her, she had a crush on me, but everyone knew I was in love with someone else who lived far away." Marcus obviously meant Violet, but she didn't want to make this conversation about her, so she nodded, and he continued, "I was a mess after I got out of boot camp. I had a one-week leave before starting my advanced individual training school, so I came back to the ranch to get over…whatever had gone wrong between us. Duke was playing in some garage band back then with Dahlia's ex-husband and talked me into coming to one of their gigs. Brie was there, and she came over to say hi. I ended up crying in my beer the whole night and telling her all about us. Or at least the version of us that I knew at the time."

Violet didn't like the feeling of jealousy blossoming inside her. Not because Marcus had shared the details of their relationship with another woman, but because Violet hadn't been able to do the same. Her mother had insisted that they needed to keep the whole thing quiet so that it didn't affect her senate reelection bid. The only other person who'd known was her dad, but he had a tendency to revert to baseball jargon during emotionally vulnerable moments. And nobody wanted to hear "Sometimes you hit a few foul balls before you get that grand slam" after a bad breakup.

Marcus rubbed the back of his neck as he continued, "Brie asked if I wanted to keep in contact while I was at AIT and assured me that she wasn't interested in some sort of rebound fling. I guess she thought I seemed like I could use a friend. Mostly we just followed each other on social media and would text every once in a while. Then, when I went on deployment, she started sending me care packages and little notes and funny cards. I never really stopped thinking about you, but talking to Brie helped keep my mind off what I'd lost. When my four years was up, I came back to Wyoming. I didn't think I'd ever be able to fall in love again after you, but she won me over. Being with her just seemed…easy."

Of course it was easy. Brie didn't have a famous mother trying to keep them physically and emotionally separated. Violet glanced at the headstone, then asked, "Do the twins get to see her family often?"

"Actually, she was raised by her grandparents. Her grandma passed away right after high school, and her grandpa moved into an assisted-living place out in Cheyenne before we started dating."

"Oh, that must've been hard for her. To feel so alone at such a young age."

Marcus nodded. "Probably, but Brie never showed

it. She was one of those glass-half-full kind of people. Always had a smile on her face, never said anything bad about anyone. My mom joked that she would've been the perfect politician's wife, but Brie never had those kinds of ambitions. Which was good, because I didn't, either. She seemed happy being married to a small-town cop and loved being a mom."

Violet heard the quiet part out loud. Brie didn't bring along the baggage of an interfering family. Unlike Violet, who had a controlling mother and who—in Marcus's mind at the time—had chosen her career over their children.

He'd fallen in love with Violet's exact opposite. She'd seen a few framed pictures of Brie and Marcus back at the main house, and even appearance wise, the women had completely different coloring and dressed very differently. A shiver of rejection made its way down Violet's spine.

"I really am sorry for your loss, Marcus. That must've been so hard on you and the boys." She bit her lip. "They must really miss their mom."

His jaw was rigid as he gave a stiff nod.

"And again, I'm sorry for interrupting your visit."

"More like a therapy session." He lifted his face to the sun before shrugging. "I'd been avoiding this place for years before my dad died. In fact, I was dreading his funeral for this very reason. I hated the reminder of what I'd lost. What my sons had lost. But that day at the graveside service, I saw her headstone without so much as a flower on it, and it made me realize that I shouldn't have allowed my hurt to keep me away. Since you've gotten here... I don't know how to explain it, but it just felt like I should be filling her in on everything going on. The boys, MJ, you. She was a good wife and mother, but more than anything else, she was always a great listener. A great partner."

Violet inhaled deeply, unsure of this raw emotion gnawing at something inside of her. It wasn't quite jealousy, despite the fact that she clearly would never be able to fill Brie's shoes when it came to being a loving mother or a doting wife—not that anyone was trying to compete with the memory of a dead woman. Nor was it the implication that Violet's sudden appearance had reopened all of Marcus's old wounds and talking to Brie was again the one thing that seemed to bring him any sort of comfort.

Rather, hearing about Marcus's wife and how much he'd loved her made Violet feel more remorse than anything else. Like she was causing him to be disloyal in some way to Brie. She never would have kissed him knowing he wasn't ready to move on.

She glanced at the freshly turned earth of Roper King's gravesite. There were two flower arrangements which were too fresh to have been leftover from the funeral weeks ago. There was also a collection of little trinkets lined up along the granite ledge, such as a set of gold pilot wings, a thirty-year sobriety chip and a small US flag in a weighted stand.

But the item that caught her attention was a freshly cut log leaning against the headstone with *RKx2* carved into the bark. Perhaps Rider had simply stopped by to visit his brother. Or maybe it was another sign from Marcus's father. It didn't matter, though. There was no way she was going to talk to him about MJ right now. In fact, maybe she'd misread the earlier signs, and Roper

King was actually trying to tell her to return to the main house and give his son space.

"Can I give you a ride back down the hill?" Marcus asked.

"No, thanks." She forced a polite smile. "I still need to finish my run."

Marcus had his own demons and hardships he needed to face without her chiming in with her two cents every time they disagreed. It was becoming increasingly clear that it wasn't Violet's place to be his voice of reason. She'd forfeited that opportunity to another woman long ago.

"You're not staying for dinner?" Aunt Freckles asked Marcus the following Friday evening when he dropped off the twins at the main house for the weekly meal that was becoming a bit too frequent. It was also a bit too tension-filled—even by King standards—now that peacekeeping Duke had returned to duty on his aircraft carrier.

"Nah. I'm covering a shift for one of my deputies who needed the night off."

"What a coincidence." Freckles pursed her coral-painted lips. "Violet won't be here for dinner, either."

"Where's she going?" Marcus asked more suspiciously than he'd intended.

"I didn't ask, seeing as how she's a grown woman and it's not my business." Freckles challenged Marcus with an impish grin.

"Is that your way of telling me that it's not my business, either?"

"Of course it's his business," Sherilee King said sarcastically as she came striding into the kitchen. "Didn't you hear, Freckles? My son is the sheriff of the whole entire county and thinks he's in charge of everything and everyone in his jurisdiction."

Marcus didn't give his mother the satisfaction of rolling his eyes. He was not going to engage in the same old argument that neither of them would win.

"Now, Sherilee, don't give the boy such a hard time for doing his job."

"Thank you, Aunt Freckles." Finally someone was on his side.

But before he could relish in his triumph, Freckles pointed an oven mitt in his direction. "And *you* don't give your mama a hard time for doing *her* job and protecting her babies."

"You mean *baby*, singular," Marcus corrected. "Only one of her young cubs is getting the full mama-bear protection, and it certainly isn't me."

"Oh, I'm protecting you, Marcus." His mother reached for the hunk of cheddar Freckles had been shredding for her baked macaroni and cheese casserole. His mom only ate dairy products when she was stressed. Or when she was annoyed. Or when she thought no one was watching. She chewed before adding, "You're just too stubborn to see it."

"You're protecting me?" Marcus snorted. "How? By undermining my job and my role in the community? Or by installing my ex-girlfriend in our family home to argue with me at every turn?"

"You think I'm enjoying all the increased tension around here?" His mom slapped a manicured hand on the counter. "Every time I turn around, you're squabbling with Violet, or Freckles is bickering with Rider.

Even my sweet Duke was getting testy on some secret phone call before he left. And then there's troublemaking Finn egging everyone on like she's an announcer at the state rodeo. My husband—the love of my life—just died, yet my home is filled with so much damn chaos and shouting I can't even hear myself think."

"You eat any more of my cheese, Sherilee, and you're going to have plenty of time alone to think. In the bathroom." Freckles took the wedge of decimated cheddar away from her sister-in-law. "Besides, Rider and I don't bicker. We engage in verbal wrestling, which isn't nearly as fun as our mattress wrestling—"

"Really, Freckles?" His mom thankfully interrupted his aunt. "Do you have to be so graphic *all* the time?"

"Stop being such a prude, Sher. You have six kids, so it's not like you didn't have a little fun in your marriage, too."

"Yeah, but I'm not going around bragging about it to the whole damn world."

"Give it a rest, you two!" Marcus suddenly went from defending himself to refereeing a forty-year dispute between the biggest verbal combatants in the entire King family. He lifted his brow at his mother. "And you accuse everyone else of arguing?"

"This isn't an argument," his mom countered. "This is a discussion. Right, Freckles?"

"Yep. Just a little conversation to clear the air."

"Oh, so now you guys decide to agree?" This time, Marcus did give in and rolled his eyes. "To gang up on me?"

"We're not ganging up on you, darlin'." Freckles tsked. "We're demonstrating healthy dialogue. Showing you there's nothing wrong with voicing your feelings and concerns."

"I talk about my feelings," he said, thinking of his trip to the cemetery the other day. It was the second visit he'd made to see Brie since his father's funeral, which was incredible progress considering he previously hadn't been there in over five years.

This time, his mother was the one rolling her eyes. "Perhaps you should try talking to someone who is alive, Marcus. Someone who will actually give you the advice you don't think you need."

"Ouch," Freckles said as she tossed some shredded cheese into a simmering pot. "That was harsh, Sherilee. True. But harsh. No wonder the kids get so frustrated with you."

"Oh, so now *you're* the expert on *my* children?" His mother and aunt continued their so-called healthy dialogue with such intensity they didn't seem to notice Marcus slipping out the back door.

His head was throbbing, his stomach was buzzing with hunger, and now he was working a night shift to avoid having dinner with a woman who wasn't even going to be there, anyway.

No. He wasn't avoiding Violet. He was just… Hell. He didn't know what he was doing. Marcus stared at his tired reflection in his rearview mirror. Talking to Brie had always used to make him feel better, but maybe his mom was right. There was a difference between venting and actually receiving feedback.

He'd told Violet that Brie had been a great listener, which was true. But his wife had also never talked about what was bothering her. She avoided conflict whenever possible and rarely challenged him with a differing opinion. Or told him something he hadn't wanted to hear. Being with Brie had been almost too easy at times. Too simple.

Yet nothing was simple anymore.

He'd always used to talk to Violet when they were younger, but it might be too late to go back to being friends now. Especially after their recent kisses proved that he couldn't keep his hands to himself whenever he was around her. That left his only options as fighting with her or avoiding her.

Unless she was avoiding him first.

Why wasn't she having dinner with his family tonight? He pulled out his phone to text her before realizing he didn't have her number.

Before he could give it another thought, a call came over his handheld radio. "Be advised we have reports of an altercation taking place at Teton Ridge High School."

It could be worse, he told himself as he drove toward the highway. Nothing could top last year when the varsity basketball team was in the playoffs and Marcus had to arrest his former math teacher for streaking across the court during the fourth quarter wearing nothing but blue and gold body paint.

Then the radio crackled to life again and the dispatcher added, "Make that two altercations. And some possible vandalism. All units, please respond."

Crap. Marcus switched on his siren before advising dispatch he was en route. At least this was a public-disturbance call that didn't involve anyone from his family.

If Violet had to sit through one more antagonistic family meal with Marcus, she'd probably scream loud enough to shatter the crystal chandelier in the formal dining room of the main house. Last Friday, Connor Remington, the new owner of one of the neighboring ranches, had come to dinner and had spent the whole evening exchanging flirtatious glances with Dahlia. But the only glances Violet received across the table that night were seething glares from Marcus, who had just found out that she'd filed a motion for discovery to have his department's Breathalyzer tested for accuracy. Apparently, he didn't appreciate the insinuation that his equipment wasn't maintained properly.

Not that Violet was an entirely innocent party when it came to their petty bickering. She'd known the Breathalyzer results were likely accurate because MJ had admitted to her that he'd had quite a bit to drink before getting arrested. Still, she wouldn't be doing her job if she didn't pursue every possible avenue of defense. Besides, if she was too busy fighting with Marcus, then she didn't have time to think about how damn attractive he always looked in his sheriff's uniform.

At least that had been her initial strategy dealing with her ex-boyfriend who was making her feel all sorts of things she probably shouldn't.

Now, though, her strategy was to escape him altogether by hiding out in an overheated and overcrowded high-school gymnasium, watching a high-stakes basketball game she had absolutely zero interest in.

She couldn't even claim that she was only there hoping to find some character witnesses for MJ's case. When Roper King had become vice president, MJ had been forced to move to Washington, DC, and attend a private school, where he hadn't exactly excelled.

No, Violet had come to the game because the only thing to do on a cold Friday night in Teton Ridge was to get a drink at Big Millie's or go to a high-school sporting event. And since she'd already been to the saloon, she'd thought she'd give basketball a try. Plus, she might run into Reed Nakamoto or Judge Calhoun at the game, which would hopefully give them the impression that she wasn't a total outsider from the big city.

It wasn't until halftime that Violet finally saw Judge Calhoun. She was behind him in line at the concession stand, and one of the parents wearing a Fling Rock High School sweatshirt dropped a tray of nachos on the judge's brand-new white high-top sneakers. Some heated words were exchanged, and the next thing Violet knew, punches were flying and she and another woman were pulling the judge from a brawl he'd caused by his overreaction to a few accidental drops of nacho cheese.

Several other parents stepped in to break up the fight, but the sound of approaching sirens could already be heard from the parking lot. The small concession area of the gym filled as the bleachers cleared and everyone came to see what was going on. There was a lot of finger-pointing over who'd thrown the first punch, and eventually Violet found her way to a nearby bench to try to wipe off the ketchup that had gotten all over her suede boot when someone lost their hot dog in the altercation.

"That's the woman who saw everything go down, Sheriff," Violet heard a woman say, and her stomach dropped.

No, she thought to herself, refusing to look up so her eyes wouldn't confirm what her gut was already telling her. He wasn't supposed to be on duty. He was supposed to be having dinner at the Twin Kings. But when she saw the black utility boots approach her, Violet knew exactly whose legs would be attached to them.

Marcus.

"Oh, hey," Violet said a little too nonchalantly. She crumpled the red-stained napkins in her hand as she stood to meet him.

"Are you bleeding?" he asked, concern evident in his blue eyes as he searched her face for injuries. Her heart did a little flip. She liked this compassionate and nonaccusatory version of Marcus.

"No. It's just ketchup. The lady in line behind me got drenched with orange soda, so I'll consider myself lucky."

Marcus scrubbed at the lower half of his face, but not before she saw the grin he was trying to hold back. When he got his expression under control, he said, "I wish you'd told me that you were coming to the game tonight. I would've warned you to avoid the concession stand and the restrooms during halftime."

"The restrooms, too, huh?"

"Oh, yeah. People take their high-school games pretty seriously around here. Broman is currently dealing with the fight in the ladies' room, and I've got two other deputies searching for some seniors in the parking lot who were letting the air out of the tires on any car with a Fling Rock bumper sticker."

"Well, kids can pull stupid pranks when school pride is on the line."

"No, not seniors in high school. Senior citizens." Marcus bit his lower lip, probably to keep himself from joining Violet as she snorted with repressed laughter. He was the sheriff and had to maintain at least the image of being in control of an otherwise chaotic situation. "I knew I shouldn't have volunteered to cover this shift tonight."

So she'd been right, and he wasn't supposed to be on duty. Not that she was trying to keep track of his schedule. "At least you can't blame me for adding to your troubles this time."

"No, but I heard you were at the center of it. Mrs. Singh said you two broke up the fight in here."

"Who?" Violet craned her neck to see around his shoulder.

Marcus pointed to the woman who'd helped Violet hold the judge back. She was using a napkin to blot orange soda off a letterman's jacket embroidered with a beaker and the words *TRHS Science Squad*. "Mrs. Singh. The chemistry teacher."

"Oh, right." The crowd was finally dispersing, and it sounded like the second half of the game was beginning. Violet squinted at the handful of people watching them, including the scowling parent from the rival high school who'd spilled the nachos on the judge. "What happened to Judge Calhoun?"

"He should be in the back of a patrol car by now."

"No!" Violet's head jerked back to face him. "Did you seriously arrest a judge, Marcus? The one presiding over your brother's case?"

Marcus rested his hands on his duty belt. "Did he throw the first punch?"

"Yes."

"Violet, I told you that I do things by the book, and nobody in this town gets special treatment. It'll be up to the prosecutor's office to decide if they want to file charges."

What had been an almost comical situation had

suddenly taken a very serious turn. A dull ache formed above Violet's temple as she considered the possible ramifications of this. "But there are only two circuit judges for the entire county. And one already recused herself from the case. If Calhoun gets removed from the bench due to judicial misconduct, it could take months for the state to appoint someone else to hear MJ's case."

Marcus rolled his shoulders dismissively. "Then it takes months."

She searched his eyes for some clue that he was hoping to delay the trial to get her to give up and return to Dallas. "I'm not leaving just because the trial date gets extended. Do you seriously think you can play nice and get along with me for that long?"

"Probably not," he admitted. "But it's out of my hands. I have to do my job, Vi. Even if the end result means prolonging all this damn sexual tension between us."

A tingle went down the back of her neck. At least he was acknowledging that he was having the same reaction to her presence as she was having to his. Really, she should be relieved that, as the sheriff, he was acting impartially and beyond reproach. Judge Calhoun really should be held to the same standards as everyone else in town.

Violet gave herself a little shake. "Fine. Do you need my witness statement?"

"Actually, do you think you can come to the station and give it? We're short staffed, and I don't want our volunteer Rod processing Calhoun's book and release all by himself."

Violet's stomach fluttered in hunger. In her efforts to avoid him at the family meal, Violet had missed out on one of Freckles's home-cooked dinners only to get herself caught up in the middle of some small-town basketball rivalry. Now she was starving, and she was going to end up spending the bulk of her evening with the very guy she'd been trying to dodge in the first place.

"Sure," she said before she could overthink it. "But I'm going to stop at Biscuit Betty's on my way there. I haven't had dinner yet, and suddenly nachos and hot dogs don't sound all that appetizing."

"Perfect. Will you grab me a chicken biscuit while you're there? Maybe a side of potato wedges?"

She tilted her head, not sure if she was quite ready to play *that* nicely yet. "Will you stop pretending to ignore me whenever we're in public?"

"I'm not ignoring you." His voice grew low and seductive as he stepped closer to her. "In fact, I'm very aware of your presence, and it takes every scrap of control I possess not to pull you into my arms and kiss you senseless every damn time I see you. But we both have opposing jobs to do, and people expect us to stay in our lanes and not get too chummy."

She stared at him in shock. "So all those times you start arguments with me, that's just for show?"

"Don't get me wrong, I like arguing with you." He smiled. "I just like kissing you more."

Marcus winked at her before walking away to interview the remaining witnesses. Violet's stomach went from rumbling to doing somersaults. If she were being honest with herself, she enjoyed kissing him more than arguing with him, as well.

But since he'd pointed out that they were supposed to be at odds, she couldn't very well bring him dinner without raising a few eyebrows. So when she stopped at Biscuit Betty's on her way to the station, she ordered enough food to feed the dispatcher, the volunteer and all the deputies on duty. Then she thought about Judge Calhoun and anyone else the Ridgecrest County Sheriff's Department might've arrested at the game and doubled her order.

When the young server gave her the total amount due, Violet smiled and said, "Sheriff King wanted you to put it all on his tab."

CHAPTER NINE

THERE WAS NO kissing for Marcus last Friday night after the brawl at the high-school basketball game. Judge Calhoun had been booked at the station and then released, but instead of going home, the man had sat at the front desk with Rod discussing the difficulty of getting stains out of white leather sneakers. Of course, Calhoun was talking about cheese sauce, and Rod was talking about blood splatters. But at least there were no hard feelings from the judge regarding his arrest. In fact, he said he had been planning to retire soon anyway so he could fulfill his lifelong dream of attending a game at every NBA stadium in the country.

Violet delivered the chicken biscuit as promised—as well as enough food to feed everyone who'd ever worked within a two block radius of the county buildings—and then gave her statement. But Marcus's deputies had processed five other arrests from that night, a record for his small department, and he hadn't been able to talk to her alone.

He got his bill from Biscuit Betty's the following day and nearly laughed at his ex-girlfriend's audacity. No wonder two of the people they'd brought in had jokingly asked Violet to be their attorney. He had no idea if she'd agreed to represent them, but she was certainly busy doing something, because he'd seen her at least three times that week filing documents at the courthouse.

It wasn't until the following Friday that Marcus finally got a chance to talk to Violet alone. Or at least not in front of the entire town.

His sister Tessa had been on the Junior Olympic diving team when an accident in high school had derailed her career. Agent Wyatt had secured the use of the heated indoor pool every day this week after the rec center closed to the public so that Tessa could practice diving again. Their mom and Aunt Freckles had insisted on turning this week's family dinner into a pool party and picked up a dozen pizzas from the Pepperoni Stampede in town.

"I thought you weren't going to ignore me in public anymore," Violet said to Marcus after the boys jumped into the water.

"I'm not ignoring you," he replied, still in his uniform. He'd stopped by the cabin after work to grab the boys' swimsuits but didn't want to make them wait while he changed. "I'm standing right here talking to you. In a public building."

"Technically. But you know that I'm referring to the four times you saw me at the courthouse this past week."

"I only saw you three times," he corrected before realizing he'd walked right into her trap.

One corner of her mouth turned up in a gotcha grin. "So then, why didn't you speak to me?"

"About what?" He lifted his eyebrow with a challenge of his own. "Did you want me to discuss the red lipstick you were wearing on Tuesday morning and how it's my absolute favorite color on you? Or perhaps we could've talked about the high heels you were wearing on Wednesday afternoon and how they made your legs look a million inches long? Maybe I should've complimented your windblown hair yesterday? Told you that it reminded me of the time I pulled it out of all those bobby pins at your homecoming dance right before we—"

She shoved a half-eaten slice of Hawaiian pizza into his mouth to keep him from saying anything else in front of the kids, who were splashing around in the shallow end. "Ew, I hate pineapple on pizza."

"I know." She wiped her hands on a napkin as they stood shoulder to shoulder. "So the only thing you can think of talking to me about when you see me in town is my appearance?"

Marcus finished chewing before replying, "It's not the *only* thing. But it was either that or ask you whether you had agreed to represent the same people my deputies had just arrested the previous weekend. I figured the first topic would get you all heated and aroused, and the second would get you all heated and pissed off. As much as I like to see you all hot and bothered, I figured it was best to not say anything when there were so many people around."

"You were right about the second, but not about the first. Both topics would've been condescending with zero chance of arousal."

"Really?" he asked, trying to get her to make eye contact with him. When she wouldn't, he smiled to himself. "Then why are you aroused right now?"

Violet carefully studied something off in the distance, refusing to give him so much as a side-eye. "Who says I am?"

"Your neck is all flushed, and your cheeks are getting rosy."

She swiped the back of her hand across her face, as though she could wipe away her telltale blush. "It's just warm in here. There's not much air circulation."

She'd shed her tailored suit jacket earlier, and he tilted his own head forward, purposely dropping his gaze to her breasts. Or more specifically, to her hardened nipples, which were perfectly outlined under the thin fabric of her silky white blouse. He waited for her to notice the subject of his gaze, then lowered his mouth closer to her ear and whispered, "That usually only happens when you're cold. Or when you're aroused."

She gasped and quickly crossed her arms over her chest.

"Hey, you asked." He smiled innocently then took another bite of pizza. Dang. He forgot about the pineapple. He tossed the piece into a nearby trash.

When he returned to where she was standing, she was the one smiling innocently. "For the record, I *did* agree to represent two of the people you guys arrested last week."

"So you're staying in town longer?"

"We'll see. Judge Calhoun will likely plead guilty to a lesser charge because he's anxious to avoid trial and start his retirement trip."

"Are you kidding me? You agreed to represent Calhoun?"

"Yes. But I charged him a notably high retainer. The other client I'm representing pro bono."

"Who's that?" Marcus asked, yet he had a feeling he already knew the answer.

"Rose Roosevelt."

Marcus smacked his palm to his forehead. "The woman who accosted the ref in the locker room after the game?"

"No, the concerned mom who followed the referee off the court to explain that his bad call was going to affect her son's stats, which would in turn affect his chances of earning a much-needed college scholarship."

"Violet. Rose's son plays second-string center and can't block a shot without fouling someone. Jumping on the referee's back and trying to put him in a choke hold isn't going to get the kid a college scholarship."

"Marcus, she's a single mom."

"Who committed an assault and battery."

"Allegedly," Violet corrected him.

Marcus rolled his eyes. "So are you taking the case because you feel sorry for her? Or are you doing it just to have something else to argue about with me?"

"You know—" Violet made a tsking sound before shaking her head "—arguing with you really isn't as enthralling for me as you seem to believe it is."

"Then why do you keep coming up with new ways to do it?" he asked.

"Have you ever stopped to think that maybe you're just spoiling for a fight?" she replied. But before he could reply, Jack interrupted them.

"Hey, Violet, watch this!" his son shouted before he did a cannonball into the water.

"That was great." She smiled and gave a little clap, which only encouraged Jack to want to show off more daring tricks. After each one, the boy would look to her for more applause.

"Hey, Violet." Jordan bounced up and down on his toes. "I'm trying to figure out how much lung capacity I got. Time me to see how long I can hold my breath."

Marcus and Violet stood side by side a foot away from the pool's edge. There was a huge clock on the opposite wall, but Violet kept glancing at her wristwatch, giving Marcus the impression that she was counting down the seconds until she could politely leave.

"Do you want to come swimming with us, Violet?" Jordan asked when he emerged from the water thirty seconds later. "I watched a video on how to do CPR so I can save you if you start drowning."

"Well, that's very reassuring, Jordan, but I didn't bring a swimsuit."

Jack lifted his goggles. "You could borrow one from Aunt Tessa or Aunt Finn."

Great. Marcus could barely take his eyes off Violet when she was wearing business attire. If she put on a bathing suit, everyone in this rec center would be watching him to see his reaction. In fact, his mom and aunt were all the way on the other side of the pool, making no secret of their interest in his and Violet's current interaction. He knew she didn't have the heart to tell either of his sons no, so he spoke up. "Hey, buddy, Violet would rather hang out up here on the deck and watch you guys play."

Both boys pouted, their little shoulders sagging in defeat. Violet, who clearly wasn't used to telling children no, whipped her head in Marcus's direction. "How do you know what I'd rather do?"

He pivoted as he stepped in front of her, blocking

his sons from witnessing yet another one of their disagreements. Facing her, he whispered, "Really, Vi? I'm
trying to get you off the hook here."

"I don't need you to get me off any hooks, Marcus.
You don't get to decide what I do, and you certainly
don't get to speak on my behalf."

"Oh, come on." He put both of his hands on top of
his head as he lifted his face to the ceiling in frustration. "This is a prime example of you once again finding
some bogus reason to argue with me. If you had wanted
to go swimming, then you clearly would've brought a
bathing suit."

"Hmm. Maybe you're right." Violet took a step closer
to him and slowly lifted her hands to his shoulders, letting her palms gently slide down to his chest. "And if
you *hadn't* wanted to go swimming, then clearly you
wouldn't have acted like such an overbearing ass."

The next thing Marcus knew, he was falling backward with too much force to regain his balance. He
heard the powerful splash before feeling the heavily
chlorinated water surround him and pull him below
the surface. Luckily, he was in the shallow end and was
able to quickly find his footing and stand up. Unluck-
ily, he was still dressed in his full uniform, heavy boots
and duty belt full of gear, including his semiautomatic
handgun and full ammo cartridges.

When he shook the water out of his ears, he could
hear the twins and his niece Amelia shrieking with
laughter. Or maybe that was Finn and Aunt Freckles.
The acoustics of the tiled walls caused all the howling
and cheering to echo around him.

Violet remained at the edge of the pool, humor re-
flecting in her eyes as she stared down her nose at him,

the upward tilt of her mouth smugly reassuring him that she wasn't the least bit sorry that she'd shoved him into the pool. She must've seen him lift his hand to the surface because she quickly jumped back before he could send a retaliatory spray of water in her direction. She even had the nerve to giggle at her superior reflexes before taunting him. "You missed."

"You're safe for now," Marcus promised her. "Just remember. Revenge is a dish best served cold."

Violet watched him intently, though, clearly not trusting him to not come after her for payback. He took advantage of her rapt attention by unzipping his soaked jacket and pitching it onto the deck. Next, he worked on the buttons of his uniform shirt, maintaining eye contact with Violet as he shrugged out of the waterlogged fabric and threw it on top of the jacket. He had to peel his white T-shirt off his torso and over his head before adding it to the pile, but his effort was rewarded when he saw Violet's tongue dart out as she licked her lips.

Good. Now she might understand why he'd been so reluctant to approach her in town when he already couldn't take his eyes off her. Satisfaction, and maybe a touch of pride, caused his chest muscles to stand at attention. When she jerked her eyes up to meet his, he gave her a satisfied wink.

Then, because he hadn't gone swimming with his sons since summer break, he turned to the kids and asked, "Who wants to play rocket launcher?"

"So now that Tessa's gone back to Washington, DC—" Freckles stood in front of Violet holding a small tray with a chicken-pesto sandwich, pasta salad and a slice of homemade strawberry-rhubarb pie "—Roper's old study is available for use. It might be a little more comfortable than this."

Violet moved aside some papers on the wicker patio table so Marcus's aunt could put down the tray. "Actually, I'm pretty comfortable out here in the pool house. But I'll gladly move into the study if that makes it easier for you to bring me lunch. Your pie is still the best, Freckles."

Violet had long ago given up on trying to convince the older woman that she didn't need to provide lunch every day, let alone bring it across the yard and to the pool house. It was clear that Freckles was missing her restaurant back in Idaho and truly enjoyed serving home-cooked meals to whoever she thought needed it.

"Oh, you know me, darlin'. I like the chance to come outside and get away from Sherilee bugging me in the kitchen."

"Good. Because the Wi-Fi is surprisingly strong out here, and it's much quieter away from the rest of the family. Plus, the twins already helped me decorate." Violet pointed to the numerous drawings taped to the shelves that used to hold sunscreen and beach towels, as well as the pine-cone and feather collections lining the wet bar.

"Those boys are really taken with you." Freckles plopped herself down on one of the cushioned chaise lounge chairs, extending her feet in front of her. The eighty-year-old woman was wearing five-inch wedged sandals, and Violet wanted to know how she managed to walk in those things. "You know, according to Rider, Marcus has never brought a woman home since Brie passed."

"I think we both know he didn't bring me home,

either." Violet unfolded the napkin and put it in her lap. Besides, just because he hadn't brought a woman to the Twin Kings didn't mean he hadn't dated anyone since his wife's death. Not that it was any of Violet's business.

"Oh, you know what I'm talking 'bout, darlin'. Those boys lost their mama before they even knew her. Now they have you here giving them all your attention."

Violet's hands went all cold and clammy, and she nearly dropped her fork. She was the furthest thing from being a mother figure to anyone and wouldn't know how to act like one even if she'd tried. She cleared her throat. "They've grown up with Finn and Dahlia and even Sherilee taking care of them."

"Yeah, but it's different having a woman here who isn't related to their daddy. Plus, they're smart boys. They can tell there's something going on with you and Marcus. Just like the rest of us can."

"Really? Because here I was thinking that their dad and I can't even stand to be in the same room as each other."

"Yeah. About that. The boys' birthday party is coming up. Sherilee has already blown through her secret stash of ice cream, stress-eating over the event. This is the first party she's thrown since the funeral, and a lot of townspeople will be here. Any chance you and my nephew can call a cease-fire for the day?"

Violet was gripping her sandwich so firmly a slice of chicken fell onto her lap. "Actually, I planned to fly back to Texas next week to take care of some personal business."

"You know, I always thought that was interesting. You living in Dallas."

"What do you mean? Lots of people live there."

"Sure they do. But your mama's family is from San Antonio. You went to boarding school in Washington, DC, college in California and law school in Boston." Freckles didn't miss a beat. And she'd once accused *Marcus* of creeping around the internet. "So why put down roots in Dallas?"

"I wouldn't say I put down roots exactly." Violet had a feeling the canny older woman was trying to steer this conversation somewhere, so she answered cautiously. "I have a nice condo and a good job, but I could be a public defender anywhere. Most of my friends from school are spread all over the globe. I guess Dallas just seemed to be a nice middle ground, so to speak."

"You mean it was far enough away from your mama in Washington but also close enough in her home state that she couldn't give you too much of a hard time. I get it. I did the same thing when I wanted to get out from under my parents' thumbs." Freckles arched one orange-tinted brow. "So when are you gonna tell her you're here?"

Great. Now the rest of the King family thought Violet was afraid to confront her mother, too. She wasn't, but that didn't mean that she could simply handle the senator the same way she handled everything else. Violet sat up straighter. "I'll see my mom next Friday night, and I'll tell her then. Unfortunately, I won't be back in time for the party."

"But the twins will be heartbroken if you're not here." Freckles clutched one manicured hand dramatically to the left side of her enormous bosom, which was barely contained in a hot-pink velour tracksuit.

Violet remembered the first time Marcus's sons had invited her to their birthday party. It was the afternoon of Roper's funeral. The boys had talked nonstop about it since then, and she'd never told them that she wouldn't be attending. She sighed. "They'll be more heartbroken if I'm fighting with their dad the whole time."

"Marcus isn't going to fight with you in front of all the guests." Freckles stood up easily in her heels and walked to the door. Before she left, she added, "After all, he learned his lesson about getting mouthy with you after his little dip in the pool last week."

Ugh.

Violet had tried not to think of the incident at the rec center. Sure, she'd been impressed with how little reaction Marcus had shown after she'd shoved him into the pool. In fact, he'd been such a good sport he'd stayed in the water and played with the kids, launching them into the air as they squealed in excitement.

But not before he'd all but done a quasi-striptease for her benefit. Sure, he'd wanted to get out of his wet clothes, and nobody else at the rec center had probably thought anything of it. However, the way he'd watched Violet as he'd slowly peeled off his shirt would've been downright provocative if they hadn't had most of the King family and half the Secret Service team surrounding them.

She shook her head to clear her mind of the mental image. Instead, she tried to remember the twins' excitement at having their dad play with them and insisting that she watch them do backflips off his broad shoulders. Freckles was right. Jack and Jordan, for whatever reason, really seemed to enjoy having Violet around. It probably would break their hearts if she was a no-show for their party.

Okay, so she'd go home, attend her mom's fundraiser

and then come back for their birthday. Maybe a week or so apart—truly apart and not running into each other on the ranch or in town—would give her and Marcus time to cool themselves down enough that a cease-fire wouldn't even be necessary.

"I promise to be back before the party," Violet told Jack when she walked them out to the back porch on Sunday evening after dinner.

"But what if you're not back in time?" Jordan wanted to know.

"Then I'll call you." She looked to Marcus for some backup. However, his expression was almost as skeptical as his two sons'.

"But what if you forget?" Jack asked.

"Then you can call and remind me." She knew the boys were fond of her, but when she announced at dinner that she would be going to Texas for the week, she hadn't expected them to declare that they would miss her. She was touched that they cared so much, and yet she was also sad that they clearly had their doubts about her returning. Of course, they would have separation issues given the death of their mother and, more recently, their grandfather.

"Can I call you to tell you what we did in our science lab this week?" Jordan asked.

She smiled. "Of course."

Jack squeezed her hand. "Can I call you to tell you how many laps I ran during PE?"

"I'll be waiting by my phone." She squeezed back.

"Can we call you to tell you how many times Uncle Rider says a bad word?"

"Maybe that would be better in a text message. I

have a feeling he's going to say quite a few while I'm gone."

"Okay, boys." Marcus bit back a grin. "Give Violet a hug and then hop in the car. It's a school night, and we still need to hunt down Jack's missing library book that's due tomorrow."

Violet wanted to hold on to the children and never let go. But their hugs were over too soon as they raced to their father's patrol vehicle.

Marcus didn't immediately follow his sons, and Violet suddenly wondered if he was expecting a goodbye hug, as well. Instead, he asked, "So are you going to tell your mom I said hi?"

Contrary to his accusation—and Freckles's assumption—Violet had every intention of telling her mom she'd been staying in Wyoming to handle MJ's case. Telling her about Marcus would be a whole other issue.

"That might not be the first thing I say to her," Violet replied. After all, she had to be strategic about when and how the discussion happened. "But I'm sure your name will come up at some point, Marcus. The thing you have to keep in mind about my mother is that she's a United States senator. She's been shutting down her opposition on the Capitol floor at the national level and brokering trade deals at the global level since both of us were in diapers. It doesn't take courage to confront my mom—it takes skill."

He shoved his hands in his pockets, staring down at his boots. "Look, if something comes up and you can't make it back before the birthday party, that's okay. The boys will be fine."

The fact that he was already giving her permission to disappoint his children didn't sit well with her. Were his expectations of her really that low? She used her finger to lift his chin until his eyes locked on hers. "I'll see them on Saturday. You can bet on that."

On Monday, she'd spent most of the flight to Dallas going over how she was going to approach the topic with her mom. Then she'd rewritten and rehearsed her speech several more times before Friday's big event.

"You look beautiful, angel," Violet's father said when she descended the stairs at the hotel ballroom. The black-tie fundraiser was in full swing with hundreds of elegantly dressed guests enjoying the open bar and decadent appetizers, while a ten-piece orchestra played big-band dance tunes. Her dad gave her a tight squeeze, then kissed both of her cheeks. "That mountain air has been agreeing with you."

Violet narrowed her eyes. "You know."

"I had a hunch something was up when you didn't leave the funeral with me and your mom that day. That hunch grew when I realized you were only responding to my texts instead of FaceTiming with me like you normally do. Then I stopped by your office last week after my sportscast to surprise you with lunch, and your assistant filled me in."

Scanning the room, Violet saw her mother talking to a well-known socialite who was feeding bits of beef Wellington to the Pomeranian in her arms. "Did you tell Mom?"

"Do I look like a rookie playing in the minor leagues?"

She reached up and straightened her dad's bow tie. "No. You look very handsome. As usual. So, do you think she's going to overreact?"

"Not tonight. There'll be too many important donors here to keep her from batting an eye at any curveball you send her way. But don't be surprised when she calls you tomorrow to lecture you about your life choices."

"I already did my scouting report," she said, easily reverting to the familiar baseball euphemisms of her childhood. "I talked to her press secretary. Mom has a packed schedule the next two days, and then you guys fly to Geneva for that climate meeting with the United Nations."

"Smart girl." Her dad gave her a pat on the back. "You locked in your game-day strategy."

"Game-day strategy for what?" her mom asked, having escaped the socialite with the fluffy dog.

"My new case," Violet said before kissing her mother's cheek. "Is that dress from the designer I suggested?"

Unable to resist a compliment, her mom ran a hand over the red sequins. "Yes. You were right about the color. I needed to update my style."

"I usually am right about most things, Mom." Violet smiled as the conversation began exactly as she'd planned it. But then she saw someone out of the corner of her eye and completely forgot what she was going to say next.

Congressman Davis Townsend was standing with a gray-haired couple on the other side of the dance floor, but he was staring directly at Violet. The last time Violet had seen him, Marcus had been escorting him from the Twin Kings. Crap. There was no way a kiss up like Townsend wouldn't make his way over here eventually.

Plus, her dad had now slipped away to the buffet table and she might not get another one-on-one opportunity like this tonight. She needed to explain the

Twin Kings situation to her mom before the congressman brought it up. Instead, she blurted, "Did you tell Marcus's father that I had an abortion?"

"Violet," her mother admonished between clenched teeth. "Now isn't the time to discuss this."

Crap. She'd been saving that topic for later in the conversation, but now she'd have to adapt and forge ahead. "Well, we could have discussed it fourteen years ago, but you took matters into your own hands then. So now we can talk about it on my terms. I'll start. You shouldn't have lied about what happened. Even if you thought you were doing it for my own good."

"For the record, I never used the *A* word," her mom said as she smiled at someone across the room and did a finger wave. "It's not my fault the boy chose to believe what he wanted."

"Why would he believe anything else? He never got any of my letters at boot camp." Violet narrowed her eyes. "Or did you have something to do with that, as well?"

This time, her mother did gasp before quickly recovering her composure. "Of course I didn't have anything to do with that. In fact, I picked up the phone several times to call the base commander and demand that they put Marcus on the phone immediately. I almost flew out there in person to knock some sense into him for ignoring your letters like that. You think I wanted to see my only daughter suffering?"

"Well, you certainly didn't want to see us together. You were ultimately responsible for his silence afterward and didn't do anything to change that. Why didn't you ever approve of him, Mom?"

"Because no matter how well-connected his family

was, I knew he was going to hold you back. He made no secret that he hated politics and desired nothing more than a small-town life. I wanted so much more for you."

It was turning into the same argument they'd had a million times before. Violet sighed. "But I wanted *him*."

"I know you did, angel." Her mom reached out and gently stroked Violet's bare upper arm. "You don't think I remember how devastated you were? I was there. I saw what you went through. If I could've taken on that heartache for you, I would've traded spots in a second. But there was nothing I could do to ease your pain. The next time I ran into Roper King, I wasn't about to give him or his son the satisfaction of thinking you were still pining in agony for some childhood crush. So, yes, I implied that you'd handled things and moved on with your life."

"He was a lot more than a childhood crush, Mom. Marcus loved me and was just as devastated as I was."

"Then why didn't he come and see you? Why didn't he fight for you?"

"Probably the same reason I didn't fight for him," Violet admitted, her heart still heavy as she wrestled with that truth. "We were young and hurting and didn't know how to overcome the obstacle of someone who was trying to keep us apart." She looked at her mother squarely. "Just keep in mind neither one of us are children anymore."

Her mother straightened, once again schooling her expression from concerned mother to perfectly composed senator. "I know. I saw him staring at you at Roper King's funeral. He's still handsome, I'll give you that. But if I hadn't intervened back then, you'd be living on a ranch in the middle of Wyoming right now with no hope of a judicial career, let alone a political one."

Violet took a glass of champagne from the tray of a passing server. "Funny you should mention that, Mom. Because I'm currently living on a ranch in the middle of Wyoming with absolutely no intention of doing any other job than the one I'm currently doing."

For the second time of the evening, her mother gasped, and she whipped her head toward Violet. "You're kidding me."

"Senator Cortez-Hill." Davis Townsend had finally descended on them. "What a beautiful party."

"Congressman." Her mom quickly recovered with a forced smile. "Have you met my daughter, Violet?"

"We saw each other a couple of weeks ago at the Twin Kings, but we weren't formally introduced." The man's smirk suggested he wasn't as embarrassed as he should've been, which meant he was hoping to gain something by bringing up their unfortunate meeting now. "Although, you didn't look quite as…put-together in the stables that day as you do tonight."

There it was. The man was trying to establish some sort of pretense of a friendship with Violet that would get him one step closer to her very powerful mother. His mistake was in thinking that Violet would be so embarrassed by being caught in a compromising position with Marcus, she would feel resigned to play along with his little game.

"Oh, was that you?" Violet blinked innocently, enjoying the way his fake grin faltered at thinking someone didn't recognize him. "Normally, the Secret Service provides those of us living on the Twin Kings with a daily list of *authorized* guests expected to visit. I don't remember your name ever being on it. Now, if you'll excuse me, I see one of my former law-school professors over by the bar, and I wanted to consult with her on several federal trespassing statutes I'm currently researching."

Violet lifted her head victoriously, walking away just as another donor approached her mom. She'd gotten thrown off her course for a second back there, but she was leaving the fundraiser having accomplished what she'd set out to do.

Overall, her trip to Dallas had been a success. Violet had spent some time in her office updating her co-counsel on several outstanding cases. She'd watered the plants at her condo and sorted through the mail that her neighbor had been putting aside for her. She'd even had after-work drinks with a few friends from work. But most importantly, Violet had confronted her mother about interfering in her relationship with Marcus all those years ago and made it clear that she would be in Wyoming for the foreseeable future.

Now all she had to do was fly back to Twin Kings and get through a birthday party for a couple of seven-year-olds without shoving their father's head in the cake.

How hard could it be?

CHAPTER TEN

"MY MOM SAID she and Aunt Freckles brokered a temporary truce with you for the day," Marcus told Violet Saturday afternoon as he tried to wrestle a disposable paper tablecloth into place without tearing it.

"I believe Freckles's word was *cease-fire*," Violet said, lunging to catch the cardboard dinosaur centerpiece before it hit the ground. "Maybe you should use some tape to keep the wind from blowing stuff all over the place?"

"Or maybe we should've just had the party at the Pepperoni Stampede like we do every year?" Marcus looked up at the deceptively clear blue sky, hoping the forecasted March rainstorm wouldn't arrive a day early. "Nobody hosts a kid's birthday outdoors in Wyoming until after spring."

"The boys wanted an inflatable obstacle course and a *Jurassic Park* theme. That's kind of hard to pull off at the local pizza place." Violet used a toy brontosaurus as a paperweight to hold the flimsy centerpiece in place. "Besides, your mom needs something to focus on besides MJ's court case."

"Oh, is my mother driving you nuts?" Marcus couldn't

help giving her an I-told-you-so look. "Who would've ever imagined that?"

"Mrs. King tried to invite the new judge to the party, Marcus. It's totally inappropriate."

"So is letting MJ have Kendra Broman here as his plus-one," he pointed out. "I heard you were the one pushing for that."

"They're under strict orders to stay in plain sight under the party tent at all times. Besides, there'll be at least a hundred people here watching them."

"Like that ever stopped us?" Marcus said.

Her shoulders gave a little shudder, as though a shiver of awareness had just raced down her spine. Instead of taking the bait, though, she moved on to the next table with the decorations blown into disarray. Marcus jogged over to the box of party supplies Finn had delivered earlier and found a roll of tape.

"Here," he said, passing the tape to her before holding the blue paper tablecloth steady. "Let's try your idea."

They worked together quietly for several minutes, and it felt almost…nice. By the time they got halfway through the decorations, though, Marcus couldn't stop himself from asking the question he'd been dying to know. "So how was your trip to Dallas?"

"It was productive," Violet replied, studying his face. "But what you really want to know is if I spoke to my mom. I did. She admitted that she'd purposely misled you after you got out of boot camp."

"You didn't believe me?"

"No, I did. But I still needed to confront her on it."

"Did she apologize?"

Violet crinkled her nose as she focused on untangling a plastic T. rex from the strings in the *Happy Birthday* banner. "Of course not. Nor will she. My mother will always think she acted in my best interest. But at least now she knows that I'm aware of her interference and that you and I are moving past that."

"Moving past that?" Marcus's hands stilled and his throat constricted. He had to swallow several times before he could ask, "As in getting back together?"

"I meant moving on and getting closure."

"Oh," he said, surprised at the sudden hollowness inside his rib cage. That couldn't be disappointment, could it?

Violet met his eyes across the table, her grin somewhat mischievous. "But I *might've* let her believe that we were getting back together."

His chest pinged back to life, yet he refused to sound as hopeful as he felt. "And why would you do that?"

"Because it'll serve her right to think her efforts to keep us apart all those years ago were in vain." Violet knelt to tape a corner of the tablecloth to the leg of the folding table. She was still on her knees when she smiled up at him. "Plus, every so often, I need to remind her that she isn't in control of my life."

Oh, man, Marcus was a sucker for that smile. It was infectious, and he couldn't help but grin in response. "So let me get this straight. You're using me to piss off the senator?"

"Do you mind?"

"It depends," he said, squatting in front of her. He heard the breath catch in her throat, and he lifted his hand to push a strand of hair behind her ear. "What do I get out of this deal?"

"Hey, Dad," Jack hollered as he zipped through the open field and toward the tables at a full run. He tripped, then got back up and resumed his breakneck pace. "The inflatables are here!"

Jordan was a few paces behind his brother. "I think we should have rules for the bounce house. Like only one person at a time. So nobody gets hurt."

"Are you sure you'd rather be a doctor instead of a lawyer?" Violet asked the boy.

"Why can't I be both?" Jordan replied, causing a burst of pride in his dad.

"I'm gonna be a monster-truck driver when I grow up," Jack said, then both boys sprinted back toward the driveway.

Marcus stared at Violet as she watched his sons. Her soft expression could only be described as smitten. She sighed. "It's hard to believe they're only seven."

"Tell me about it." He jerked his thumb toward the party-rental trucks. "Anyway, I better go see about the delivery. Maybe make sure nobody brought a dunk tank. I wouldn't want you to send me into the water again."

"Are you kidding?" Violet chuckled as her eyes scanned the length of him. A current of awareness raced through him as she made her appraisal. "I never get to see you in anything other than your uniform. I plan to take a break from arguing with the sheriff today and simply enjoy watching you in your dad jeans."

"These aren't dad jeans." Marcus feigned outrage as he rose to his feet. "They're actually quite fashionable."

"I meant that they're jeans and you're in dad mode today. I'm going to sit back and appreciate both."

"In that case, I'll try to give you something worth watching." Strutting away, he did his best impression of strutting down an imaginary runway, relishing the way her laughter echoed in his ears as he moved on to the next task.

It turned out Violet didn't simply sit back during the party at all—either as a spectator or a guest. She finished decorating the tables, read over the waivers for the inflatable course before ensuring each parent signed one as soon as they arrived, helped Freckles carry out platters of food and then took a turn as the line judge during Finn's impromptu dodgeball contest.

Marcus didn't get a single second to talk to her because there was constantly something that needed to be done. Anytime he did get a chance to slow down for a second, there was Melissa Parker trying to corner him and invite him to yet another Social Singles event. In fact, he'd just escaped her when he passed the empty bounce house and noticed one of the stakes had come out of the ground. That couldn't be good. He fixed it, then poked his head inside the safety netting and was surprised to see Violet sitting cross-legged in the corner.

"Vi?" he asked as he awkwardly climbed inside toward her. "Are you okay?"

"Yep." She held up her canvas sneaker. "This went missing during the potato-sack race. Amelia told me she saw Keegan Parker throw a bunch of shoes into the bounce house. It was so quiet in here, I figured I deserved a few minutes of downtime after getting trampled during the piñata."

"Yeah, standing in front of the rope line at the exact second the candy busts out is a rookie mistake." Marcus plopped beside her, causing Violet to bounce into him. She didn't immediately straighten so they ended up leaning against each other. Or sagging against each other, depending on who asked. "It's almost as dangerous as taking the stick away from the blindfolded kid who won't stop swinging."

"Are birthday parties always this much work?"

"Only when my children invite half the town and Finn organizes the games. As soon as that first minivan full of guests arrived, I was already cursing myself for not taking my mom up on her offer to hire a professional event planner to do everything."

"Why didn't you?"

"Because it was supposed to be a simple seventh-birthday party, and I've always wanted my kids to have as normal a childhood as they could. Unfortunately, their Gan Gan doesn't seem to have any concept of what constitutes *normal*."

Violet chuckled. She leaned her head back against the netted wall behind them, and Marcus caught a glimpse of half of her face. He did a double take, then lifted his hand to her chin. "What happened to your cheek?"

"Oh, I was going for prehistoric fairy, but the face painter ran out of glitter for the scales and went back to her car to get more supplies. The water-balloon battle broke out behind me, and I decided it was every person for themselves at that point. I made a run for it and have been hiding in here ever since."

He used his thumb to caress her jaw, which was smeared with greenish-brown face paint. "You are such a good sport. A lot of the other moms decided to hang back under the heat lamps in the tent drinking Dahlia's Irish coffees. Yet you're out playing with the kids and getting your hands—and face—dirty in the process. No wonder my sons adore you."

Something flashed in her eyes, but she quickly blinked it away. "If I'd realized cocktails and heat lamps were an option, I might've planned my day differently. But I'm not a mom, so I didn't really know what I was getting myself into."

She'd tried to make a joke out of it, but he heard the sadness in her voice and wanted to kick himself. "No, it has nothing to do with you being a mom or not. And I shouldn't have made an insensitive comparison like that. It was more of a reflection on who you are as a person. You treat the twins as though they're on the same playing field as you. You never talk down to them or make them feel as though their opinions don't matter just because they're children. But you also don't expect them to be perfect little adults all the time. They know you respect them as individuals, and that makes them want to be around you even more. What I'm trying to say is…" He paused long enough to swallow down his own emotion. "Thank you for being yourself with my children and for letting them be themselves with you."

Her lashes grew damp, and she wiped the corner of her eye. "I appreciate you telling me that. Most of the time, I feel like I'm just trying to keep up with them. They're so smart and so compassionate, and I love how everything is black and white with them. I know this is weird, but sometimes it feels as if they're the ones teaching me how to be a better version of myself."

"Well, I already like this version of you," Marcus said as he lowered his face to hers. But before his lips could touch hers, something thumped the back of his head. It was another avalanche of footwear.

"Stop stealing all our shoes, Keegan," Jack yelled as he chased a bigger boy across the field.

"Hey, Dad, Miz Parker is looking for you again," Jordan said as he popped his head inside the bounce house. "Oh, hi, Violet. I didn't know you guys were playing in here."

"We weren't really playing, we were—" Marcus got cut off when several more kids tumbled into the bounce house and sent him and Violet careening into the air. She managed to get to her feet before Marcus did and shot him an unapologetic grin before hopping in sync with the other kids.

"Popcorn in the middle," someone cried out as the group formed a jumping circle around him. The higher they got, the more he flipped and flopped like a kernel of corn in a hot pan of oil, unable to get himself upright.

"Pop! Pop! Pop!"

Violet's smile was wide, and her voice joined the chants a bit too eagerly.

Marcus would've rolled his eyes if he wasn't already so dizzy. Yeah, she seemed to be keeping up with his sons just fine.

"How are you still standing upright?" Violet asked Freckles as she padded into the kitchen an hour after the birthday party had ended. The older woman was still buzzing around the counters, putting leftover food into storage containers and loading the dishwasher. Violet couldn't remember the last time she'd been this exhausted. How did the children have so much energy?

"Because I know how to pace myself, darlin'." Freckles handed Violet a glass of cabernet and a chocolate cupcake. "You were running around with those kiddos nonstop today. Did you even sit down once?"

She flashed back to her ten minutes alone in the

bounce house with Marcus. But before she had time to give their near kiss too much thought, Uncle Rider spoke up from his slumped position on one of the kitchen chairs.

"How 'bout me? I 'bout threw out my damn back lifting dozens of little buckaroos on and off the ponies all afternoon. Or maybe I hurt it when I went down that blasted slide on the inflatable obstacle course."

"I'm surprised you could get that—" Freckles pointed a serving spoon directly at Rider's very prominent belly "—ten-pound belt buckle of yours over the rope wall."

"Figures you'd know how much this buckle weighs, considering how many times you've taken it off—"

Violet quickly interrupted Rider. "One nice thing about a small-town community is having most of the guests stay after the party to help clean up." She took a long gulp of her wine, letting the liquid relax her from the inside out.

"You can say that again." Freckles snapped a lid onto a plastic container full of smoked brisket. "Speaking of cleanup, I see you were finally able to get that face paint off."

"After quite a bit of scrubbing and a lot of hot water," Violet replied before biting into her cupcake. Freckles had given her some industrial-strength makeup remover and insisted she go take a shower while Marcus loaded all the unwrapped gifts into his SUV to take back to their cabin. She wondered if he was still at the main house or if he'd already gone home. She took another drink of wine, then said, "I saw the boys and Amelia setting up their sleeping bags in the den. Are they staying the night?"

"Yep. They were so hyped-up on sugar and overstimulation I told Marcus to leave them here for a sleepover so he could go on back to his cabin and enjoy a little bit of peace and quiet. Oh, no." Freckles frowned. "I can't believe I forgot."

Normally, the woman was all smiles and sassy comebacks, so seeing creases of concern rather than laugh lines around her mouth immediately made Violet pause. "What's wrong?"

"I just realized I forgot to send Marcus home with any food. I didn't see him eat a thing today at the party, and Lord knows what that man has in the fridge at that cabin of his. Rider, grab the keys so you can run some leftovers to him."

Rider made a grumbling sound as his hefty frame slouched even lower in his chair. "Woman, I don't think I could walk to my truck right this second, let alone climb inside it."

"Well, I can't drive in the dark with my sense of direction," Freckles replied.

"You don't seem to get lost finding *my* cabin every night," Rider mumbled before clearing his throat. "But, yeah, I guess Marcus's place is a little farther out."

Both pairs of eyes swung toward Violet, and she held up her palms. "Don't look at me. I don't know how to get there."

"Rider can draw you a map." Freckles batted her false eyelashes. "Please, darlin'. You know I'm gonna worry myself sick if one of my kiddos goes hungry."

Violet swallowed down the remainder of her wine to keep herself from pointing out that the so-called kiddo in question was a grown man who knew how to get himself to the market in town. But Freckles was the same woman who insisted on bringing a tray of food to Violet every day in the pool house whenever she worked through lunch. Plus, a small part of her wanted to see where Marcus lived.

"Fine," Violet said before stifling a yawn. "Let me go get my boots and jacket."

She had to act at least a little put out, otherwise they might get the impression that she was eager to see Marcus. When she returned to the kitchen, she picked up the very detailed map Rider had somehow managed to draw in a short amount of time, as well as a large brown paper bag loaded with enough food to feed half the cattle hands on the Twin Kings. On her way out the door, she grabbed the keys to one of the ranch trucks because there was no way she wanted anyone seeing her rental car coming or going from Marcus's place.

The sun had set over an hour ago, but even the star-filled Wyoming sky couldn't hide the fact that Marcus's cabin wasn't a cabin at all. It didn't have a single log or river rock making up its architecture like most of the other buildings on the ranch. Rather, it was a large one-story spread in a modern hacienda style with high arches, white stucco walls and a red tile roof. It reminded her of her grandfather's estate outside of San Antonio.

The front door opened before she'd even made it out of the driver's side, and the sight of Marcus standing there shirtless on his porch took her breath away.

Nope, those certainly were *not* dad jeans.

"Are the boys okay?" he asked, his eyes searching the dimly lit interior of the truck as he crossed the cold ground in his bare feet.

"Yes! Sorry to worry you. Freckles sent me to deliver some dinner. She was convinced you might starve to death if I didn't come straightaway with barbecued ribs, smoked brisket and what feels like ten pounds of corn bread."

"Well, that was very thoughtful of my aunt," Marcus said as he easily took the heavy bag from Violet, "considering she just stocked my freezer yesterday with a tray of lasagna, a tub of beef stew and at least eight chicken pot pies."

Violet squeezed her eyes shut before shaking her head. "Why do I feel like I've totally been played?"

"Because Freckles is just as crafty as my mom and twice as subtle. Especially when she gets Rider to play along with her schemes. Did you eat dinner yet?"

"I didn't even have time to eat lunch today. I'm operating on half a cupcake and a glass of wine, which probably explains why I so easily fell for your aunt and uncle's ploy to get me out here."

"Well, we wouldn't want all their strategizing to go to waste." Marcus jerked his chin toward his front door. "Come inside, and I'll share some of this potato salad with you."

Following him into his house would be a huge mistake. They could barely control themselves around each other when there were people right outside his office or the stables or even the bounce house. His place was at least a mile away from anyone accidentally stumbling in on them, offering a false sense of security from the risk of getting caught.

Which, now that she thought about it, actually made it the perfect place to finally lose control. Nobody would have to know. They could release some of their pent-up sexual tension and maybe get whatever this was out of their systems.

Violet took one step. Then another. Before she knew it, Marcus had the front door closed behind her, and the bag of food was forgotten on the floor as he pulled her into his arms. Apparently, his thoughts had been on the exact same page as hers, because he angled his mouth over hers and murmured, "Just this once."

Violet would've nodded earnestly, but he was already kissing her. Holding her face securely in place as his tongue stroked hers, encouraging her lips to open wider to accommodate him. She allowed her hands the opportunity to finally explore the bare skin of his chest and then his wide shoulders. She'd been aching to trace the ridges of his defined muscles and feel the silky dark blond hair under her fingertips, but it wasn't enough. If his body felt this good against her palms, it would feel even better against all of her.

Without breaking the kiss, she tore off her coat and went to work yanking her top higher. In her haste, one arm got stuck in her sleeve, and Marcus pulled away long enough to help her get first her sweater and then her camisole over her head. When she was standing in front of him in just her bra and her jeans, he stared appreciatively at her breasts before lifting his eyes back to hers.

"Are you sure?" he asked, his voice low and raspy.

She nodded before unclasping her bra. "But we can't let anybody find out."

His only response was to reach behind her and flip the dead bolt into the locked position. She pulled his mouth down to hers again and sighed as her aching nipples finally pressed against the hard planes of his chest. Marcus lifted her in his arms, and she wrapped her legs around his waist as he carried her through the entryway and toward what must have been the formal living room. She caught a glimpse of them in the mirror hanging over the fireplace mantel, both of them still wearing their jeans.

As he lowered her onto an oversize sectional, Violet's fingers wrestled with the button on her waistband and then her zipper. She couldn't get her pants over her hips soon enough. Marcus was undoing his fly just as eagerly but then paused. "It's been a while since I've done this. The lab results from my last physical were clear, but I don't have any protection."

They were both older and wiser this time around and knew better than to leave birth control to chance. She relaxed against the sofa cushions and said, "I've had my IUD for a few years, and I got screened when I saw my doctor in Dallas earlier this week. Just in case…"

"Just in case you couldn't keep your hands off me?" Marcus asked playfully as he finally shoved his own jeans lower. His arousal sprang forward, and Violet slid her palms down his rib cage and then to his narrow hips, pulling him closer.

"It's not my hands you need to worry about," she said breathlessly as he settled himself between her thighs.

"I know. It's that wonderful mouth of yours." He claimed her lips in another kiss as he entered her.

Violet shuddered at the familiar sensation of Marcus filling her. It had been fourteen long years since they'd done this together, but it felt as normal to her as breathing. He pulled back slightly, and she drew her knees up on either side of him, causing his next thrust to go even deeper.

Marcus groaned before setting a tentative pace. But Violet didn't want to go slowly. This ache, this coil of unsatisfied need, had been building inside of her ever since she'd seen him again. Now that her release was finally within her grasp, she wanted to race to it.

Clinging to his shoulders, she rocked her hips in a faster tempo. His breath quickened while hers came out in short pants. His arms slid under her waist, pulling her tighter against him right as she shattered through the finish line.

"You know, I can't ever remember a time when we actually took our time making love," Marcus told Violet as he lit a fire in the fireplace. He'd been so incredibly spent in her embrace that he'd remained there for nearly fifteen minutes before realizing that if they stayed like that any longer, they might catch a cold. "When we were younger, there was always such a rush because we were afraid of getting caught."

"I'm still afraid of getting caught." Violet pulled a decorative throw blanket over herself. "The last couple of times we started anything, someone in your family walked in and nearly busted us."

Marcus never bothered to use this room since it was supposed to be for formal occasions. Suddenly, though, he couldn't imagine a more formal occasion than having Violet back in his arms. And she looked so beautiful lounging there in her afterglow, he had no intention of carrying her back to his rather informal bedroom.

"Well, I can assure you that the twins won't bust us tonight. Once they fall asleep, they're out cold until the morning." The fire blazed to life behind him, instantly warming his bare backside as he turned toward her. "So we've got at least a few hours to slow things down for round three."

"Round three? Did I miss the second round?" Violet stretched, one dusky nipple popping out from under the blanket. Marcus felt himself stirring to attention already.

"No," he said before rejoining her on the sofa and pulling her onto his lap. "That round is starting right now. Then we can refuel with some dinner before we take our time."

Violet laughed throatily as she hooked one leg around his hip and lifted herself astride him. It wasn't until midnight that they finally dragged themselves to the kitchen to reheat the food they'd abandoned by the front door. Along with most of Violet's clothes.

"You're right," Violet said as she stood in front of his open fridge. "This thing is so well stocked, I can't even find room for these leftover containers. And it's not even premade meals in here."

"I'm actually a pretty decent cook, you know."

"Since when?" Violet arched a brow.

"Since always." He grabbed their heated plates from the microwave and carried them to the living room. Violet followed with two glasses of wine.

"You never cooked for me," she said as they settled under the blanket in front of the fire.

"Because we usually only saw each other when we were on vacations with our parents," Marcus reminded her. "There were always restaurants or private chefs around."

"You didn't have a private chef here on the Twin Kings?"

"We have a cook for the ranch hands at the bunkhouse. But my dad never liked anyone but family in our kitchen. His grandma ran a moonshine operation out of Big Millie's Saloon during Prohibition and was extremely suspicious of strangers snooping around what she referred to as her *recipes*. She instituted this rule that only people with the King last name were allowed to cook in the family kitchen."

"But there were caterers at the funeral," Violet said, oblivious to the smear of barbecue sauce on her chin. "I know because I caught a ride with one to my hotel in Jackson Hole."

"Yeah, my mom pushed for caterers to be an exception when my dad first started running for office and they had to host occasional parties on the ranch. My dad did a lot of the cooking, but after he became governor, he never really had the time. And nobody wanted to eat what my mom came up with for meals."

"So you had to learn to cook for yourself?"

He nodded, swallowing a bite of corn bread. "And my siblings, when my parents were on the campaign trail. But only if we didn't feel like eating in the bunkhouse. The rule only applies to the main house."

"How did I not know that? That's a pretty big responsibility, Marcus."

He shrugged. "I'm the oldest. It comes with the big-brother role."

"Is taking care of them still your responsibility?"

"Logically, no. But old habits die hard."

They ate several more bites in silence before Violet paused and faced him. "Even MJ? Other than the time he threw up on the Ferris wheel at the county fair, I don't ever recall you having to babysit him or hang out with him at all when we were teenagers."

A familiar guilt gnawed at Marcus. "He was born when I was fourteen. I remember being mortified to tell my friends that my parents were having another baby because then everyone would know that my mom and dad were still having sex. And eww. Who wanted to admit that to their buddies? MJ was an infant, and I was starting high school. I was busy with homework and playing sports and doing all those leadership camps in summer, seeing you whenever I could get the chance. I rarely took care of him. MJ went wherever my mom went, and she and my dad were traveling a lot more for his campaigns. Us older kids stayed here with Rider, although he and Freckles were already separated by then. I joined the Marines and was gone for four years. When I came home, MJ was spending more time at the governor's mansion in Cheyenne than here in Twin Kings. After that I had my own family, and he and my folks moved to DC and, well, we just never really bonded."

"Do you think his arrest is going to help you in the bonding process?"

He sighed. "No. Maybe. All I know is that I should've been a better big brother to him back then, and I wasn't. I'm doing what I can now."

Violet studied him over the rim of her wineglass. "What if MJ doesn't want a big brother? The same way you resented having a little brother all those years ago."

"I didn't resent it, exactly." He thought about MJ bringing up the story about going on the carnival ride alone so Marcus could sit with Violet. The guilt settled in deeper. "I just had other things going on. I'm trying to make it up to him."

"Okay, think about it this way." She tucked her feet under her legs. "The first five Kings were an already-established, tight-knit group before he came along. You and MJ might've had the same parents, but you grew up under such different circumstances. He doesn't have all those shared experiences that bonded you older siblings. In a way, it's almost as though MJ was inadvertently raised as an only child. When you look at it from his viewpoint, it's not fair to suddenly insert yourself into a role that existed in name only. Especially not after he lost his father so recently."

"I lost my father, too."

"Yes. But you had thirty-two years with Roper King. MJ only had eighteen. I remember you when you were that same age, Marcus, and you would've been just as lost as your brother is now. You need to give him time and space to deal with things in his own way."

This. This is what his mom had meant when she'd said that Marcus needed someone who wouldn't just listen to him but would tell him the things he needed to hear. He'd been so focused on his own guilt for not being a better big brother to MJ, he hadn't stopped to think of what it had been like for the teen to feel as though he'd never really fit in with the rest of them.

Still. That didn't mean Marcus was going to sit back and let MJ ruin his own life. But maybe Violet was right and he'd been approaching it from the wrong angle this whole time.

"Hey." He gave her a quick kiss, then wiped the sauce off her chin. "Thank you."

"For what?"

"For making me see things from a different perspective. For challenging me."

She took his plate from him and set it beside hers on the coffee table. Then she returned his kiss. "And here I thought *you* were the challenging one."

"I tried to be. But you've clearly already worn me down."

"I hope you're not too worn-down. I was promised a round three."

Marcus groaned before proving that he was a man of his word.

They never even made it to the bedroom before dawn slowly crept up on them. The sun shone into the wide windows of the living room, and Violet stirred in his arms, then fell right back to sleep wedged between him and the sofa cushions. After the birthday party yesterday and then all their lovemaking last night, she had to be exhausted. Marcus eased himself from the sectional without waking her and went to the kitchen to start the coffee maker before getting in the shower.

When she'd shown up at his door yesterday evening, Marcus had told himself that it would just be this one time. But now that they'd spent the night together, there was no way that he would be satisfied. Maybe the twins would want a sleepover at the main house again tonight. No, that wouldn't work. It was Sunday, which meant they had school tomorrow.

He'd call and check on them when he got out of the shower, and if his mom insisted on keeping them for the day, then maybe he could convince Violet to stay a little longer.

But when he came out of the bathroom, Violet was already wide-awake and talking to someone on her phone. Marcus could only hear one side of the conversation, yet that didn't make him feel like any less of an eavesdropper. Especially since Violet seemed to be on the receiving end of an interrogation.

"No, Mom, I flew back to Wyoming Friday night

after the fundraiser," Violet said, and Marcus's blood couldn't decide if it wanted to run hot or cold.

"I'll be staying here until after MJ's trial." Then another pause.

"Of course they have other attorneys in Wyoming. But I'm doing this as a favor to their family, which is the least I can do after you interfered in their oldest son's life all those years ago. Plus, Sherilee is trying to keep it out of the press, which I know you can relate to, considering you didn't want anyone knowing what *your* daughter was doing when she was that same age." Wow. That was both strong and logical. Good for Violet.

"Yes, Marcus is here." At this, he straightened his spine and took a few steps closer to announce his presence. But something held him back.

"He lives on the Twin Kings, so I see him quite regularly." Violet's tone was practically boastful, so maybe she really did want to get her mom all riled up. Another point for Violet.

"I don't know if we're getting back together, but—" There was a heavy sigh, which meant the senator must've interrupted her. Marcus held his breath as he waited for Violet to defend him. To defend their relationship.

Instead, Violet replied, "I know my life is in Dallas, Mom. I have no intention of throwing away my career. Speaking of careers, what time is your speech with the Girls in Technology organization?"

The subject had changed and that was it. Feeling deflated, Marcus let out the breath he didn't realize he'd been holding. Violet had been so close to telling her mother to mind her own business, but then she'd done what she always did with the senator: acknowledge the concerns without denying them and then steer the conversation to a neutral topic. Marcus almost didn't recognize this version of her, since he hadn't seen it on display since they were teens. He'd gotten too accustomed to the Violet who'd passionately argued with him about something as inconsequential as a William Shakespeare play or the suitability of pineapple as a topping for pizza.

Or maybe she wasn't fighting her mother on the issue because she was in complete agreement with the woman. Either way, Violet clearly planned to return to Texas when MJ's case was over. Marcus was no longer a naive recruit at boot camp holding on to the hope that they had a future together. They both wanted different things out of life, and that was okay.

However, there was one thing they'd never really talked about, and he wasn't quite ready to let her leave until they had.

He went to the kitchen to pour them both some coffee, then returned to the living room to find her dressed in her clothes from the night before. He handed her a cup, then sat beside her and tried to keep his voice as bland as possible.

"Listen. Um, you mentioned something last night. About having an IUD. And I was just wondering…" He swallowed past the apprehension that threatened to cut off his words. He had to know. "Is having kids still a possibility for you? I mean physically?"

He heard the slight catch in her throat, almost a hiccup sound, and hurried to explain himself. "God, I didn't mean that to sound so intrusive. It's just that we've discussed what happened with us after the miscarriage, but we never really talked about…you know, the actual thing itself."

Violet bit her lower lip, then looked around the empty house, as though to confirm their conversation wasn't going to be overheard. Or interrupted again. "As far as I know, yes, I can still have kids. But there could be risks, and I don't know if I could handle going through that again."

He slipped his free hand into hers, pulling their joined fingers onto his lap. "Will you tell me what happened?"

It took her a few seconds, but finally she nodded. "When you left for boot camp, I thought I was only a few weeks along. At my first doctor's appointment, though, they did an ultrasound and told me I was at eleven weeks. With twins. It's probably a good thing you didn't get that initial letter at boot camp because I was already freaking out that this was more than we'd anticipated, and I didn't want to tell my parents yet. But I didn't hear back from you, so I started thinking that maybe you were more panicked than me. I sent another letter the following week, trying to sound more upbeat and positive. By that time, I'd convinced myself that we were so blessed and were going to be amazing parents, and I'd even started thinking about decorating a nursery in some imagined home we didn't even have yet. But still no response from you."

While Marcus gently held her palm in one of his hands, his other fist tightly gripped the mug handle, wishing he could go back fourteen years ago and punch someone. "Most of my drill instructors were pretty decent, and I was so careful not to let anyone know who my father was because I didn't want them to treat me differently. But we had this one staff sergeant who was such a jerk. One of those guys who kept track of how many recruits he could make cry in a day. He figured out who I was early on. He must've been smart enough to allow all the envelopes with the name King on the return address through, because I never got suspicious that anyone was messing with my mail. They took our phones away as soon as we checked in on the base, and we never had internet access. It killed me not knowing what was going on with you, but other guys in my unit were getting breakup letters and I tried to be relieved that at least you hadn't sent me one of those. I did manage to write you a couple of times. I'm guessing you didn't get any mail from me, either?"

Violet shook her head, then sighed. "It's not like you could've done anything about it anyway. When I got my next ultrasound at fourteen weeks, they could only hear one heartbeat. The doctor explained that since our twins were identical, they were sharing the same placenta and sometimes only one of them got enough nutrients to survive. She tried to reassure me that I could still carry the surviving baby to term but said that we'd have to do a procedure to remove the other one since it was too late in my pregnancy for my body to naturally expel it."

"Oh my God, Violet. I can't even imagine…" Marcus swallowed the knot in his throat. "I am so sorry that you had to go through that alone. I should've been there."

Her eyes were damp, but her chin jutted forward. "I'm not going to lie. That was one of several thoughts that went through my mind. 'How can I do this without Marcus?' 'How am I going to tell him that I lost one of his babies?' Then it was 'How dare he not be here to go through this with me!'"

"Aw, Violet." Marcus let go of her hand long enough to put his arm around her and pull her closer. "I know that neither one of us had planned on being parents so young. The pregnancy was a shock, but it was also thrilling. Thinking about you and our child—I didn't know it was more than one at the time—was what got me through boot camp. I wanted to have a family with you. But I would never have blamed you for the miscarriage."

"Now I know that. But at the time, I was such a mess of emotions in that exam room, the nurse had to call my mom since she was the only person listed on my emergency-contact form. I'd been such a coward for not telling my parents about the pregnancy before then. But my mom never said a word. She arrived right as they were about to take me in for surgery. At first, the procedure went as expected and I tried to console myself with the fact that we would still have one baby. But they kept me in the hospital overnight because there was too much bleeding, and by the next day, the second baby was gone. I was devastated and inconsolable, but I was also postpartum, and a heavy fog of depression set in along with everything else."

He stayed silent, letting her continue.

"That first week out of the hospital was a blur. I was just an empty shell. My mom had to hold a cup of water up to my lips to get me to drink fluids. She brushed my hair and changed my pads because even getting myself to the bathroom was an overwhelming task. Eventually, the depression lifted as my hormones evened out, but then came the denial and the anger and all those other stages of grief you hear about. The odd thing was, it was my mother who defended you. Who told me that you were probably under too much stress with boot camp and a potential military deployment. When I didn't hear back from you, well... We all know what happened after that."

He let out a deep, shuddering breath. "I know that we can't go back and change things, but..." Pausing, he dragged his hand through his still-damp hair. "Man, I wish I would've been smarter and more understanding, and not so damn stubborn."

"Me, too. We both were young, and our emotions got the better of us."

He lifted one brow. "You say that like we're not going to let our emotions get the best of us this time."

"That's because we're not, Marcus. This..." She pointed at him and then back at herself before making a circular motion at the rumpled blanket on the ground. "This is just us getting the physical stuff out of the way so that we can think clearly about everything else going on in our lives. We both have people depending on us, and we can't afford to get too caught up in what might've been."

Marcus knew better than anyone that there were no guarantees in relationships. By now he'd built enough of a wall around his heart that he wasn't going to leave his happiness up to fate. He would have to be satisfied with making the best of their time together while they had it.

CHAPTER ELEVEN

"Explain to me again why your mom and Freckles think that *all* of you need to go to Washington, DC, to get Tessa and Agent Wyatt together," Violet asked Marcus as they stood under the hot spray of the shower inside the pool house.

It was supposed to have been just one night of love-making. At least that's what Violet had told herself. But then one night had turned into a hot-and-steamy thirty minutes in the front seat of his patrol unit, which had led to an interesting encounter in the dusty file room at the courthouse. Now it was almost a game for Violet and Marcus to find secret locations where nobody would discover what they were up to. Her office at the pool house was usually off-limits because it was too close to the main house, and when the boys came home from school, it was the first place they looked for her. But it was still morning and Sherilee and Freckles had left the ranch for the day to talk Dahlia into what sounded like an ill-conceived plan. Romantic, Violet thought, but also very ill-conceived.

Marcus rinsed the soap off his face, then resumed his explanation. "My mom is getting the Presidential Medal of Freedom at the White House for all her charity work when she was the second lady. If the whole family isn't there, Tessa will immediately get suspicious. Even Duke is taking leave to fly in."

"How's Duke doing, by the way?" Violet switched spots with him, so she could rinse off, as well. "He seemed pretty sad when he left the ranch."

"I think something is going on with him and Tom. I tried to bring it up when he was here, but he said he couldn't talk about it."

"That's rough."

"It was," Marcus agreed. "Actually, it was kind of a punch in the gut because we've always talked to each other about everything."

"I meant that's rough for Duke." Violet squeezed the excess water out of her hair. "But sure, let's make it about another bruise to your already-fragile big-brother ego."

"I agree with you one time about one sibling and you never let me live it down." Marcus cut in front of her to block the hot water. She turned the faucet to cold then ran for her towel, leaving him to yelp as she jumped out of the spray.

"So how long are you guys going to be gone?" she asked, trying not to stare at his abs as he rubbed the dry towel over them.

"Just one night. We fly out in the morning, stay the night in DC, then bring the jet back on Sunday."

"I bet MJ will be excited to get away from the ranch for a while. Even if it's only for twenty-four hours."

"That's one of the reasons why I can't take the boys. MJ has a lot of old school buddies in Washington, and he always used to slip his Secret Service tail when he was living there. I'm going to need to keep him occupied so he can't get into any more trouble."

She noticed that Marcus said *keep him occupied*, which implied participating in an activity together rather than acting as his jailer. That was progress at least. She bent forward to wrap her wet hair in a separate towel. Someone was going to start wondering why Violet was going through so many beach towels when the outside pool was only forty degrees. When she flipped back up, she asked, "So then, who's going to watch the twins?"

Marcus tucked his chin and gave her a wide-eyed helpless stare.

Violet gulped. "Me?"

"That would be amazing, Vi," he said a bit too quickly. "Thanks so much for offering."

She narrowed her eyes. "You know full well that wasn't an offer. I've never so much as babysat a child, let alone supervised two of them for twenty-four hours straight. At least not by myself."

"But you hang out with the boys all the time, and they love being around you. Plus, they'll be sleeping for at least nine hours of your shift. Probably."

"Shift?" Violet crossed her arms. "Am I getting paid for this?"

"I can pay you in other ways." He began kissing her neck, and she giggled before hearing a noise outside. They jumped apart, neither one of them wanting anyone to catch them. After several heart-pounding seconds of nobody knocking on the sliding glass doors, Violet finally let out a relieved breath.

"We can talk more about the details tonight," Marcus said as he pulled on his uniform pants. "I'll owe you big for this. And so will Tessa, if things work out between her and Agent Wyatt."

The rest of the afternoon, Violet vacillated between being thrilled and being nervous as hell. She was flattered that Marcus trusted her enough to leave his sons in her care. At the same time, she was seriously concerned that Marcus trusted her enough to leave his sons in her care. What was she going to do with two seven-year-olds for a whole day?

The situation got even more complicated when Marcus called her later that night to fill her in on the latest. Apparently, Dahlia's ex-husband, Micah, was going to be coming into town to stay with their daughter.

"The thing is," Marcus continued, "Dahlia's apartment above Big Millie's is only two bedrooms, and even though she and Micah get along great, she thinks it would be awkward for him to sleep at her place. Micah and Amelia are going to stay at the main house at the Twin Kings. So would you mind staying at my cabin with the boys?"

Micah Deacon was a famous musician, but Violet had never met the man. According to Dahlia, Micah was a doting father who was as active as he could be in Amelia's life, considering he lived in Nashville for work and spent a lot of time on tour with his band. It sounded like Micah could probably use some quality alone time with his daughter. Plus, Violet didn't like the idea of having a stranger witness all the babysitting mistakes she was bound to make with Jack and Jordan.

She tossed and turned all night trying not to think of all the things that could go wrong. When that failed to lessen her anxiety, she took one of her migraine pills and figured she might as well get a couple of hours of sleep before reporting for her so-called shift.

The following morning when she arrived at the cabin, Violet wished she had insisted on staying at the main house. Jack and Jordan were, of course, thrilled to see her, but Marcus was rushed and unfocused and kept rattling off last-minute instructions as he put away a box of cereal in the fridge and a gallon of milk in the pantry. She followed him from the kitchen to the front entry and then back to the kitchen when he realized he'd left his suitcase by the recycle bin.

"If you need the first-aid kit, it's in the right-side cabinet in the master bathroom," he said as they made their way to the front door. Again. "But if it's something more serious, then just drive to the hospital in Jackson. They already have both boys' insurance cards on file because we make a lot of trips there. If it's worthy of 9-1-1... Crap, I forgot Rod was covering for the dispatcher this weekend. Try not to call 9-1-1."

Violet gulped. "Is this supposed to be putting me at ease?"

"Don't worry. You guys *should* do fine." His emphasis on the word *should* wasn't any more reassuring. But he continued babbling out instructions. "Freckles stocked the fridge again, but the boys might try and talk you into going to the Pepperoni Stampede. I keep a bag of quarters in the top drawer of the mudroom for the arcade games. But don't let Jordan near the salad bar because the manager gets annoyed when he starts talking about salmonella and *E. coli* in front of the other customers. And Jack isn't allowed to use the claw machine because one time he climbed inside and...never mind. I'm supposed to be at the airfield in ten minutes. Okay, what am I forgetting?"

It suddenly occurred to her that Marcus was just as nervous about leaving his children overnight as she was about watching them. Surely, that had to be more stressful for him than anything she was going through. She threw back her shoulders with a confidence she didn't quite feel and asked, "So where should I sleep?"

"Oh." He paused. Then looked over his shoulder toward the formal living room where they'd slept the one and only time she'd been to his house. He took the small travel bag she'd packed and said, "Follow me."

They went past the dining room and then a smaller family room where the boys were sprawled out with blankets watching TV and eating cereal. An arched hallway led to what must be the bedrooms, and Marcus turned into the first doorway on the right. The room was furnished nicely, but it was also very nondescript. There were no photos, no books, no personal touches to give it the appearance of actually having been lived in. It was a guest room.

Okay. So Marcus was sticking her in a guest room. Violet wasn't sure what she'd been expecting, but her heart sank. No. She wasn't going to make a big deal out of it. It was probably better for the boys to see her sleeping in here rather than in their father's bed, anyway. How would she explain that sort of thing to them?

He set her bag on the dresser, then pulled her into his arms and gave her a deep kiss. "I really wish I could make this goodbye a little longer, but I'm already running late. Call me if you need anything."

And with that, he was gone.

Violet resisted the urge to go down the hallway to

explore the rest of the bedrooms. Instead, she tentatively approached the family room, took a deep breath and asked the twins, "So what do you guys want to do today?"

There were several outlandish ideas and a few disagreements, but in the end, Violet sat down at the coffee table in the family room with a yellow legal pad and treated this discussion as she would any other settlement conference.

"Okay, so Jack's suggested activities are bungee jumping, dirt-bike racing and going to that new axe-throwing place in Jackson Hole. Jordan, your suggestions are the Discovery Center, dinosaur-bone excavating and going to the pharmacy in town to use their blood-pressure machine." Violet waited until both kids nodded in agreement before continuing. "Now, let's see which of these options are going to work best for our needs. According to the Let Loose Adventures website, you have to be fourteen to jump off the bridge over Snake River. The Discovery Center looks interesting, but it's all the way in Casper, and we'll never make it back in time to watch that superhero detective show you guys were telling me about."

It took another thirty minutes of negotiating, but they finally compromised on taking one of the four-seater ATVs—with Violet, not Jack, driving—out exploring for caves and ancient artifacts. Jack was very impressed with her ability to do what he called *sick burnouts*, and Jordan was very excited to find a femur bone he was convinced belonged to a nineteenth-century buffalo, as well as several arrowheads. One of the boys' birthday gifts had been a pair of Nerf bows and pad-tipped arrows. So Violet set up an impromptu archery range, which was way safer than throwing axes, and held still while Jack attempted to shoot an apple off her head. On their way to dinner at the Pepperoni Stampede, they stopped by the pharmacy, and Jordan explained to her that her blood pressure was—surprisingly—in the normal range at 105 over 68.

It turned out, the only person who had sustained any sort of injury that day was Violet. And it wasn't until after she'd put the boys to bed and gone back to the kitchen to open a bottle of wine, intending to toast herself to a successful day of babysitting. A little too anxious to celebrate her victory, her thumb slipped on the condensation of the bottle, and she jabbed herself with the corkscrew.

It was a small gash, but started bleeding again every time she bumped it. Marcus had said the first-aid kit was in the master bathroom; however, Violet had been trying to avoid that particular part of the house.

It was either go get a bandage or risk having Jordan wake up and see a pile of discarded paper towels soaked with her blood. The poor boy would probably insist on giving her stitches himself. Violet steeled her spine and quietly made her way down the hallway.

When she got to the door, though, a heaviness made her stomach queasy.

The king-size bed was covered with a fluffy floral-patterned comforter and throw pillows in assorted sizes and colors. There was a silver frame on the dresser holding a different wedding photo than the one she'd seen in the main house. In this picture, Marcus and Brie were happily staring into each other's eyes. Just when Violet had gotten over feeling like an impostor babysitter this morning, she now felt like an intruder in another woman's house.

Turning to the bathroom, she quickly made her away across the plush rug, wanting to get in and out of there as soon as she could. She knelt and opened the right-side cabinet, reluctant to see any other personal items, and was relieved that the only thing on the shelf was the first-aid kit. She quickly found a bandage and wrapped it around her thumb, before deciding to grab a couple more for backup. She certainly didn't want to come back in here if she didn't have to. But when she stood up in front of the vanity mirror, she could see the reflection of the enormous walk-in closet directly behind her. The door was slightly ajar, and behind it, a row of Brie's clothes were still hanging there.

So this was the reason Marcus hadn't taken her to his bed that first night she'd spent here. And why he'd installed her in the guest room today. The master bedroom wasn't necessarily a shrine to his dead wife, but her presence could still be felt.

Violet's phone rang in her pocket, startling her. She saw Marcus's name on the screen and swallowed down her panic. There was no way he could possibly know that she'd been in the master bedroom snooping around.

No. This wasn't snooping.

It was discovery. She had known all along how much he'd loved Brie. This only served as a reminder that Violet could not allow herself to fall for a man who was no longer hers.

"Hello," Violet said, when she finally picked up. Marcus had waited for so many rings, he'd half expected the call to go to voice mail. But hearing her voice on the other end sent a wave of contentment through him.

"How're the boys?" Marcus leaned back against the pillows of his hotel bed.

"Asleep. We had a fun and busy day. I'll send you some of the pictures I took. How is everything going over there?"

"Good, actually. My mom and Freckles's plan actually worked. Grayson proposed to Tessa right there in the Rose Garden, and the media finally got the buzzworthy story they'd been waiting for. MJ and I went out to dinner, just the two of us, and then he took me to this random yoga studio on the other side of the Potomac. He said he used to go there when he wanted to get away from all the tourists and what he called *the political noise*. I had no idea he was into yoga."

"Good! I'm glad you guys are spending some time together and getting to know each other."

"I know, I know. As much as it pains me to admit it, you were right about our relationship." Marcus grinned listening to her chuckle in response. "But don't get too used to hearing me say it. Your client still has to go before the new judge."

Secretly, Marcus was hoping for another delay in the trial. The longer Violet stayed on at the Twin Kings, the more time he had to convince her to... What? Give up her life and career and move to a small town in Wyoming to be with a single dad who'd once broken her heart?

"Don't worry," she replied. "I'm looking forward to our day in court. I might even decide to call you as a character witness on your brother's behalf."

"Good try, counselor. But I think I've already proven

that I'd make a terrible character witness. I'm as impartial as I can be when it comes to enforcing the law." Marcus rubbed the back of his neck, debating whether he should even risk saying his idea out loud. Why not? If it meant keeping her in town longer, it was worth a shot. He cleared his throat. "In fact, with the way my family has been behaving lately, I might even have a couple of new clients for you."

"Oh, no. What happened?"

"Do you want me to tell you as the sheriff? Or as a big brother who couldn't stop laughing when I first heard the story?"

"Definitely the big-brother version."

"You know how Dahlia has been seeing that new rancher out on the Rocking D? The one who my mom made stay for dinner a couple of Fridays ago?"

"Connor Remington?" Violet asked. "I thought I was the only one who'd figured out that there was something going on between him and your sister."

"I'm pretty sure everyone knows." Just like they all had probably figured out he and Violet were sneaking around again. "Anyway, somehow my sweet little niece Amelia convinced both Micah and Connor to rescue some stuffed animal from Jay Grover's place. When he wasn't home."

Violet's jaw dropped. "You mean to tell me that your sister's boyfriend and her ex-husband broke into someone's house? *Together?* And you're laughing about it?"

Marcus snorted. "I don't know why I think it's so funny. Dahlia is furious. Deputy Broman is annoyed because my family is indirectly involved. Again. And I'm out of town and can't do a thing about any of it."

"No, you can't," she agreed. "Which might be a good thing. You don't always have to be the fixer."

He let out an exaggerated breath. "I wish I could fix us, Vi."

There was no response, and he looked at his phone to see if the call had been disconnected. It hadn't. "Are you there?"

"I'm here." Her voice was soft, hesitant.

Had he gone too far?

"Are you going to answer my question?" he asked.

"Was it a question? Because it sounded like a statement."

"I guess it was." He ran his hand through his hair. "What I should've said was *Do you think I can fix us?*"

"No." Her one-word response would've sent him to his knees if he wasn't already lying down. Then she continued, "I think that you alone can't do anything, Marcus. If anything needs to be fixed, it would take both of us to do it."

Okay. That sounded slightly more promising. "Do you think we should try?"

"Before I answer that, let me ask *you* a question."

"Go for it."

She paused, further increasing the suspense already zapping through his nerve endings. Then she threw him for a loop by asking, "Why didn't you ever take me to your bed?"

"What are you talking about?"

"Here at your house. We slept in the living room the first night. Then, today, you put my stuff in the guest room. Is there a reason you don't want me in your bed?"

"That *is* my bed, Vi. That's the room I use at the cabin," he said. When she didn't respond right away, he added, "Go look in the closet. All my uniforms are in there."

He could hear some background noise and then the unmistakable slide of the closet doors.

"Oh. You don't use the master bedroom?" As soon as she said the word *master*, he pictured the room in his head and wished he hadn't waited so long to go through Brie's stuff.

"No. But I know what you're thinking."

"What am I thinking, Marcus?"

"That I'm some sorry sap that can't move on from the memory of his dead wife."

"Are you?"

A blast of air expelled from his mouth. "When Brie died, it hit me hard. She was my best friend and the mother of my children. Sure, living in our house without her was overwhelming at the time. I had two toddlers and a full-time job. Moving into the main house with the rest of my family there as a sort of built-in backup helped me get through those first couple of months. I told myself that the twins and I would move back into the cabin at some point, and I even talked to Dahlia about helping me redecorate. But she'd just had Amelia and was in the middle of refurbishing Big Millie's. Eventually, months turned into years, and I became the sheriff. Looking out for everyone else took priority. A couple of winters ago, Tessa's TV network was holding a national coat drive, and I thought it would be the perfect time to finally go through Brie's clothes and give them away. Finn came to help me, and we made it halfway through the closet when I got a call from the preschool telling me that Jack got his head stuck in the opening of the puppet theater."

He heard what might've been a snort of laughter on the other end.

"Anyway, I thought Finn had stayed back to finish the job, not that it was her responsibility. It wasn't until you moved into the main house that the boys and I returned to the cabin full-time. I didn't really want the boys running in and out of the master bedroom and getting sad seeing all their mom's stuff. So I took the spare bedroom and figured I'd get around to dealing with the rest later."

"Oh."

That was it? Marcus thought. All Violet could say was *oh*?

No. He wasn't going to be the only one put on the spot in this conversation. If they were going to talk about the things standing between them, then he had a few things he wanted some clarity on, as well. "Now can I ask you a question?"

"Hold on. I'm still processing," Violet replied. Processing what? Whether she believed him or whether she thought he was holding on to way too much baggage? At least thirty more seconds went by and then she said, "Okay. Go ahead and ask."

"Does your mom still think you're moving back to Dallas when MJ's case is over?"

"I didn't tell her that I wasn't."

"You might want to consider talking to her about that," Marcus suggested.

"Why?" He could hear the dread in Violet's voice, which would've made him laugh if he wasn't worried about how she was going to react to his warning.

"Because my mom saw her at the Capital Grille today having lunch with the chairman of the foreignaffairs committee. Mom handed over her real estate agent's card and told the senator to start looking at investing in a vacation home in Jackson Hole so that she could come visit you more often."

"Crap," Violet said. Then added, "Double crap. That's my mother ringing through right now on call-waiting. I've got to do some damage control. We can talk about this tomorrow when I see you at home."

The call disconnected, and he would've been left feeling dejected that she'd referred to explaining things to her mother as *damage control*. Except he wasn't disappointed. Instead, a thrill of excitement shot through him.

She'd said *home*. Not your home. Not your family's home. Just home. As though she was already thinking of it as her own.

CHAPTER TWELVE

"WHY DO OUR moms do this, Marcus? We're thirty-two years old, and they're still using us as pawns. Clearly, we need to stage some sort of intervention to prove once and for all that neither one of them are calling the shots on our relationship."

Violet was pacing back and forth in his office after Connor's and Micah's bail hearings. The charges were probably going to be dropped, but that didn't mean Violet was backing down as his adversary. At least not in public. But first she needed to deal with the latest development of their quarreling mothers.

"Our relationship?" he asked. "You mean the one we're currently involved in?"

"Sure. That one."

"No, Violet. I want to hear you say it."

"Don't you think we're a little too old for me to call you my boyfriend?"

"You think I'm your boyfriend," he sang. "That means you wanna be my girlfriend."

"This is so mature." Violet narrowed her eyes. "Besides, when we were on the courthouse steps a few minutes ago, I didn't hear you telling Dahlia, Connor and Micah that I was your girlfriend."

"MJ's trial starts tomorrow, and we were out in the open. Everyone expects us to stick with the routine that we can't get along. No special favors, remember? As soon as that's over, we can come clean and let everyone know."

"Do you seriously think your family doesn't already know what's going on with us?" This was the first time they'd been able to speak alone since he'd returned from Washington, and neither one had wanted to mention what was said during that emotional phone call the night before. "If your mom is giving my mom business cards for Jackson Hole real estate agents, then she knows."

"Not everyone in my family has figured out that I'm your boyfriend."

"Stop calling yourself that." Violet tried to sound disapproving, but deep down, her stomach got all fluttery when he said the word.

"Make me," he said, acting even more juvenile as he slipped his hands around her waist and pulled her closer.

Violet's attempt at a stern expression turned into a sigh as he traced his lips down her neck in a series of light kisses. A booming knock sounded on his door, and they jumped apart before Rod entered the office.

"Here's that surveillance footage a so-called anonymous source gave the DA to get those charges reduced to trespassing." The V-shaped crease between Rod's overgrown eyebrows was meant to remind Violet that he didn't approve of defense attorneys fraternizing with law-enforcement officers. The few times she'd been at the sheriff's station, the older volunteer's hawk eyes followed her wherever she went, as though he was expecting her to do something sneaky and nefarious, such as take an extra handful of M&Ms from the candy bowl on the front desk.

"Oh, thanks, Mr. D'Agostino." Violet held up a thumb drive with the video of Jay Grover breaking into his ex-wife's house the same night Micah and Connor had broken into his. Reed Nakamoto had known the case would be flimsy and had been eager to reduce the charges to trespassing well before he'd found out the alleged victim was going to make a very unreliable witness. "I brought my own copy to show the sheriff. But I'm certainly not an anonymous source. Just a concerned citizen hoping to see justice done."

"Hmph," Rod said before turning and purposely leaving the office door open. Probably so that he could keep her clearly in his sight.

"Concerned citizen?" Marcus asked. "As in a *permanent* citizen of Teton Ridge?"

Violet's stomach fluttered again, but then the sensation moved to her chest and caused a tight knot of anxiety. "I know what you're trying to get me to say, Marcus. But I'm not ready to commit to anything yet. Especially nothing as big as uprooting my life and moving to Wyoming."

An obvious cough sounded as Rod passed by the open office door on his way to the copy machine.

"Sorry about that," Marcus mumbled. "Rod thinks that every time you stop by, I'm consorting with the enemy. He's worried that you're going to use your big-city defense-attorney charm to manipulate me into doing your bidding."

"How does he know I haven't already?" Violet gave the man a friendly wave on his way back to the desk, almost enjoying feeding into his suspicions about her ulterior motives. Then she raised her voice so that Rod could hear. "So you think about what I said, Sheriff, and I'll meet you later tonight at our usual location. I'll be sure to bring that special thing you requested."

While Violet and Marcus both knew that neither of them had broken any ethical rules by being together, let him be the one to explain to his staff that their *usual location* was the main house at the Twin Kings for a family dinner. And the *special thing* he'd requested was a plum pie from Burnworth's Bakery.

Turning on her heel, she tried not to laugh at Marcus's painful groan behind her as she walked away. Too bad. He couldn't have it both ways. He couldn't call her his girlfriend in private, while at the same time want everyone else in town to think that their relationship was only professional until after the trial. He'd have to decide what he wanted—and soon.

Later that evening, Violet was sitting in the formal living room at the main house, having predinner cocktails with Tessa, Dahlia and Finn as Sherilee King shoved glossy bridal magazines under their noses. Duke had flown back to Wyoming with the family after meeting them in DC and was now trying to include Grayson, Tessa's new fiancé, and Connor, Dahlia's boyfriend, in a conversation that wasn't all about Micah's and Marcus's glory days on the high school football team.

Freckles was in the kitchen doing what she loved, and Rider was doing what he loved—taking Jack, Jordan and Amelia out for a ride on their horses. Violet tried to focus on what Sherilee was saying about bridesmaid dresses and flower arrangements, but she couldn't stop sneaking glances at Marcus. Every time their eyes met, his filled with a heat that promised what he intended to do to her once he finally got her alone.

MJ was too nervous about the trial starting tomorrow, so he'd gone back to his bedroom to be alone. And probably to call Kendra. Violet was just thinking that she should probably head back to her room, as well, and put the final tweaks on her opening statement. But before she could make her excuses, Micah strode into the room, his eyes filled with panic, and announced, "Hey, Rider and the kids aren't back yet. They were expected at the stables over thirty minutes ago."

Marcus immediately turned to Violet, and she watched all the color drain from his face. It was nearly dark, and his uncle's rides with the children never lasted this long. This wasn't good.

"I'll go find them." Connor, who had once been a tracker in the military, was the first to head to the door.

"We'll all come," Finn said, taking off after him.

Marcus was also gone before Violet could cross the room to him. Everyone was hurrying to the stables, and she tried not to think of the kids lost somewhere on the trail, all alone in the dark.

Mike Truong, the stable manager, was already saddling horses, while Marcus and Grayson were organizing who would be going on horseback and who would be taking the ATVs. Many of the riding trails on the ranch were too narrow for vehicles, and Connor and Finn immediately rode off on horseback with radios clipped to their belts.

"I'll take Dahlia to the airfield to meet the helicopter pilot," Duke said. "We'll get a searchlight up in the air so you guys on the ground can see where you're looking."

Even Freckles had come from the kitchen, prepared with granola bars and protein snacks to put in the emergency-kit backpacks. Sherilee did the same with bottles of water before hopping into the back seat of a departing ATV at the last minute. No way was the King matriarch going to sit back and wait patiently for her grandchildren to be found.

Violet stood there in the stables, watching helplessly as everyone sprang into action and got their job assignments. She couldn't ride a horse, and there were only so many ATVs. Only a few Secret Service agents remained on the ranch, and along with the other cattle hands, they knew the trails and the terrain way better than her. Other than being an extra set of eyes, she couldn't really offer the search team much value. But the boys were out there, possibly alone, and she needed to get to them as soon as possible. She didn't want to waste time changing into her running shoes, so she grabbed a flashlight and a radio from the table of supplies and was about to set out on foot when Marcus's voice stopped her.

"Violet," he shouted, anxiously looking around the stables for her.

Up until now, he'd been methodical and organized and completely in command as he gave everyone instructions. She imagined that, as the county sheriff, he'd participated in numerous search and rescues. But this was different. These were his own boys who were lost. How was he holding himself together?

"Over here," she said, rushing over to him.

There was the slightest flicker of panic in his eyes, but he quickly blinked it back when he saw her. "I'm taking Micah in one of the ATVs. I need you to stay here in case the kids and Rider come back while we're all still out there."

"Oh. Okay." Logically, Violet knew that her assignment would be just as important as the others. But she hated just sitting there not doing anything. So she pushed away her own fears and forced a confident smile she didn't quite feel. "In fact, I'll probably see them before you guys, because I'm sure they're already on their way back so they can sneak in a few of Freckles's lemon bars before dinner."

He nodded and sucked in a deep breath, probably to calm his racing thoughts. Violet pulled his head down for a parting kiss then added, "Be careful. And don't worry. When they get here, I'll take care of them. I promise."

Tessa and Grayson set up a command center in the conference room attached to the bunkhouse where the Secret Service agents stayed. The radio reception was much better there, plus there were maps and whiteboards to track everybody's progress. Freckles, who had to be just as worried about Rider as she was about the children, returned to the kitchen to prep more food in case it ended up being a long night. Not that anyone could eat at a time like this. But it was probably good to have someone stationed at the house just in case they went straight there.

Violet was left alone in the stables and found herself pacing back and forth as she waited for word. She listened intently to every transmission across the radio, her nerves becoming more frayed each time a voice came on the air to report another dead end.

No. Don't think about the word *dead*.

"Why is it taking so long?" she asked Fabio, who was hanging his head over the stall door watching her. To keep herself occupied, Violet grabbed a bucket of treats that looked like the oat clumps Marcus carried in his uniform pocket and went down the rows of stalls, feeding one to every animal who hadn't gotten to ride out for the search.

She was nearly back to Fabio's stall when it dawned on her that she was supposed to be afraid of horses. Her spirits perked up, but before she could celebrate her small victory, the radio cracked to life.

"I have the boys." Finn's announcement caused Violet to jump up in celebration, sending a few extra oat treats Fabio's way. "They were southwest of the Peabody Trail. They're tired and thirsty, but still in their saddles."

"Where's Amelia?" Micah demanded, the engine of his and Marcus's ATV revving in the background of the radio transmission.

"The boys say Rider got hurt and couldn't ride," Finn advised. "Amelia stayed to watch over him while the boys rode back to the stables to get help. But they got lost."

"Do they know where they left Amelia and Rider?" This time it was Dahlia's voice, but Violet couldn't tell if she was in the helicopter already.

"Negative," Finn said. "We'll get these two back to Violet. You guys keep looking."

Violet wanted to weep in relief that the boys were safe, but there were still two people missing. Plus, Marcus had to stay with Micah. He couldn't abandon the search for Amelia and Rider just because his own sons had been found.

"I'll take care of them," she repeated her promise from earlier to Fabio.

The engine of an ATV grew louder, and Violet ran to the stable doors. An agent was driving with one boy in the front seat and the other in the back sitting next to MJ. Even in the fading light, she could see the drying trail of tears down Jack's dirty cheeks as he frantically unbuckled and launched himself out of the vehicle and directly into Violet's arms.

Her heart went to pieces, and she wanted to hold the child close to her until she could make sure he was truly safe. But she also had to check on his brother. Jordan was the usually cautious twin, but he wasn't even unbuckling himself. He was sitting stiffly in his seat, MJ speaking quietly to him.

Freckles was hurrying across the driveway with a plate of cookies and a stack of blankets. Violet set Jack on his feet, letting Freckles wrap him in a quilt and crush him in a hug, her own sparkle-stained tears running down her face.

Violet immediately went to Jordan's side. She noticed he had a piece of fabric holding his right arm in makeshift sling. "What's wrong, Jordan?"

The boy was pale, and his lips made a grimaced line as he refused to answer.

She looked at MJ, who ran a hand through his hair before shrugging. "When we were transferring him from his horse to the ATV, his arm hit the roll bar, and he let out a scream. He wouldn't let any of us check it out. I could tell he was in a ton of pain from the bumpy ride, so I convinced him to let me use this sling to hold it in place."

"Want me to call for an ambulance?" an agent asked her.

"No," Jordan yelled, finally finding his voice. He turned pleading eyes to Violet.

Everyone was looking at her to make a decision that really wasn't hers to make. Deep down, though, she had a feeling she knew exactly what was wrong. "Let's get you out of that seat and get you something to eat. Then, you can tell me how you're feeling."

The boy squished his face in pain as Violet eased the holster seat belt away from the shoulder of his injured arm. Violet didn't think she was strong enough to lift him without jostling him even more, so MJ helped. When he was out of the ATV, MJ walked him to the bench just outside the stables and sat him down next to his brother.

Freckles went back to the main house to get some lemonade in case the boys were dehydrated. The agent explained that he had to go back and get their horses, and MJ added, "I should return to the search. Are you sure you're good here?"

"We got it." When the ATV pulled away, Violet knelt in front of Jordan. "Are you ready to tell me why you don't want anyone to look at your arm?"

Jordan sniffed, tears filling his eyes. "Uncle Rider got hurt real bad. The fire department only has one ambulance, and Uncle Rider needs it more than me."

"That's very thoughtful of you, Jordan. But you might have a pretty serious injury there yourself. Don't you think we need to get that fixed?"

He bit his lower lip, and Violet realized she had to try a different tactic. She turned to the boy's twin, who was lovingly drying Jordan's tears with a corner of the blanket.

"You're pretty good at diagnosing stuff, Jack. What do you think is wrong?"

Jack, who never paid attention to any of the medical documentaries his twin watched, shrugged. "Maybe he sprained his wrist?"

"It's not my wrist. It's a sub-cromal pinge-oment," Jordan corrected.

Violet had absolutely no idea what that was, but it

sounded serious. And painful. She'd promised Marcus that she'd take care of his sons, and that was exactly what she was going to do. "How about if instead of calling an ambulance, I drive you to the hospital? Your dad can meet us there after they find Rider and make sure he's in good hands."

The boy tried to shrug but winced in pain. Violet held her breath, not wanting to push his decision. "Okay, I guess."

Aunt Freckles was returning with two insulated cups and a couple of bottles of water tucked into her apron pockets.

"All right, then. Aunt Freckles, can you please load up the snacks and the blankets in the car for us?" Violet forced her voice into a calmness she didn't feel. "We're just going to go on a little drive over to the hospital and let the doctors take a peek at Jordan's sub pingement situation."

"I don't need an ambulance," Jordan insisted to the older woman, as though she hadn't been listening in on the radio this whole time and knew full well that Rider was in trouble.

"Of course you don't, darlin'." Freckles smiled her wide grin, her bright lipstick proving to be much longer lasting against tears than her smeared mascara.

"You'll like the CT-scan machine, Jord," Jack eagerly told his twin as Violet pulled onto the main highway. Jack then rattled off all the emergency-room procedures that he'd experienced in the past five years. Instead of being distracted, though, Jordan's little face grew even more pale as he listened in terror.

Violet pushed her foot harder on the gas and prayed she was making the right choice.

CHAPTER THIRTEEN

MARCUS KNEW THIS emergency room almost as well as he knew the Ridgecrest County Courthouse. The desk nurse greeted him and, before he could ask, said, "They're in room 107."

"Thanks, Cathy," he replied, striding down the hall.

When he got to 107, the door was open, and the curtain partition was pushed aside. Violet was sitting in a chair beside the bed, showing Jordan a video on her phone. Pausing a second, he watched them without saying anything. He let the wave of relief crash through him and sent up a silent prayer of thanks that they were all okay.

"Dad!" Jack paused from spinning in circles on the doctor's stool. "It wasn't me this time."

"So I heard." Marcus had found out over the radio that his sons were safe, but it wasn't the same as seeing them with his own eyes. He squeezed Jack to him before turning to look at the hospital bed. Not wanting to cause any discomfort to Jordan, Marcus had to settle for ruffling his hair. "How's the patient doing?"

"Sorry I got hurt, Dad. Is Uncle Rider okay?" Of course Jordan would be more concerned about his dad's feelings and his uncle's condition than his own.

"Don't be sorry, buddy. Accidents happen. Uncle Rider is in surgery right now, but he should be fine. Amelia is fine, too. She's with Aunt Dahlia and everyone else in the lobby, waiting to hear from the surgeon. But I'm more worried about you. What's going on in here?"

Jordan looked at the digital machine beside him. "My blood pressure is in the normal range. Pulse and oxygen are fine. They already did an MRI, and we have to wait for the results."

"In fact, the doctor should've been here a while ago." Violet stood. "Maybe I should go down the hall and find her."

"Hey." Marcus took several steps toward the foot of the bed and grabbed Violet's hand before she could leave. He lowered his voice. "MJ said he could tell it was bad, but Jordan wouldn't say anything. Thank you for taking charge."

"Of course." Violet squeezed his fingers in response, but she made a subtle side-eye look toward the boys, as though she was warning Marcus that they had an audience.

They locked eyes for several seconds, and then Jordan asked, "Are you guys gonna kiss?"

Violet immediately tried to pull away, but Marcus wouldn't release her hand. He maintained eye contact with her while asking his sons, "Why? Do you want us to?"

"Yes!" Both of the boys cheered, but Jack did so with more energy and crashed his spinning stool into the blood-pressure machine.

He lifted his brows at Violet. "They want us to kiss."

"How about we just shake instead?" They were

already holding hands, so Violet pumped her arm dramatically.

"No!" the boys chorused. Jordan even giggled.

"We could compromise with a hug?" Marcus suggested, pulling Violet into his arms. God, she felt good. After everything he'd been through tonight, he didn't know how much he'd needed to hold her until she was pressed against him. Apparently, she'd needed a hug just as badly, because she wrapped her own arms around his neck and let her head fall to his shoulder.

"Uh, excuse me, Mrs. King?" A young doctor that Marcus didn't recognize stood in the doorway holding a clipboard. Violet pulled away from his embrace and looked around the room in confusion before finally realizing the newcomer was speaking to her. "I'm Dr. Yu, and I just got your son's MRI scans from the radiology department. Is now a good time for me to come in?"

"Oh, I'm not... He's not my..." Violet started, but Jordan prevented her from saying anything else.

"Is it a sub-cromal pinge-oment?"

The doctor tilted her head to the side. "How do you know what subacromial impingement is?"

Violet finally managed a reply. "He does a lot of medical research."

"Well, you're close. It's actually a dislocation. Do you know what that is?"

"Yes, but I didn't hear a popping sound," Jordan replied. "Shouldn't I have heard a popping sound?"

"Not always." The doctor turned to Violet. "So how did the injury happen?"

"Oh." Violet waited for Marcus to take the lead on speaking to the doctor, but he'd only just arrived and still wasn't sure what exactly had happened. Dr. Yu looked expectantly at Violet. "Uh, he and his brother were riding on their horses, and the trail was getting dark. They had to go under a low-hanging branch, and Jordan was worried Jack wouldn't see it. So he reached to push it out of the way, and his sleeve got caught. The horse kept going, and his arm got jerked backward."

"Ouch," Dr. Yu said, and Marcus winced in agreement. "I know the physician's assistant already did a cursory eval, but do you mind if I examine him?"

The doctor continued to direct most of her attention to either Jordan or Violet, who she clearly assumed was the mother of the twins. Marcus would've been slightly insulted that his role as the father had been dismissed in favor of the mother if he hadn't been enjoying watching Violet easily answer the questions.

"Okay, Dad." Dr. Yu finally spoke to Marcus. "I'm going to need you to sit behind Jordan and help him stay in position like this."

"Mom—" Dr. Yu said to Violet, and at this point nobody corrected her "—I'm going to need you to hold Jordan's good hand in yours so he can squeeze it real tight. Now, I'm going to simply rotate your arm and move everything back into place on the count of three."

"Wait. Can I do it?" Jack asked.

"No!" Marcus, Dr. Yu and Jordan all yelled at the same time.

"Maybe I should take Jack out to—" Violet started, but Jordan interrupted.

His eyes were wide, and his small fingers were digging into her hand. "Please stay with me."

"Of course I'll stay with—"

Pop!

Dr. Yu had taken advantage of the distraction, and Jordan barely made a yelp.

"Was that it?" the boy asked.

"Yep. All done. You did great." The doctor again looked at Violet. "He's going to need to keep it elevated and iced. Do you have children's ibuprofen at home?"

"We can stop at the pharmacy and get some," she replied easily.

"Does he play any sports?"

"He's supposed to start baseball next week."

"You'll have to tell his coach that he can participate in the running drills, but no throwing for at least four weeks."

"Got it," Violet said, then looked at Marcus. "Hear that, Coach? No throwing for four weeks."

The doctor finally glanced at Marcus, and he wanted to tell her that he was also her patient's parent, not just the coach. But with the exception of being the muscle to hold Jordan in place, all the questions and directions were given to Violet. Which was really for the best because Marcus was too emotionally drained to remember all the instructions.

"He'll have to wear a sling for a few days. Do you need a note for school?"

"Any documentation you could give us would be great," Violet said, always thinking of the legalities.

"That didn't take as long as last time when I got my cast," Jack said when the doctor finally left. "Can we get some ice cream on the way home?"

"Sure," Violet said without even consulting Marcus. For a woman who'd been reluctant to babysit for a few hours, she was certainly warming up to the motherly role she'd been thrust into.

Cathy, the desk nurse, at least gave Marcus one parental duty. He got to sign the discharge paperwork.

The four of them left the emergency room and stopped in the hospital lobby to check in with the rest of the family. Duke saw them coming and signaled Marcus and Violet over to talk, while Jordan showed off his new sling to everyone else.

"Rider's out of surgery, but they're going to keep him in ICU."

"ICU?" Marcus shuddered. Connor had found Rider and Amelia first, but Marcus and Micah had arrived soon after. Rider had still been pretty lucid when they'd called for medical transport.

Duke nodded. "He broke a rib, and it punctured one of his lungs. Freckles is back there now with him. The surgeon said the prognosis is good, but I didn't want to say anything in front of your kids because I know Jordan would worry."

"You're a good uncle," Marcus said, then pulled his brother in for a fierce hug. His second hug of the evening. "I know I usually don't say this, but I'm glad you're in town."

"Why? Because I'm the only one in the family with a pilot's license and could provide aerial support during the search?"

"No, because Kendra Broman just came in the door, and someone needs to make sure her daddy doesn't come in here looking for MJ."

"Big brother isn't going to stick around and keep watch on everyone?" Duke asked, and Violet snorted. "This is certainly unexpected."

"I'm taking the rest of the night off. I need a few hours alone with my family to focus on what I almost lost." Marcus wrapped his arm around Violet's waist and pulled her against his side. "Come on, boys. We're heading back to our cabin."

Violet should've been in her room at the main house planning for her opening statement at the trial tomorrow. Instead, she was at Marcus's house kissing a very sleepy Jordan good-night. Jack had fallen asleep in the truck on the way home with his half-eaten ice-cream cone in his hand, and Marcus was trying to get his chocolate-stained shirt off without waking him.

When she and Marcus left the room and shut off the hallway light, he asked, "Beer or wine?"

"Definitely wine."

He went into the kitchen, and she collapsed on the living-room sofa, thinking over everything that had happened that night. When he returned with her glass, she asked, "Why did you let the doctor think that I was Jordan's mom?"

"Because you were acting like his mom."

"I wasn't trying to be," she insisted, not wanting Marcus to think she was angling to take the place of his children's mother. She wouldn't have even known how to fill that role.

"I know. I meant you were doing all the things that parents normally do in those situations. My brain was still on overload from earlier, so I was grateful one of us could properly function. You were great at comforting him and making decisions and advocating for him."

"Well, he was doing a pretty good job advocating for himself. Man, that boy knows his medical terminology."

Marcus chuckled, then took a sip of his beer. "He also knows that he can count on you. He could've easily told Finn or MJ about his arm, but he waited and told you. Not that he didn't trust his aunt and uncle to take care of him. But because he knew that you would listen to his concerns and not override him or tell him he was silly for not wanting to call for an ambulance. I told you before that my boys not only adore you, they respect you."

Violet knew the conversation would have to take place sooner or later. She couldn't let the twins think that she was going to continue being in their lives if she had even the slightest doubt that things might not work out with their father.

She took a deep breath and faced him. "You told me that one of the reasons you married Brie was because she was so easy to get along with. But Marcus, I'm not her, and I'm never going to be her."

"Have I ever made you feel as though you needed to be? As though I didn't want you to be completely yourself?"

"The girl I used to be, or the woman I am now? Because I've changed a lot since then."

"Like you're more argumentative? Believe me, I've noticed."

"Do you know how I got this way?" she asked.

His mouth lowered into a frown. "Because I hurt you."

"Yes and no. It's important that you understand that even if we get back together, even if we try to move past all the hurt we once caused each other," she paused so that he would know that she, too, was taking some responsibility for their breakup, "there are going to be times when we still won't agree."

He lifted his knee onto the cushions to better face

her. "Then help me to understand where you're coming from."

"We both know that my mother is overbearing and controlling and—" Violet exhaled "—frankly, a lot like *your* mother. Except you grew up with other siblings, who taught you how to argue, how to fight back. I had the desire, but I didn't have the training or the courage. Even back then, there was a part of me that knew I shouldn't have given up so easily. That I should have fought harder for you. Or at least fought harder to confront you. But I was young and hurt, and before I knew it, you were gone. I convinced myself that you might not be worth fighting for, but that I was. In law school, I finally found my voice. I learned how to negotiate, how to persuade and, more importantly, how to argue. And I was good at it. Distinguished law firms recruited me. The district attorney told me I could have my choice of assignments. My mom had arranged for me to clerk with the Supreme Court. You know what I chose, though?"

"To represent the people who you thought needed you most?"

"Well, that was a small part of it. But mostly I became a public defender because those were the hardest cases to win. I needed the challenge. I needed the fight because I had spent too much of my life not fighting for the things I believed in."

He picked up her hand. "Did you believe in us?"

"Back then?" She only paused to take a breath. "One hundred percent."

"What about now?" he asked.

"Right now?"

"Yes, Violet Cortez-Hill. Do you believe that we can figure out a way to fight for each other this time?"

"What are you saying, Marcus?" She didn't want anything to be said in the heat of passion or in jest. They both needed to lay all their cards out and talk about their expectations.

He cupped her cheek in his hand. "At one time in my life, I thought I wanted things to be easy. I don't regret my marriage to Brie because she gave me what I needed at the time. Truthfully, we gave each other what we needed. Plus, she gave me my children. But now I need something else in my life. I need you, Violet. My boys need you. Hell, my whole family needs you. I know that things won't be perfect and that we will have our ups and downs. I wouldn't expect anything less from you. You bring out the best in me, and you challenge me to be the kind of man that I want my sons to be. I loved the girl you once were, but I love the woman you've become even more."

Her heart filled with a lightness, and her mind was spinning. Marcus loved her. He wanted her in his life. Normally, she knew all the right things to say. But right now, all she could manage was "I love you, too."

"Then stay here," he said, before picking her up and carrying her to his bedroom. She had a feeling he meant stay in Wyoming, not just in his bed. And as he shut the door behind them, she realized there was nowhere else she'd rather be.

Except preparing for trial tomorrow. Ugh. They'd just had an intense, adrenaline-fueled night, topped by an emotionally healing conversation about their future, and Violet was going to have to leave to get ready to oppose Marcus in court in the morning. Well, not Marcus exactly. Just the deputy who worked for him and the county prosecutor.

When Marcus started kissing her, though, Violet decided that she could probably stay one more hour. Maybe two.

Before dawn the following morning, Marcus was thinking about what he was going to cook Violet for breakfast when a pounding knock came from his front door. If something had happened to Rider in the middle of the night, one of his family members would've called.

"I'll go see who it is," he told Violet when she stirred in his arms. "But I'm not going to keep it a secret that you're here."

Last night, she'd told him she loved him. This morning, the boys would wake up and see she'd spent the night. After the trial ended, everyone would know that they were together, and they could stop all this sneaking around.

Turned out, there was no need to pretend otherwise. When Marcus opened the door, MJ was on the other side and strode inside. "Is Violet awake? I need to talk to her."

"Is everything okay?" Violet asked, coming down the hall in the sweater she'd been wearing last night—inside out—and a pair of Marcus's boxer shorts. Her hair was in a messy ponytail, and her face was filled with concern. "Is it Rider?"

"Oh, um, sorry. Rider is good. He was already awake and asking Freckles to sneak some biscuits and gravy into the hospital for him. The surgeon is moving him out of the intensive care unit later this morning. But that's not why I'm here. I want to plead guilty today."

"Whoa," Violet said, not so subtly jerking her chin toward Marcus. "This might be a conversation that needs to take place somewhere else to maintain attorney–client privilege."

"I can go get some coffee started," Marcus offered, but MJ cut him off.

"No. I want you to hear this. You were right. I needed to grow up and start taking responsibility for my actions. Dad had always steered me in the right direction, and I used to sit back and let him. I know that sounds like a cry for attention, and maybe it was. But the more I acted like I needed guidance, the more Dad gave me. Then, right after my high-school graduation, Dad seemed distracted. You guys were all busy with your own lives when he first got sick, but I knew something was up with his health before then. I put off college last fall because I wanted to stay close to him. I thought that maybe if he thought I needed him badly enough, he'd fight whatever was wrong with him and stick around. When he died, though, I started thinking that maybe I should've been the one to fix him, rather than the other way around."

Sounded like Marcus wasn't the only one in the family who thought he needed to fix things. But he let MJ continue.

"I was angry and I was emotional and I was stupid. I shouldn't have gotten drunk after the funeral, and I shouldn't have punched Deputy Broman. Dad would've wanted me to accept the consequences of my actions, and I'm doing him a big disservice and causing everyone else in the family a bunch of grief by drawing out this trial any longer than it needs to be."

Neither Marcus nor Violet said anything, and MJ released a big breath. "Well, now that I got that off my chest, I think I'll go get that coffee started. I bet you guys will need it for the rest of this conversation."

Marcus whispered to Violet, "Shouldn't you be giving him some sort of lawyerly advice right now?"

Violet whispered back, "I think he could use some brotherly advice more."

"Right." Marcus nodded and started toward the kitchen.

Violet caught up to him and grabbed his arm. "Except not so much advice as more of a listening ear. Just listen to his feelings, and let me handle the legal stuff."

When they arrived in the kitchen, MJ was pulling a box of sugary cereal out of the pantry. "Sweet. Mom never lets me keep Sugar Loops at the main house."

"So what happened to make you change your mind about pleading guilty?" Marcus asked, then grabbed three bowls out of the cupboard. They might all supposedly be grown-ups now, but nobody said no to Sugar Loops.

"You know when you took that yoga class with me in Arlington?"

"*Took* the class?" Violet brought the milk container to the table. "Marcus, you said you went there, but you never told me you actually did yoga."

"You want me to show you my planks?" He flexed his arms.

"Ew, gross." MJ set the box down so he could plug his ears. "You guys sound like Uncle Rider and Aunt Freckles."

"No, we don't!" Marcus shuddered, then shook his head. "Anyway, you started thinking about changing your plea when we were in DC?"

"Yeah. You were asking me about my electives in

high school, and I told you about that biomedical science class. You said it sounded pretty interesting. So I started doing a little bit of research, but there's no way I could go to school for all the years it would take to be a doctor. Then last night when Jordan got hurt, I made him that sling, and it helped. Agent Franks and I made it back to where Rider was just before the medical evac team got there, and I got to ride in the helicopter with them. Man, I watched them save Rider's life, and I thought, hey, I could do this, too. I stayed up talking to Kendra at the hospital, and she convinced me I should become a medic. One of the guys on the flight last night told me that he was in the Army Reserve and that EMTs can pretty much get any job they want if they have a combat background. I have to figure out if the military will take me with a criminal record, though."

"Have you met our mother?" Marcus asked. "She has half of the joint chiefs of staff on her speed dial."

"I want to go about it the right way, though," MJ said, which made Marcus even more proud. "I don't want any special favors because I'm a King."

Violet finally spoke up. "Now this is where I come in with the legal advice." She explained that misdemeanors could often get expunged from the record after time was served. She thought she could get Reed Nakamoto to agree to twelve months of probation, and if MJ successfully completed that, she could file a motion to expunge. After that, the recruiter's office would have to decide whether or not they'd be willing to accept MJ, but who were any of them kidding? Sherilee King would make some phone calls whether any of them wanted her to or not.

* * *

By the end of the day, Violet had gotten MJ only six months of probation—with credit for house arrest the past three months he'd been confined to the Twin Kings—she'd picked up the twins from school and she'd stopped by the Pepperoni Stampede to pick up dinner for the four of them.

"Day one and you're already setting the bar pretty high for this girlfriend gig," Marcus said when he opened the pizza box. "Wait. Did you get pineapples on purpose?"

"Maybe," she replied with a sly grin, then yelped when he started chasing her around the kitchen table. "I told you I wasn't going to make things too easy for you."

He changed directions at the last minute and caught her in his arms. She was now laughing breathlessly, and the boys started chanting, "Kiss her! Kiss her!"

But she took matters into her own hands and kissed him. The boys cheered, and she whispered, "I love you, Marcus King."

His heart felt as though it was going to explode. When the boys heard the opening song to their favorite movie, they took the pizza box into the family room, leaving Marcus and Violet in the kitchen.

"Do you love me enough to stay together even when we live so far apart?"

"The main house isn't all that far," she replied. "Not even a whole mile."

"I meant when you go back to Texas," he said, trying not to hold his breath. "To your career and your life."

"As long as there's a courthouse nearby, my career can be anywhere I want it to be, Marcus. And since you and the boys are in Wyoming, then I guess my life will be here, as well."

"Are you serious?" He grinned, his wildest dreams coming true before his eyes. "You're staying here at the Twin Kings with us?"

"Yes. But on one condition."

"Name it," Marcus said.

"We hire a wedding planner. There's no way I'm running interference between our mothers when they start trying to get the upper hand on reception venues and invite lists."

His laughter echoed in the kitchen. "Is that a proposal, Miss Cortez-Hill?" he asked. "Are you asking me to be your husband?"

"No, it's the preliminary stages of a pending negotiation. We can wait until after the boys go to bed before you deliver your counteroffer."

"No counteroffer," he replied. "I accept. I'm not letting you get away ever again."

EPILOGUE

"I DON'T KNOW why you can't get married at the First Congregation of Teton Ridge like everyone else in the family," Sherilee said to Marcus after most of the guests had left. The immediate King family was still sitting around several large tables at Big Millie's, which had been closed tonight so that Tessa and Grayson could hold their wedding rehearsal dinner there, much to Sherilee's chagrin. "You could still have your reception in Texas at a later date if it's so important to Senator Cortez-Hill."

"I got this," Violet whispered, then patted Marcus's knee before turning to his mom. "Mrs. King, my mother is already heartbroken that I'm moving to Wyoming full-time to open my own law practice. The least we can do is compromise by following *my* family's tradition and have the ceremony at St. Thomas's in San Antonio. Look on the bright side, though. Think of how crazy Aunt Freckles is going to drive my mom when it comes to planning the reception dinner."

Sherilee seemed to mull the idea over. "I might pay to see that. But I'll talk to our church secretary about their open dates. Just in case."

Marcus pressed his smiling mouth against Violet's

forehead. "Good try, counselor. You can't win every case."

"I didn't get married at the First Congregation." Dahlia raised her hand from behind the bar. She and Connor had enjoyed a very small, outdoor ceremony at his ranch, the Rocking D.

"Not this time, you didn't," Finn mumbled from her stool where she was nursing a melting margarita.

"Don't be jealous that your twin has got you beat two times over when it comes to finding great guys," Micah said.

"*One* great guy," Finn corrected, then turned to Connor who was helping his wife wash glasses behind the bar. "You're a saint for putting up with Dahlia's ex-husband, Con."

"Someday you'll have your chance to walk down the aisle, too, Finn." Micah was one of the few people who could really get under the tough cowgirl's skin. "As soon as you can find someone who wants to put up with your sassy attitude."

Tessa held up her hands in a time-out sign. "Can we please have at least one night with no major family arguments?"

"Nope."

"No way."

"Yeah, right." A chorus around the bar.

"Keep in mind, Mom," Marcus said, his voice raised as he slung an arm around his younger brother, "MJ is going to be my best man, and it'll be easier for him to attend the wedding after he gets out of boot camp if we get married in Texas."

The heavy oak door opened, and all eyes turned toward the entrance.

"Sorry we're late," Duke said as he and Tom shrugged out of their coats. Tom was wearing his dress blues, and Duke was still in his flight suit. But at least they were together.

Amelia, Dahlia's daughter who often asked more questions than Jack and Jordan combined, yelled across the room, "Hey, Uncle Duke and Uncle Tom. Do you guys have your baby yet?"

There were several gasps as everyone's heads pivoted from Amelia to Duke to Tom and then back to Amelia again. Finally, Duke smiled and put his arm around his husband.

"So you guys might've noticed that we haven't really been ourselves lately. For a while now, Tom and I have been looking into adoption. We had gone through the whole background process and were hopeful a couple of times, but then things would fall through at the last minute. It was pretty heart-crushing, and we were about ready to throw in the towel on the whole idea of ever becoming parents. But…"

"But?" Sherilee was clasping her hands together hopefully. It was no secret that she wanted as many grandchildren as possible.

"But then someone came through with the incredibly selfless offer to be our surrogate and, well, there's going to be a new addition to the family in six months."

Their mother squealed and danced around in a circle with whoops of happiness. Everyone else joined in with hugs of congratulations, and Dahlia popped the cork from a bottle of champagne.

"Wait!" Sherilee yelled over the noise. "You haven't told us anything about this surrogate. Who is she? Where does she live? What's her vitamin regimen?

Does she do Pilates? I'm going to need the name of her obstetrician and her nutritionist."

"Why don't you ask her yourself?" Duke said, then nodded to where Finn was sitting quietly at the bar, apparently drinking lemonade out of her margarita glass.

"You… You're… Wow…" Micah stuttered, putting into words what everyone else in the room was feeling. Completely stunned.

"It's not like I had anything else going on, anyway," Finn snapped at him. Then she pushed herself off the bar stool. "Besides, I couldn't let my other siblings get all the attention."

There was more cheering and more champagne and more hugs.

Violet wrapped her arm around Marcus's waist and whispered in his ear, "Maybe we should wait to make our announcement. I don't want to take away from Duke and Tom's special moment."

Marcus lovingly placed a hand on her belly. "You are going to be the most beautiful bride, and I promise that I am going to be the most amazing father to our children."

Violet lifted her chin toward where Jack and Jordan were playing swords with the pool cues. "You already are."

* * * * *

COMING SOON!

We really hope you enjoyed reading this book.
If you're looking for more romance, be sure to
head to the shops when new books are
available on

Thursday 8th
July

To see which titles are coming soon, please visit

millsandboon.co.uk/nextmonth

LET'S TALK
Romance

For exclusive extracts, competitions
and special offers, find us online:

MILLS & BOON
A ROMANCE FOR EVERY READER

- **FREE** delivery direct to your door

- **EXCLUSIVE** offers every month

- **SAVE** up to 25% on pre-paid subscriptions

SUBSCRIBE AND SAVE

millsandboon.co.uk/Subscribe